GOOD GAME, WELL PLAYED ™

RACHAEL SMITH
AUTHOR

KATHERINE LOBO
ARTIST

JUSTIN BIRCH
LETTERER

CHLOE BRAILSFORD
SENSITIVITY READER

CHRIS SANCHEZ
EDITOR

DAVID REYES
BOOK & LOGO DESIGNER

LAURA CHACÓN
FOUNDER

MARK LONDON
CEO AND CHIEF CREATIVE OFFICER

MARK IRWIN
VP OF BUSINESS DEVELOPMENT

CHRIS FERNANDEZ
PUBLISHER

CECILIA MEDINA
CHIEF FINANCIAL OFFICER

ALLISON POND
MARKETING DIRECTOR

MANNY CASTELLANOS
SALES & RETAILER RELATIONS

GIOVANNA T. OROZCO
PRODUCTION MANAGER

MIGUEL ANGEL ZAPATA
DESIGN DIRECTOR

CHRIS SANCHEZ
SENIOR EDITOR

CHAS! PANGBURN
SENIOR EDITOR

MAYA LOPEZ
MARKETING MANAGER

BRIAN HAWKINS
ASSISTANT EDITOR

DIANA BERMÚDEZ
GRAPHIC DESIGNER

DAVID REYES
GRAPHIC DESIGNER

ADRIANA T. OROZCO
INTERACTIVE MEDIA DESIGNER

NICOLÁS ZEA ARIAS
AUDIOVISUAL PRODUCTION

FRANK SILVA
EXECUTIVE ASSISTANT

PEDRO HERRERA
RETAIL ASSOCIATE

STEPHANIE HIDALGO
OFFICE MANAGER

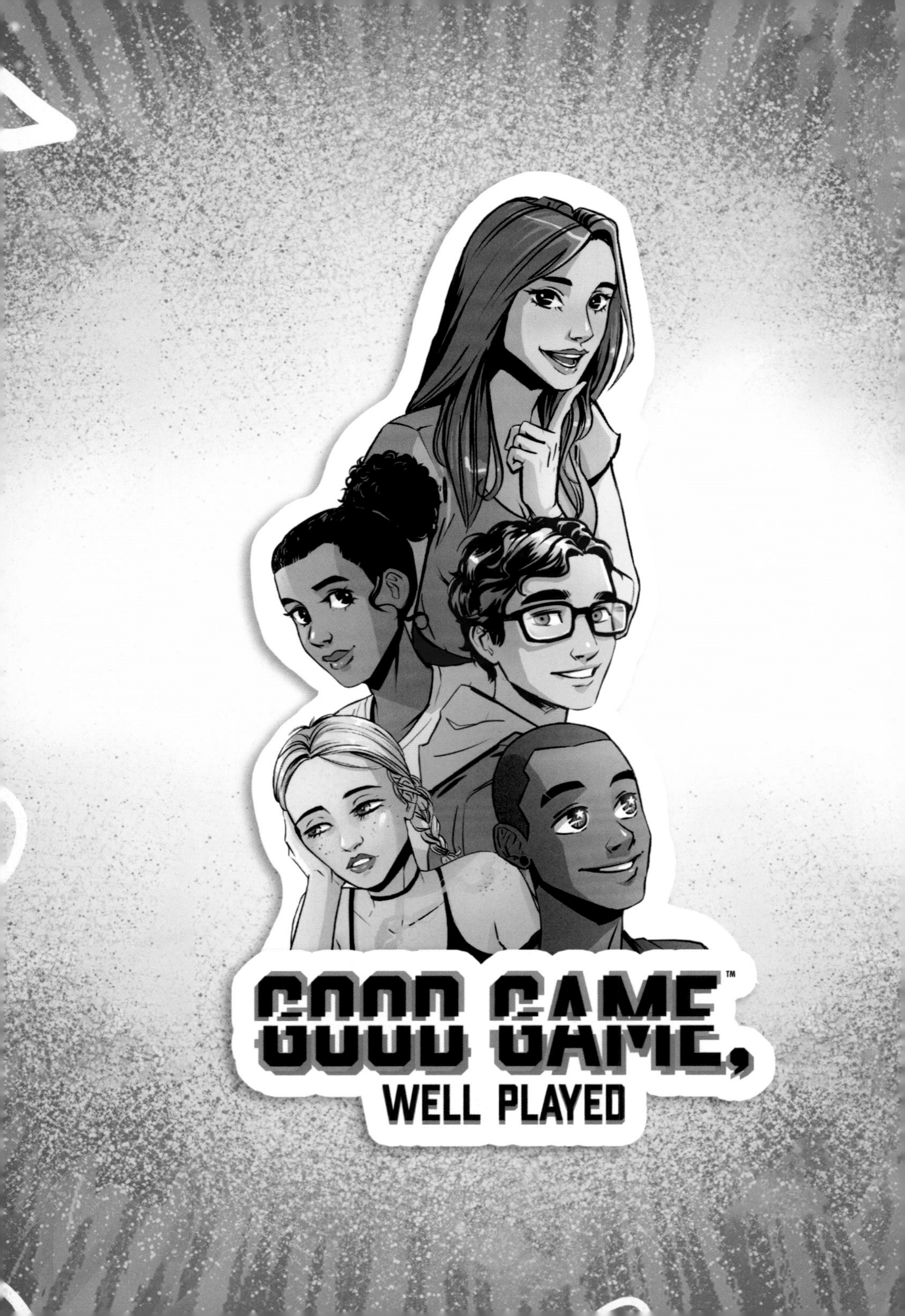
GOOD GAME,™
WELL PLAYED

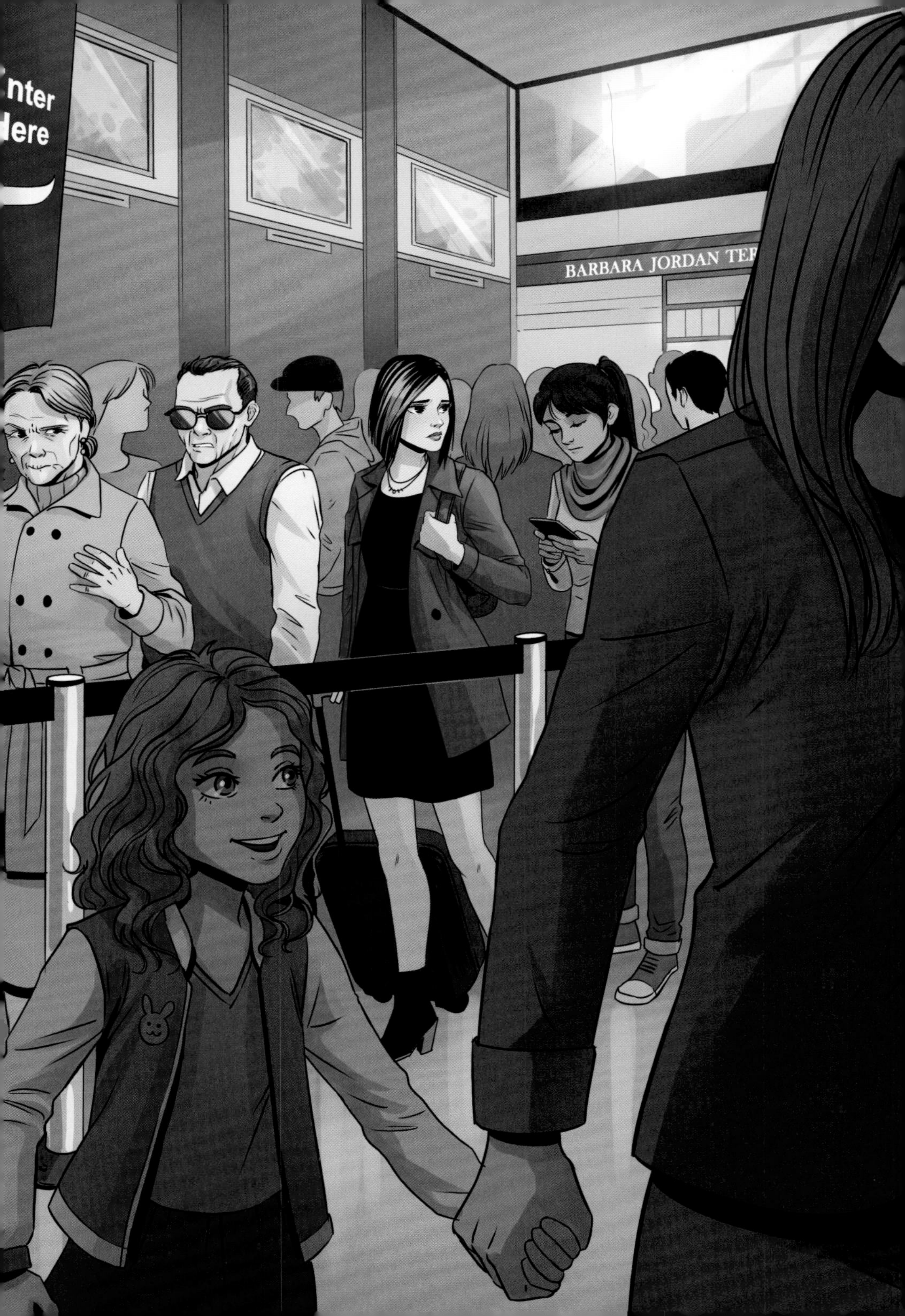

nter
Here
BARBARA JORDAN TER

AUTUMN 2009
AUSTIN, TX

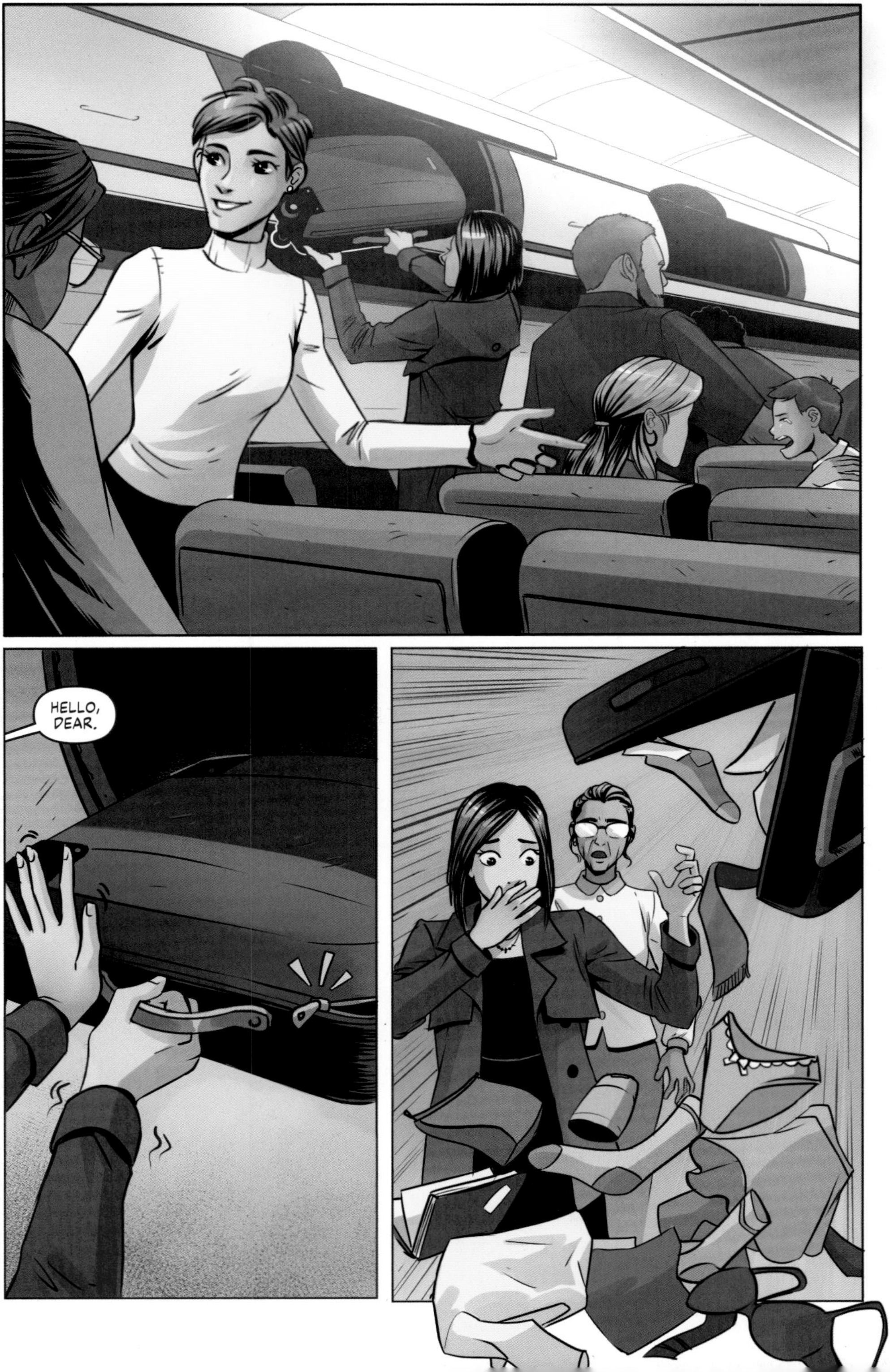
HELLO, DEAR.

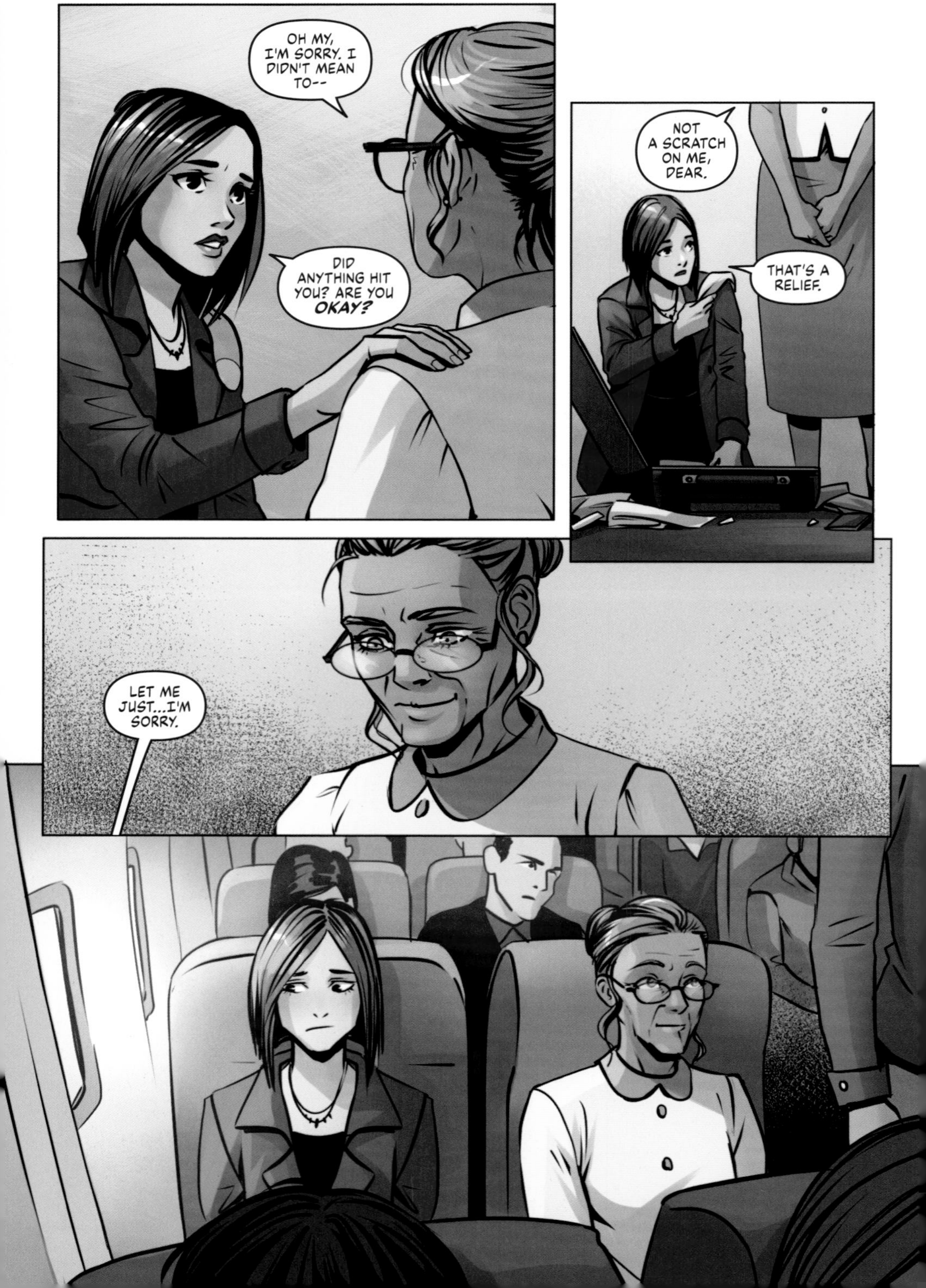
OH MY, I'M SORRY. I DIDN'T MEAN TO--
DID ANYTHING HIT YOU? ARE YOU **OKAY?**
NOT A SCRATCH ON ME, DEAR.
THAT'S A RELIEF.
LET ME JUST...I'M SORRY.

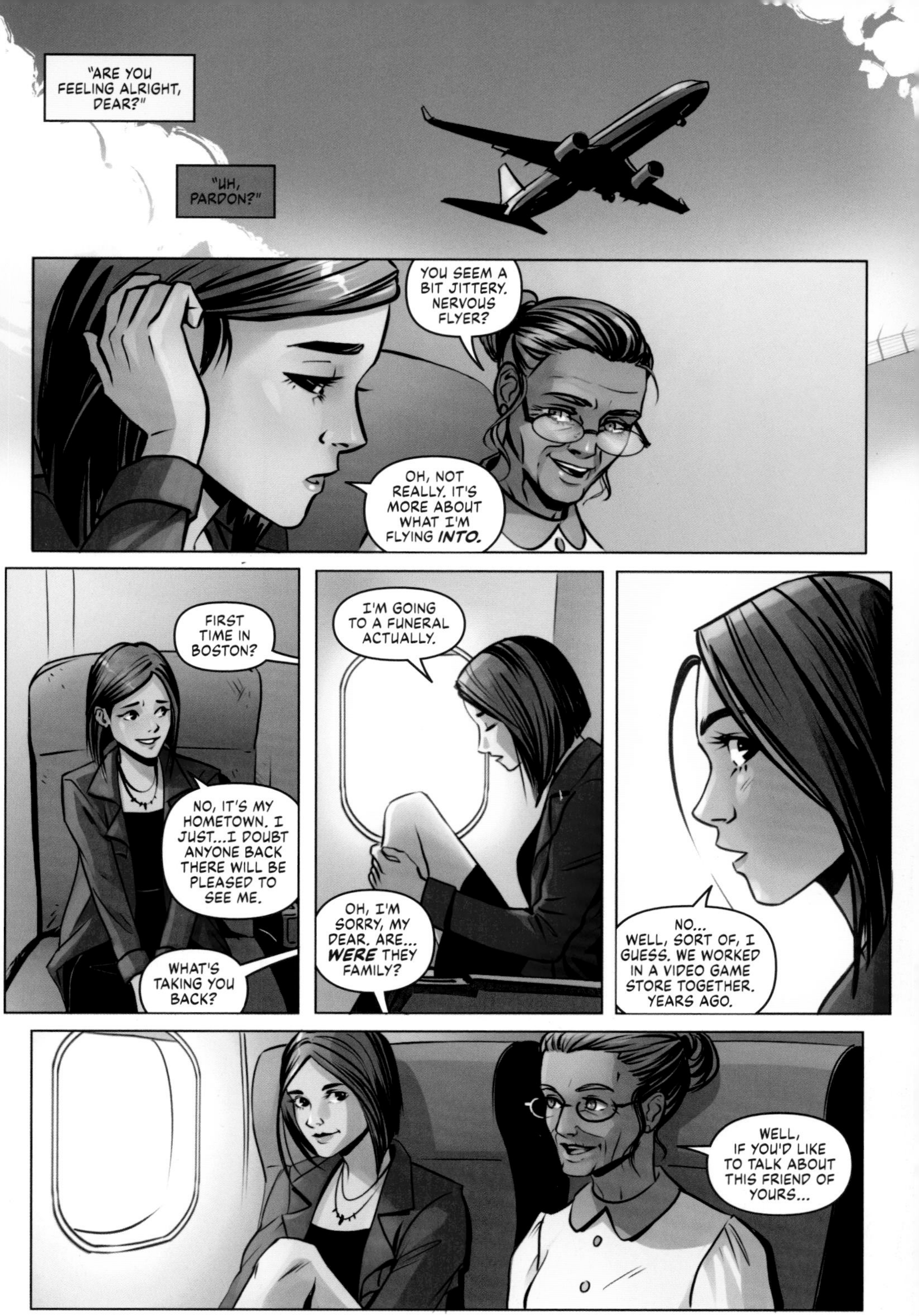
"ARE YOU FEELING ALRIGHT, DEAR?"
"UH, PARDON?"
YOU SEEM A BIT JITTERY. NERVOUS FLYER?
OH, NOT REALLY. IT'S MORE ABOUT WHAT I'M FLYING *INTO.*
FIRST TIME IN BOSTON?
NO, IT'S MY HOMETOWN. I JUST...I DOUBT ANYONE BACK THERE WILL BE PLEASED TO SEE ME.
WHAT'S TAKING YOU BACK?
I'M GOING TO A FUNERAL ACTUALLY.
OH, I'M SORRY, MY DEAR. ARE... *WERE* THEY FAMILY?
NO... WELL, SORT OF, I GUESS. WE WORKED IN A VIDEO GAME STORE TOGETHER. YEARS AGO.
WELL, IF YOU'D LIKE TO TALK ABOUT THIS FRIEND OF YOURS...

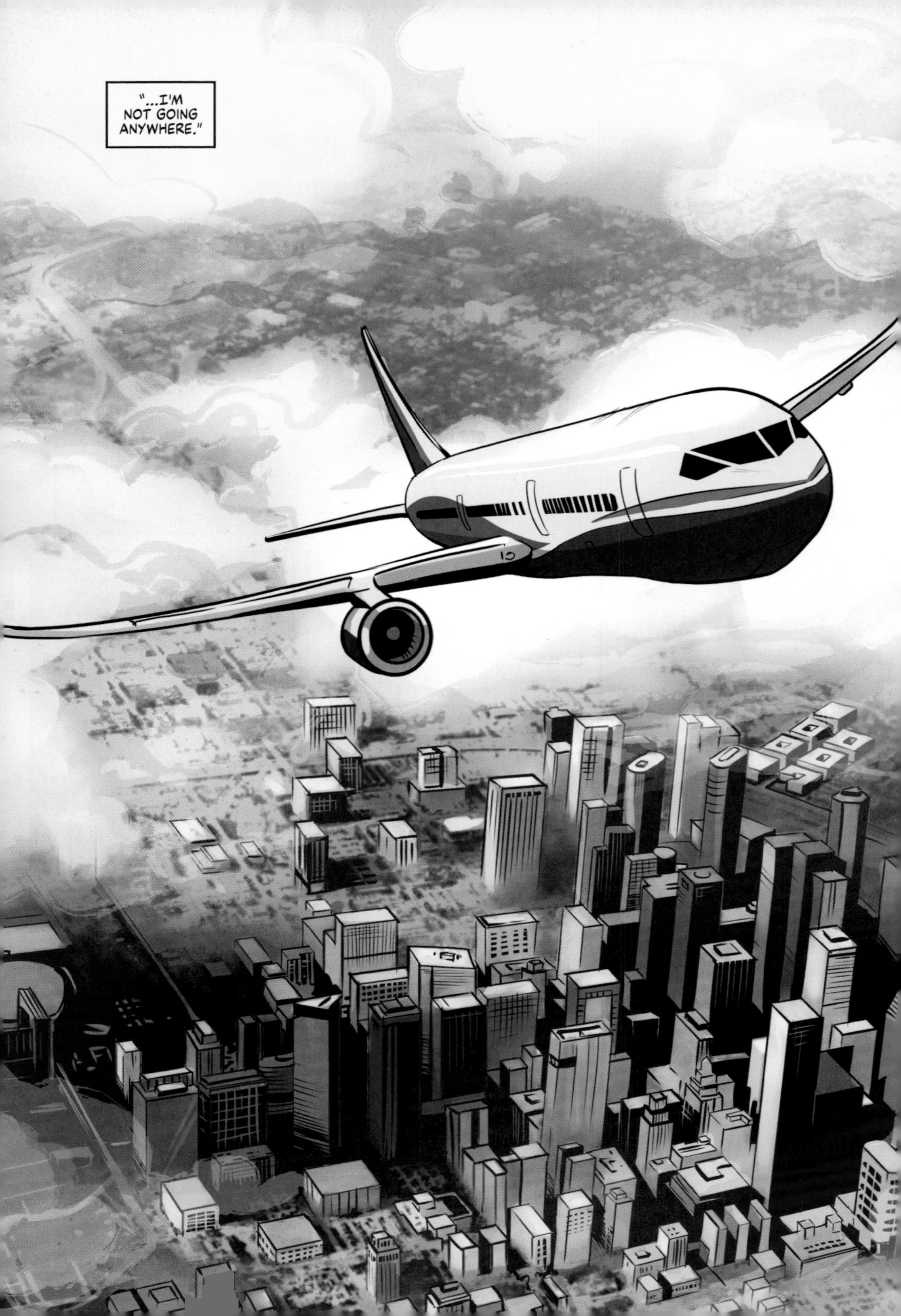
"...I'M NOT GOING ANYWHERE."

SUMMER 1999
BOSTON, MA

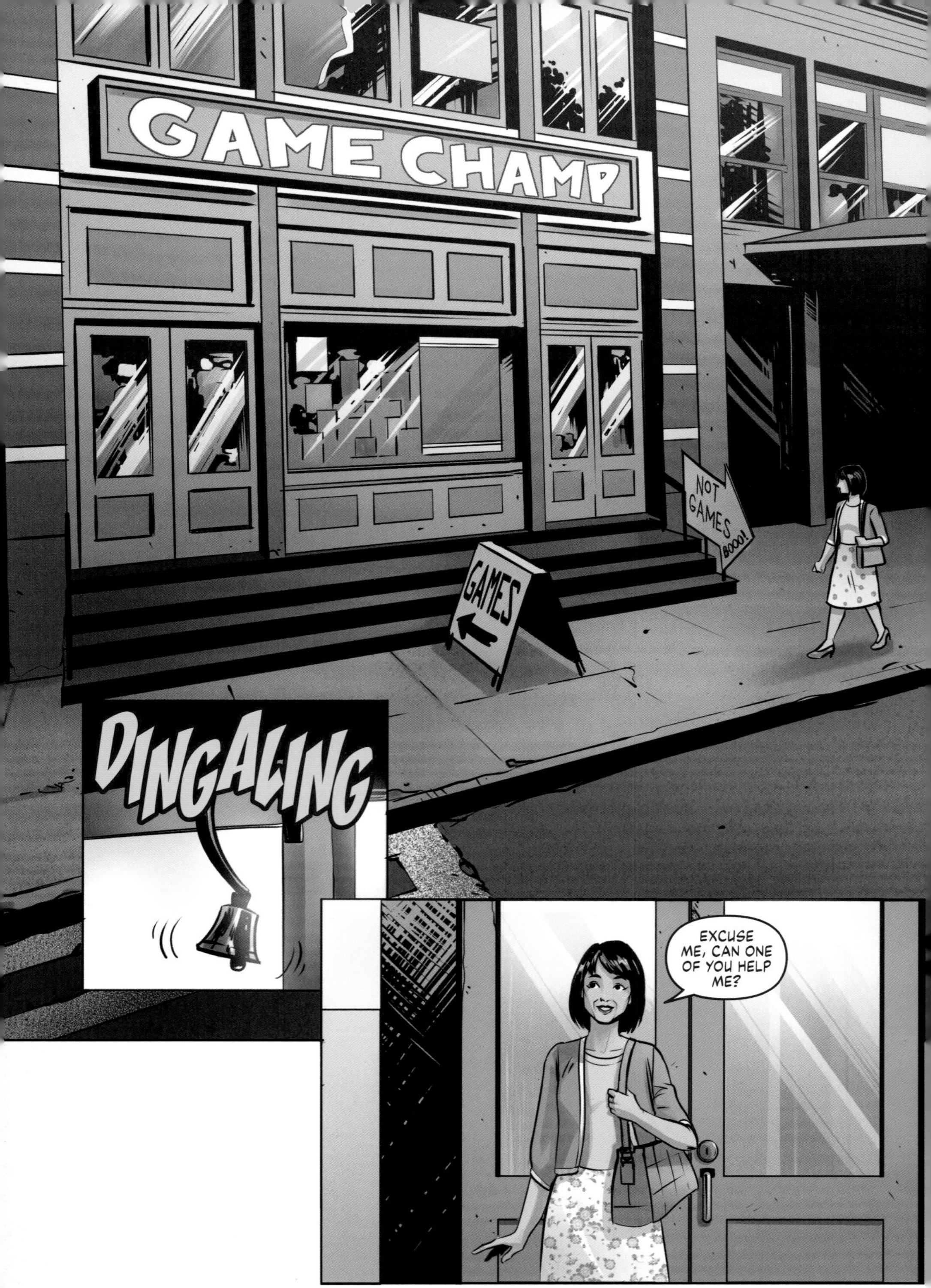
GAME CHAMP
NOT GAMES BOOO!
GAMES
DINGALING
EXCUSE ME, CAN ONE OF YOU HELP ME?

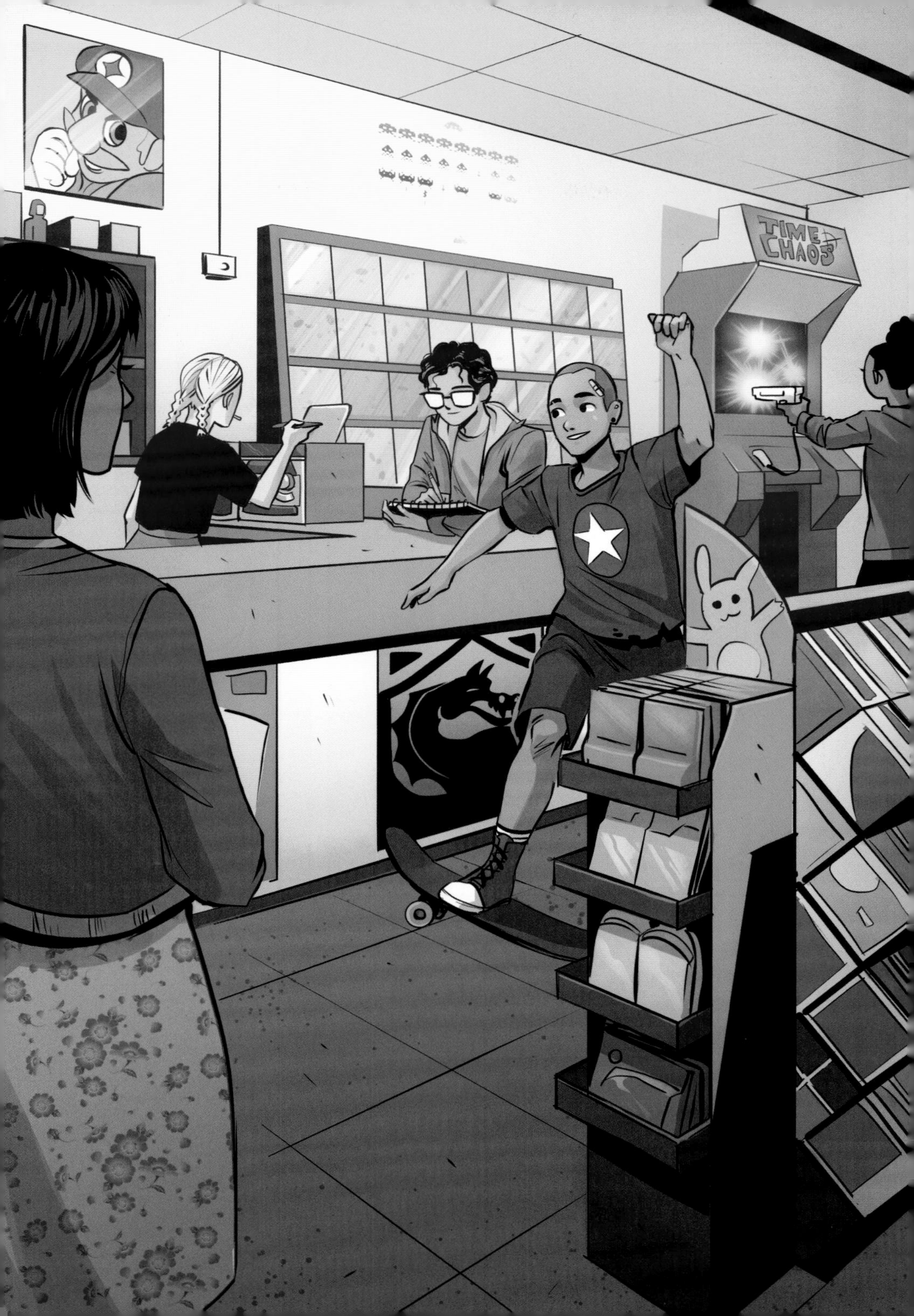
TIME CHAOS

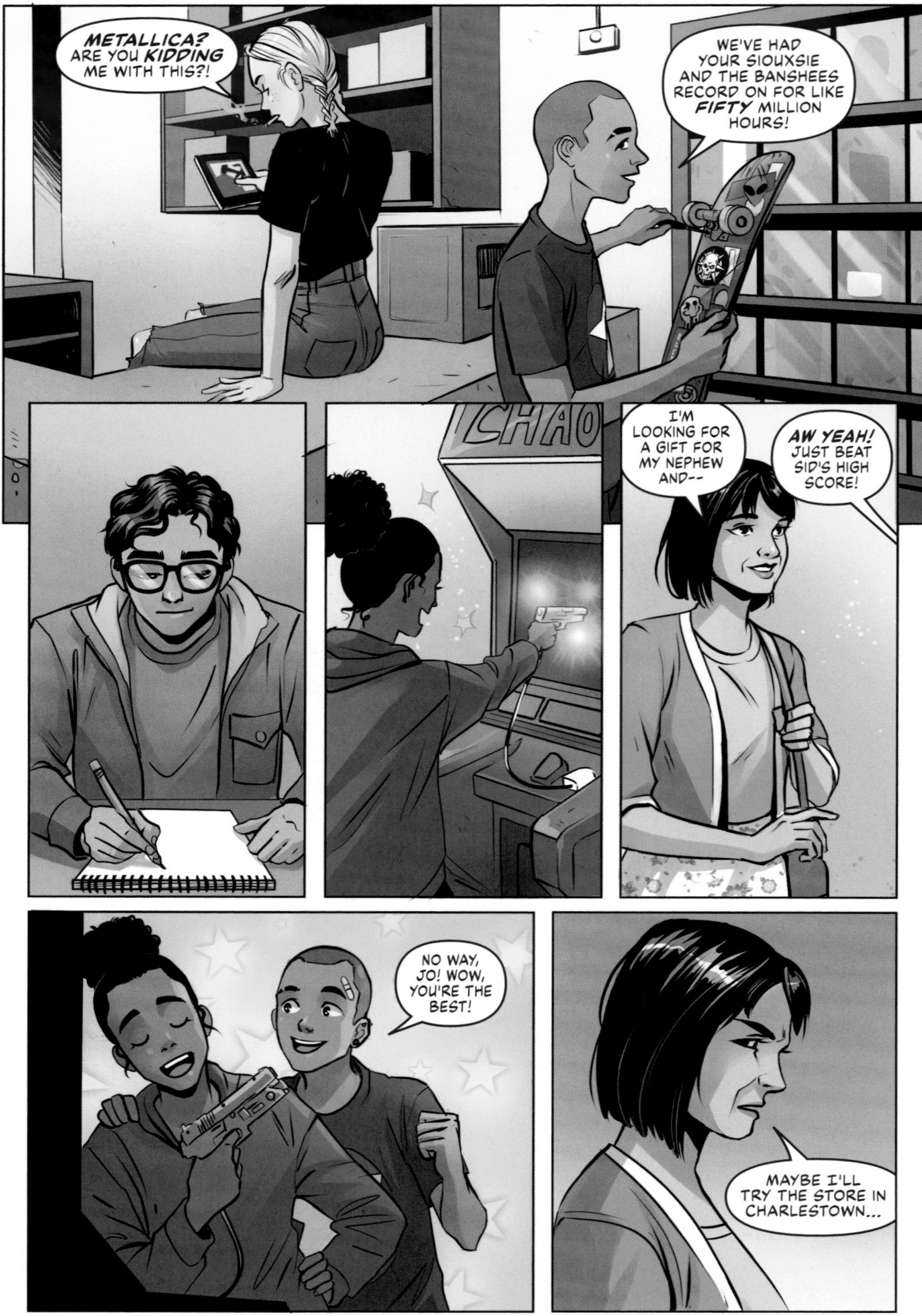
METALLICA? ARE YOU KIDDING ME WITH THIS?!
WE'VE HAD YOUR SIOUXSIE AND THE BANSHEES RECORD ON FOR LIKE FIFTY MILLION HOURS!
CHAO
I'M LOOKING FOR A GIFT FOR MY NEPHEW AND--
AW YEAH! JUST BEAT SID'S HIGH SCORE!
NO WAY, JO! WOW, YOU'RE THE BEST!
MAYBE I'LL TRY THE STORE IN CHARLESTOWN...

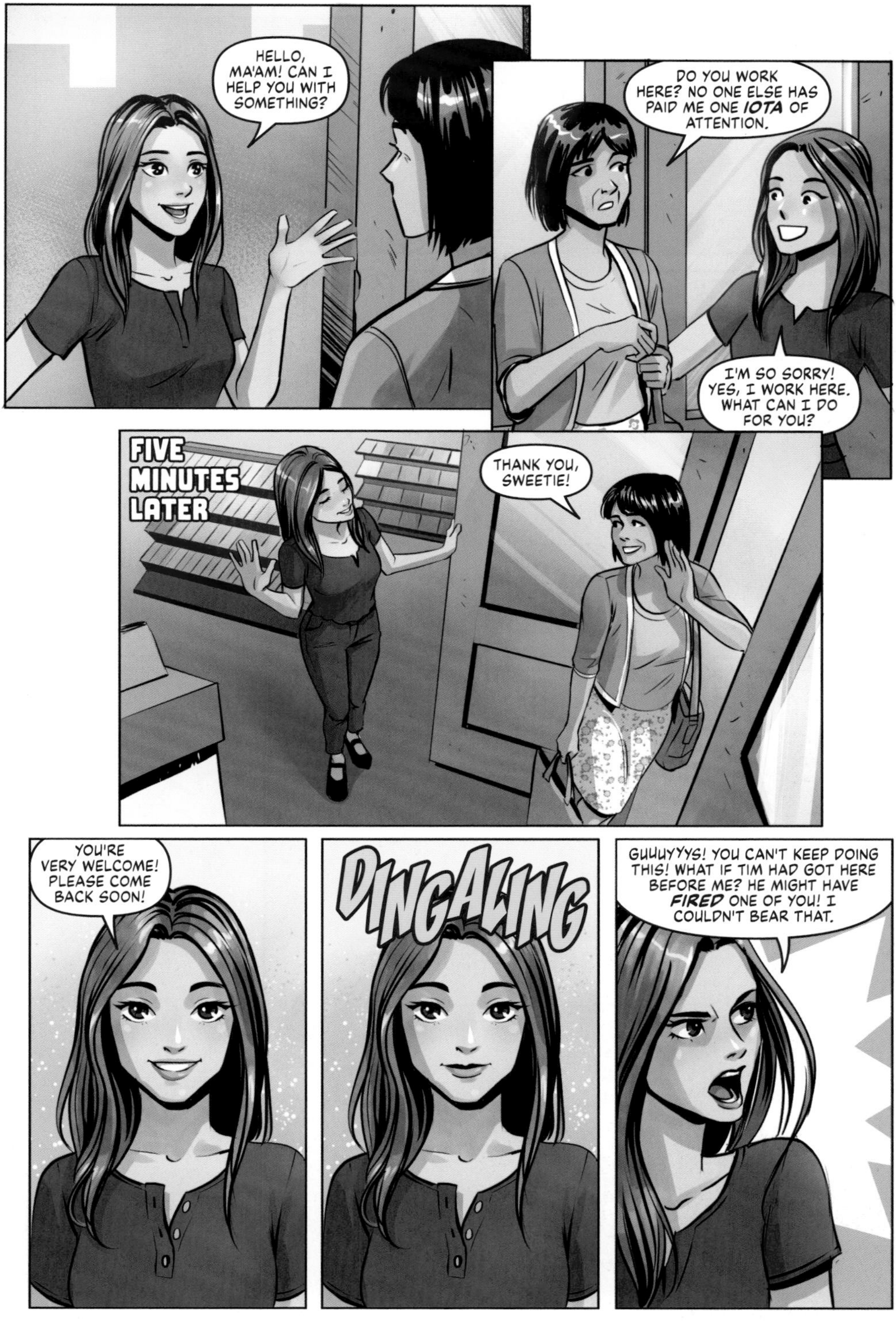
HELLO, MA'AM! CAN I HELP YOU WITH SOMETHING?
DO YOU WORK HERE? NO ONE ELSE HAS PAID ME ONE *IOTA* OF ATTENTION.
I'M SO SORRY! YES, I WORK HERE. WHAT CAN I DO FOR YOU?
FIVE MINUTES LATER
THANK YOU, SWEETIE!
YOU'RE VERY WELCOME! PLEASE COME BACK SOON!
DINGALING
GUUUYYYS! YOU CAN'T KEEP DOING THIS! WHAT IF TIM HAD GOT HERE BEFORE ME? HE MIGHT HAVE *FIRED* ONE OF YOU! I COULDN'T BEAR THAT.

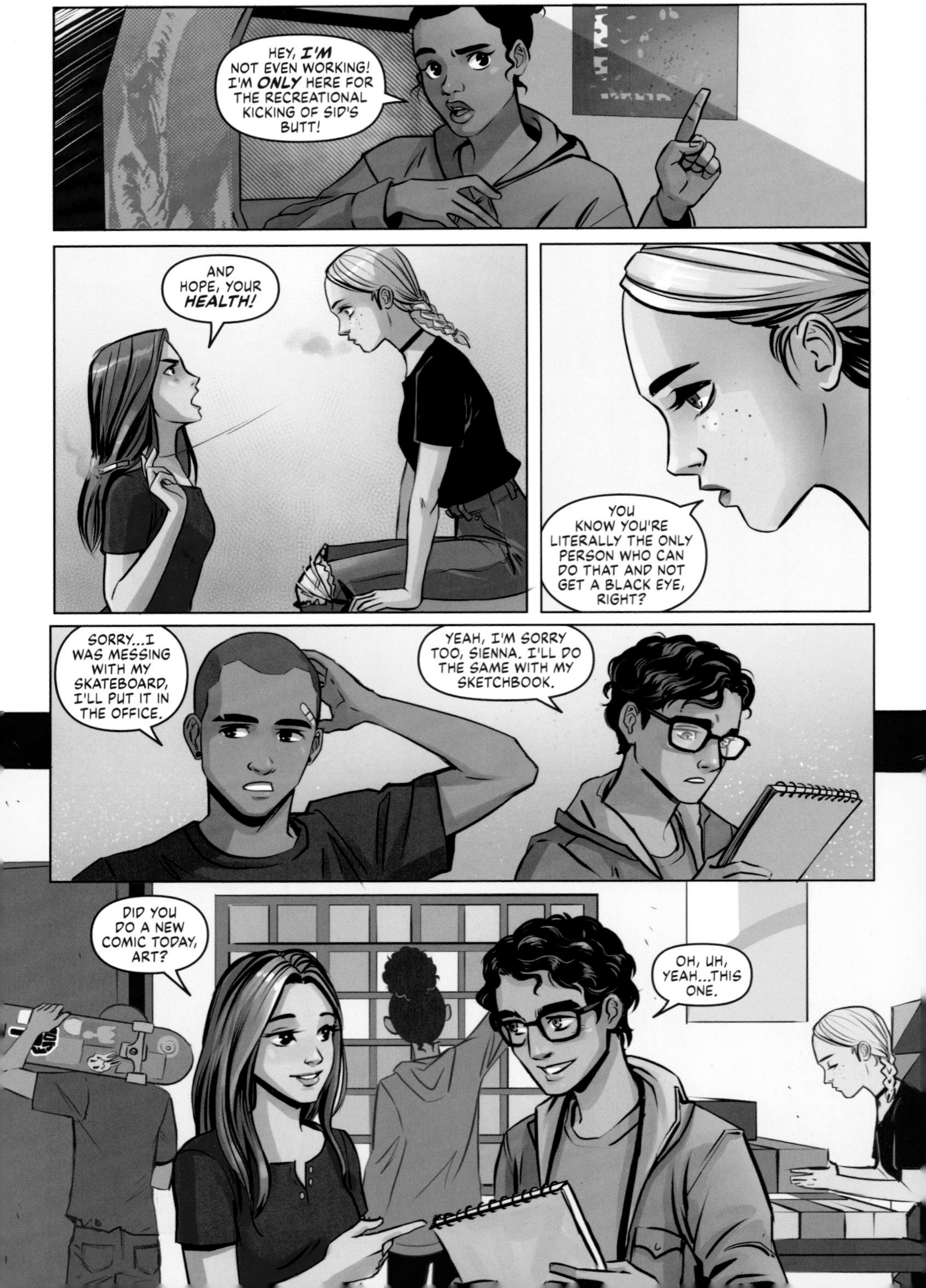

HEY, ***I'M*** NOT EVEN WORKING! I'M ***ONLY*** HERE FOR THE RECREATIONAL KICKING OF SID'S BUTT!
AND HOPE, YOUR ***HEALTH!***
YOU KNOW YOU'RE LITERALLY THE ONLY PERSON WHO CAN DO THAT AND NOT GET A BLACK EYE, RIGHT?
SORRY...I WAS MESSING WITH MY SKATEBOARD, I'LL PUT IT IN THE OFFICE.
YEAH, I'M SORRY TOO, SIENNA. I'LL DO THE SAME WITH MY SKETCHBOOK.
DID YOU DO A NEW COMIC TODAY, ART?
OH, UH, YEAH...THIS ONE.

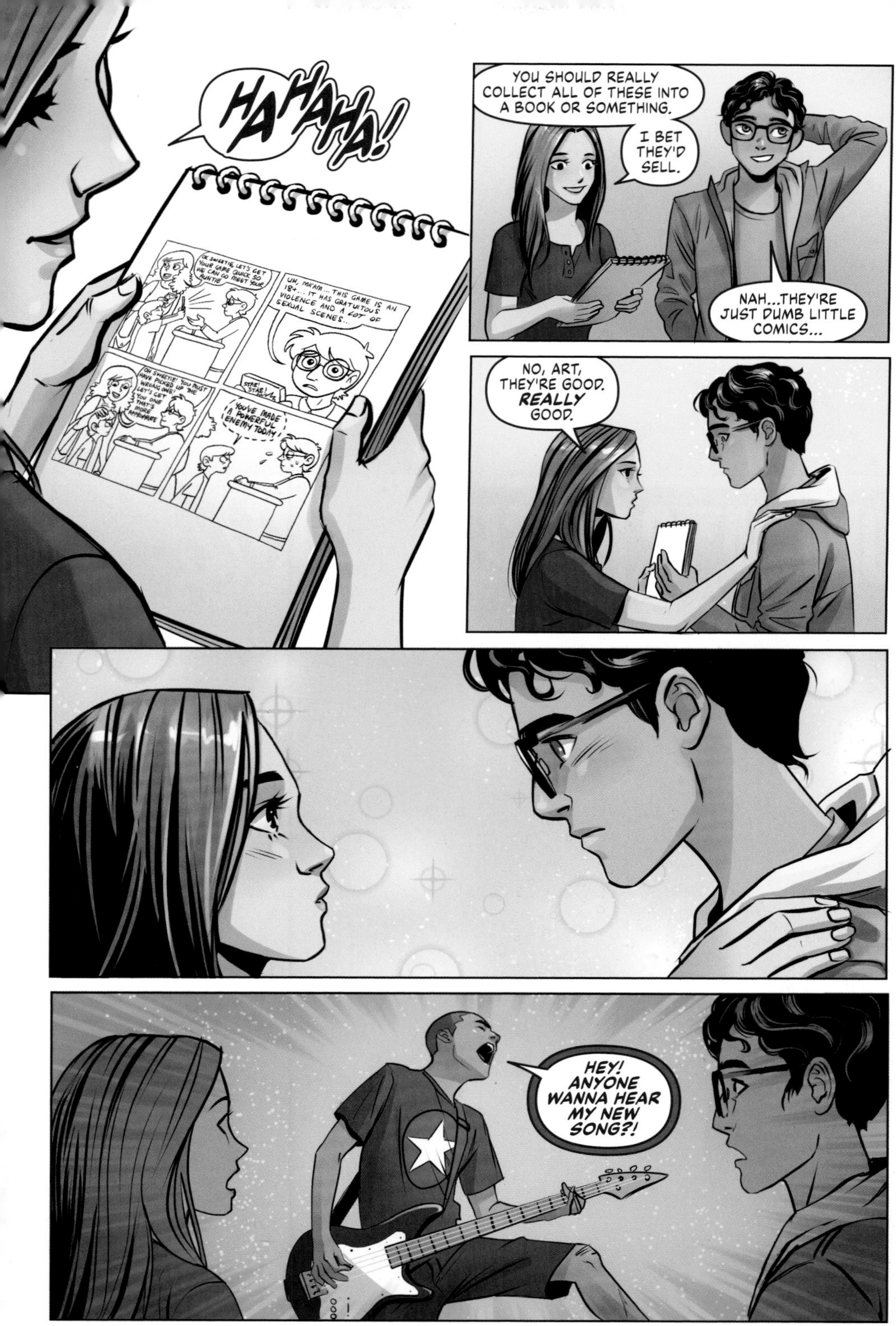
HAHAHAHA!
OK SWEETIE, LET'S GET YOUR GAME QUICK SO WE CAN GO MEET YOUR AUNTIE
UH, MA'AM... THIS GAME IS AN 18+... IT HAS GRATUITOUS VIOLENCE AND A LOT OF SEXUAL SCENES...
STAB! STAB!
OH SWEETIE! YOU MUST HAVE PICKED UP THE WRONG ONE! LET'S GET YOU ONE THAT'S MORE APPROPRIATE
YOU'VE MADE A POWERFUL ENEMY TODAY
YOU SHOULD REALLY COLLECT ALL OF THESE INTO A BOOK OR SOMETHING.
I BET THEY'D SELL.
NAH...THEY'RE JUST DUMB LITTLE COMICS...
NO, ART, THEY'RE GOOD. REALLY GOOD.
HEY! ANYONE WANNA HEAR MY NEW SONG?!

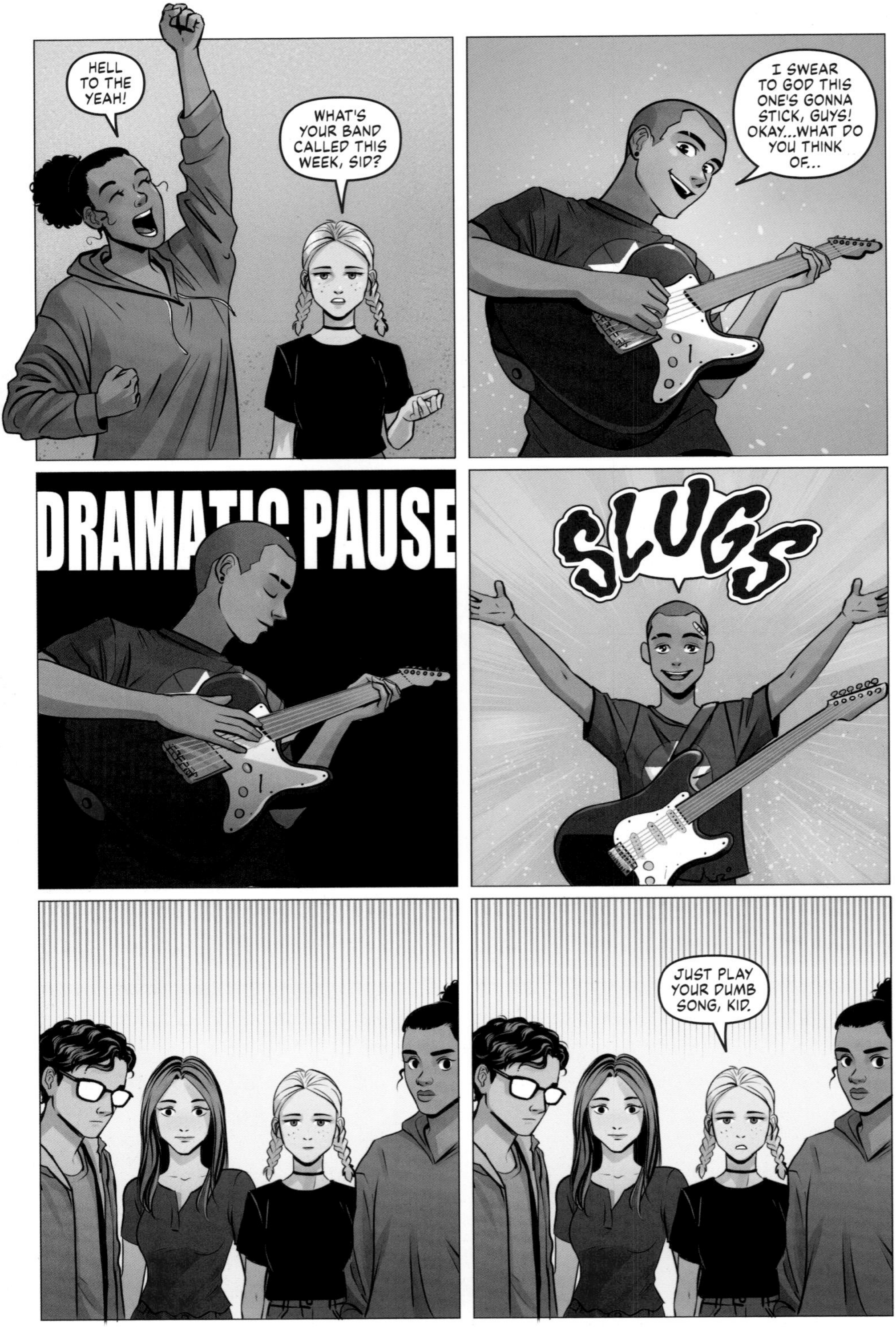
HELL TO THE YEAH!
WHAT'S YOUR BAND CALLED THIS WEEK, SID?
I SWEAR TO GOD THIS ONE'S GONNA STICK, GUYS! OKAY...WHAT DO YOU THINK OF...
DRAMATIC PAUSE
SLUGS
JUST PLAY YOUR DUMB SONG, KID.

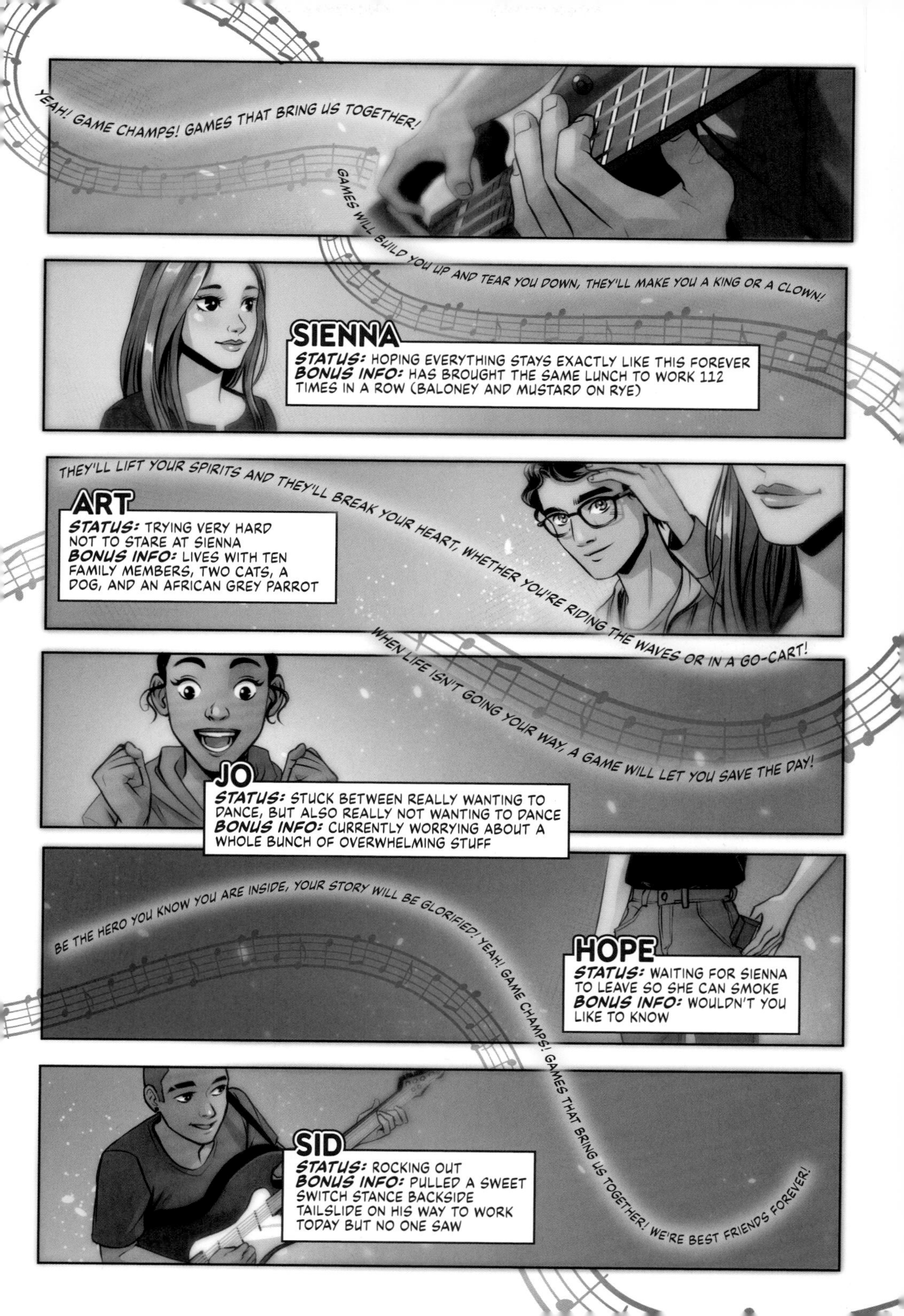

YEAH! GAME CHAMPS! GAMES THAT BRING US TOGETHER!
GAMES WILL BUILD YOU UP AND TEAR YOU DOWN, THEY'LL MAKE YOU A KING OR A CLOWN!
SIENNA
STATUS: HOPING EVERYTHING STAYS EXACTLY LIKE THIS FOREVER
BONUS INFO: HAS BROUGHT THE SAME LUNCH TO WORK 112 TIMES IN A ROW (BALONEY AND MUSTARD ON RYE)
THEY'LL LIFT YOUR SPIRITS AND THEY'LL BREAK YOUR HEART, WHETHER YOU'RE RIDING THE WAVES OR IN A GO-CART!
ART
STATUS: TRYING VERY HARD NOT TO STARE AT SIENNA
BONUS INFO: LIVES WITH TEN FAMILY MEMBERS, TWO CATS, A DOG, AND AN AFRICAN GREY PARROT
WHEN LIFE ISN'T GOING YOUR WAY, A GAME WILL LET YOU SAVE THE DAY!
JO
STATUS: STUCK BETWEEN REALLY WANTING TO DANCE, BUT ALSO REALLY NOT WANTING TO DANCE
BONUS INFO: CURRENTLY WORRYING ABOUT A WHOLE BUNCH OF OVERWHELMING STUFF
BE THE HERO YOU KNOW YOU ARE INSIDE, YOUR STORY WILL BE GLORIFIED! YEAH! GAME CHAMPS! GAMES THAT BRING US TOGETHER! WE'RE BEST FRIENDS FOREVER!
HOPE
STATUS: WAITING FOR SIENNA TO LEAVE SO SHE CAN SMOKE
BONUS INFO: WOULDN'T YOU LIKE TO KNOW
SID
STATUS: ROCKING OUT
BONUS INFO: PULLED A SWEET SWITCH STANCE BACKSIDE TAILSLIDE ON HIS WAY TO WORK TODAY BUT NO ONE SAW

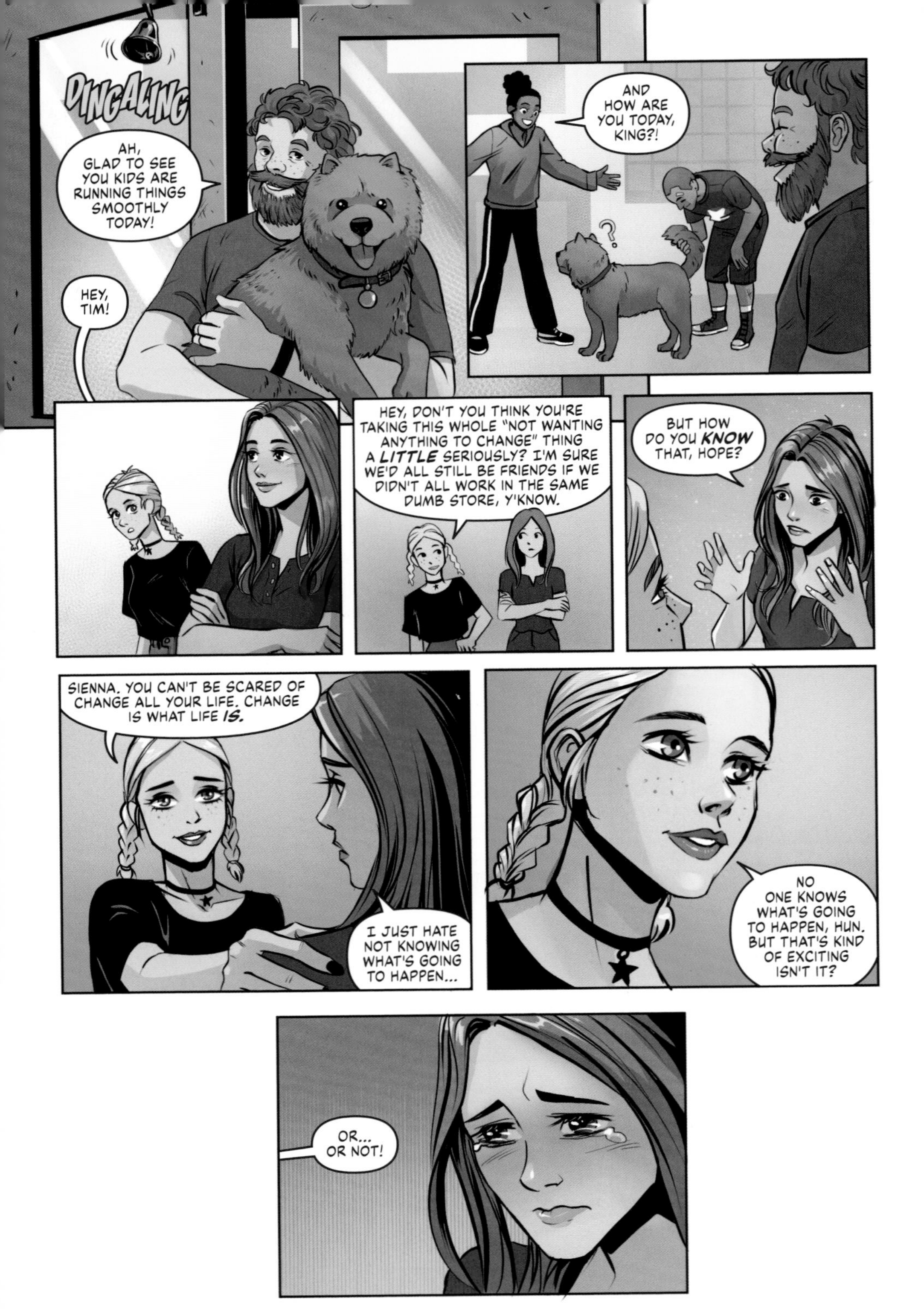
DINGALING
AH, GLAD TO SEE YOU KIDS ARE RUNNING THINGS SMOOTHLY TODAY!
HEY, TIM!
AND HOW ARE YOU TODAY, KING?!
?
HEY, DON'T YOU THINK YOU'RE TAKING THIS WHOLE "NOT WANTING ANYTHING TO CHANGE" THING A *LITTLE* SERIOUSLY? I'M SURE WE'D ALL STILL BE FRIENDS IF WE DIDN'T ALL WORK IN THE SAME DUMB STORE, Y'KNOW.
BUT HOW DO YOU *KNOW* THAT, HOPE?
SIENNA. YOU CAN'T BE SCARED OF CHANGE ALL YOUR LIFE. CHANGE IS WHAT LIFE *IS.*
I JUST HATE NOT KNOWING WHAT'S GOING TO HAPPEN...
NO ONE KNOWS WHAT'S GOING TO HAPPEN, HUN. BUT THAT'S KIND OF EXCITING ISN'T IT?
OR... OR NOT!

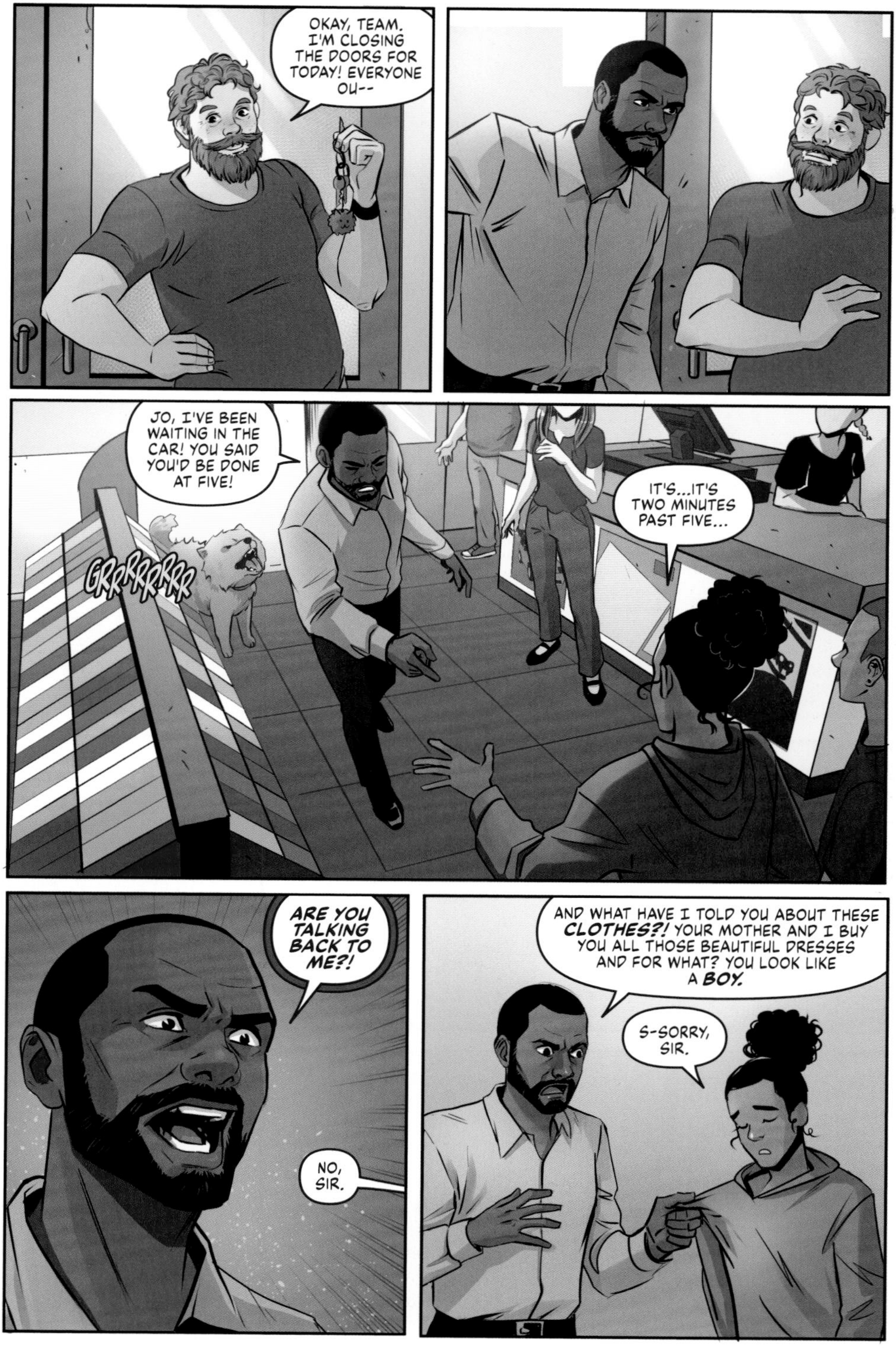
OKAY, TEAM. I'M CLOSING THE DOORS FOR TODAY! EVERYONE OU--
JO, I'VE BEEN WAITING IN THE CAR! YOU SAID YOU'D BE DONE AT FIVE!
GRRRRRRRR
IT'S...IT'S TWO MINUTES PAST FIVE...
ARE YOU TALKING BACK TO ME?!
NO, SIR.
AND WHAT HAVE I TOLD YOU ABOUT THESE CLOTHES?! YOUR MOTHER AND I BUY YOU ALL THOSE BEAUTIFUL DRESSES AND FOR WHAT? YOU LOOK LIKE A BOY.
S-SORRY, SIR.

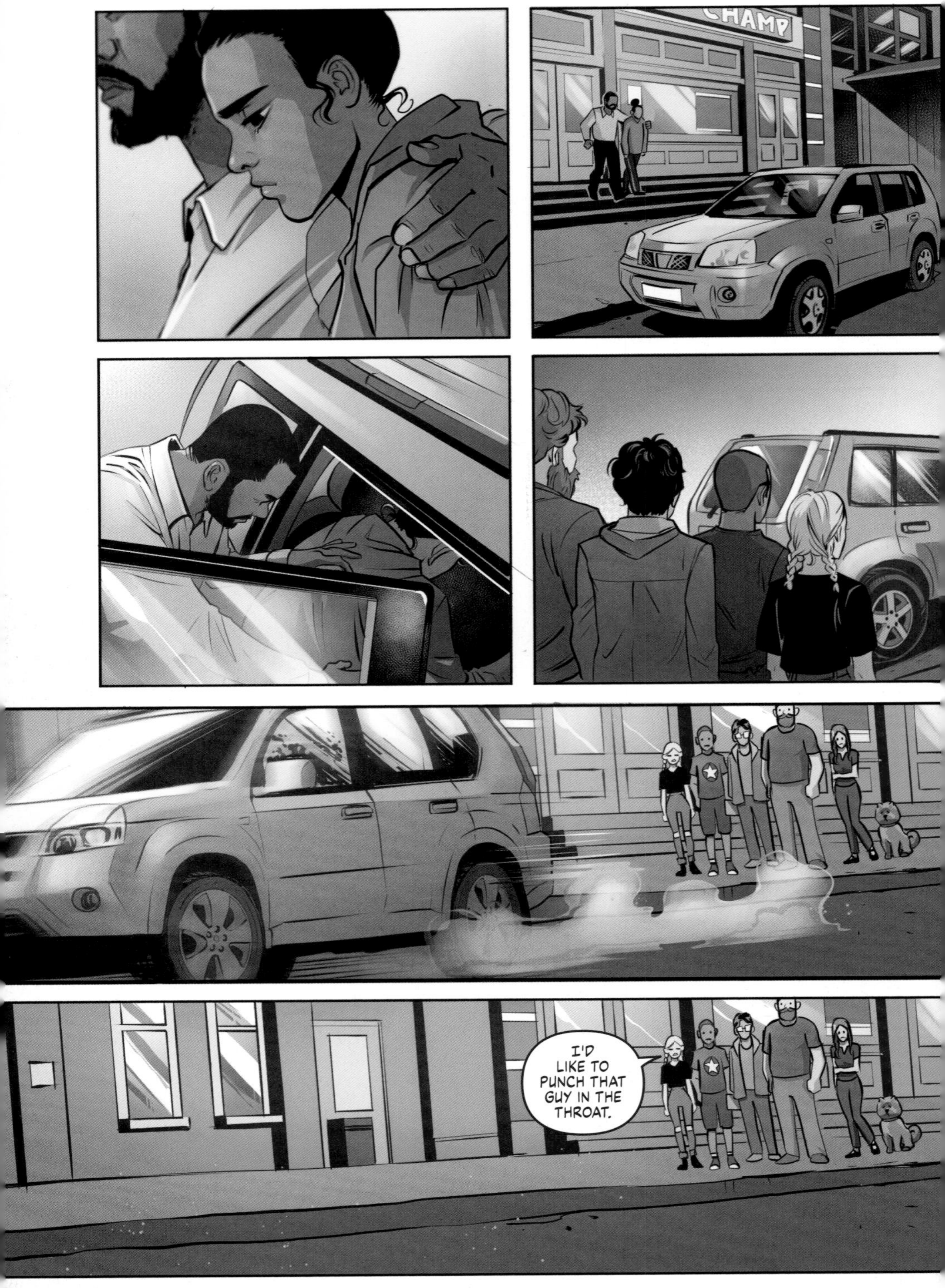
CHAMP
I'D LIKE TO PUNCH THAT GUY IN THE THROAT.

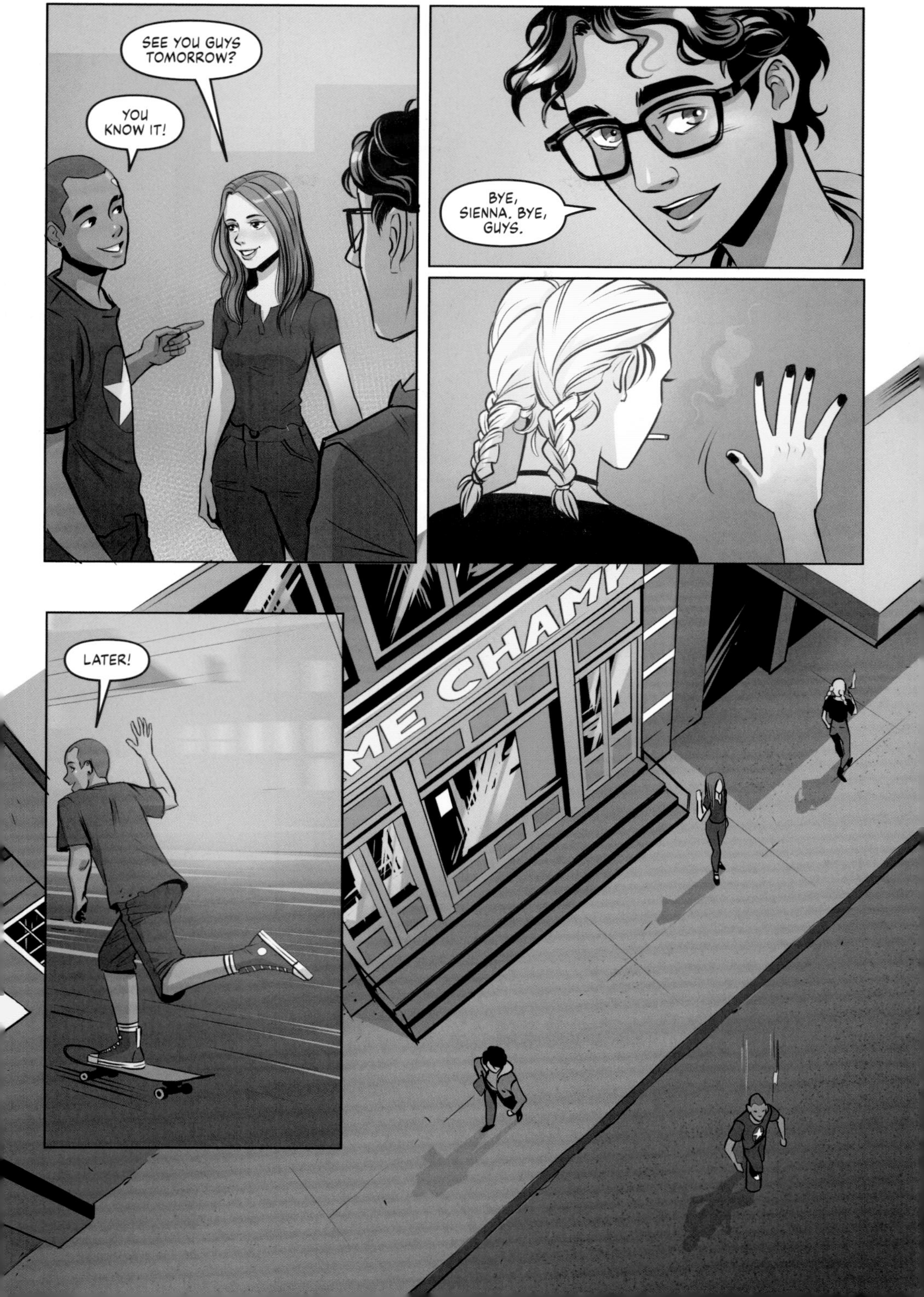
SEE YOU GUYS TOMORROW?
YOU KNOW IT!
BYE, SIENNA. BYE, GUYS.
LATER!
ME CHAMP

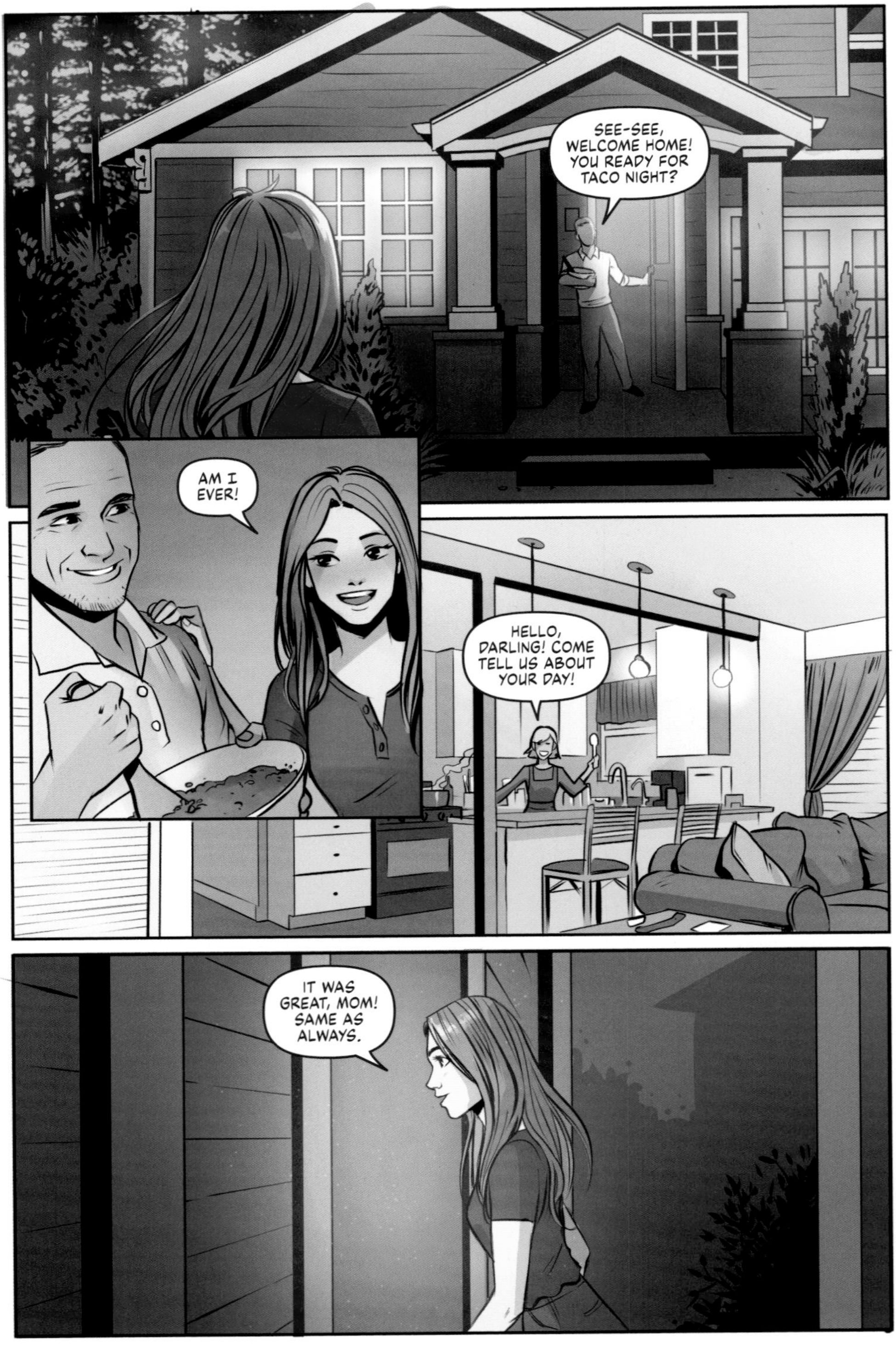
SEE-SEE, WELCOME HOME! YOU READY FOR TACO NIGHT?
AM I EVER!
HELLO, DARLING! COME TELL US ABOUT YOUR DAY!
IT WAS GREAT, MOM! SAME AS ALWAYS.

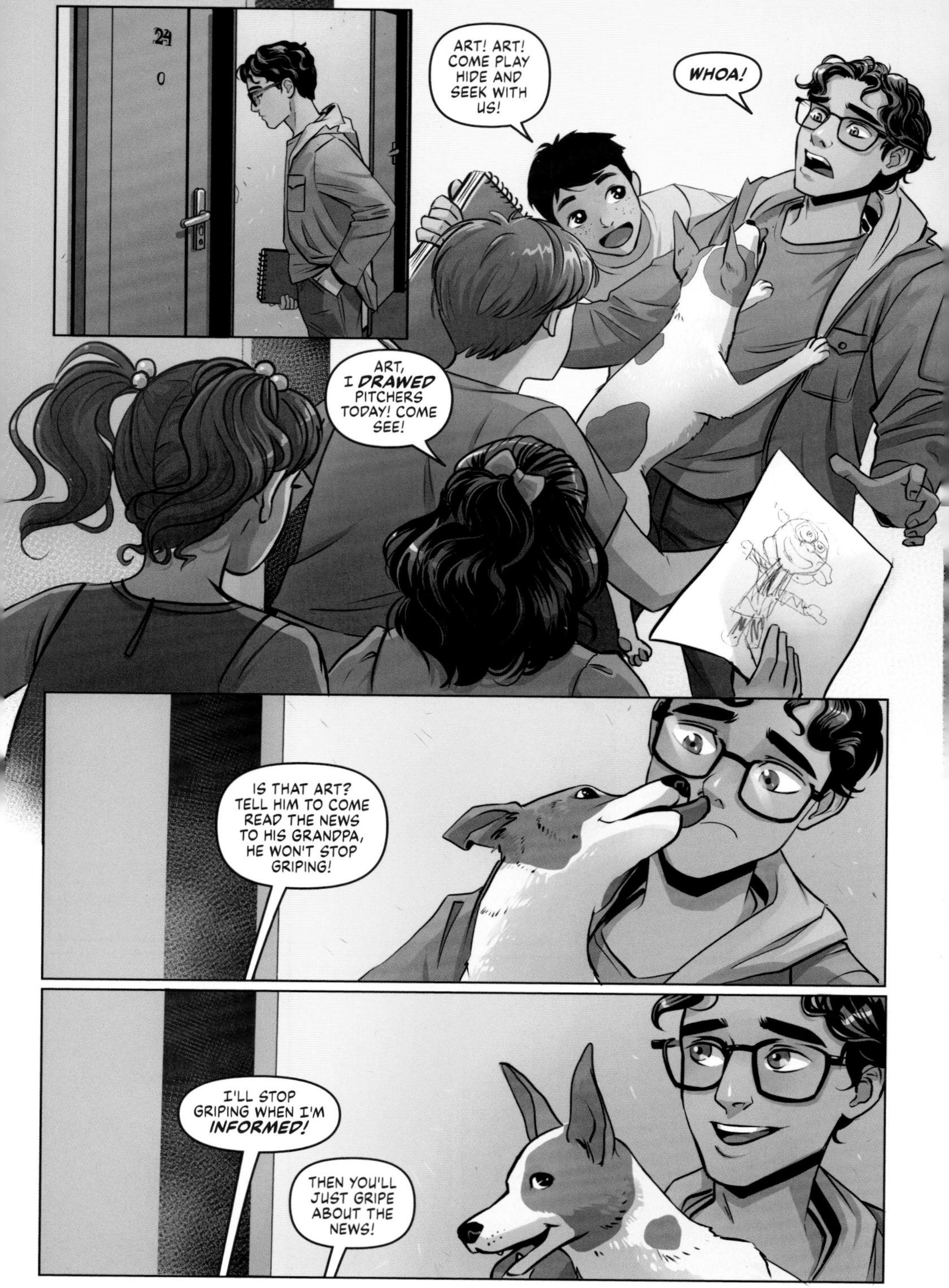
24
0
ART! ART! COME PLAY HIDE AND SEEK WITH US!
WHOA!
ART, I DRAWED PITCHERS TODAY! COME SEE!
IS THAT ART? TELL HIM TO COME READ THE NEWS TO HIS GRANDPA, HE WON'T STOP GRIPING!
I'LL STOP GRIPING WHEN I'M INFORMED!
THEN YOU'LL JUST GRIPE ABOUT THE NEWS!

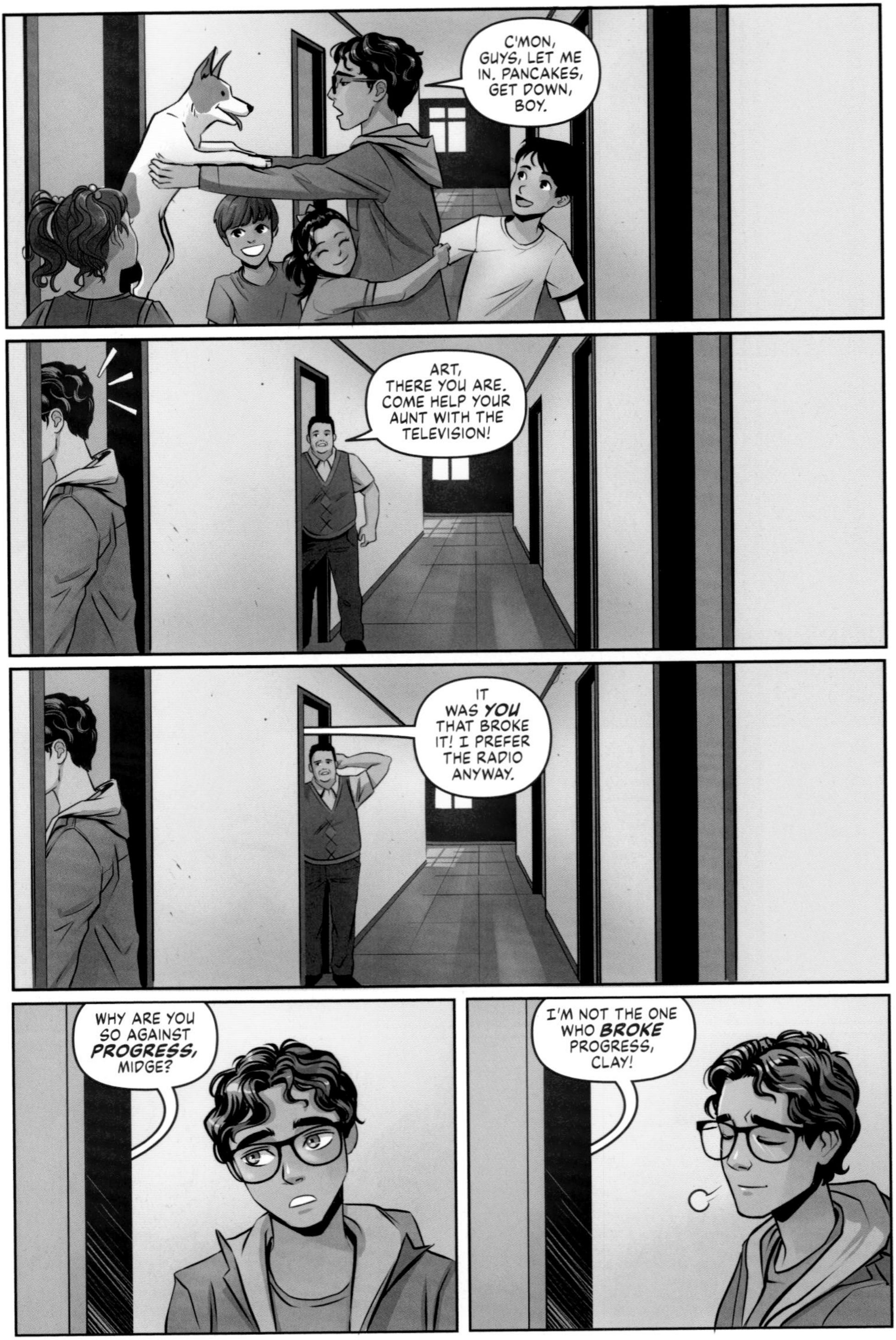
C'MON, GUYS, LET ME IN. PANCAKES, GET DOWN, BOY.
ART, THERE YOU ARE. COME HELP YOUR AUNT WITH THE TELEVISION!
IT WAS *YOU* THAT BROKE IT! I PREFER THE RADIO ANYWAY.
WHY ARE YOU SO AGAINST *PROGRESS,* MIDGE?
I'M NOT THE ONE WHO *BROKE* PROGRESS, CLAY!

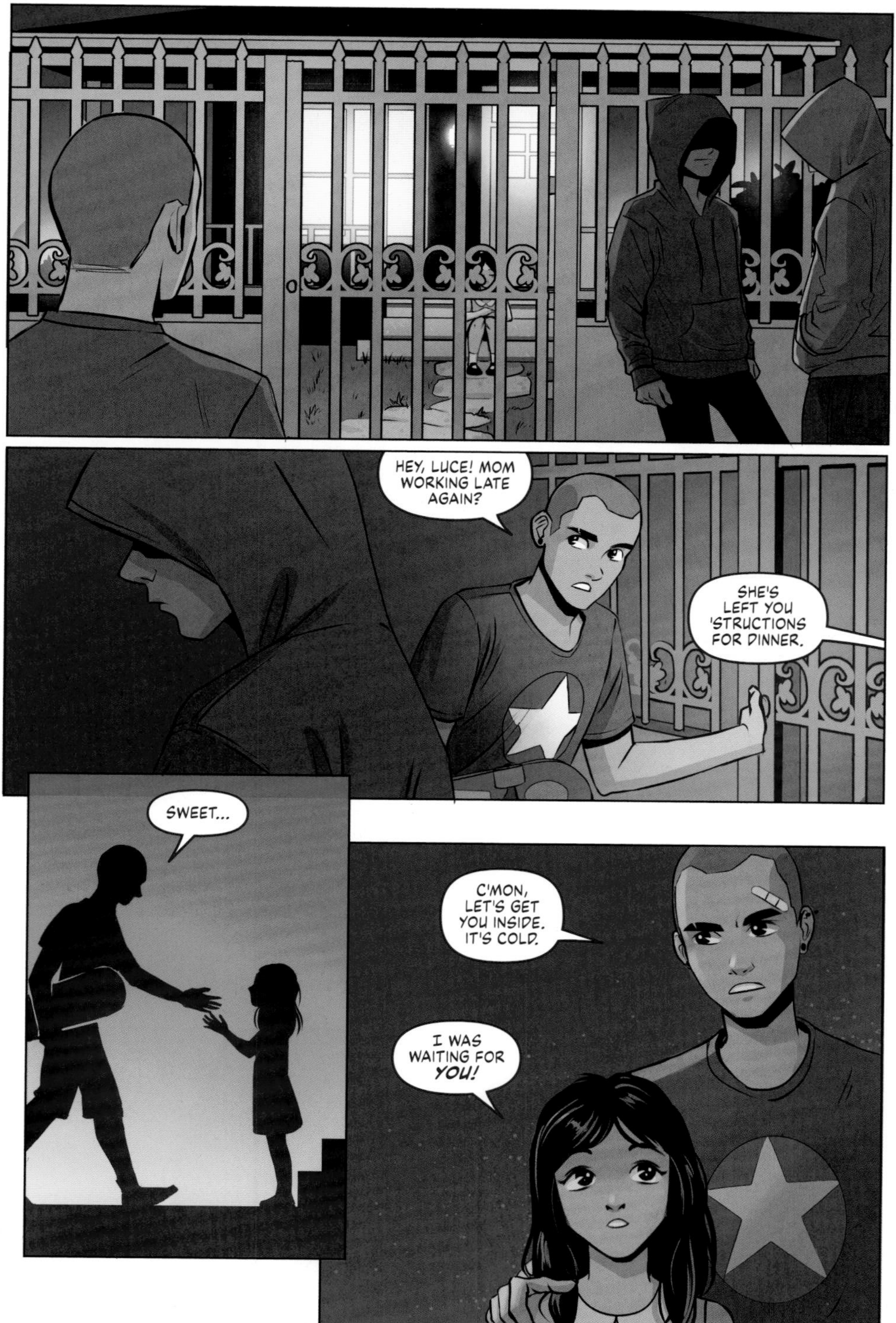
HEY, LUCE! MOM WORKING LATE AGAIN?
SHE'S LEFT YOU 'STRUCTIONS FOR DINNER.
SWEET...
C'MON, LET'S GET YOU INSIDE. IT'S COLD.
I WAS WAITING FOR *YOU!*

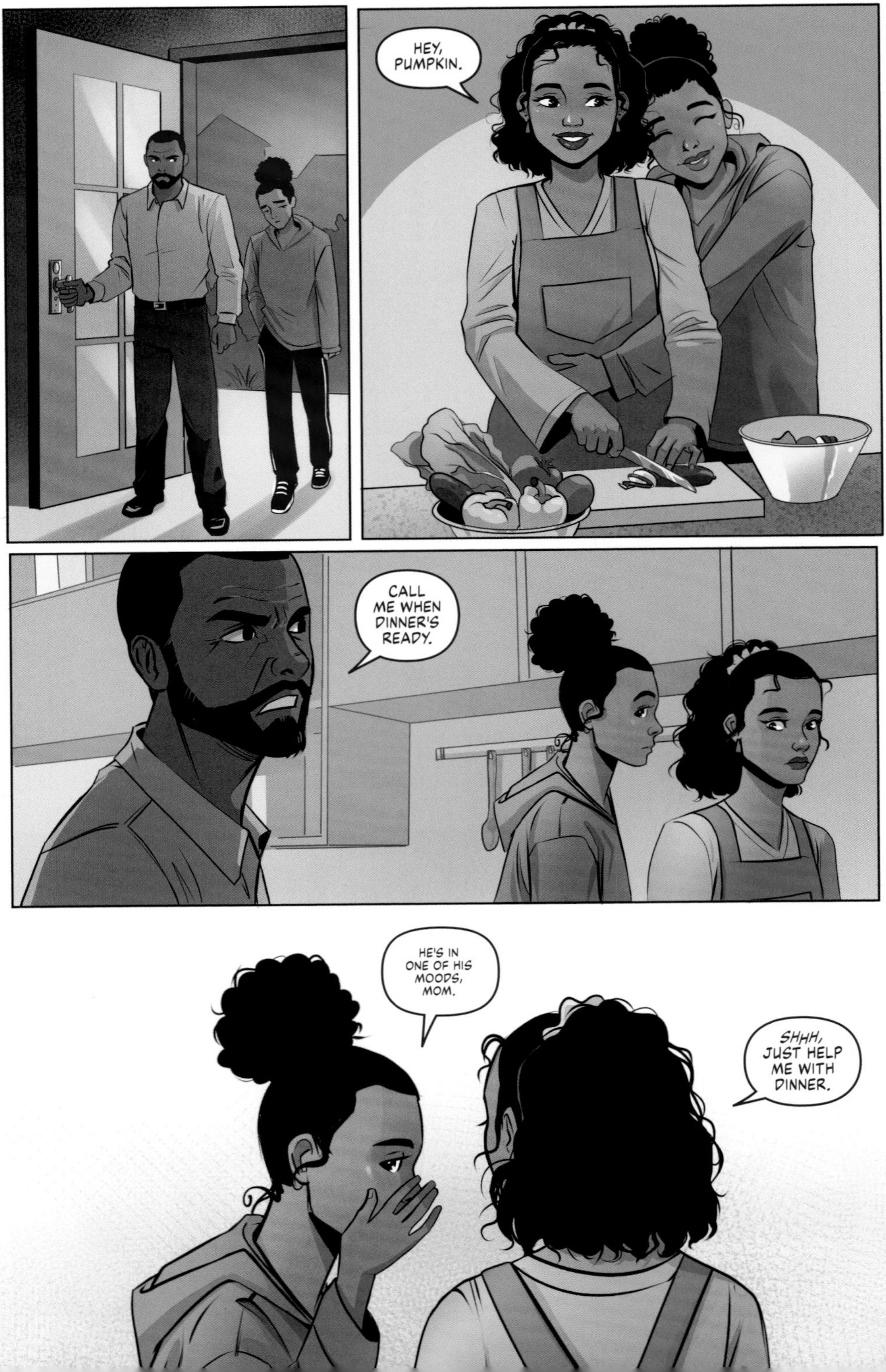
HEY, PUMPKIN.
CALL ME WHEN DINNER'S READY.
HE'S IN ONE OF HIS MOODS, MOM.
SHHH, JUST HELP ME WITH DINNER.

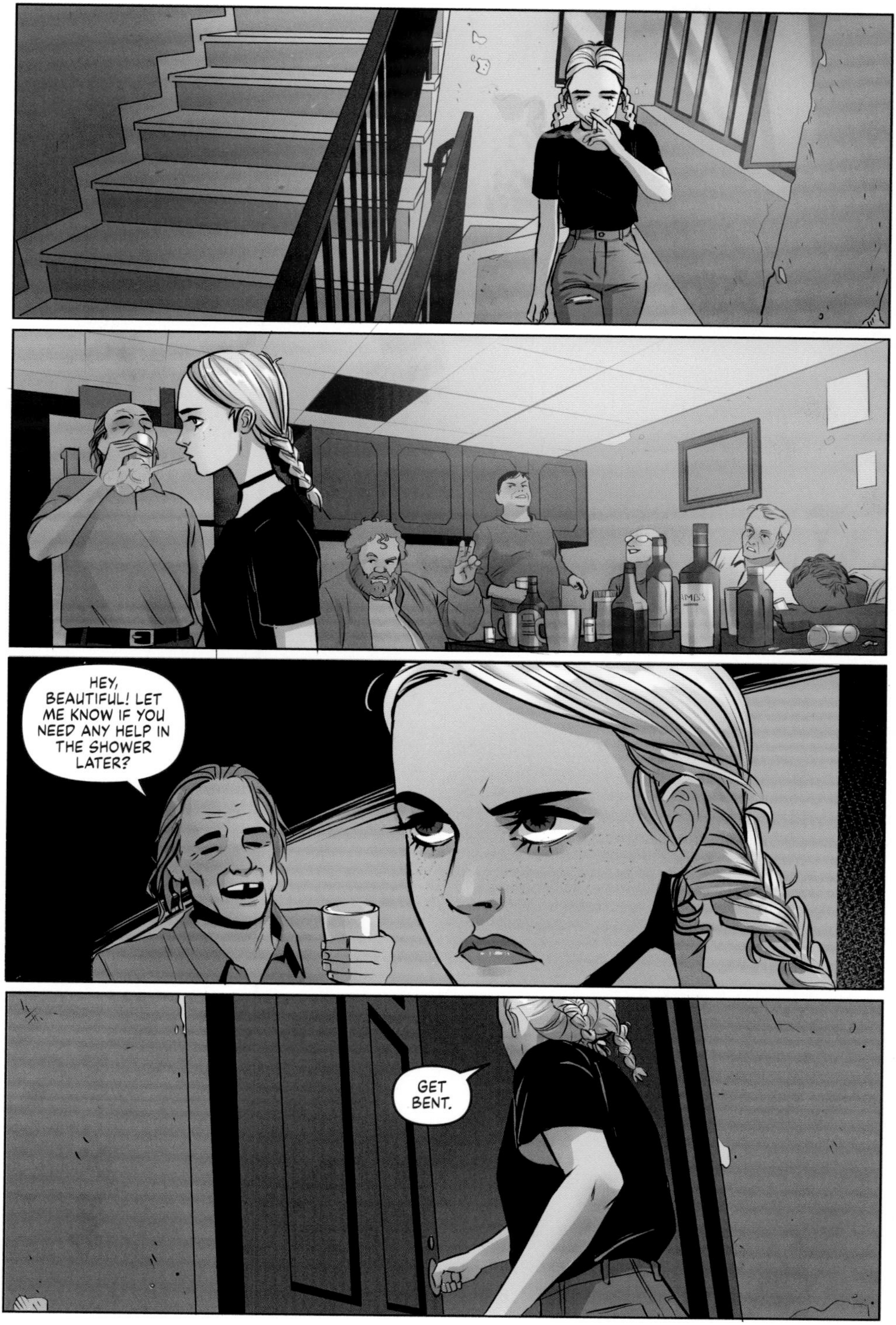
HEY, BEAUTIFUL! LET ME KNOW IF YOU NEED ANY HELP IN THE SHOWER LATER?
GET BENT.

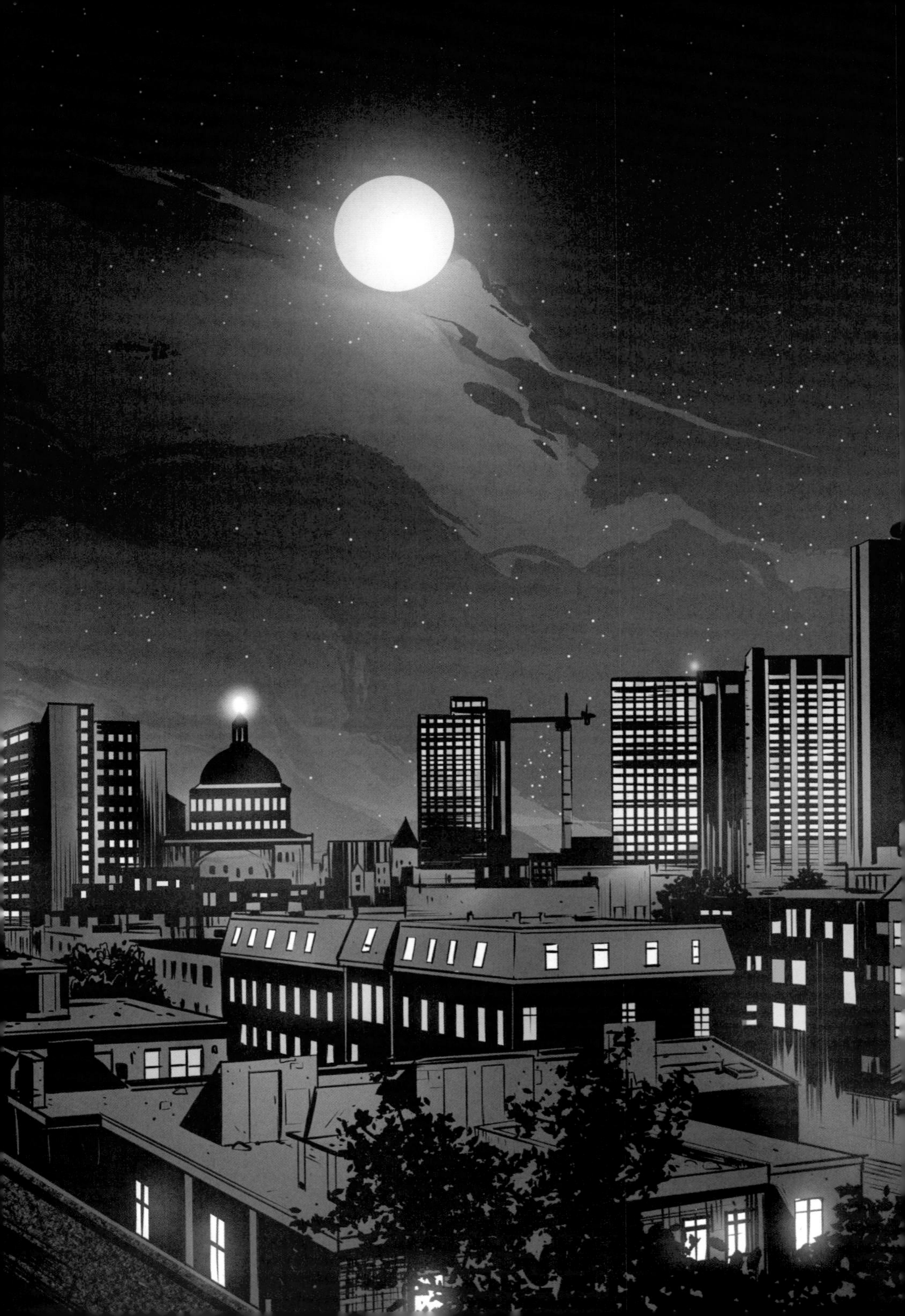

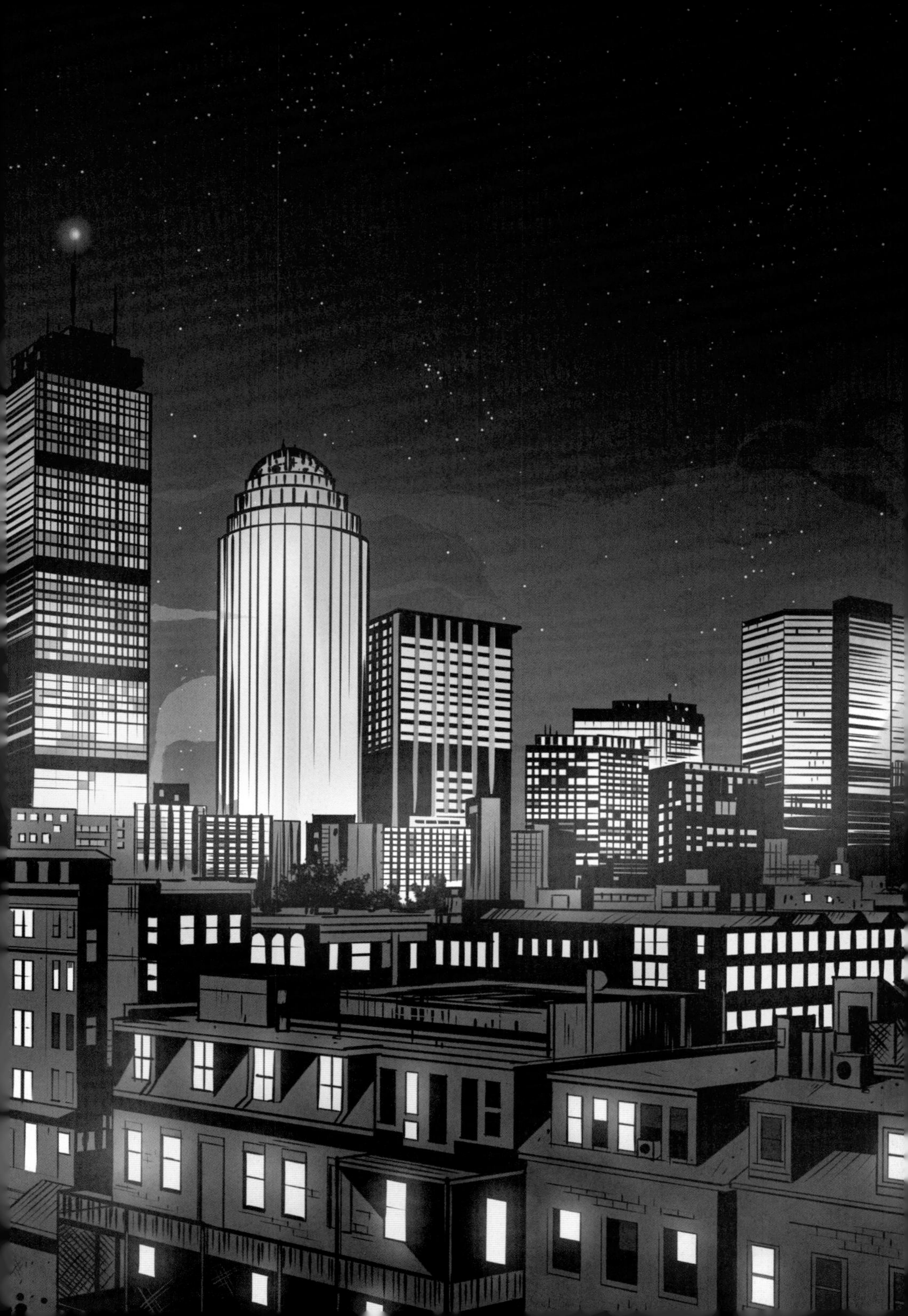

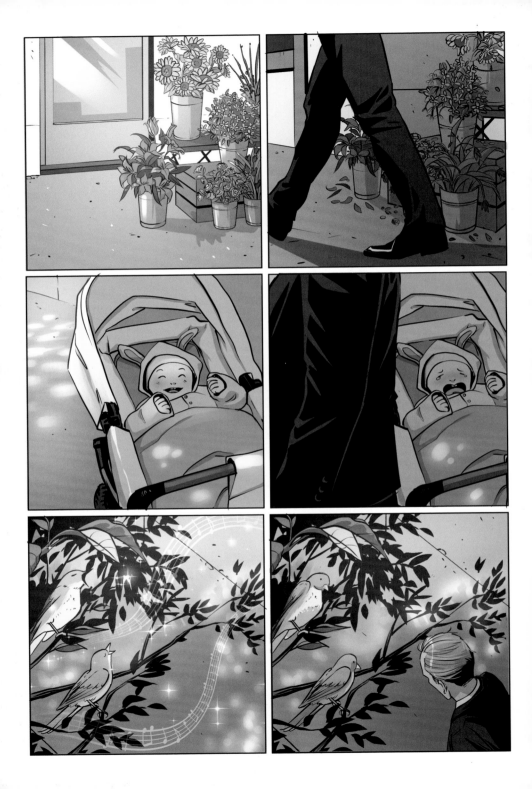

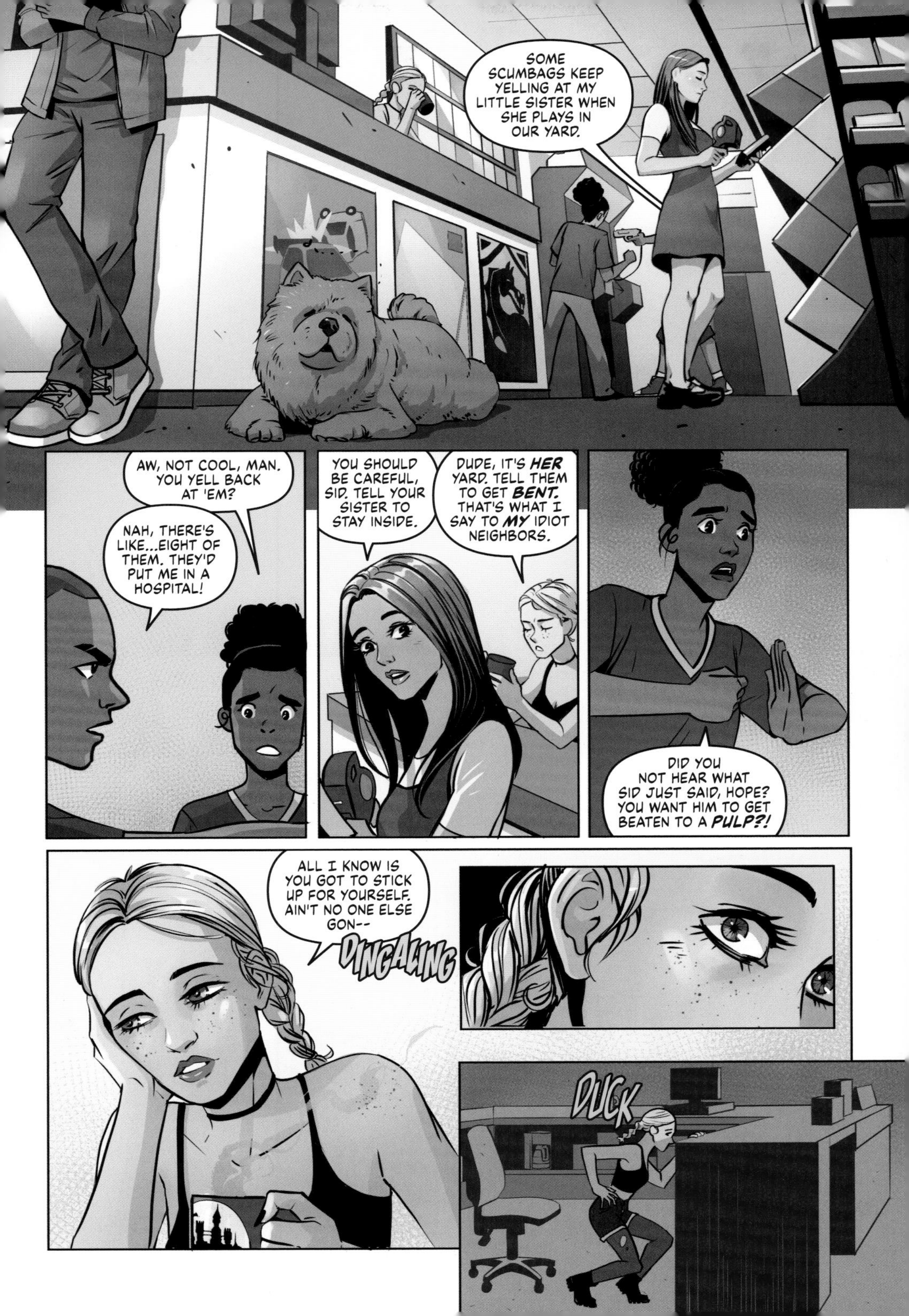
SOME SCUMBAGS KEEP YELLING AT MY LITTLE SISTER WHEN SHE PLAYS IN OUR YARD.
AW, NOT COOL, MAN. YOU YELL BACK AT 'EM?
NAH, THERE'S LIKE...EIGHT OF THEM. THEY'D PUT ME IN A HOSPITAL!
YOU SHOULD BE CAREFUL, SID. TELL YOUR SISTER TO STAY INSIDE.
DUDE, IT'S HER YARD. TELL THEM TO GET BENT. THAT'S WHAT I SAY TO MY IDIOT NEIGHBORS.
DID YOU NOT HEAR WHAT SID JUST SAID, HOPE? YOU WANT HIM TO GET BEATEN TO A PULP?!
ALL I KNOW IS YOU GOT TO STICK UP FOR YOURSELF. AIN'T NO ONE ELSE GON--
DINGALING
DUCK

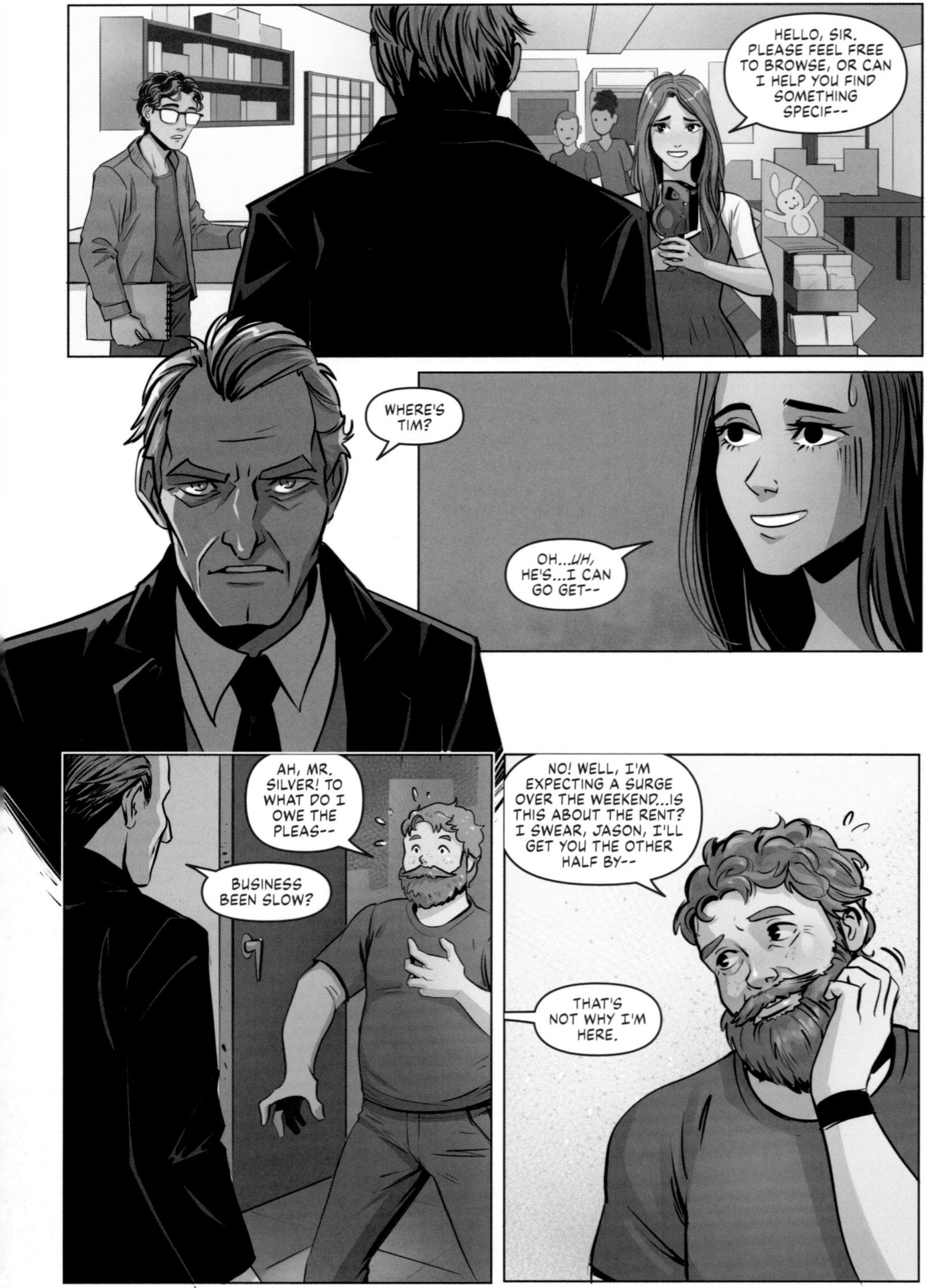
HELLO, SIR. PLEASE FEEL FREE TO BROWSE, OR CAN I HELP YOU FIND SOMETHING SPECIF--
WHERE'S TIM?
OH...*UH*, HE'S...I CAN GO GET--
AH, MR. SILVER! TO WHAT DO I OWE THE PLEAS--
BUSINESS BEEN SLOW?
NO! WELL, I'M EXPECTING A SURGE OVER THE WEEKEND...IS THIS ABOUT THE RENT? I SWEAR, JASON, I'LL GET YOU THE OTHER HALF BY--
THAT'S NOT WHY I'M HERE.

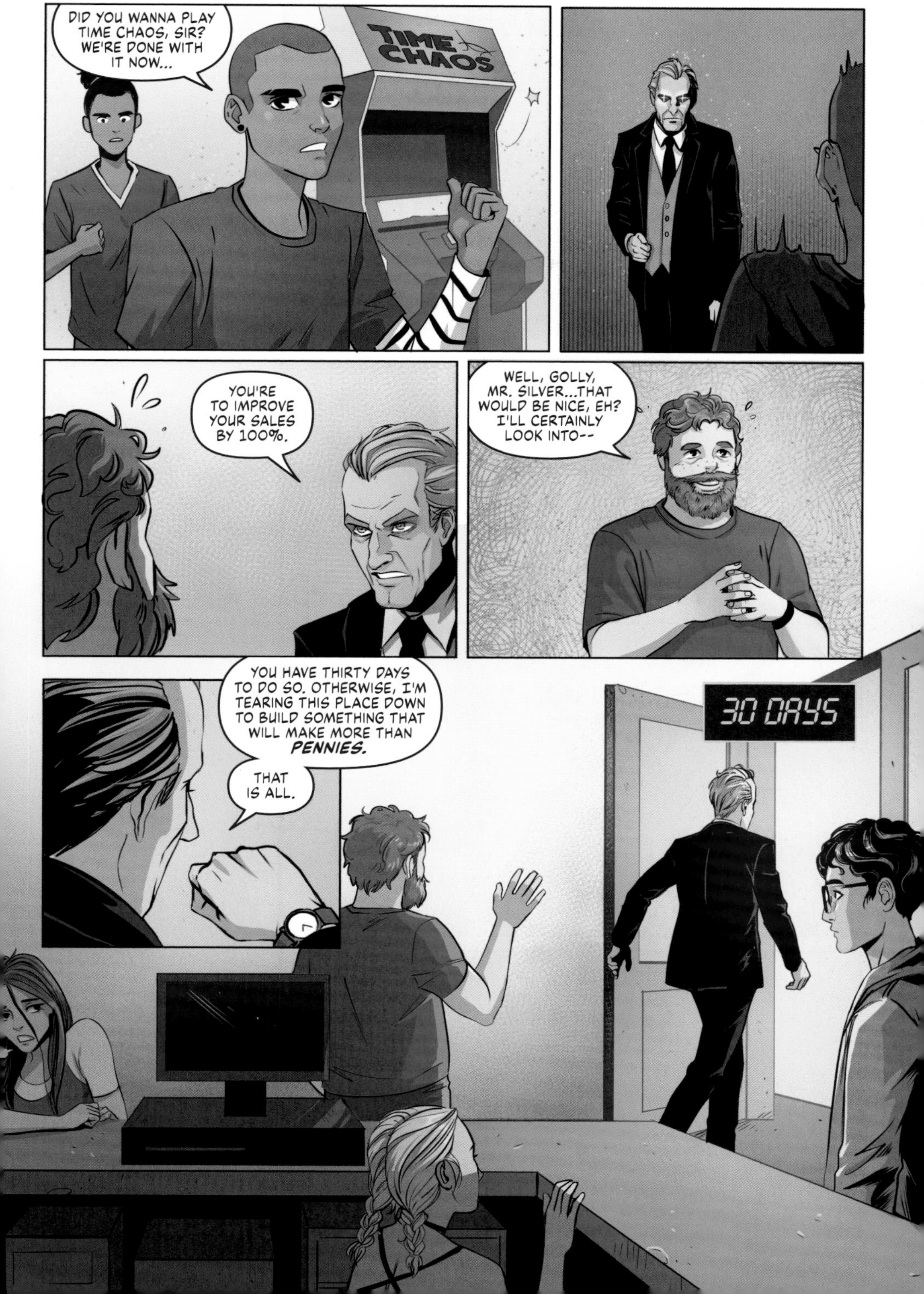
DID YOU WANNA PLAY TIME CHAOS, SIR? WE'RE DONE WITH IT NOW...
TIME CHAOS
YOU'RE TO IMPROVE YOUR SALES BY 100%.
WELL, GOLLY, MR. SILVER...THAT WOULD BE NICE, EH? I'LL CERTAINLY LOOK INTO--
YOU HAVE THIRTY DAYS TO DO SO. OTHERWISE, I'M TEARING THIS PLACE DOWN TO BUILD SOMETHING THAT WILL MAKE MORE THAN ***PENNIES.***
THAT IS ALL.
30 DAYS

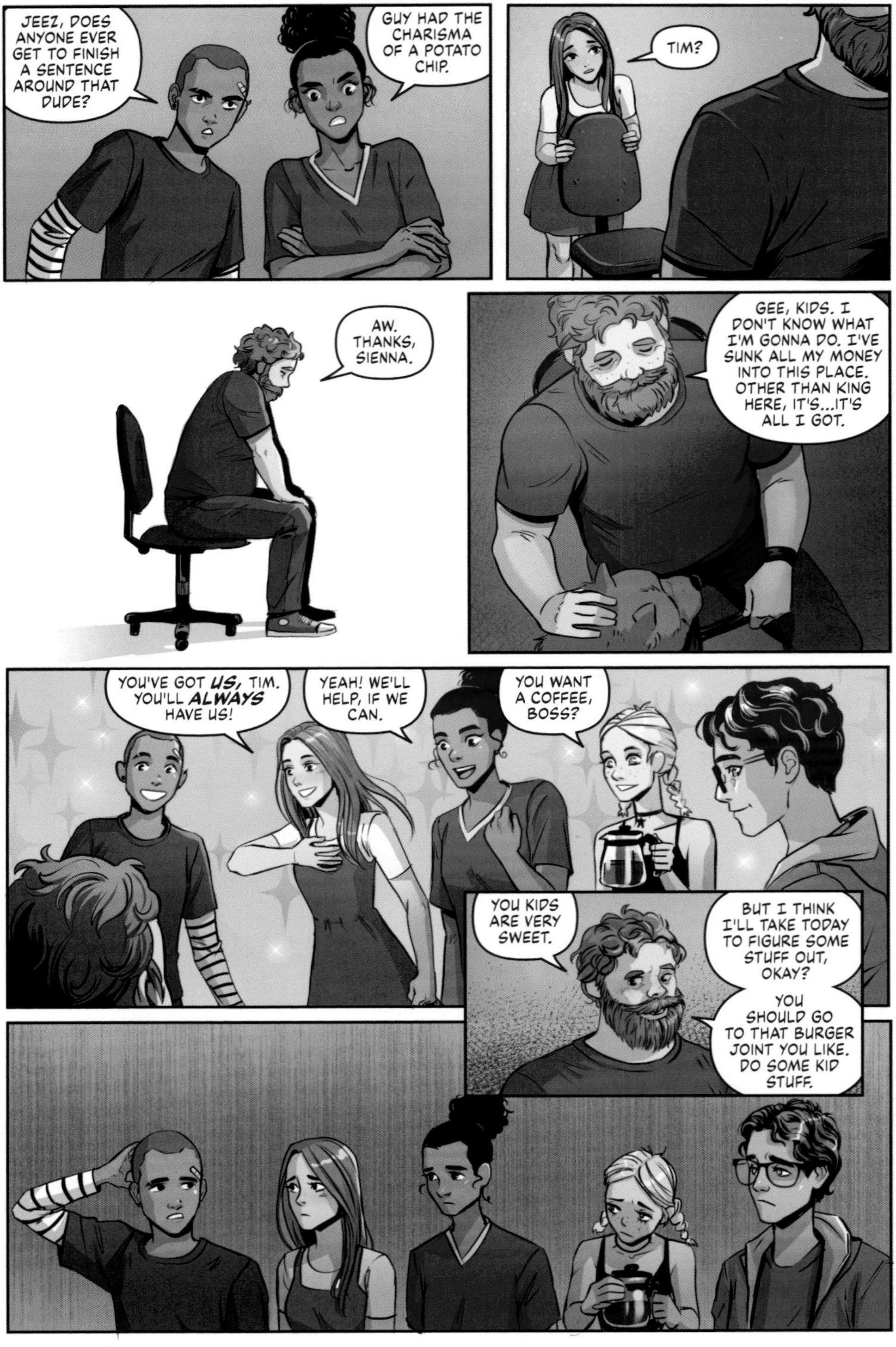
JEEZ, DOES ANYONE EVER GET TO FINISH A SENTENCE AROUND THAT DUDE?
GUY HAD THE CHARISMA OF A POTATO CHIP.
TIM?
AW. THANKS, SIENNA.
GEE, KIDS. I DON'T KNOW WHAT I'M GONNA DO. I'VE SUNK ALL MY MONEY INTO THIS PLACE. OTHER THAN KING HERE, IT'S...IT'S ALL I GOT.
YOU'VE GOT **US,** TIM. YOU'LL **ALWAYS** HAVE US!
YEAH! WE'LL HELP, IF WE CAN.
YOU WANT A COFFEE, BOSS?
YOU KIDS ARE VERY SWEET.
BUT I THINK I'LL TAKE TODAY TO FIGURE SOME STUFF OUT, OKAY?
YOU SHOULD GO TO THAT BURGER JOINT YOU LIKE. DO SOME KID STUFF.

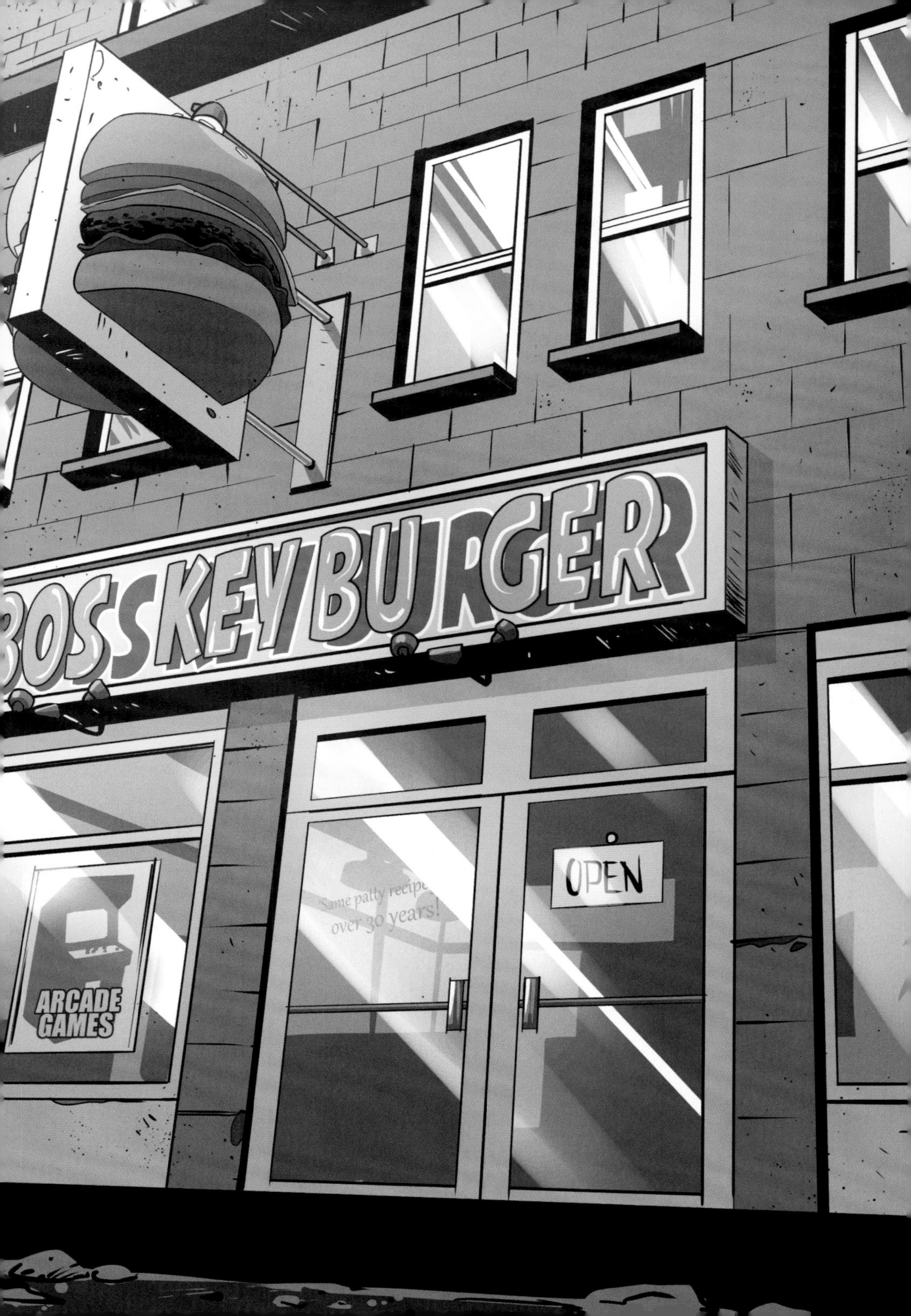
BOSSKEY BURGER
Same patty recipe
over 30 years!
OPEN
ARCADE
GAMES

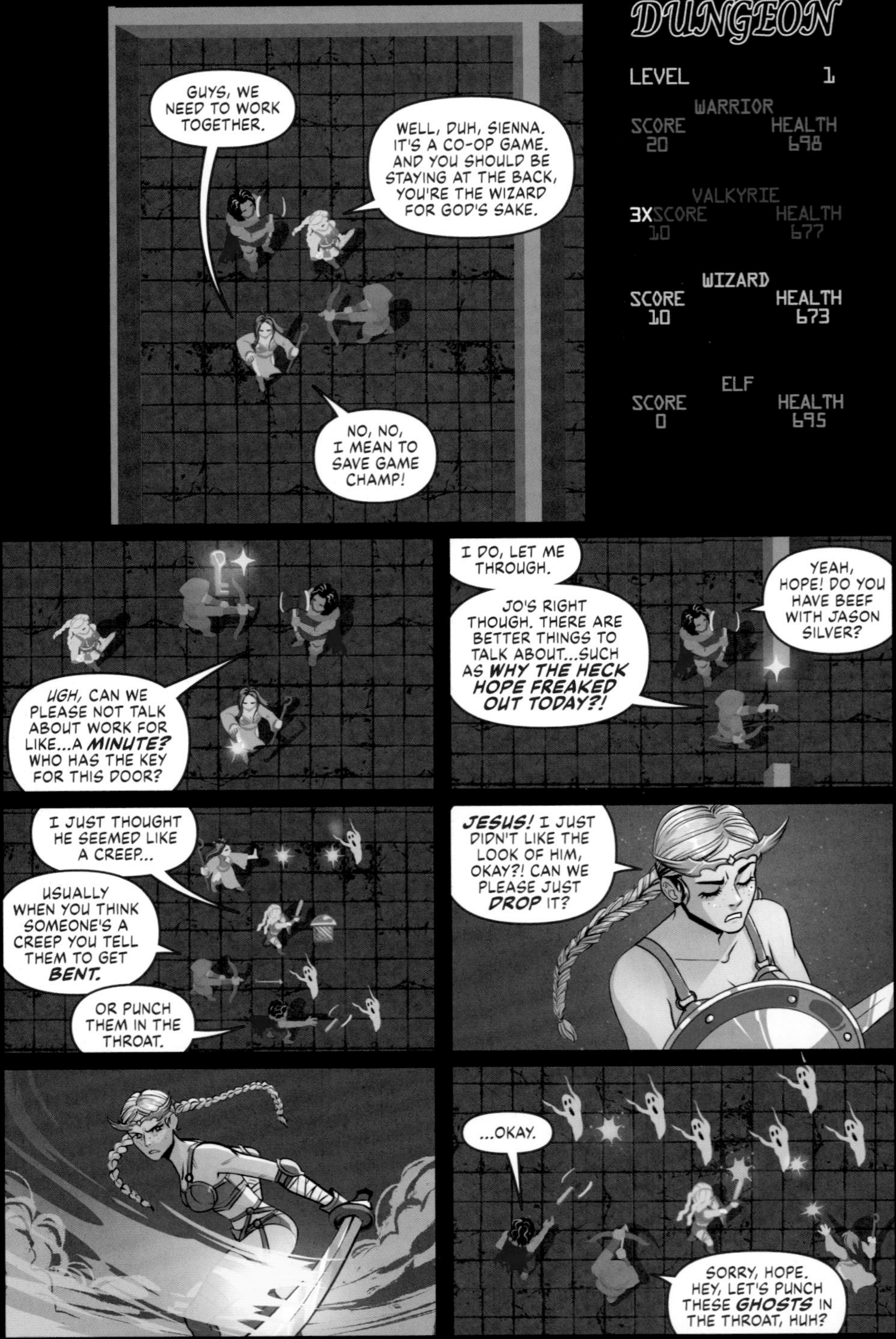
DUNGEON
LEVEL 1
WARRIOR
SCORE 20 HEALTH 698
VALKYRIE
3X SCORE 10 HEALTH 677
WIZARD
SCORE 10 HEALTH 673
ELF
SCORE 0 HEALTH 695
GUYS, WE NEED TO WORK TOGETHER.
WELL, DUH, SIENNA. IT'S A CO-OP GAME. AND YOU SHOULD BE STAYING AT THE BACK, YOU'RE THE WIZARD FOR GOD'S SAKE.
NO, NO, I MEAN TO SAVE GAME CHAMP!
UGH, CAN WE PLEASE NOT TALK ABOUT WORK FOR LIKE...A ***MINUTE?*** WHO HAS THE KEY FOR THIS DOOR?
I DO, LET ME THROUGH.
JO'S RIGHT THOUGH. THERE ARE BETTER THINGS TO TALK ABOUT...SUCH AS ***WHY THE HECK HOPE FREAKED OUT TODAY?!***
YEAH, HOPE! DO YOU HAVE BEEF WITH JASON SILVER?
I JUST THOUGHT HE SEEMED LIKE A CREEP...
USUALLY WHEN YOU THINK SOMEONE'S A CREEP YOU TELL THEM TO GET ***BENT.***
OR PUNCH THEM IN THE THROAT.
JESUS! I JUST DIDN'T LIKE THE LOOK OF HIM, OKAY?! CAN WE PLEASE JUST ***DROP*** IT?
...OKAY.
SORRY, HOPE. HEY, LET'S PUNCH THESE ***GHOSTS*** IN THE THROAT, HUH?

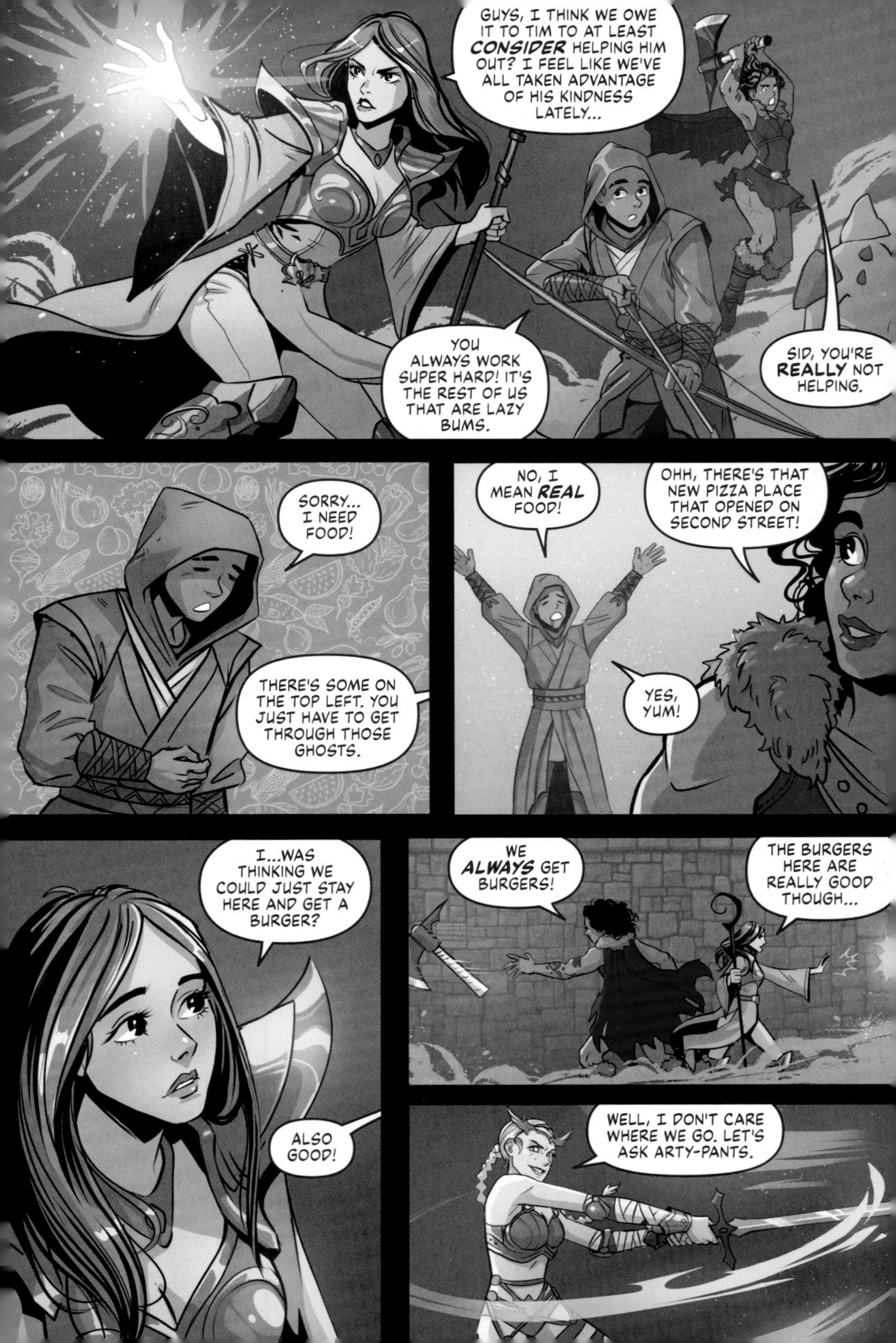
GUYS, I THINK WE OWE IT TO TIM TO AT LEAST ***CONSIDER*** HELPING HIM OUT? I FEEL LIKE WE'VE ALL TAKEN ADVANTAGE OF HIS KINDNESS LATELY...
YOU ALWAYS WORK SUPER HARD! IT'S THE REST OF US THAT ARE LAZY BUMS.
SID, YOU'RE **REALLY** NOT HELPING.
SORRY... I NEED FOOD!
THERE'S SOME ON THE TOP LEFT. YOU JUST HAVE TO GET THROUGH THOSE GHOSTS.
NO, I MEAN ***REAL*** FOOD!
OHH, THERE'S THAT NEW PIZZA PLACE THAT OPENED ON SECOND STREET!
YES, YUM!
I...WAS THINKING WE COULD JUST STAY HERE AND GET A BURGER?
ALSO GOOD!
WE ***ALWAYS*** GET BURGERS!
THE BURGERS HERE ARE REALLY GOOD THOUGH...
WELL, I DON'T CARE WHERE WE GO. LET'S ASK ARTY-PANTS.

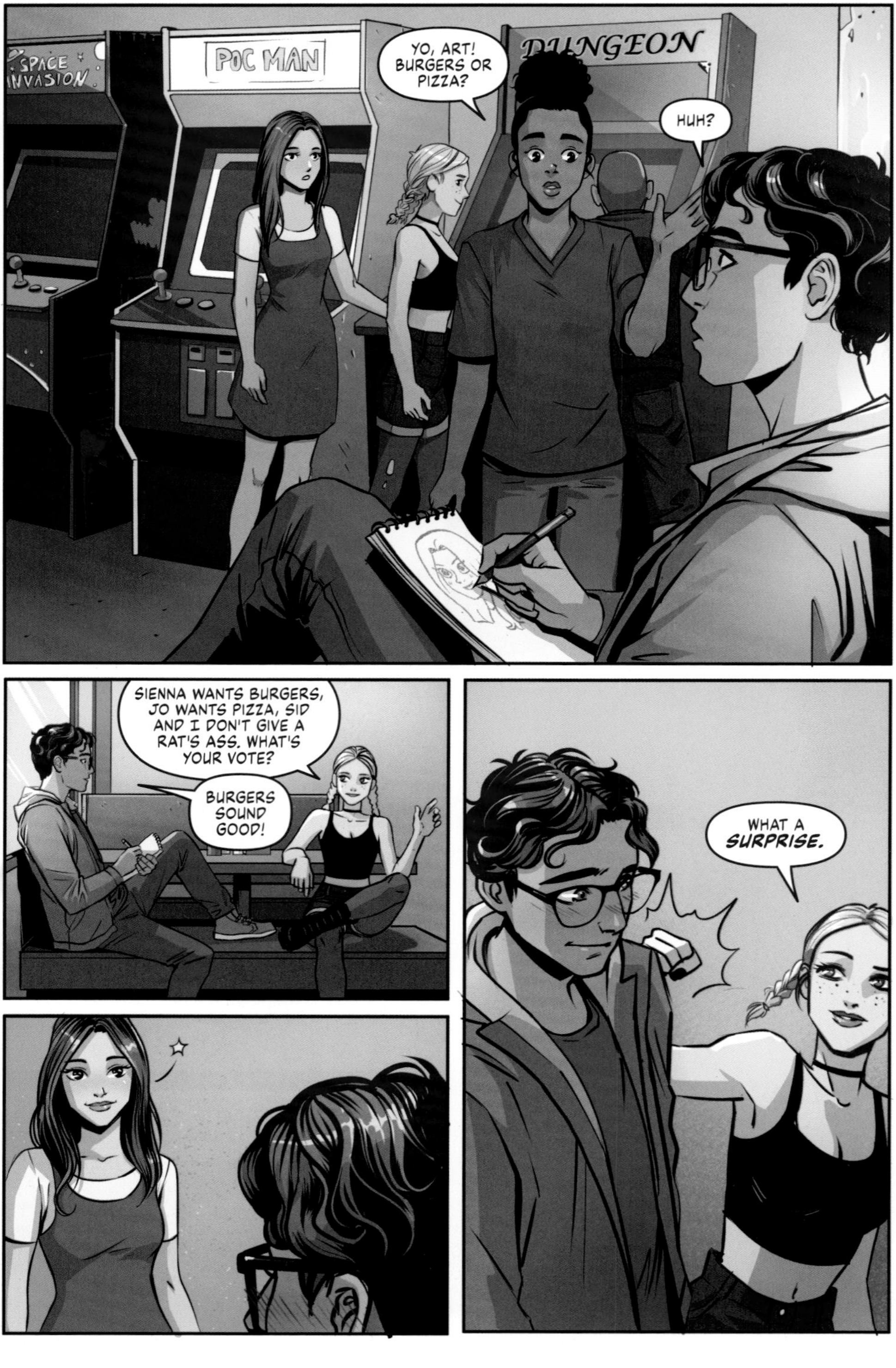
SPACE INVASION
POC MAN
DUNGEON
YO, ART! BURGERS OR PIZZA?
HUH?
SIENNA WANTS BURGERS, JO WANTS PIZZA, SID AND I DON'T GIVE A RAT'S ASS. WHAT'S YOUR VOTE?
BURGERS SOUND GOOD!
WHAT A SURPRISE.

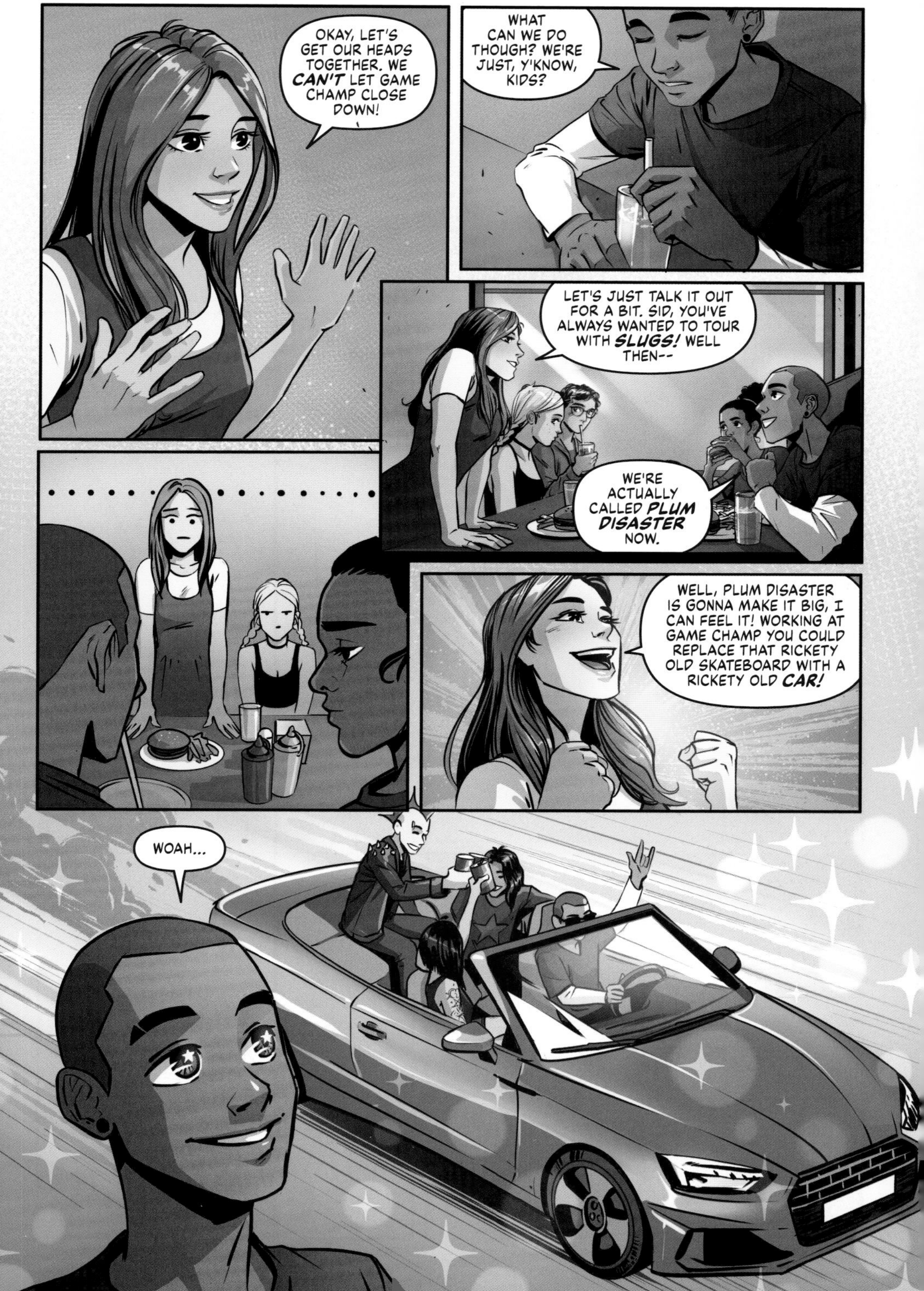
OKAY, LET'S GET OUR HEADS TOGETHER. WE CAN'T LET GAME CHAMP CLOSE DOWN!
WHAT CAN WE DO THOUGH? WE'RE JUST, Y'KNOW, KIDS?
LET'S JUST TALK IT OUT FOR A BIT. SID, YOU'VE ALWAYS WANTED TO TOUR WITH SLUGS! WELL THEN--
WE'RE ACTUALLY CALLED PLUM DISASTER NOW.
. . . .
WELL, PLUM DISASTER IS GONNA MAKE IT BIG, I CAN FEEL IT! WORKING AT GAME CHAMP YOU COULD REPLACE THAT RICKETY OLD SKATEBOARD WITH A RICKETY OLD CAR!
WOAH...

ART, GAME CHAMP IS WHERE YOU GET THE INSPIRATION FOR YOUR AMAZING COMICS. THEY ARE SO RELATABLE AND HILARIOUS!

THERE? ...OCHES

YEAH! YOU CAN TALK TO ME!

YOU!? HAHAHA! I BET YOU DON'T EVEN KNOW WHAT A JOY-STICK IS, DO YA, SWEET HEART!?

PERSONALLY, I'M A BIG FAN OF-

UM...

DON'T Y...
EN WHO
O THE
OFFEE

OW!

H-HOPE!

YOU STILL HAVE THOSE...AND KEEP THEM IN YOUR PURSE?

ANYWAY...

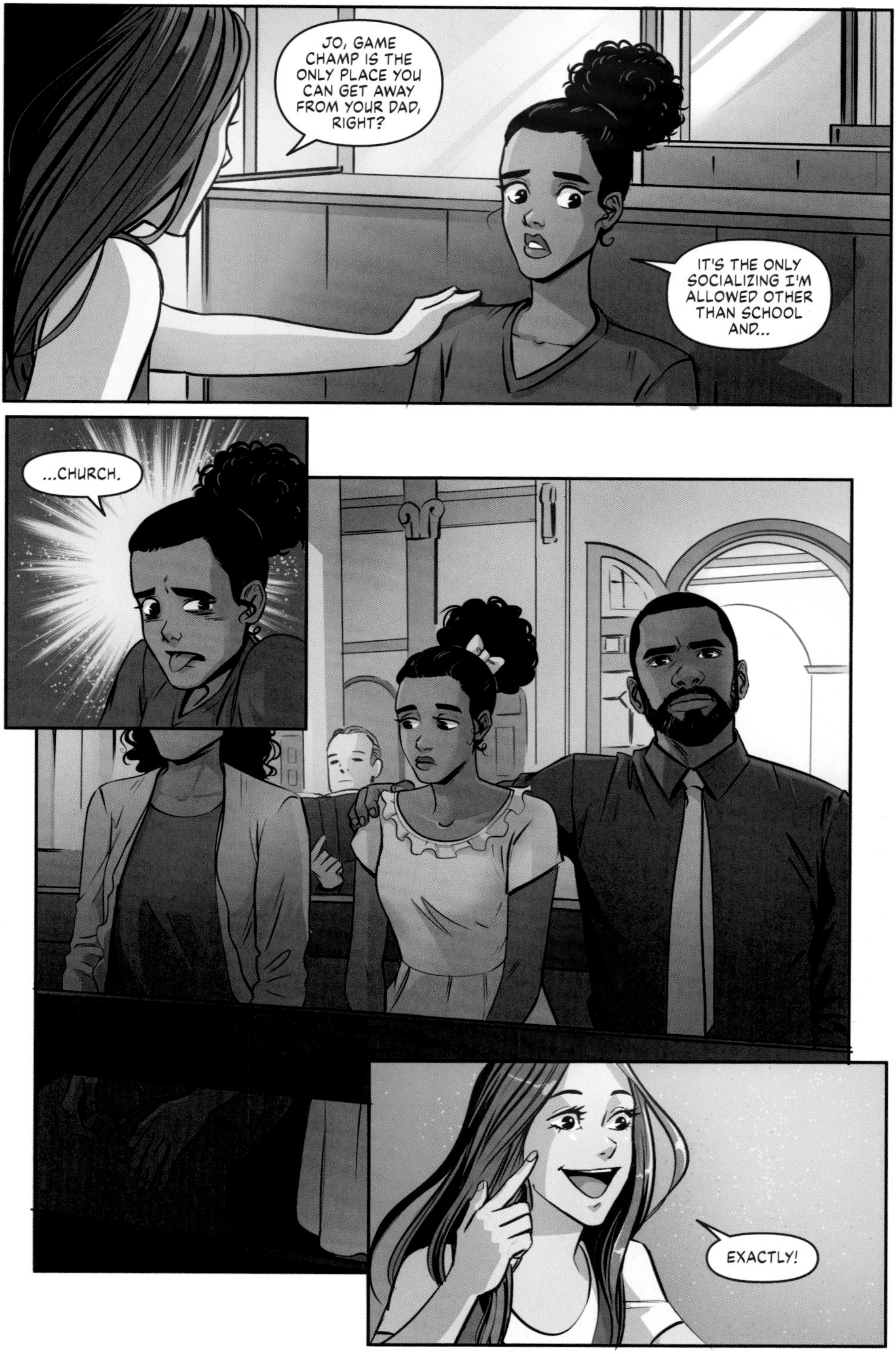
JO, GAME CHAMP IS THE ONLY PLACE YOU CAN GET AWAY FROM YOUR DAD, RIGHT?
IT'S THE ONLY SOCIALIZING I'M ALLOWED OTHER THAN SCHOOL AND...
...CHURCH.
EXACTLY!

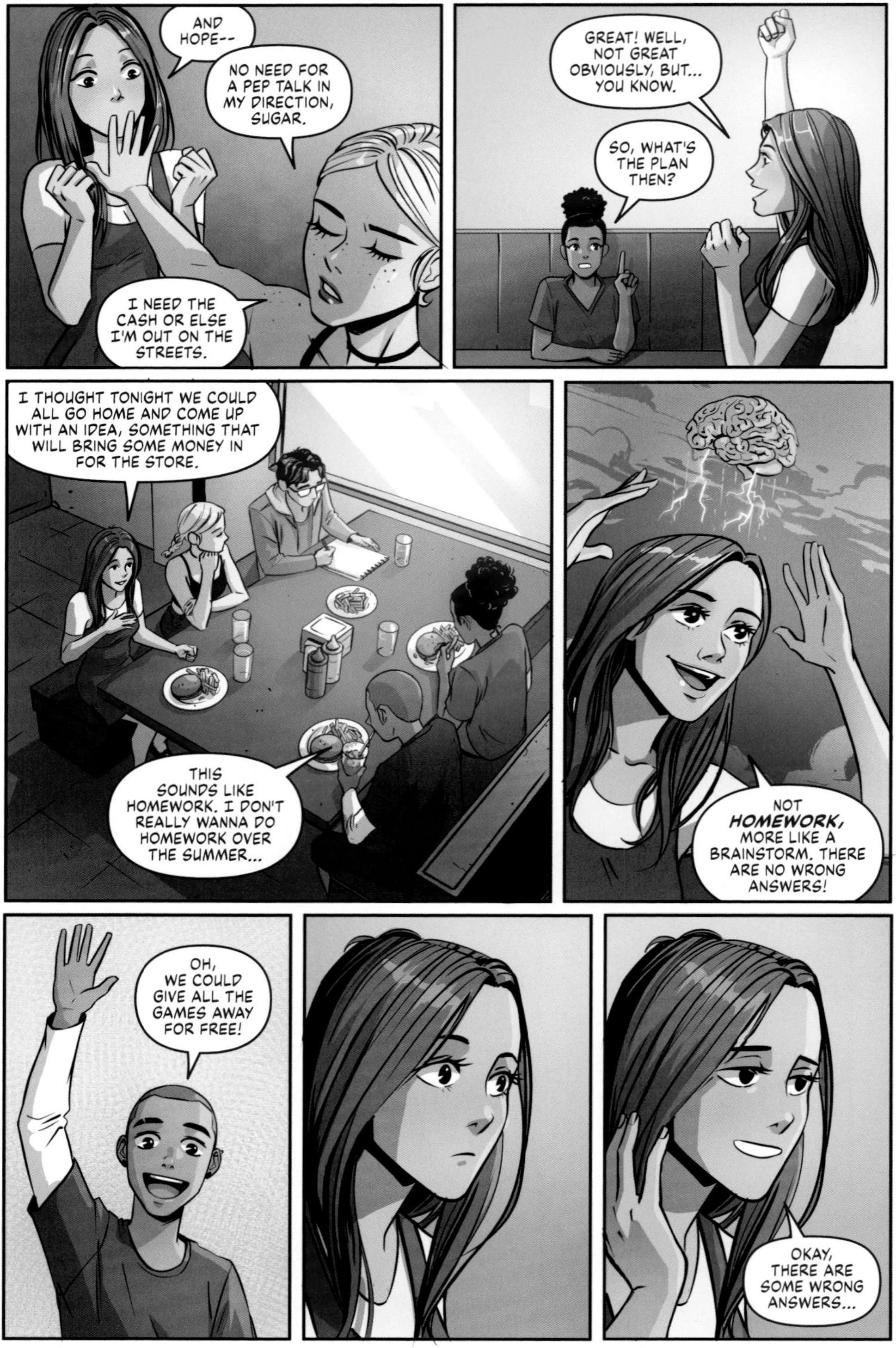
AND HOPE--
NO NEED FOR A PEP TALK IN MY DIRECTION, SUGAR.
I NEED THE CASH OR ELSE I'M OUT ON THE STREETS.
GREAT! WELL, NOT GREAT OBVIOUSLY, BUT... YOU KNOW.
SO, WHAT'S THE PLAN THEN?
I THOUGHT TONIGHT WE COULD ALL GO HOME AND COME UP WITH AN IDEA, SOMETHING THAT WILL BRING SOME MONEY IN FOR THE STORE.
THIS SOUNDS LIKE HOMEWORK. I DON'T REALLY WANNA DO HOMEWORK OVER THE SUMMER...
NOT ***HOMEWORK,*** MORE LIKE A BRAINSTORM. THERE ARE NO WRONG ANSWERS!
OH, WE COULD GIVE ALL THE GAMES AWAY FOR FREE!
OKAY, THERE ARE SOME WRONG ANSWERS...

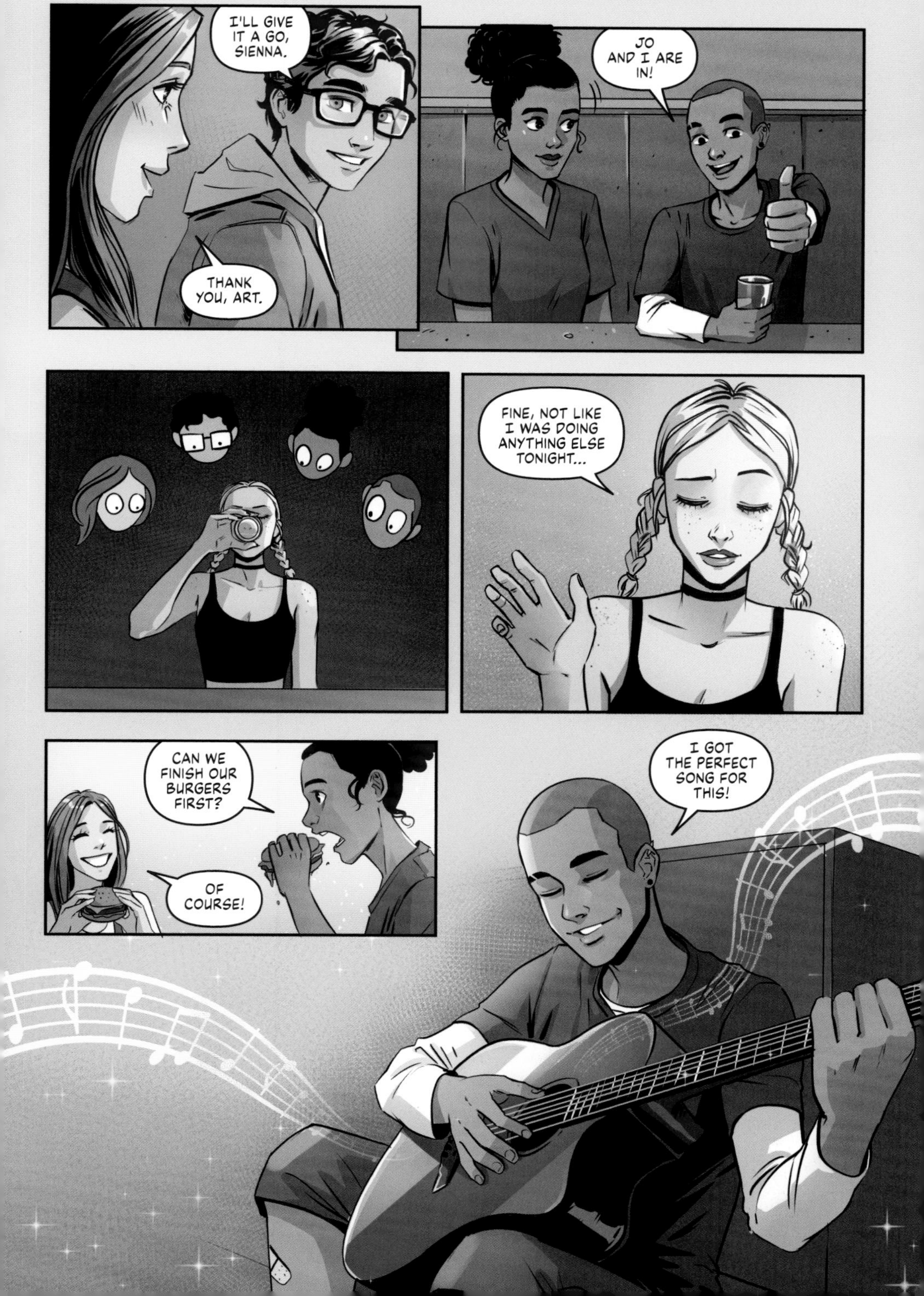
I'LL GIVE IT A GO, SIENNA.
THANK YOU, ART.
JO AND I ARE IN!
FINE, NOT LIKE I WAS DOING ANYTHING ELSE TONIGHT...
CAN WE FINISH OUR BURGERS FIRST?
OF COURSE!
I GOT THE PERFECT SONG FOR THIS!

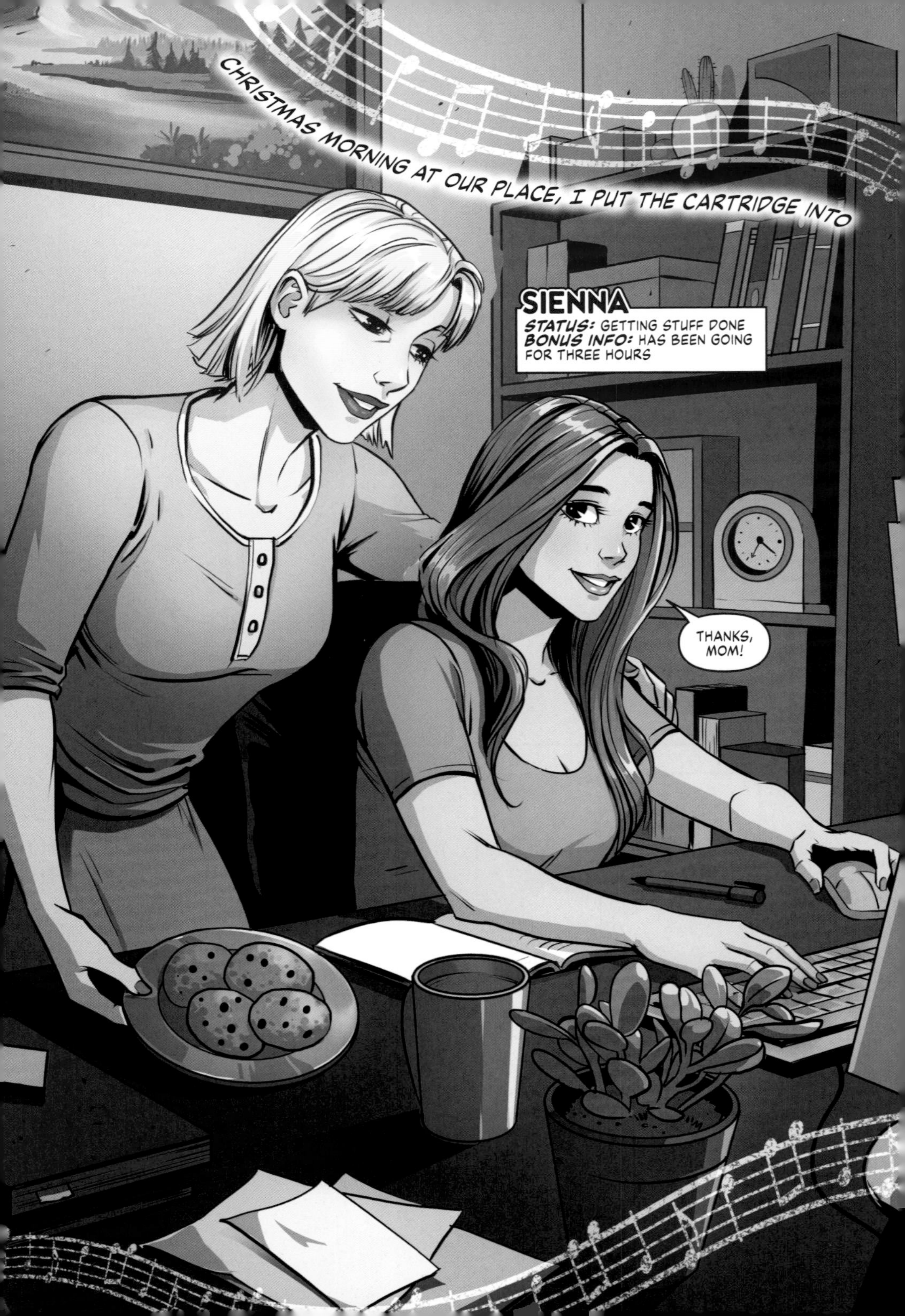
CHRISTMAS MORNING AT OUR PLACE, I PUT THE CARTRIDGE INTO
SIENNA
STATUS: GETTING STUFF DONE
BONUS INFO: HAS BEEN GOING FOR THREE HOURS
THANKS, MOM!

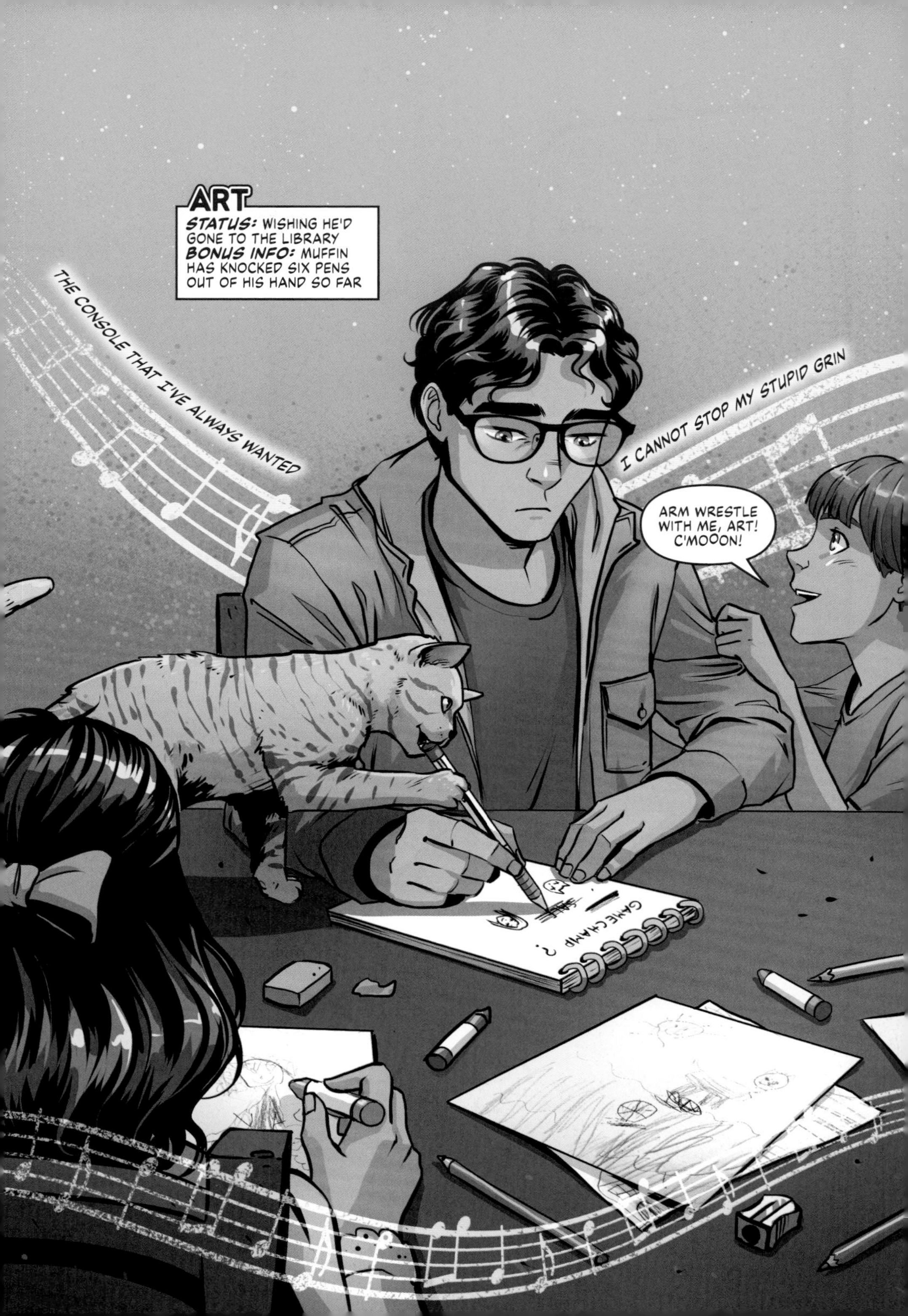
ART
STATUS: WISHING HE'D GONE TO THE LIBRARY
BONUS INFO: MUFFIN HAS KNOCKED SIX PENS OUT OF HIS HAND SO FAR
THE CONSOLE THAT I'VE ALWAYS WANTED
I CANNOT STOP MY STUPID GRIN
ARM WRESTLE WITH ME, ART! C'MOOON!
GAME CHAMP ?

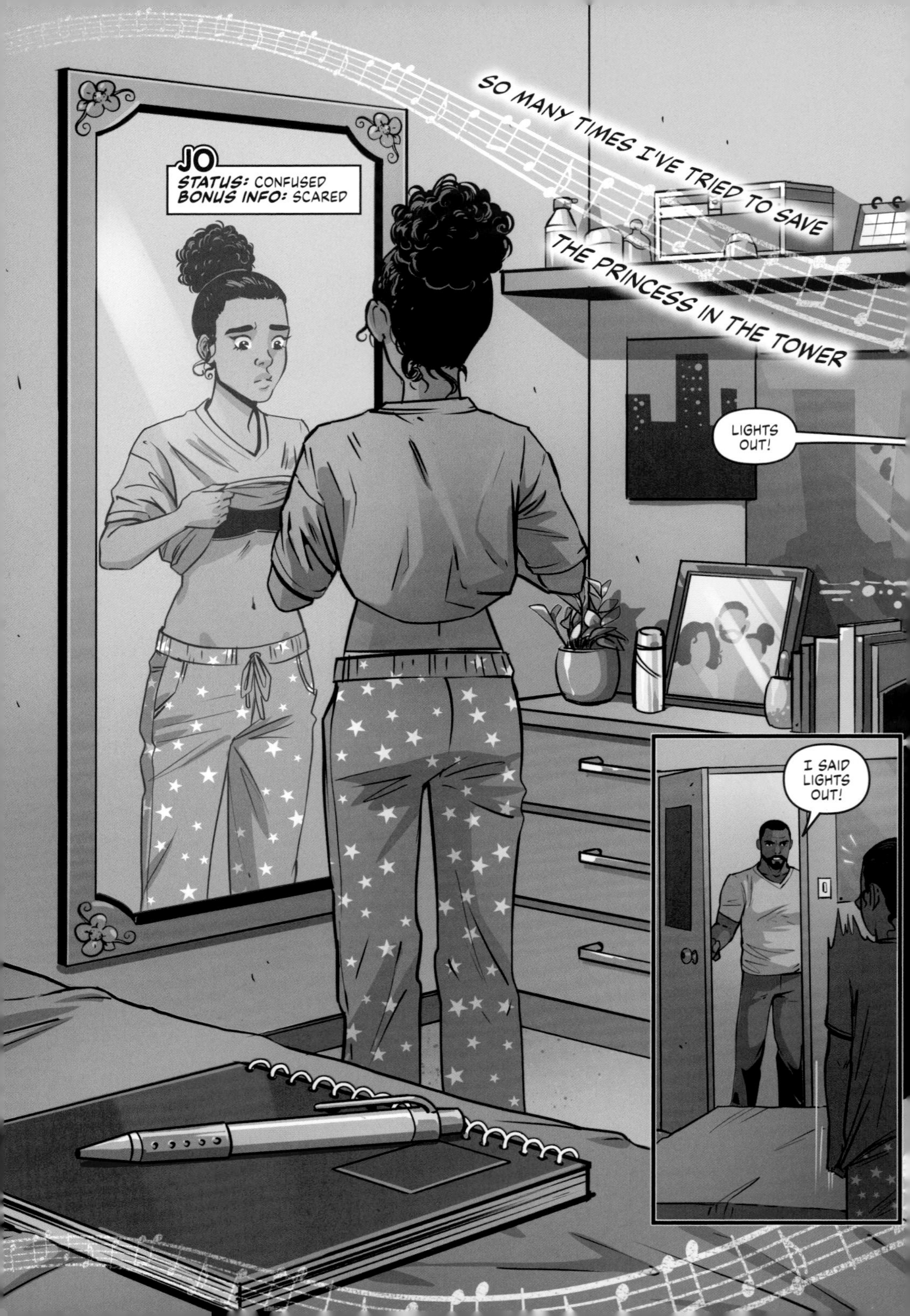
JO
STATUS: CONFUSED
BONUS INFO: SCARED
SO MANY TIMES I'VE TRIED TO SAVE
THE PRINCESS IN THE TOWER
LIGHTS OUT!
I SAID LIGHTS OUT!

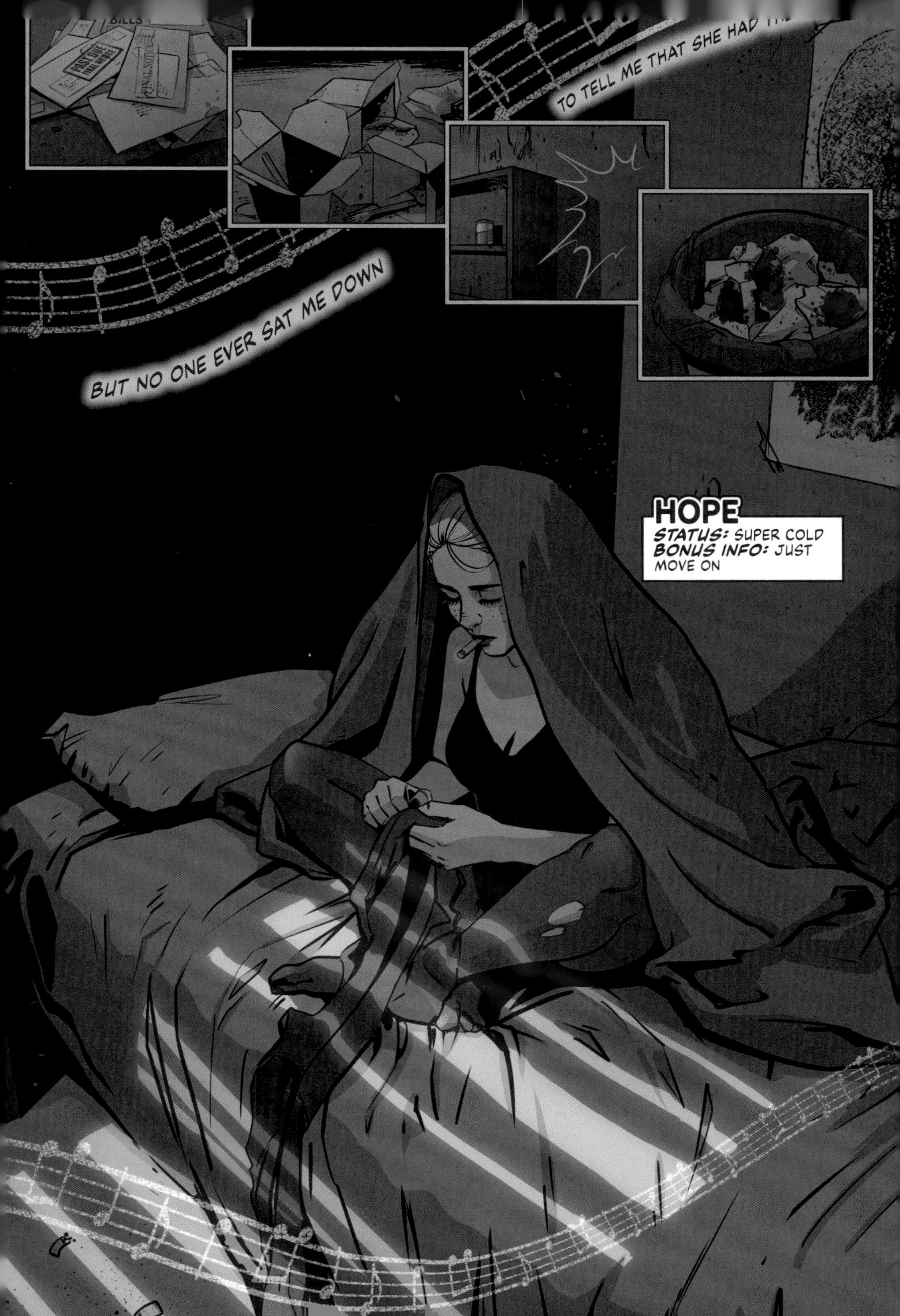
BILLS
BUT NO ONE EVER SAT ME DOWN
TO TELL ME THAT SHE HAD
HOPE
STATUS: SUPER COLD
BONUS INFO: JUST MOVE ON

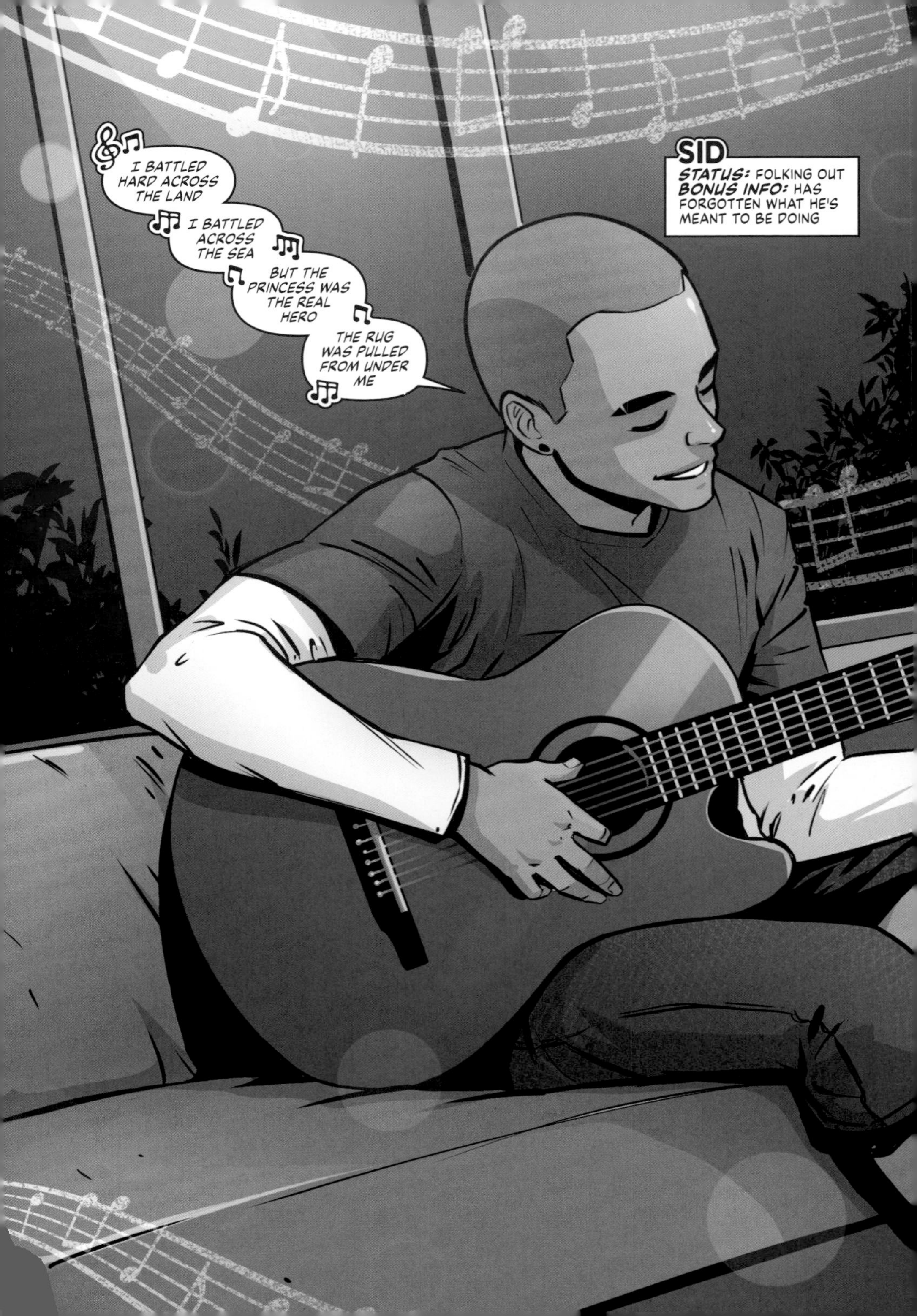
I BATTLED HARD ACROSS THE LAND
I BATTLED ACROSS THE SEA
BUT THE PRINCESS WAS THE REAL HERO
THE RUG WAS PULLED FROM UNDER ME
SID
STATUS: FOLKING OUT
BONUS INFO: HAS FORGOTTEN WHAT HE'S MEANT TO BE DOING

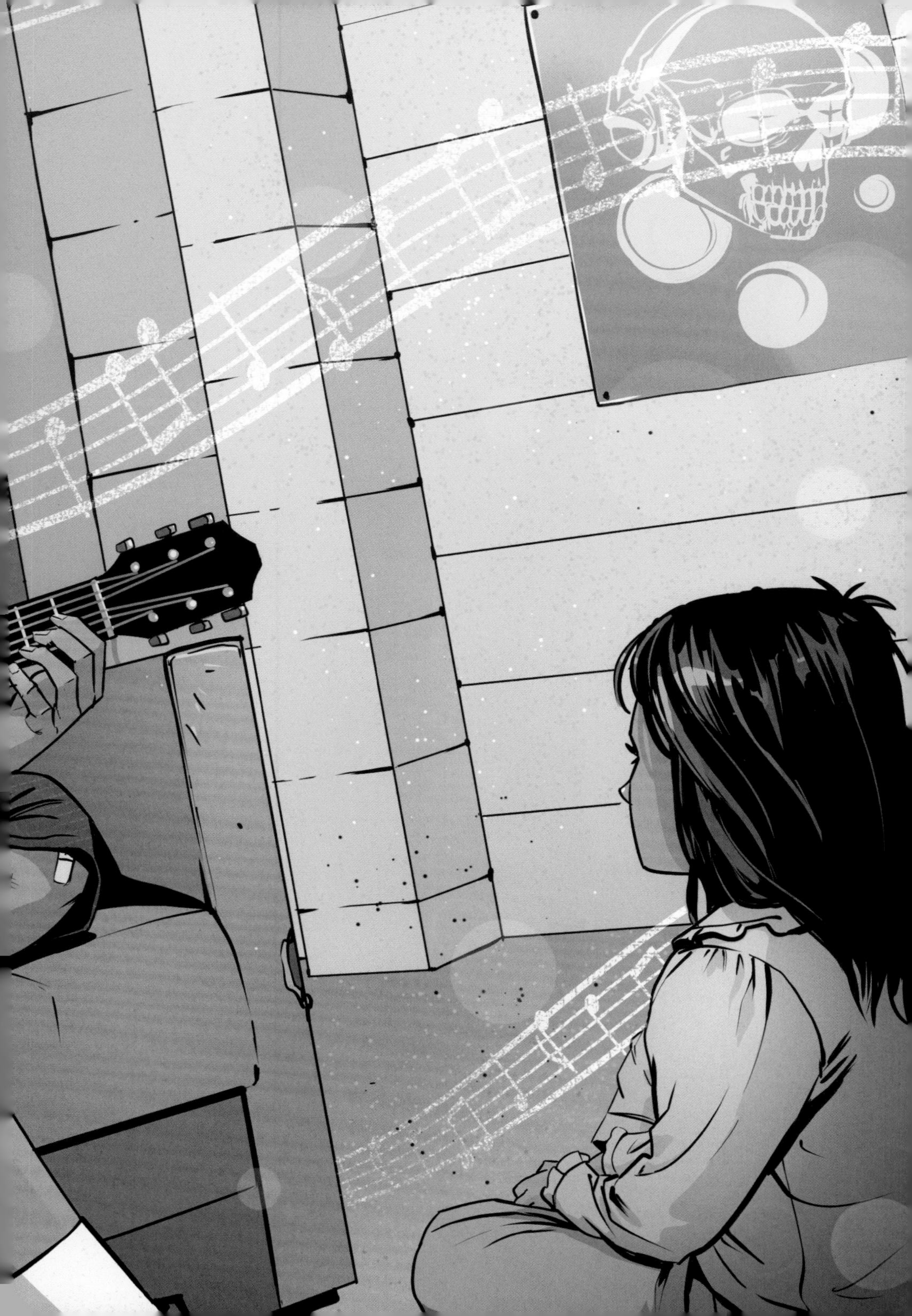

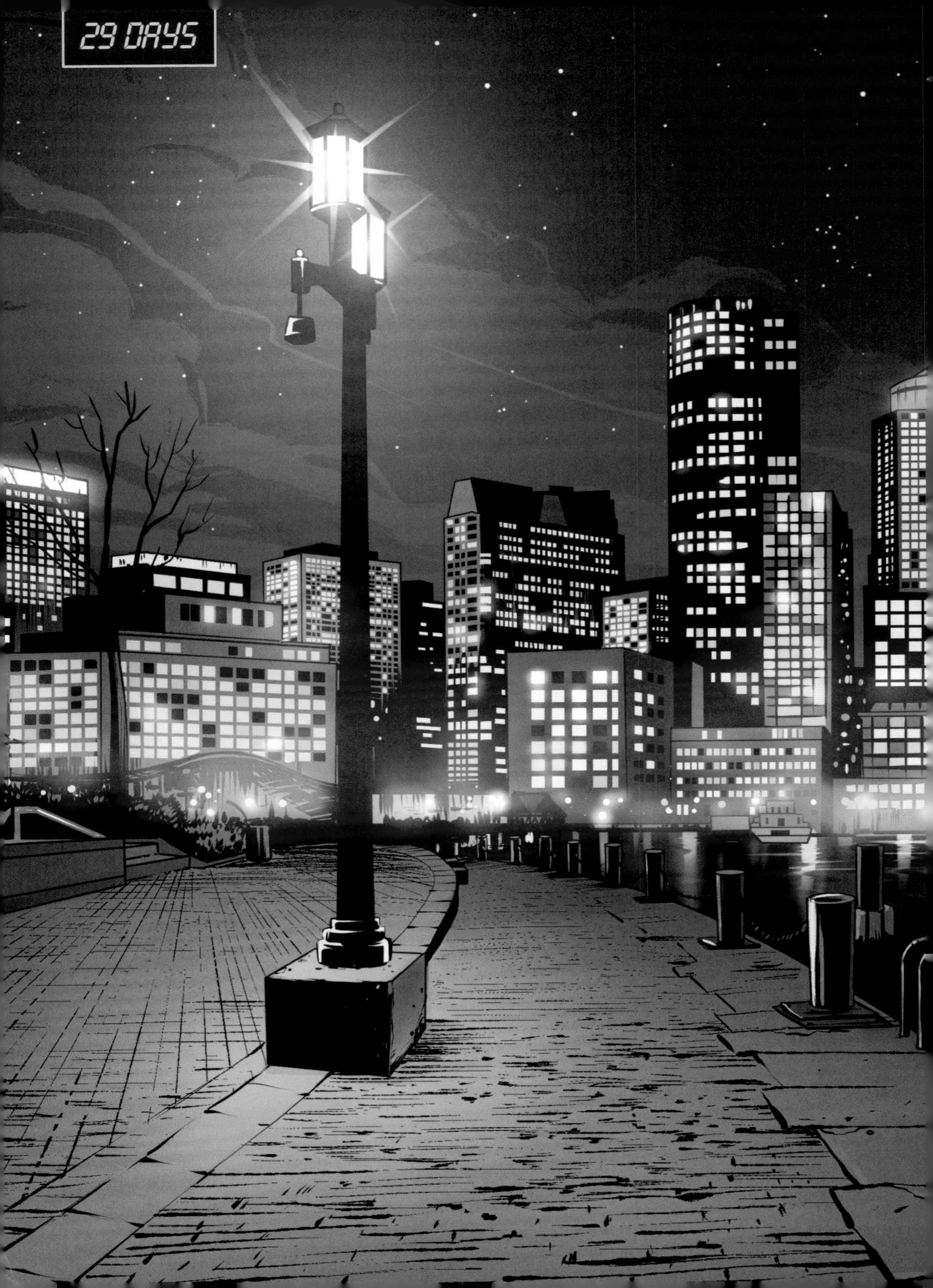
29 DAYS

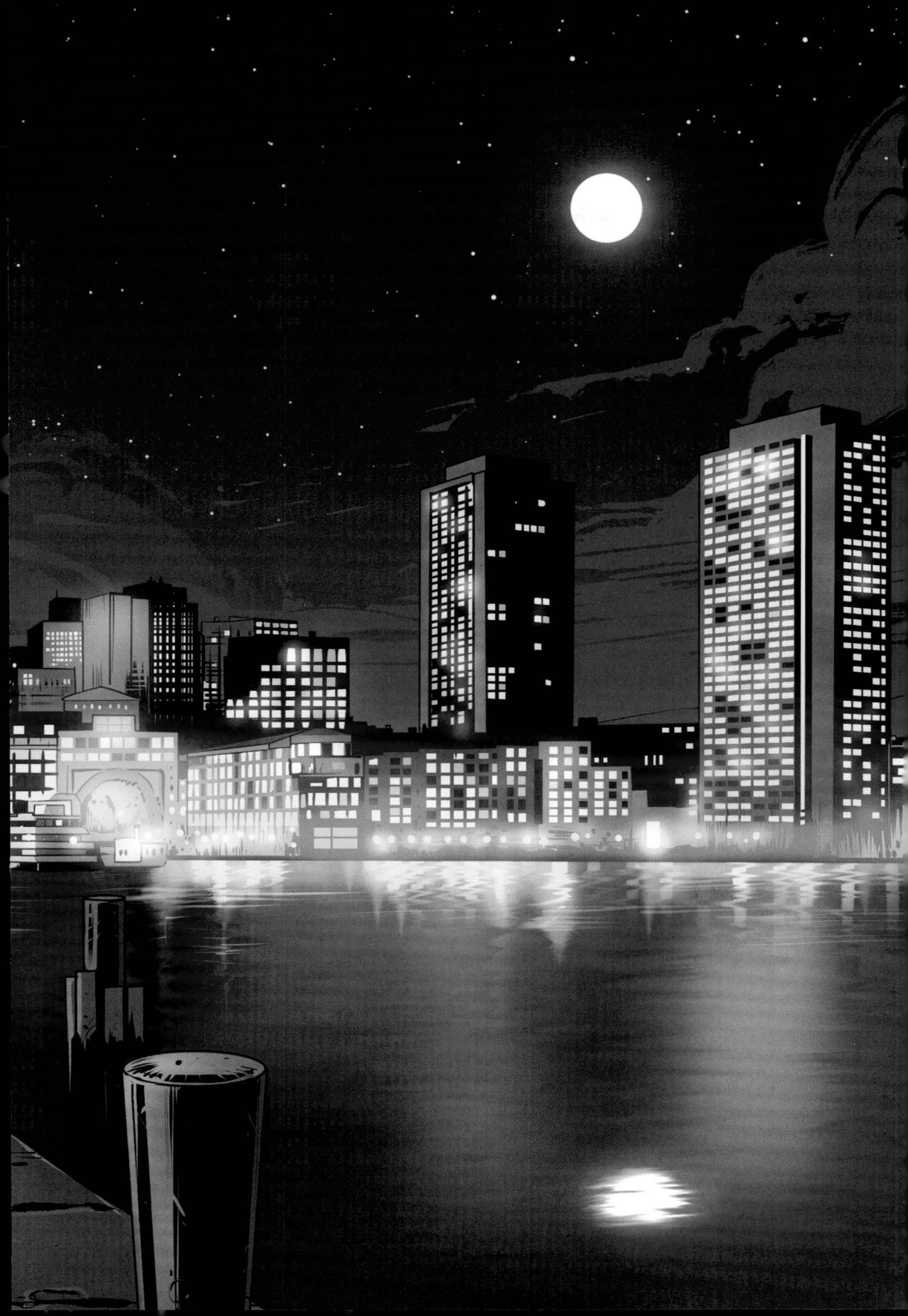

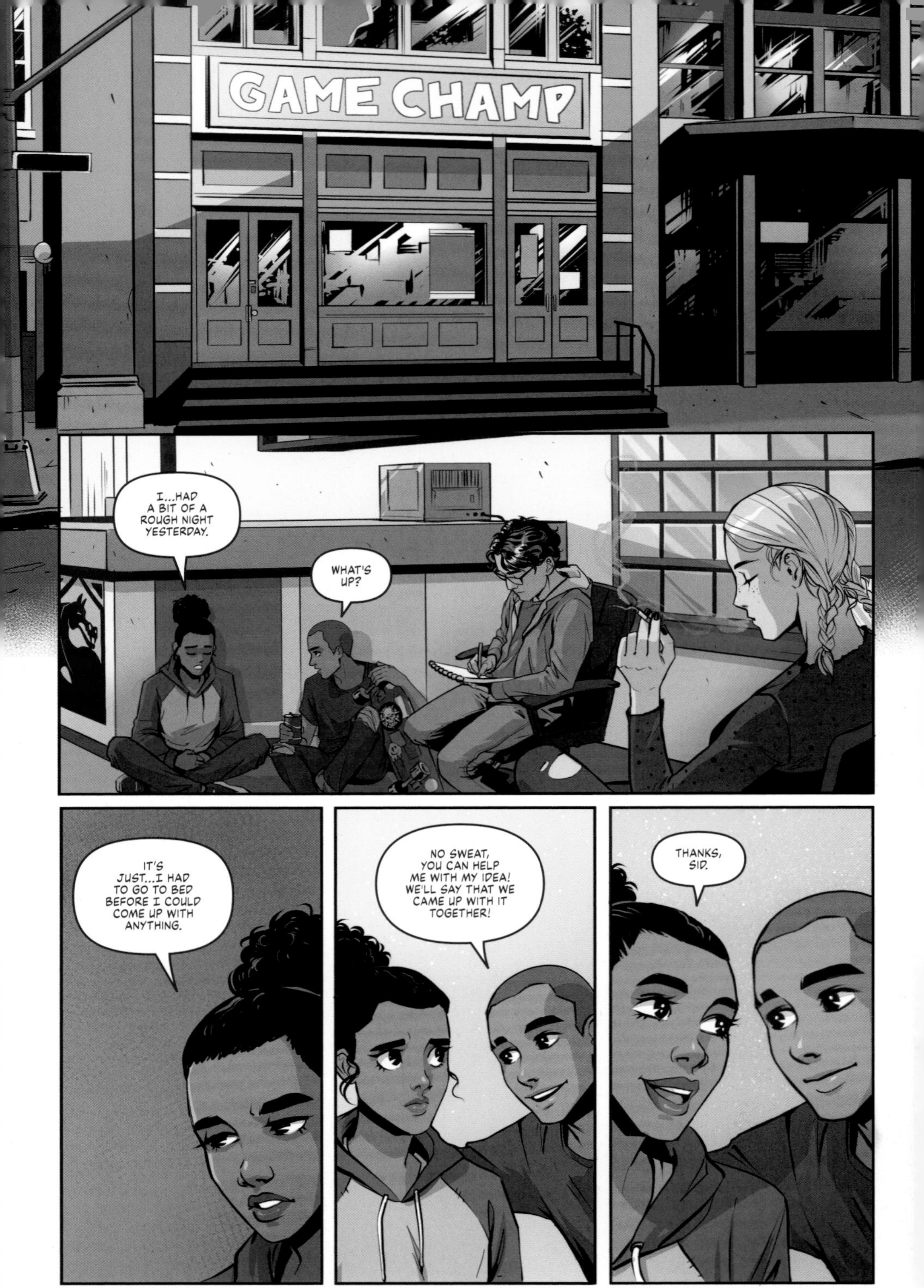
GAME CHAMP
I...HAD A BIT OF A ROUGH NIGHT YESTERDAY.
WHAT'S UP?
IT'S JUST...I HAD TO GO TO BED BEFORE I COULD COME UP WITH ANYTHING.
NO SWEAT, YOU CAN HELP ME WITH MY IDEA! WE'LL SAY THAT WE CAME UP WITH IT TOGETHER!
THANKS, SID.

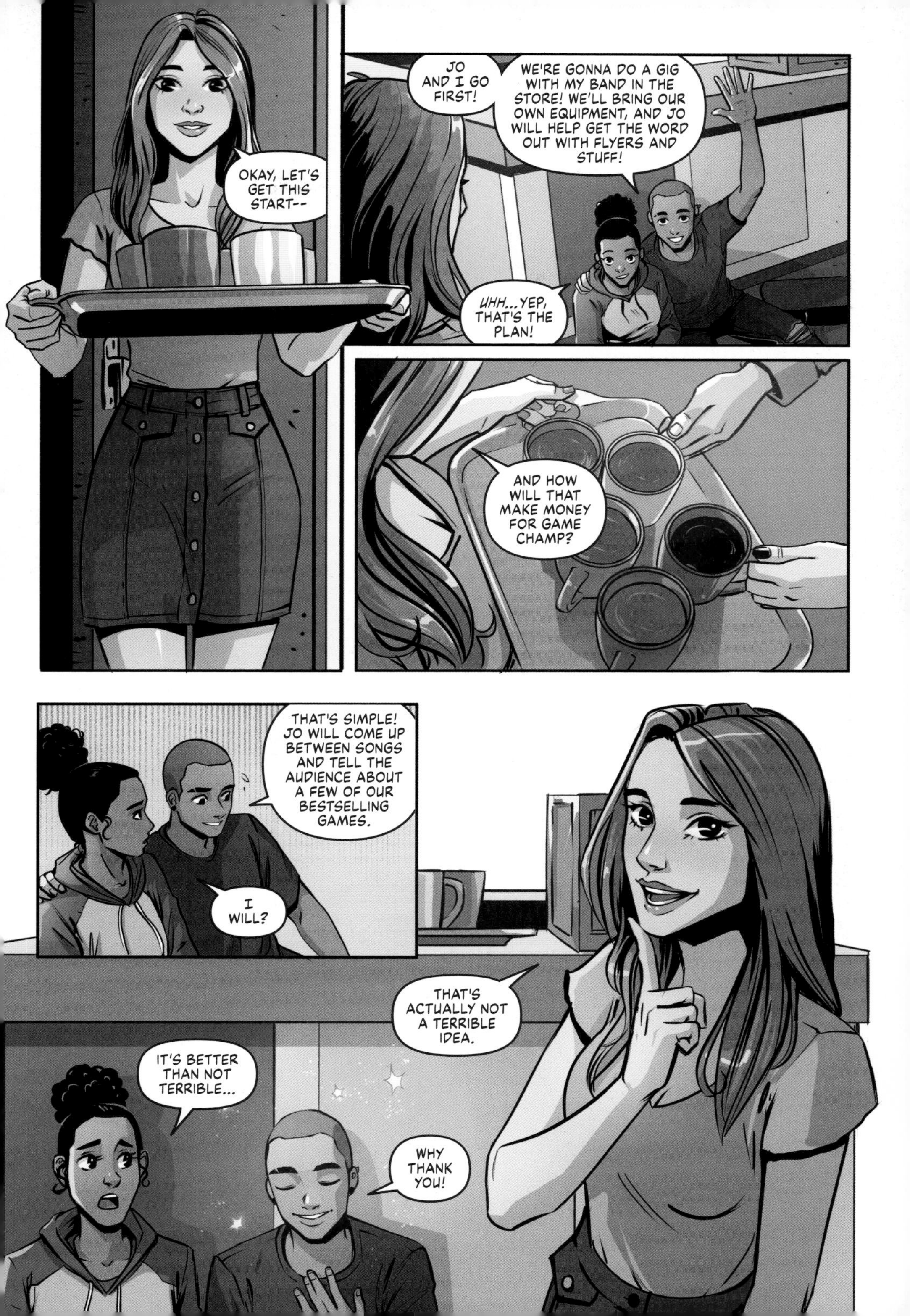
OKAY, LET'S GET THIS START--
JO AND I GO FIRST!
WE'RE GONNA DO A GIG WITH MY BAND IN THE STORE! WE'LL BRING OUR OWN EQUIPMENT, AND JO WILL HELP GET THE WORD OUT WITH FLYERS AND STUFF!
UHH...YEP, THAT'S THE PLAN!
AND HOW WILL THAT MAKE MONEY FOR GAME CHAMP?
THAT'S SIMPLE! JO WILL COME UP BETWEEN SONGS AND TELL THE AUDIENCE ABOUT A FEW OF OUR BESTSELLING GAMES.
I WILL?
THAT'S ACTUALLY NOT A TERRIBLE IDEA.
IT'S BETTER THAN NOT TERRIBLE...
WHY THANK YOU!

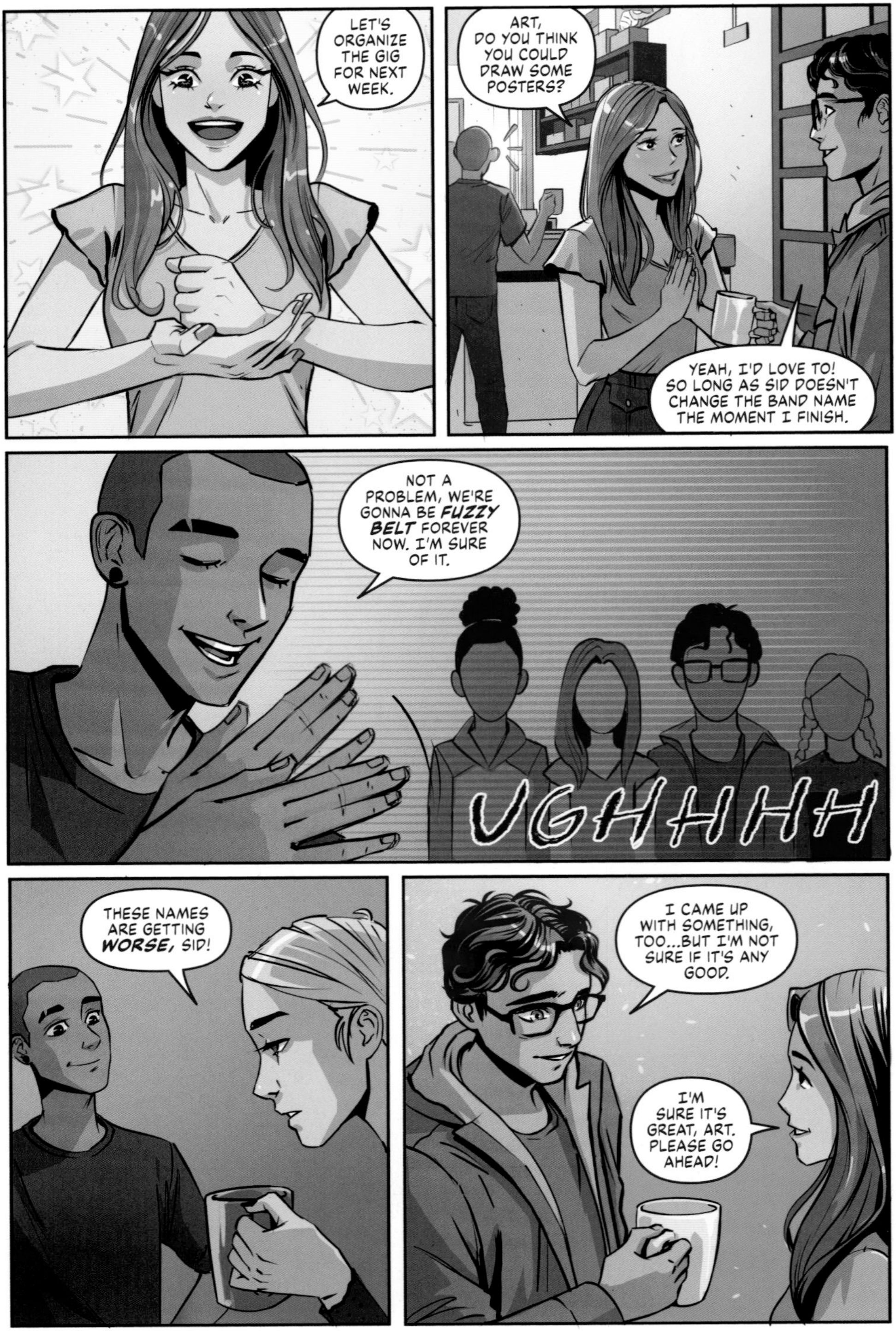
LET'S ORGANIZE THE GIG FOR NEXT WEEK.
ART, DO YOU THINK YOU COULD DRAW SOME POSTERS?
YEAH, I'D LOVE TO! SO LONG AS SID DOESN'T CHANGE THE BAND NAME THE MOMENT I FINISH.
NOT A PROBLEM, WE'RE GONNA BE FUZZY BELT FOREVER NOW. I'M SURE OF IT.
UGHHHH
THESE NAMES ARE GETTING WORSE, SID!
I CAME UP WITH SOMETHING, TOO...BUT I'M NOT SURE IF IT'S ANY GOOD.
I'M SURE IT'S GREAT, ART. PLEASE GO AHEAD!

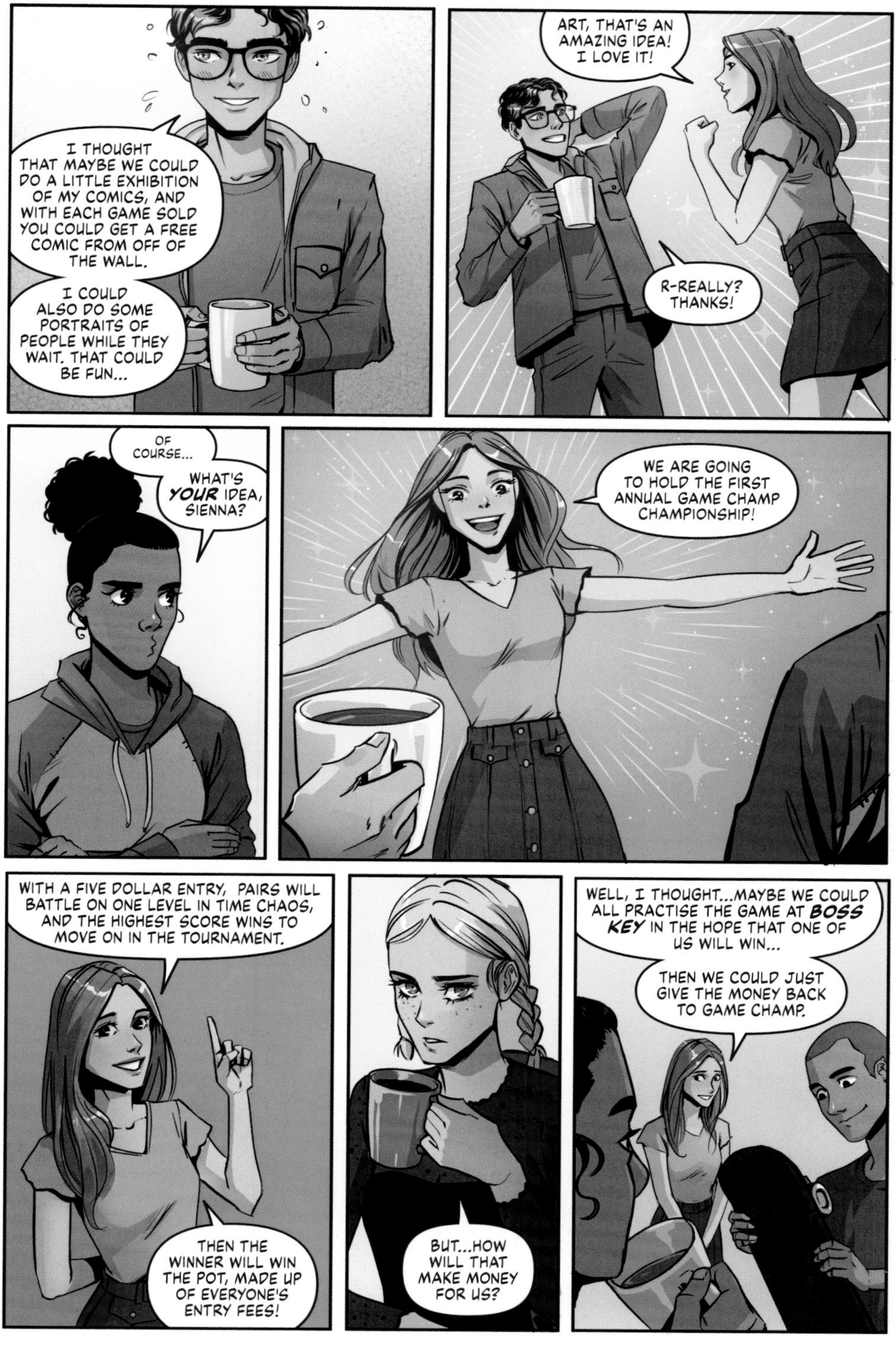
I THOUGHT THAT MAYBE WE COULD DO A LITTLE EXHIBITION OF MY COMICS, AND WITH EACH GAME SOLD YOU COULD GET A FREE COMIC FROM OFF OF THE WALL.
I COULD ALSO DO SOME PORTRAITS OF PEOPLE WHILE THEY WAIT. THAT COULD BE FUN...
ART, THAT'S AN AMAZING IDEA! I LOVE IT!
R-REALLY? THANKS!
OF COURSE...
WHAT'S *YOUR* IDEA, SIENNA?
WE ARE GOING TO HOLD THE FIRST ANNUAL GAME CHAMP CHAMPIONSHIP!
WITH A FIVE DOLLAR ENTRY, PAIRS WILL BATTLE ON ONE LEVEL IN TIME CHAOS, AND THE HIGHEST SCORE WINS TO MOVE ON IN THE TOURNAMENT.
THEN THE WINNER WILL WIN THE POT, MADE UP OF EVERYONE'S ENTRY FEES!
BUT...HOW WILL THAT MAKE MONEY FOR US?
WELL, I THOUGHT...MAYBE WE COULD ALL PRACTISE THE GAME AT *BOSS KEY* IN THE HOPE THAT ONE OF US WILL WIN...
THEN WE COULD JUST GIVE THE MONEY BACK TO GAME CHAMP.

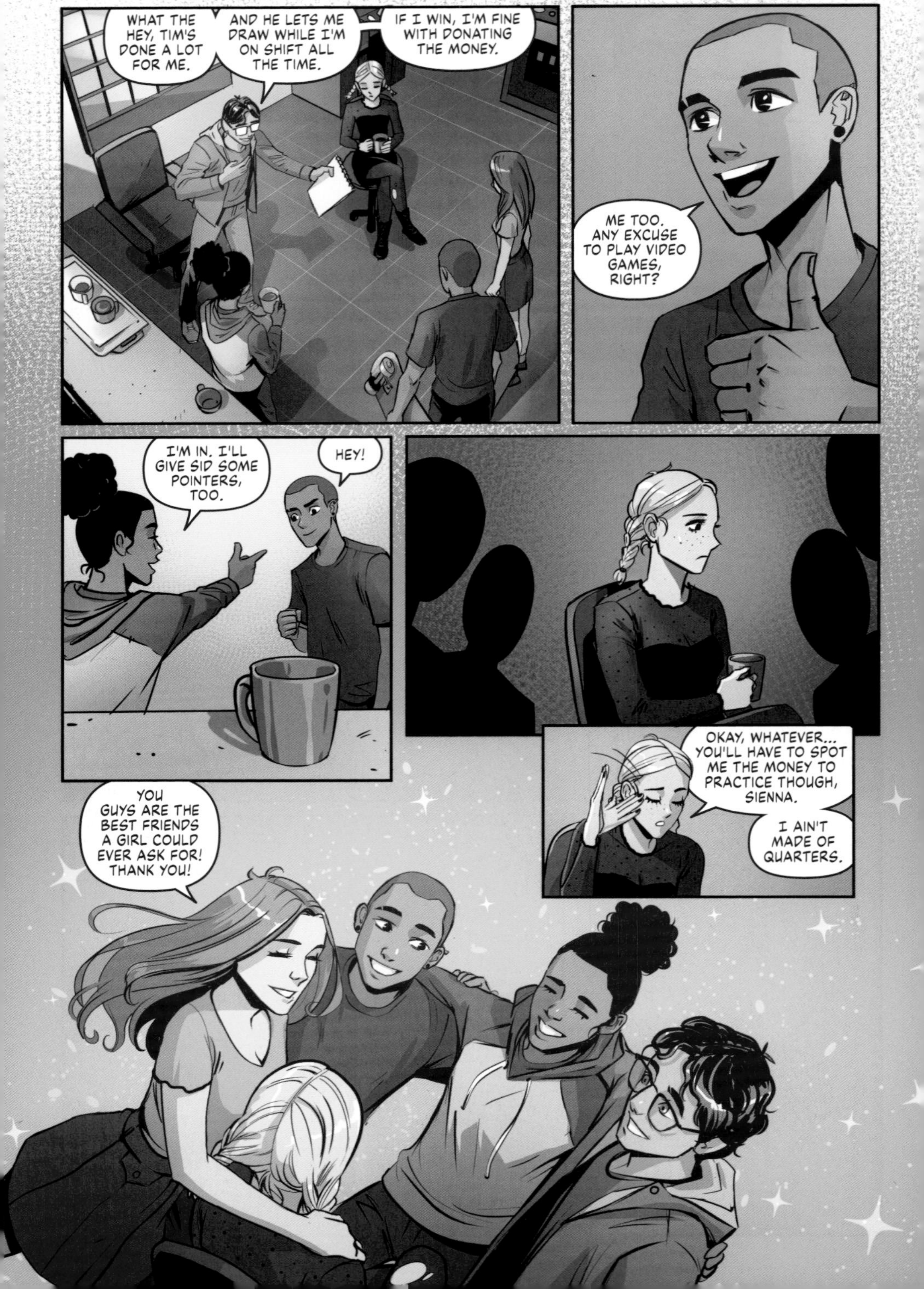
WHAT THE HEY, TIM'S DONE A LOT FOR ME.
AND HE LETS ME DRAW WHILE I'M ON SHIFT ALL THE TIME.
IF I WIN, I'M FINE WITH DONATING THE MONEY.
ME TOO. ANY EXCUSE TO PLAY VIDEO GAMES, RIGHT?
I'M IN. I'LL GIVE SID SOME POINTERS, TOO.
HEY!
OKAY, WHATEVER... YOU'LL HAVE TO SPOT ME THE MONEY TO PRACTICE THOUGH, SIENNA.
I AIN'T MADE OF QUARTERS.
YOU GUYS ARE THE BEST FRIENDS A GIRL COULD EVER ASK FOR! THANK YOU!

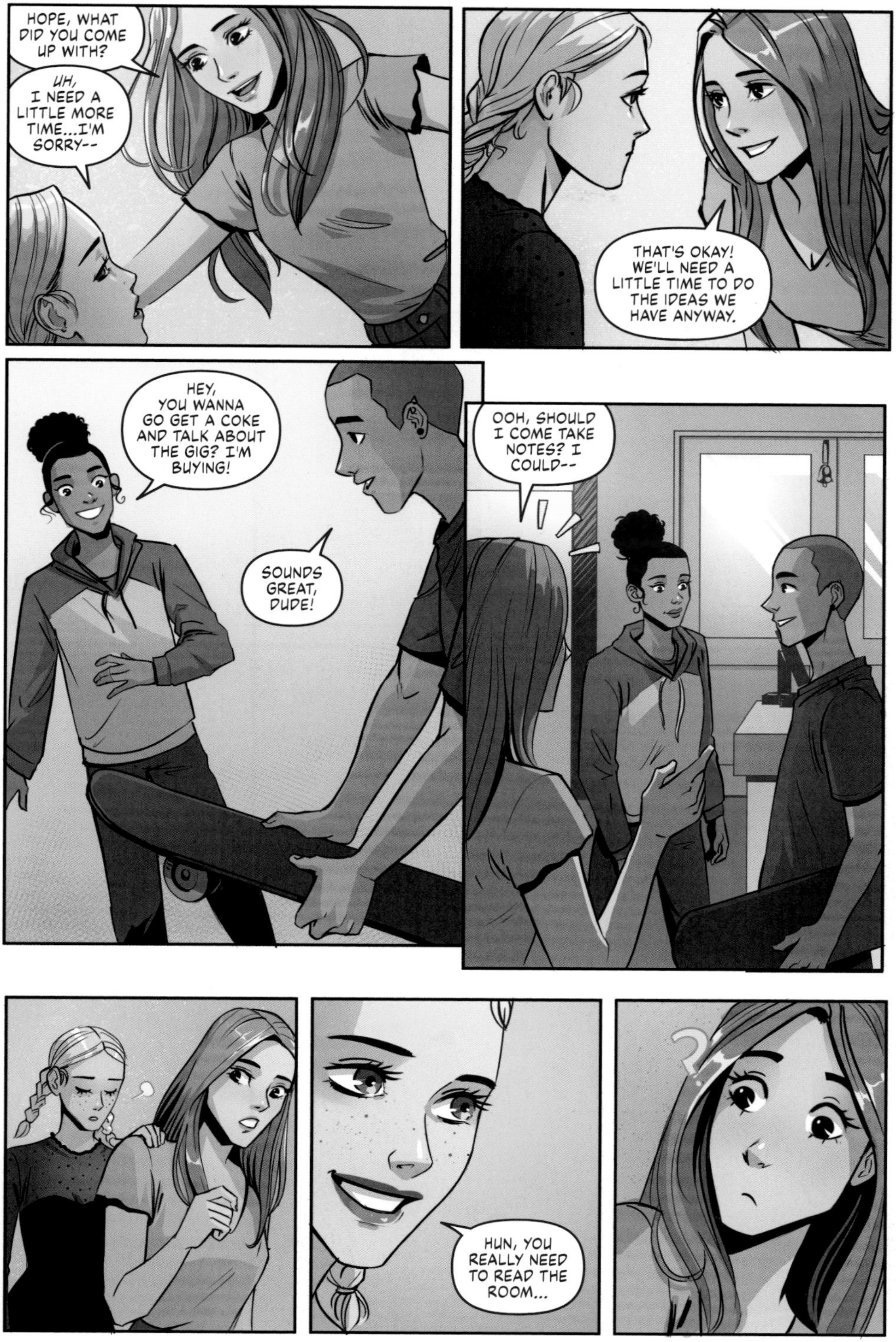
HOPE, WHAT DID YOU COME UP WITH?
UH, I NEED A LITTLE MORE TIME...I'M SORRY--
THAT'S OKAY! WE'LL NEED A LITTLE TIME TO DO THE IDEAS WE HAVE ANYWAY.
HEY, YOU WANNA GO GET A COKE AND TALK ABOUT THE GIG? I'M BUYING!
SOUNDS GREAT, DUDE!
OOH, SHOULD I COME TAKE NOTES? I COULD--
!
HUN, YOU REALLY NEED TO READ THE ROOM...
?

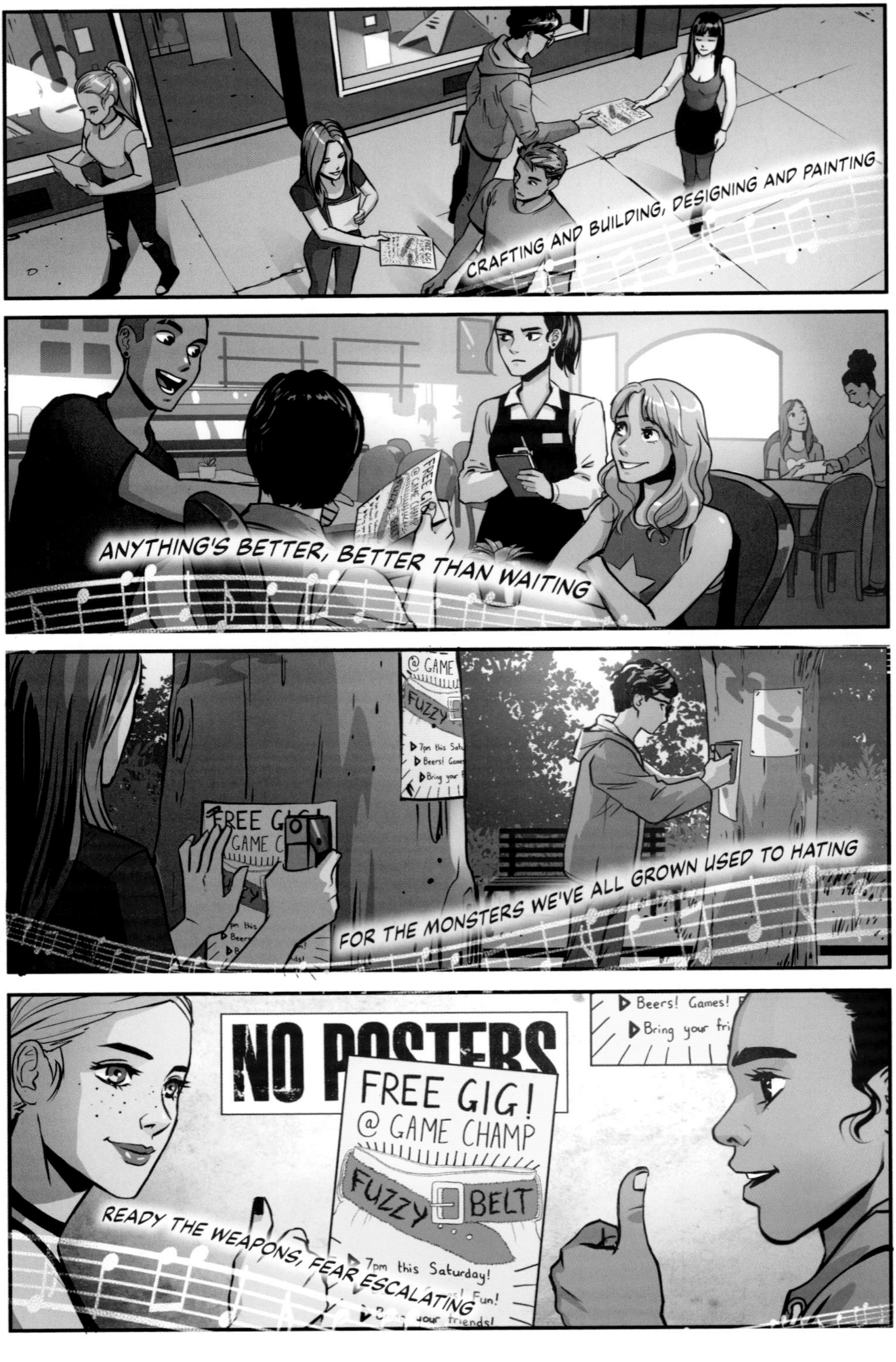
CRAFTING AND BUILDING, DESIGNING AND PAINTING
ANYTHING'S BETTER, BETTER THAN WAITING
FOR THE MONSTERS WE'VE ALL GROWN USED TO HATING
Beers! Games!
Bring your fri
FREE GIG!
@ GAME CHAMP
FUZZY BELT
7pm this Saturday!
Fun!
your friends!
READY THE WEAPONS, FEAR ESCALATING

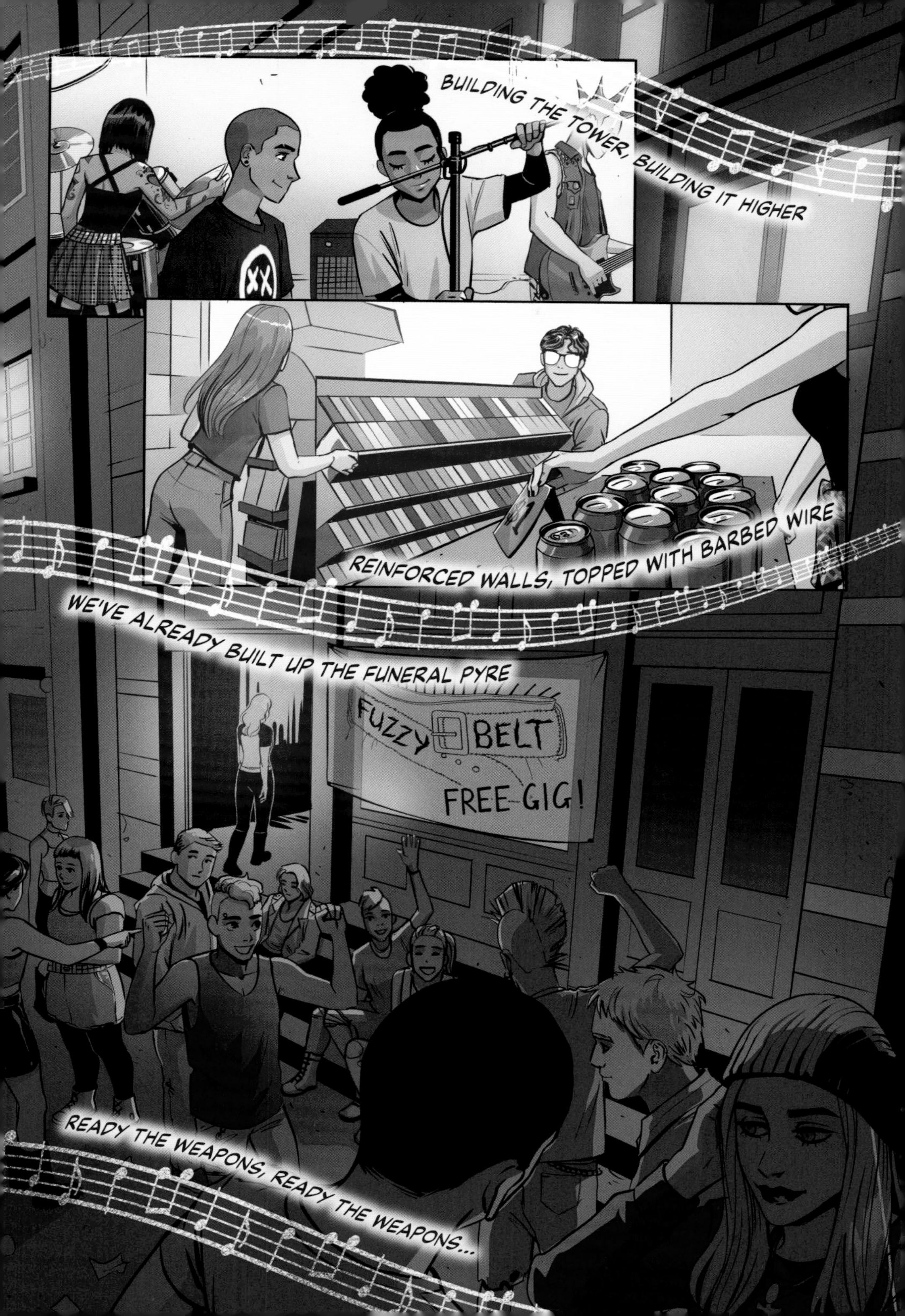
BUILDING THE TOWER, BUILDING IT HIGHER
REINFORCED WALLS, TOPPED WITH BARBED WIRE
WE'VE ALREADY BUILT UP THE FUNERAL PYRE
FUZZY BELT
FREE GIG!
READY THE WEAPONS, READY THE WEAPONS...

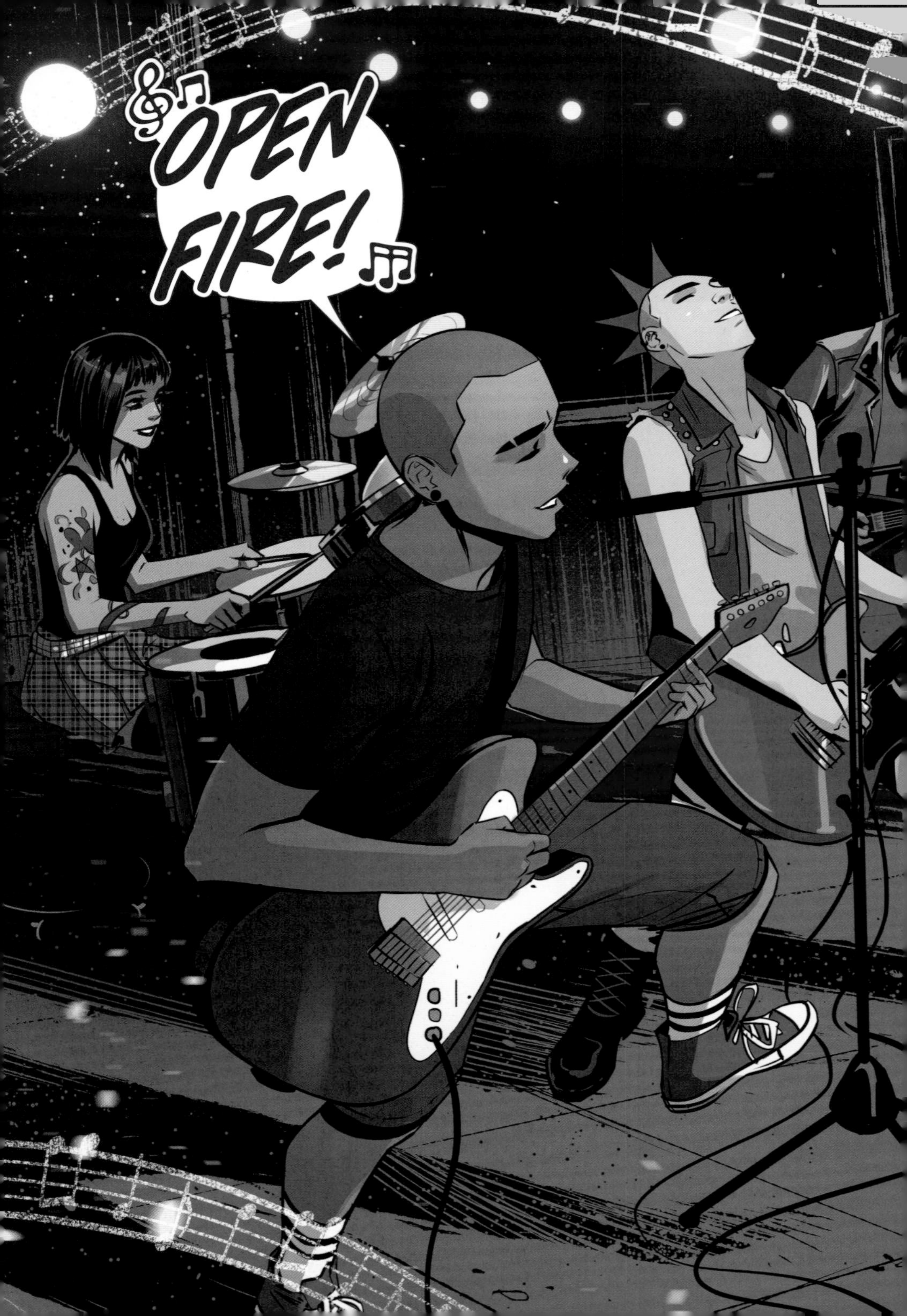
OPEN FIRE!

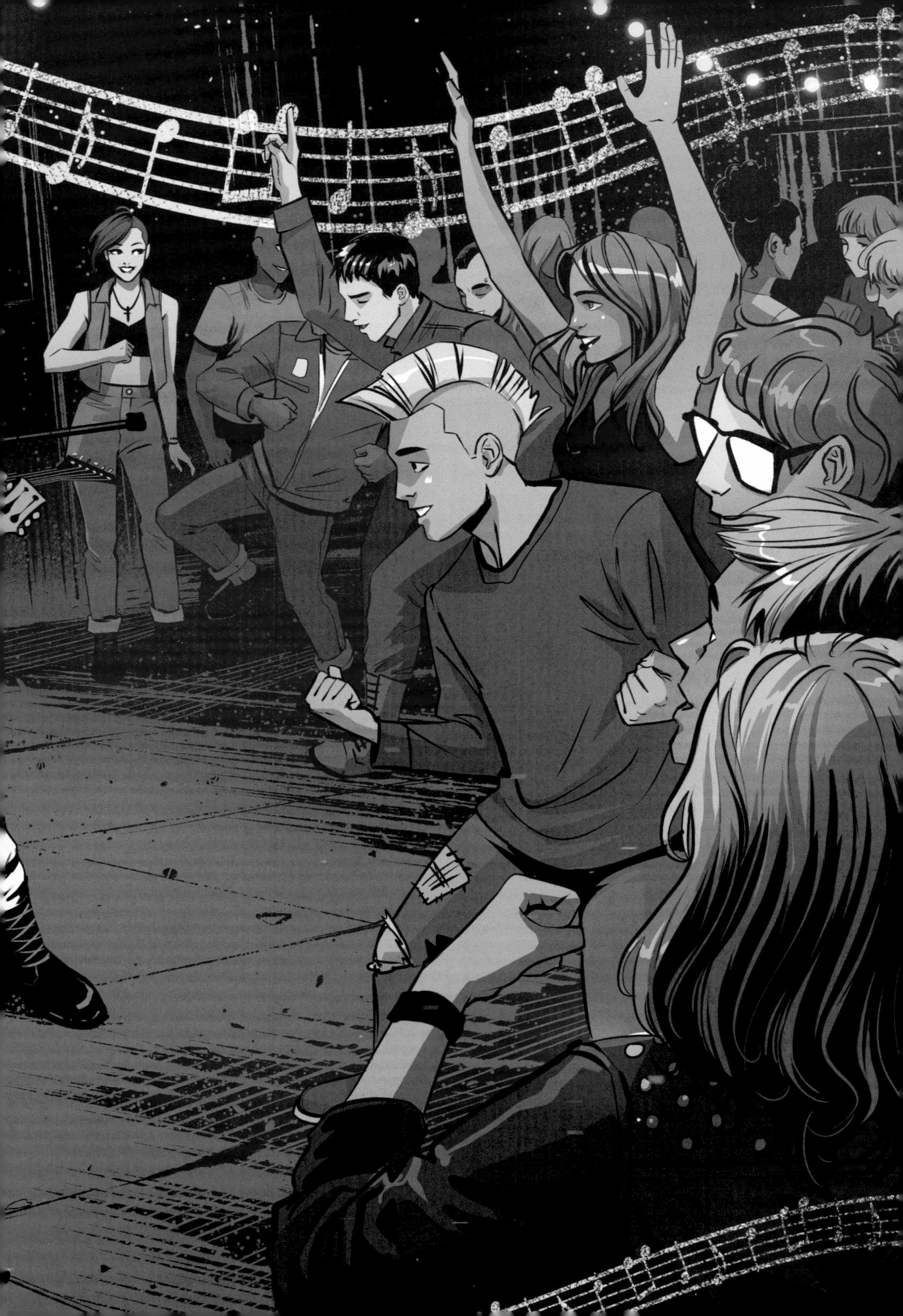

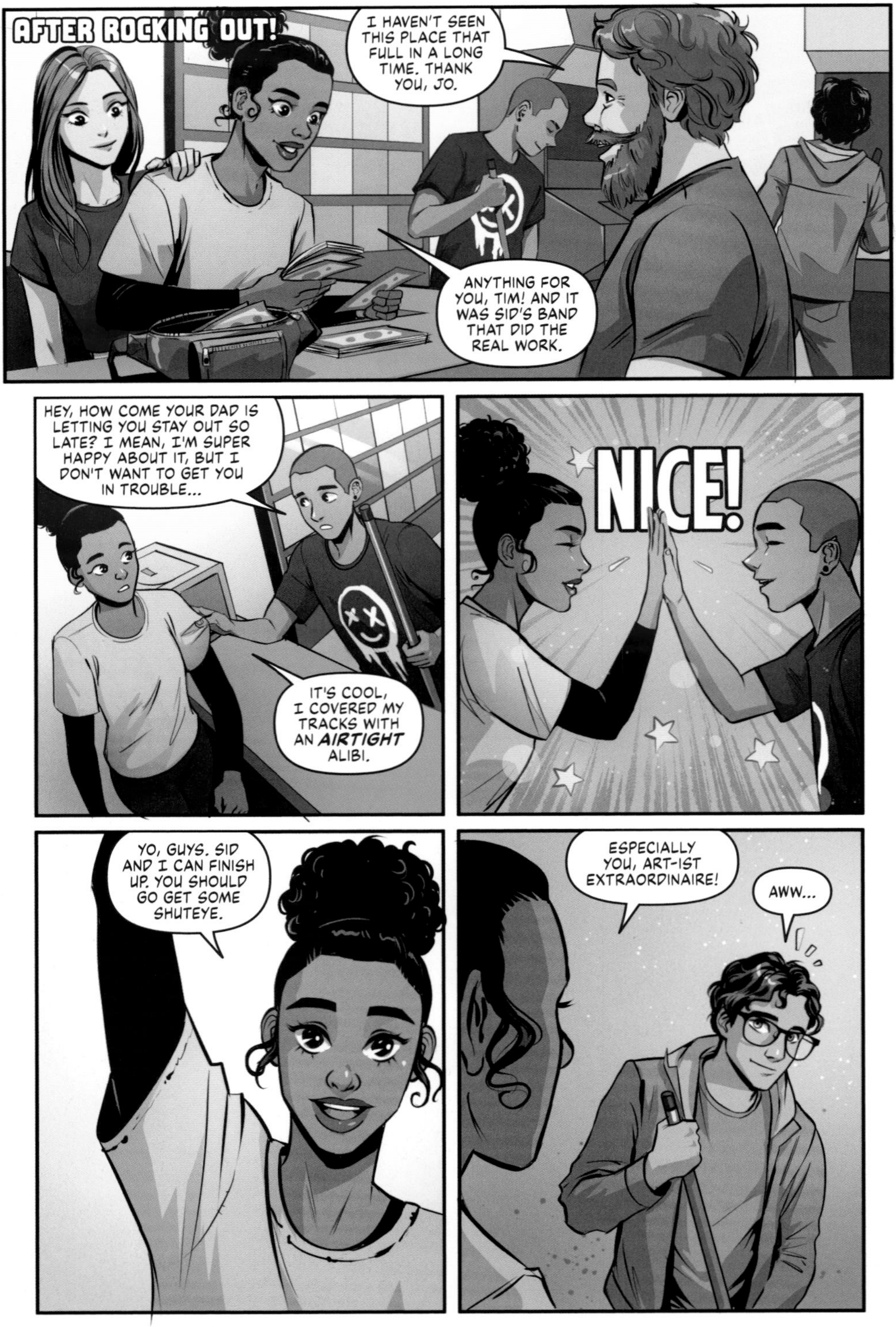
AFTER ROCKING OUT!
I HAVEN'T SEEN THIS PLACE THAT FULL IN A LONG TIME. THANK YOU, JO.
ANYTHING FOR YOU, TIM! AND IT WAS SID'S BAND THAT DID THE REAL WORK.
HEY, HOW COME YOUR DAD IS LETTING YOU STAY OUT SO LATE? I MEAN, I'M SUPER HAPPY ABOUT IT, BUT I DON'T WANT TO GET YOU IN TROUBLE...
IT'S COOL, I COVERED MY TRACKS WITH AN *AIRTIGHT* ALIBI.
NICE!
YO, GUYS. SID AND I CAN FINISH UP. YOU SHOULD GO GET SOME SHUTEYE.
ESPECIALLY YOU, ART-IST EXTRAORDINAIRE!
AWW...

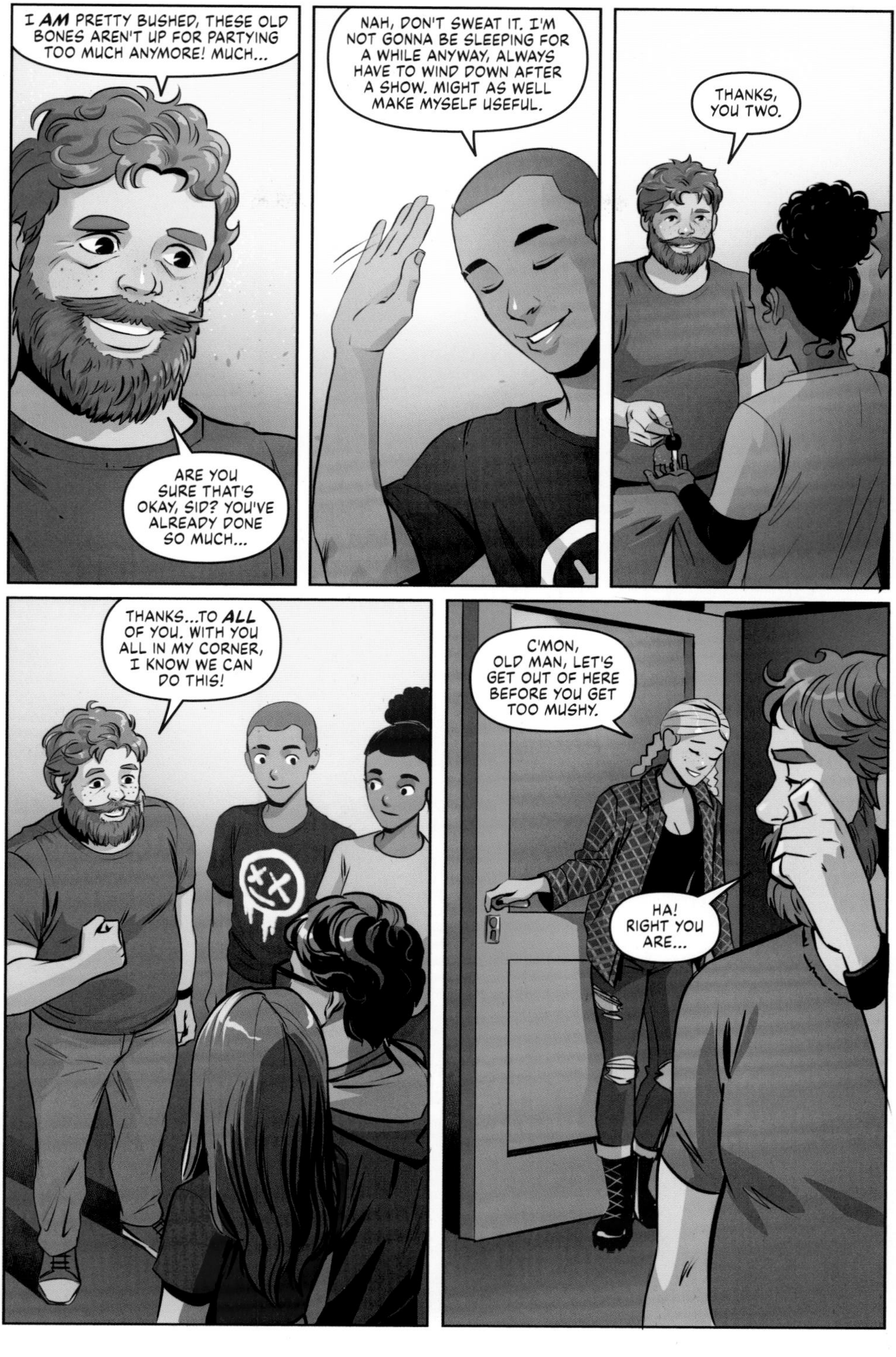
I AM PRETTY BUSHED, THESE OLD BONES AREN'T UP FOR PARTYING TOO MUCH ANYMORE! MUCH...
ARE YOU SURE THAT'S OKAY, SID? YOU'VE ALREADY DONE SO MUCH...
NAH, DON'T SWEAT IT. I'M NOT GONNA BE SLEEPING FOR A WHILE ANYWAY, ALWAYS HAVE TO WIND DOWN AFTER A SHOW. MIGHT AS WELL MAKE MYSELF USEFUL.
THANKS, YOU TWO.
THANKS...TO ALL OF YOU. WITH YOU ALL IN MY CORNER, I KNOW WE CAN DO THIS!
C'MON, OLD MAN, LET'S GET OUT OF HERE BEFORE YOU GET TOO MUSHY.
HA! RIGHT YOU ARE...

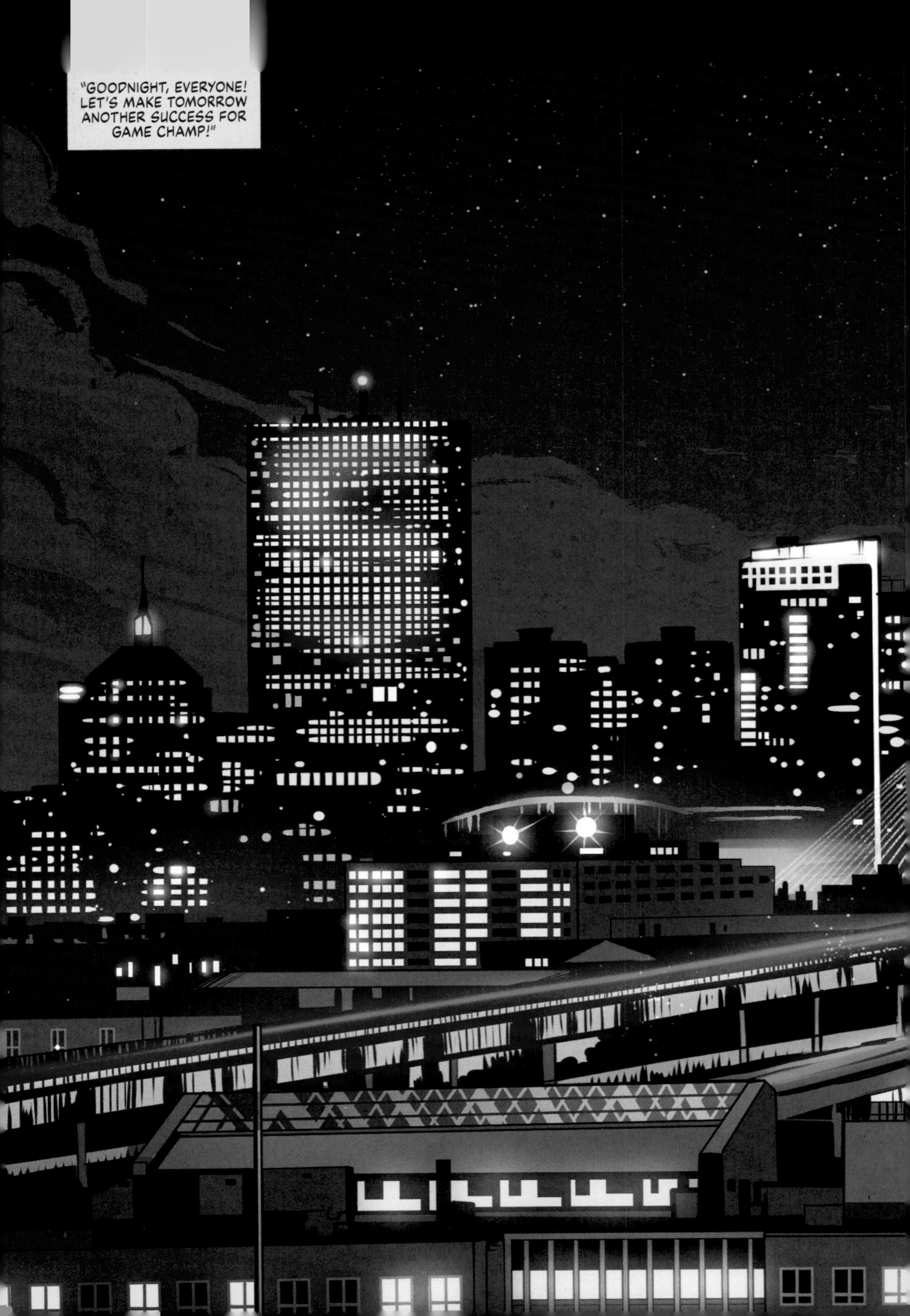
"GOODNIGHT, EVERYONE! LET'S MAKE TOMORROW ANOTHER SUCCESS FOR GAME CHAMP!"

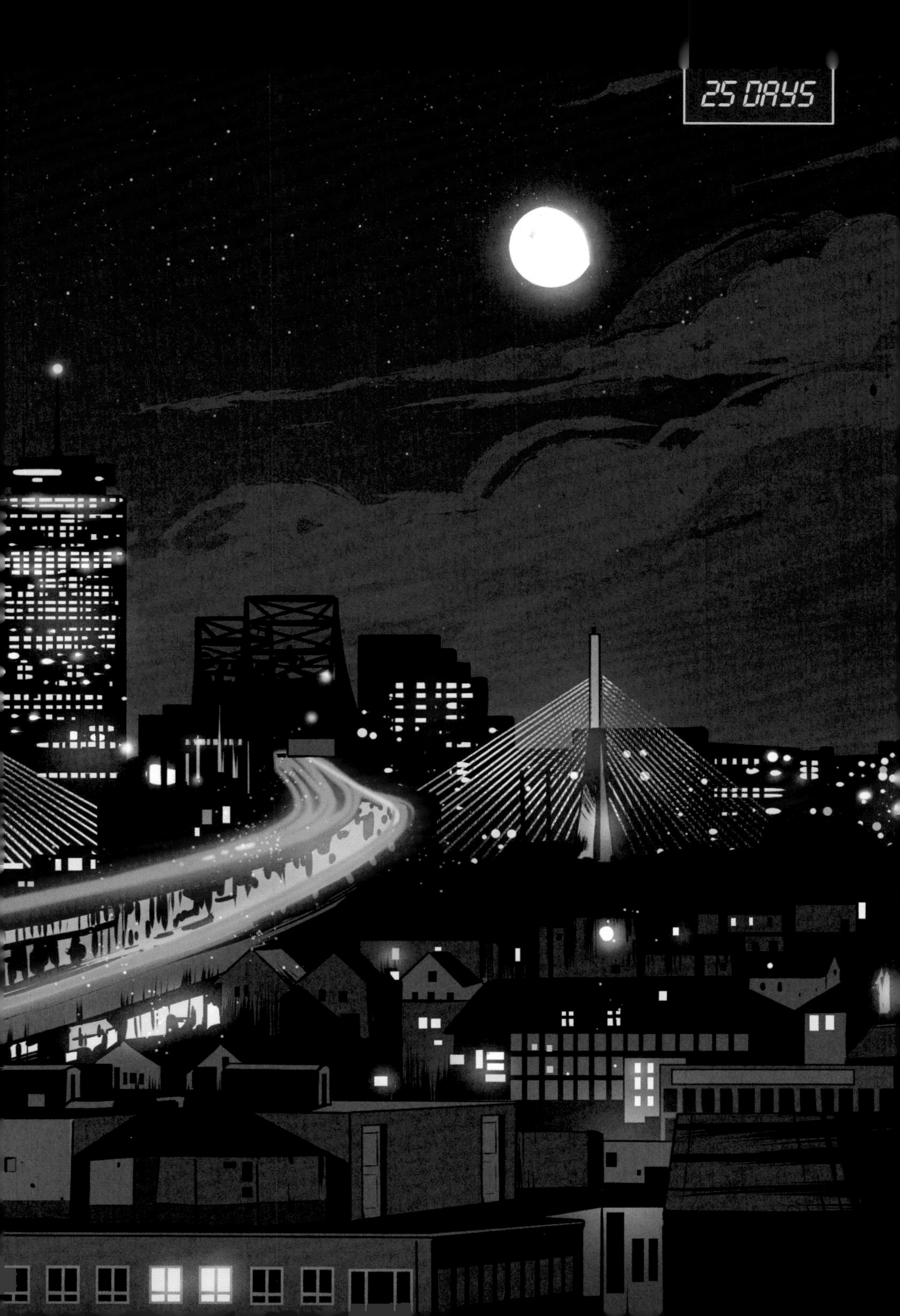
25 DAYS

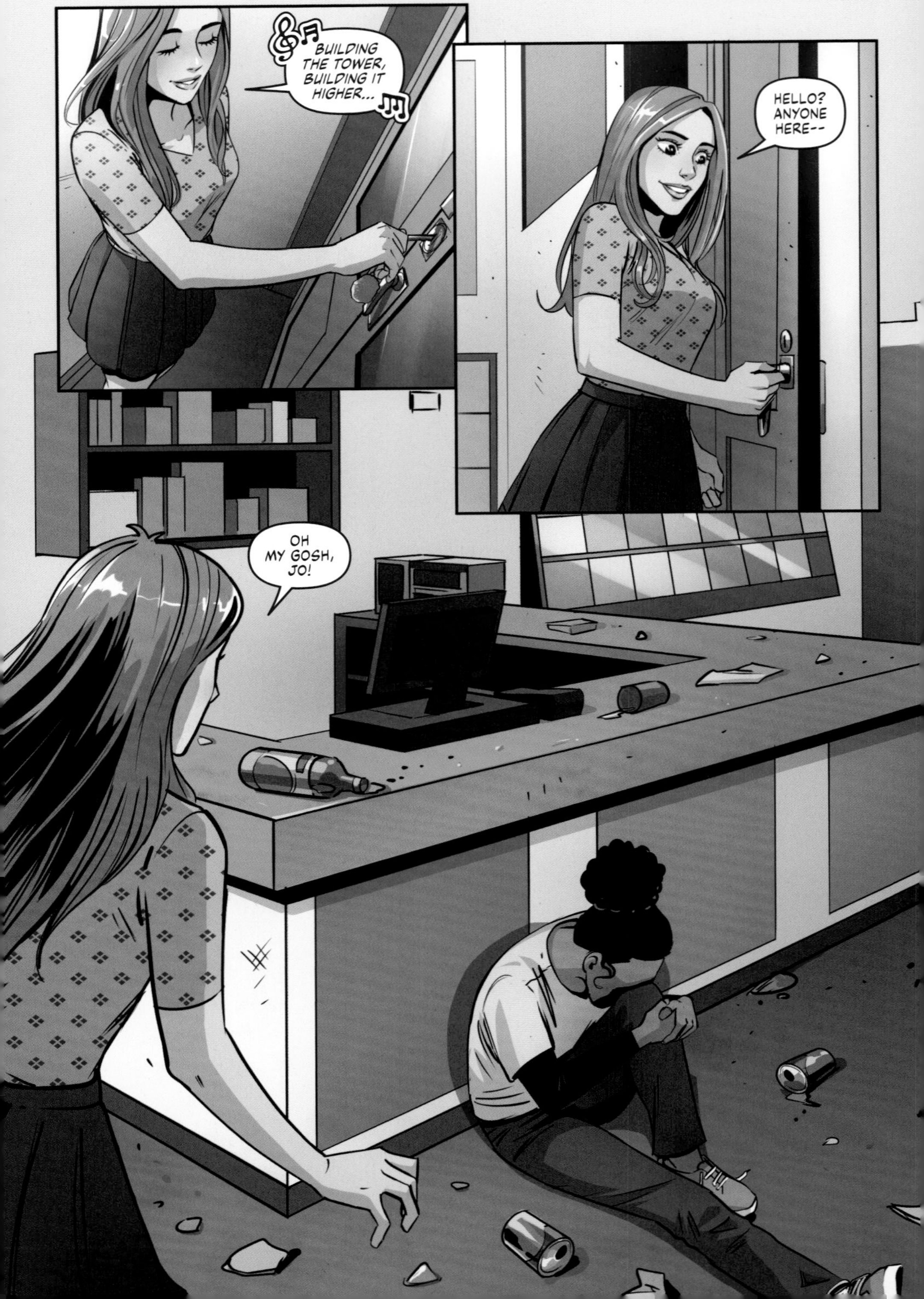
BUILDING THE TOWER, BUILDING IT HIGHER...
HELLO? ANYONE HERE--
OH MY GOSH, JO!

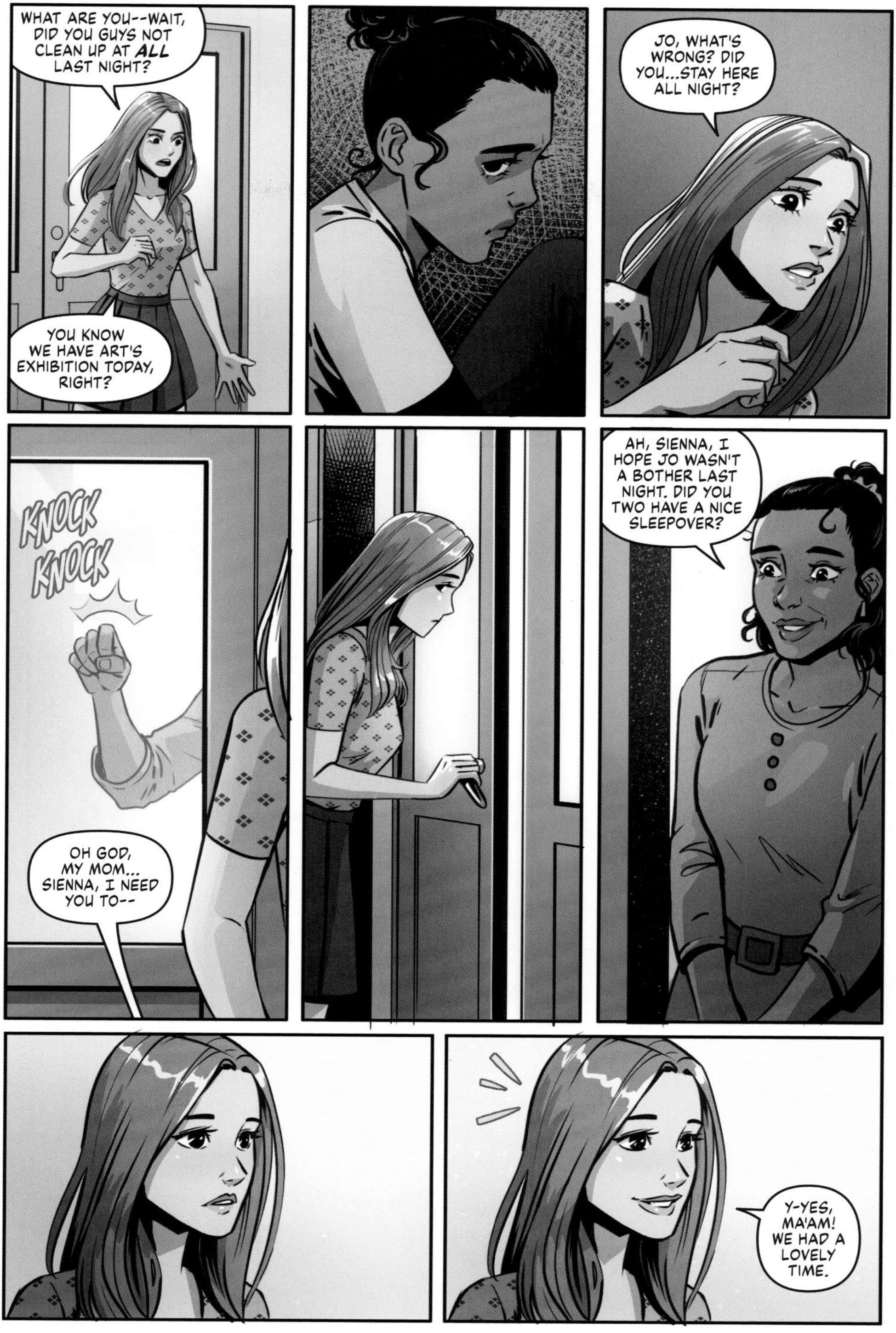
WHAT ARE YOU--WAIT, DID YOU GUYS NOT CLEAN UP AT ALL LAST NIGHT?
YOU KNOW WE HAVE ART'S EXHIBITION TODAY, RIGHT?
JO, WHAT'S WRONG? DID YOU...STAY HERE ALL NIGHT?
KNOCK KNOCK
OH GOD, MY MOM... SIENNA, I NEED YOU TO--
AH, SIENNA, I HOPE JO WASN'T A BOTHER LAST NIGHT. DID YOU TWO HAVE A NICE SLEEPOVER?
Y-YES, MA'AM! WE HAD A LOVELY TIME.

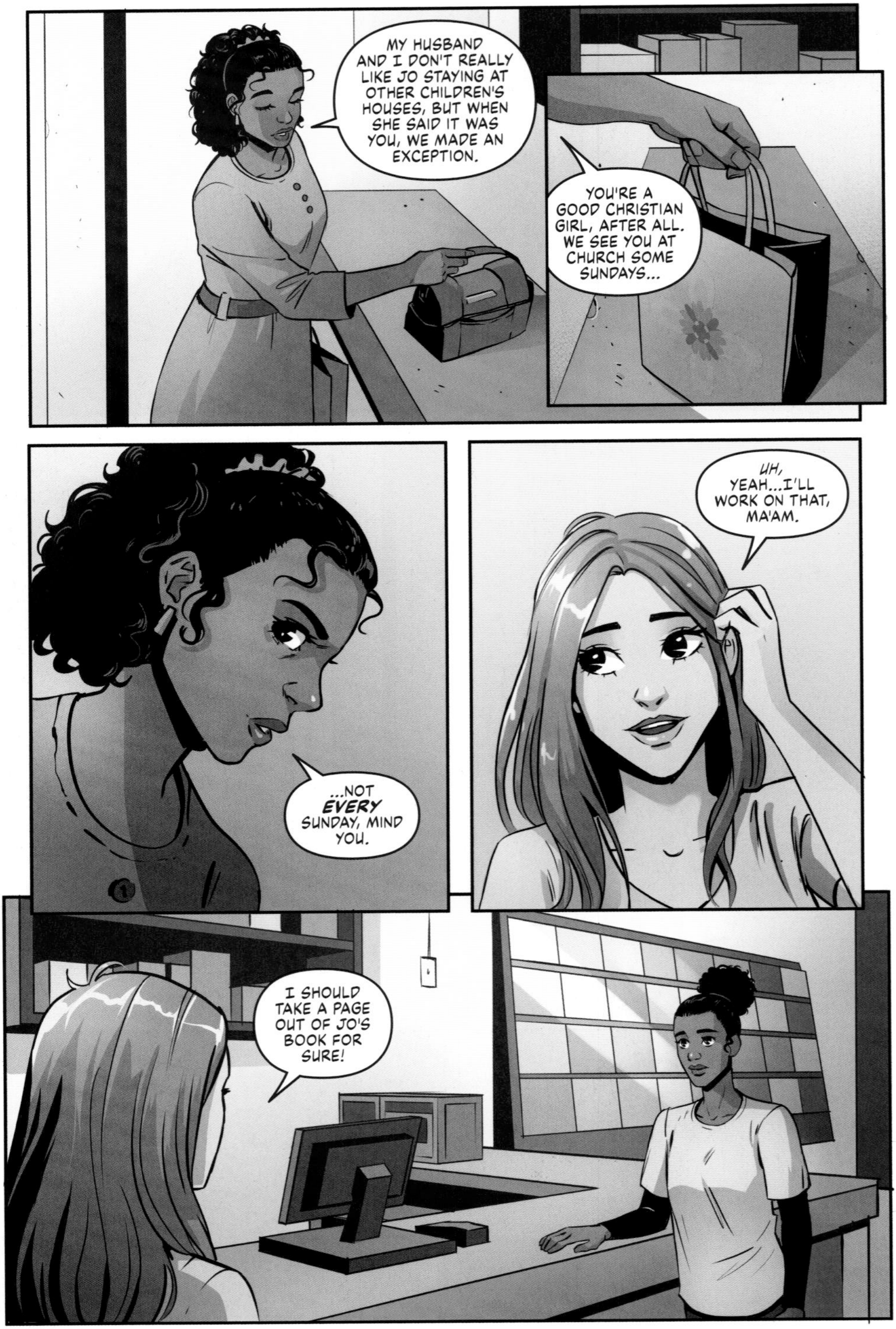
MY HUSBAND AND I DON'T REALLY LIKE JO STAYING AT OTHER CHILDREN'S HOUSES, BUT WHEN SHE SAID IT WAS YOU, WE MADE AN EXCEPTION.
YOU'RE A GOOD CHRISTIAN GIRL, AFTER ALL. WE SEE YOU AT CHURCH SOME SUNDAYS...
...NOT ***EVERY*** SUNDAY, MIND YOU.
UH, YEAH...I'LL WORK ON THAT, MA'AM.
I SHOULD TAKE A PAGE OUT OF JO'S BOOK FOR SURE!

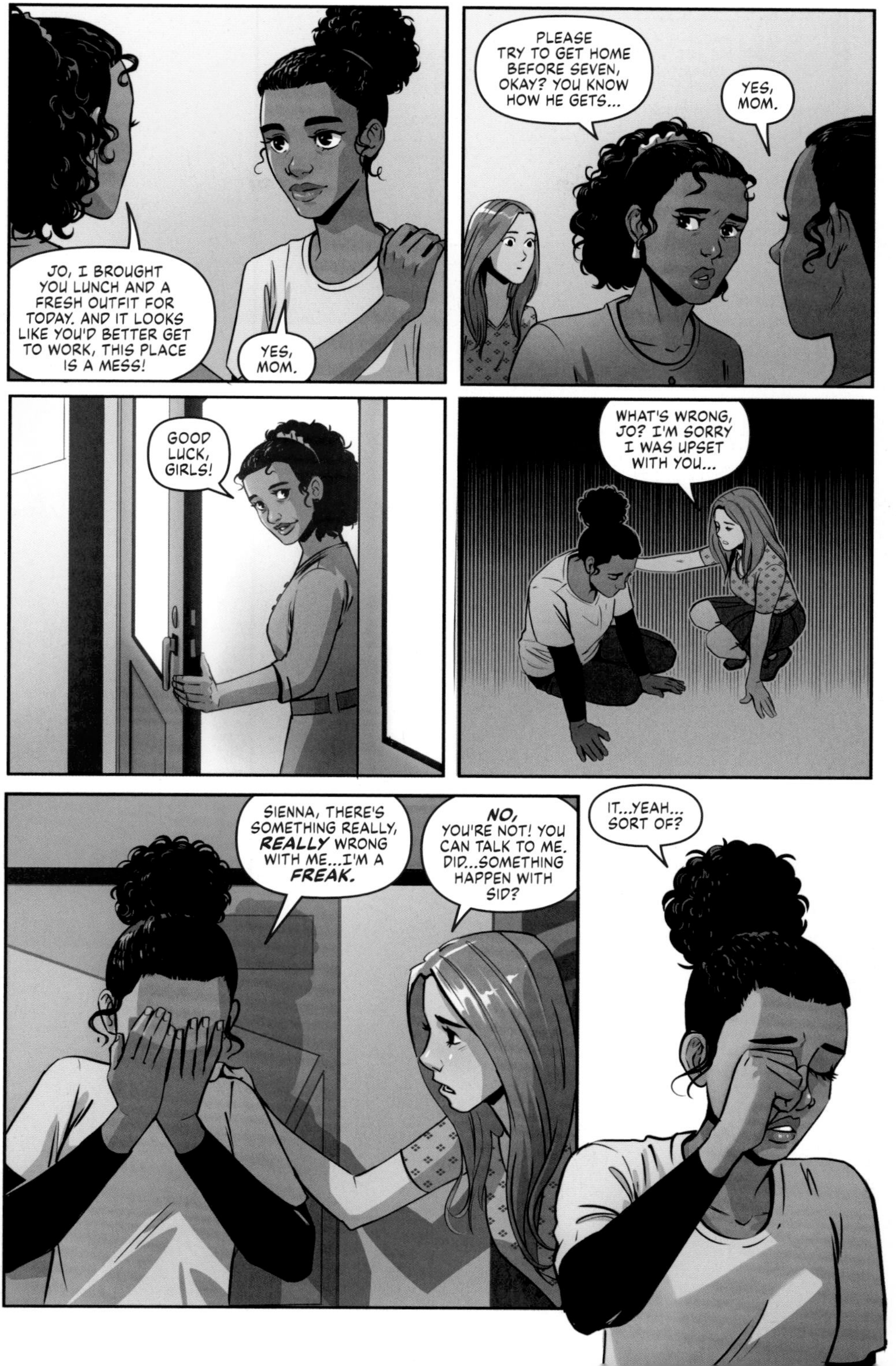
JO, I BROUGHT YOU LUNCH AND A FRESH OUTFIT FOR TODAY. AND IT LOOKS LIKE YOU'D BETTER GET TO WORK, THIS PLACE IS A MESS!
YES, MOM.
PLEASE TRY TO GET HOME BEFORE SEVEN, OKAY? YOU KNOW HOW HE GETS...
YES, MOM.
GOOD LUCK, GIRLS!
WHAT'S WRONG, JO? I'M SORRY I WAS UPSET WITH YOU...
SIENNA, THERE'S SOMETHING REALLY, **REALLY** WRONG WITH ME...I'M A **FREAK.**
NO, YOU'RE NOT! YOU CAN TALK TO ME. DID...SOMETHING HAPPEN WITH SID?
IT...YEAH... SORT OF?

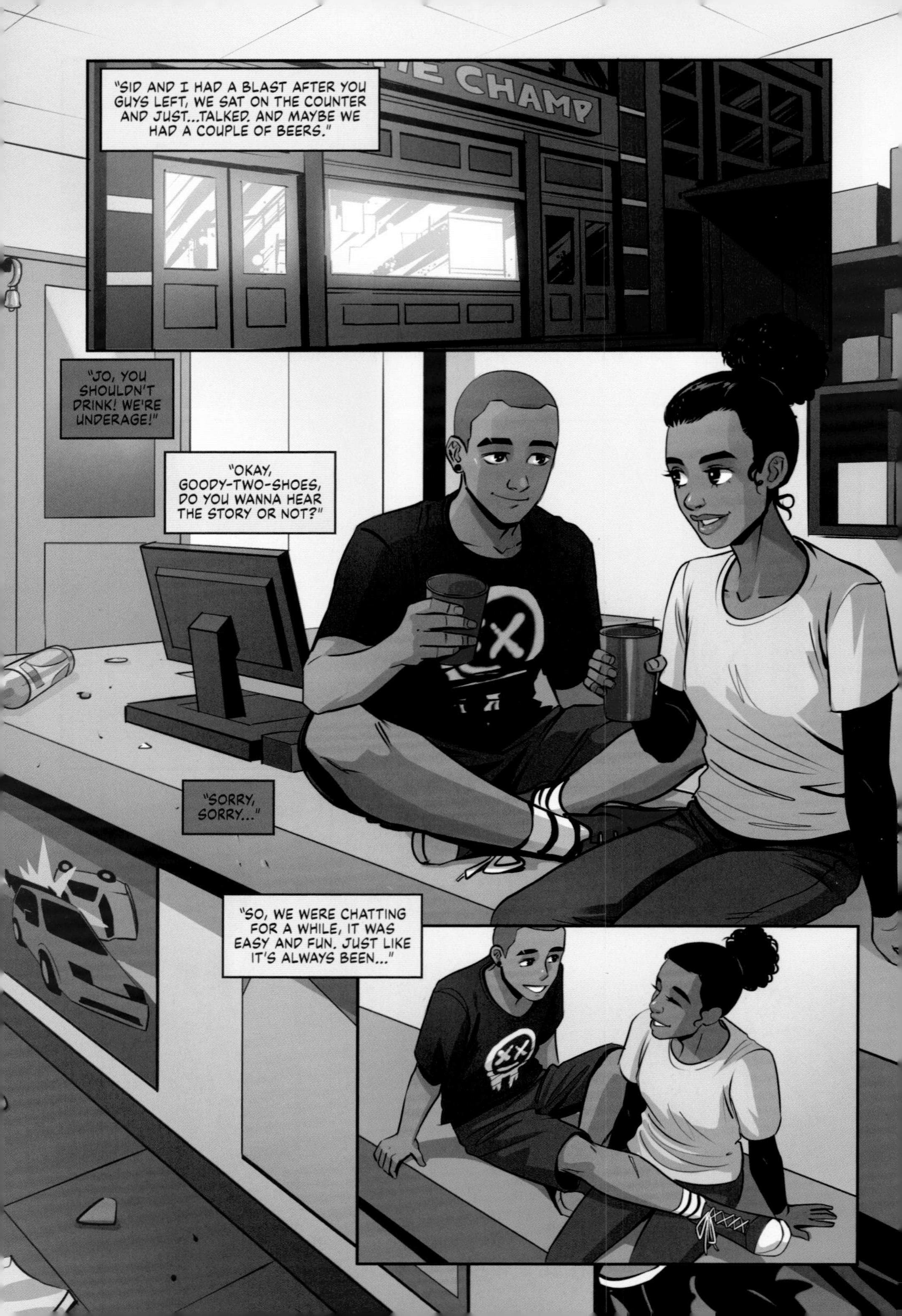
"SID AND I HAD A BLAST AFTER YOU GUYS LEFT, WE SAT ON THE COUNTER AND JUST...TALKED. AND MAYBE WE HAD A COUPLE OF BEERS."
CHAMP
"JO, YOU SHOULDN'T DRINK! WE'RE UNDERAGE!"
"OKAY, GOODY-TWO-SHOES, DO YOU WANNA HEAR THE STORY OR NOT?"
"SORRY, SORRY..."
"SO, WE WERE CHATTING FOR A WHILE, IT WAS EASY AND FUN. JUST LIKE IT'S ALWAYS BEEN..."

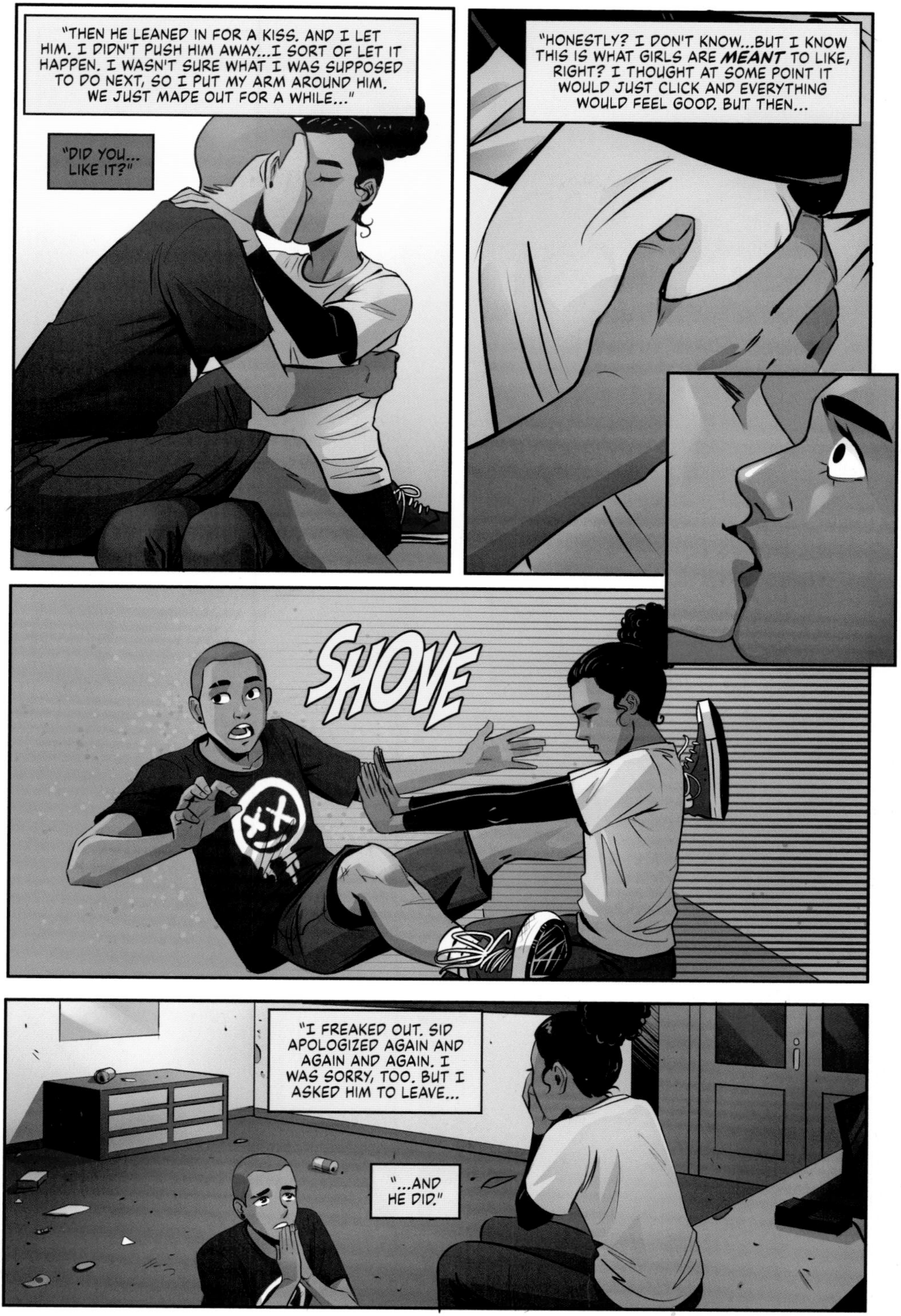
"THEN HE LEANED IN FOR A KISS. AND I LET HIM. I DIDN'T PUSH HIM AWAY...I SORT OF LET IT HAPPEN. I WASN'T SURE WHAT I WAS SUPPOSED TO DO NEXT, SO I PUT MY ARM AROUND HIM. WE JUST MADE OUT FOR A WHILE..."
"DID YOU... LIKE IT?"
"HONESTLY? I DON'T KNOW...BUT I KNOW THIS IS WHAT GIRLS ARE ***MEANT*** TO LIKE, RIGHT? I THOUGHT AT SOME POINT IT WOULD JUST CLICK AND EVERYTHING WOULD FEEL GOOD. BUT THEN...
SHOVE
"I FREAKED OUT. SID APOLOGIZED AGAIN AND AGAIN AND AGAIN. I WAS SORRY, TOO. BUT I ASKED HIM TO LEAVE...
"...AND HE DID."

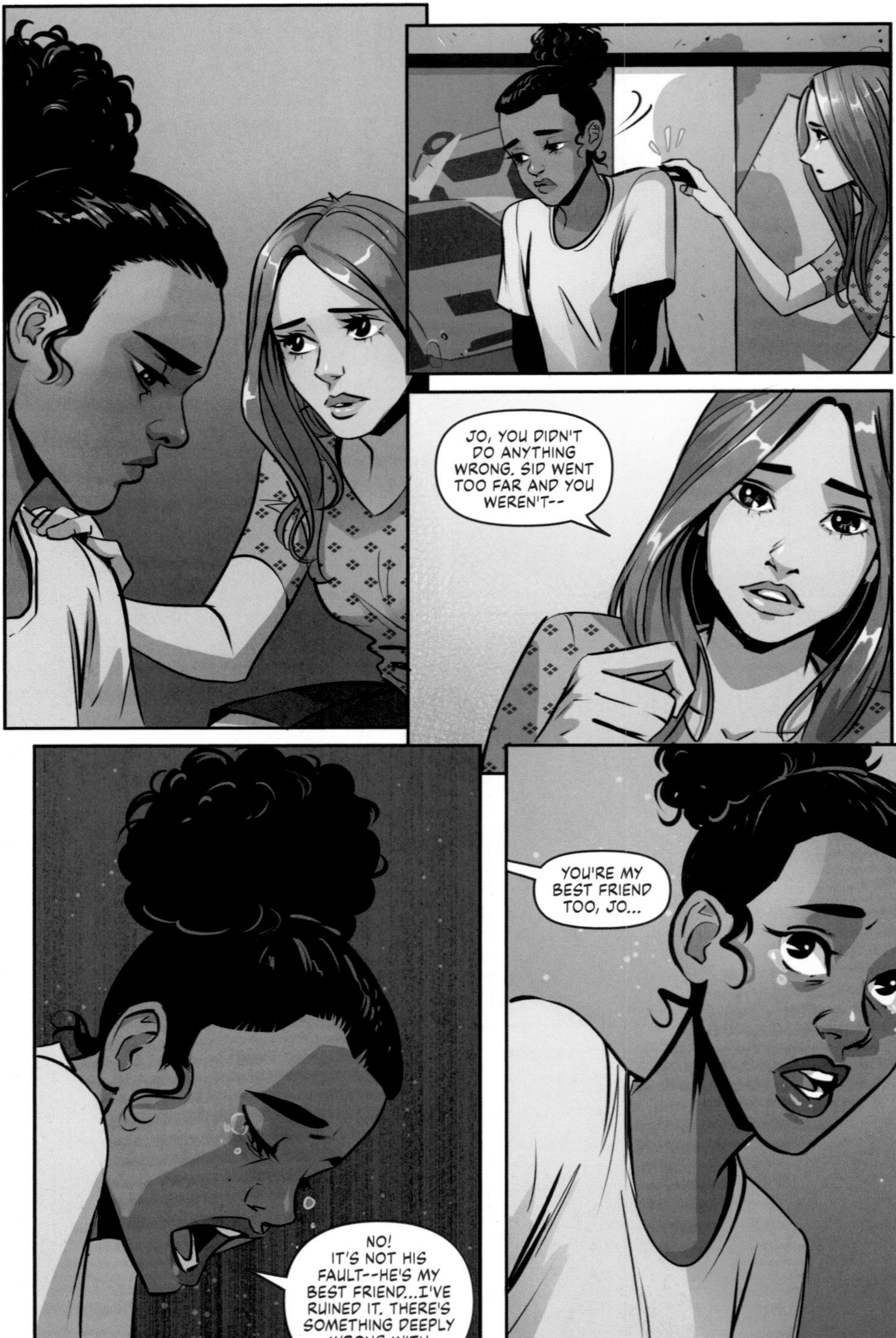
JO, YOU DIDN'T DO ANYTHING WRONG. SID WENT TOO FAR AND YOU WEREN'T--
NO! IT'S NOT HIS FAULT--HE'S MY BEST FRIEND...I'VE RUINED IT. THERE'S SOMETHING DEEPLY WRONG WITH ME...
YOU'RE MY BEST FRIEND TOO, JO...

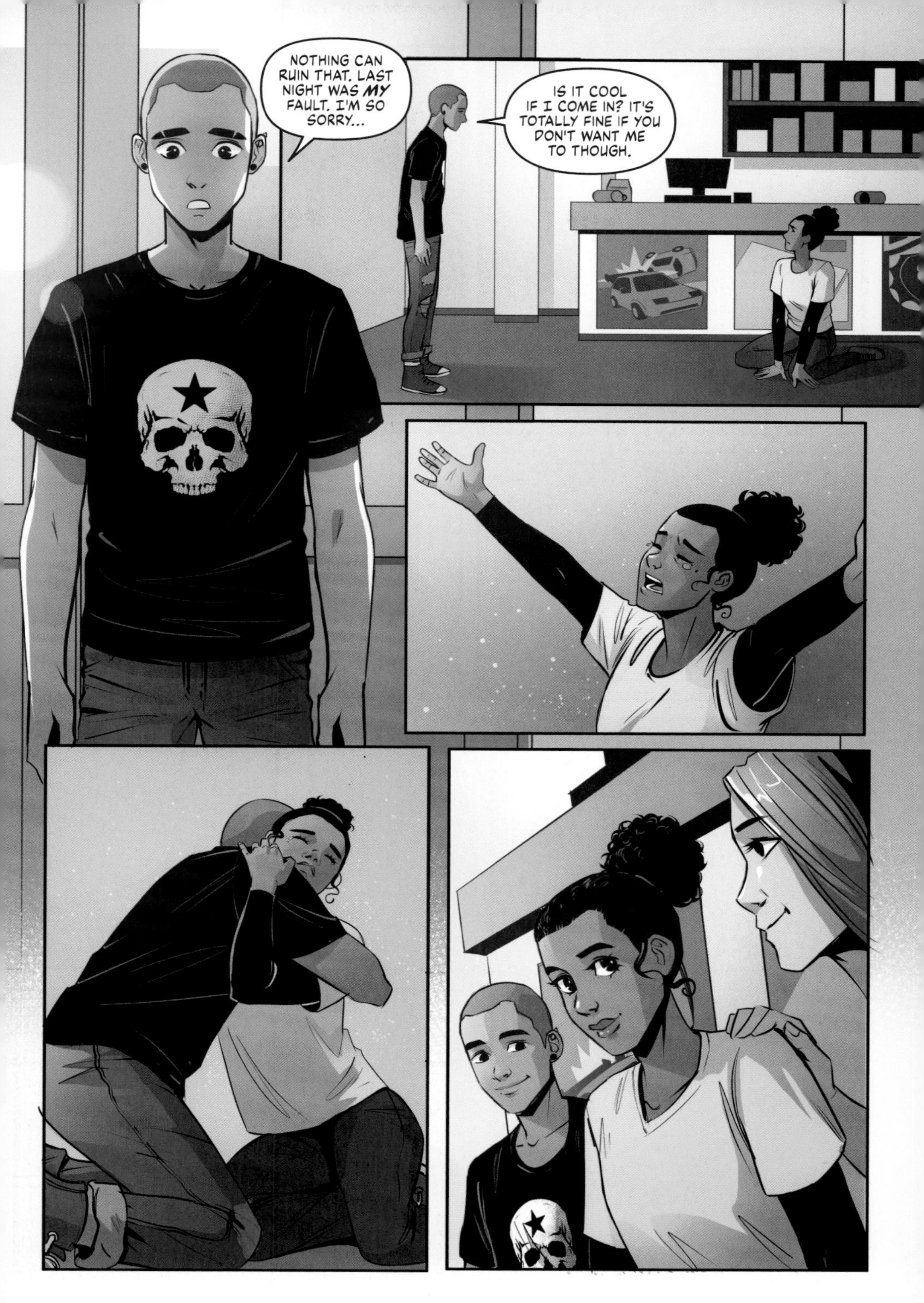
NOTHING CAN RUIN THAT. LAST NIGHT WAS MY FAULT. I'M SO SORRY...
IS IT COOL IF I COME IN? IT'S TOTALLY FINE IF YOU DON'T WANT ME TO THOUGH.

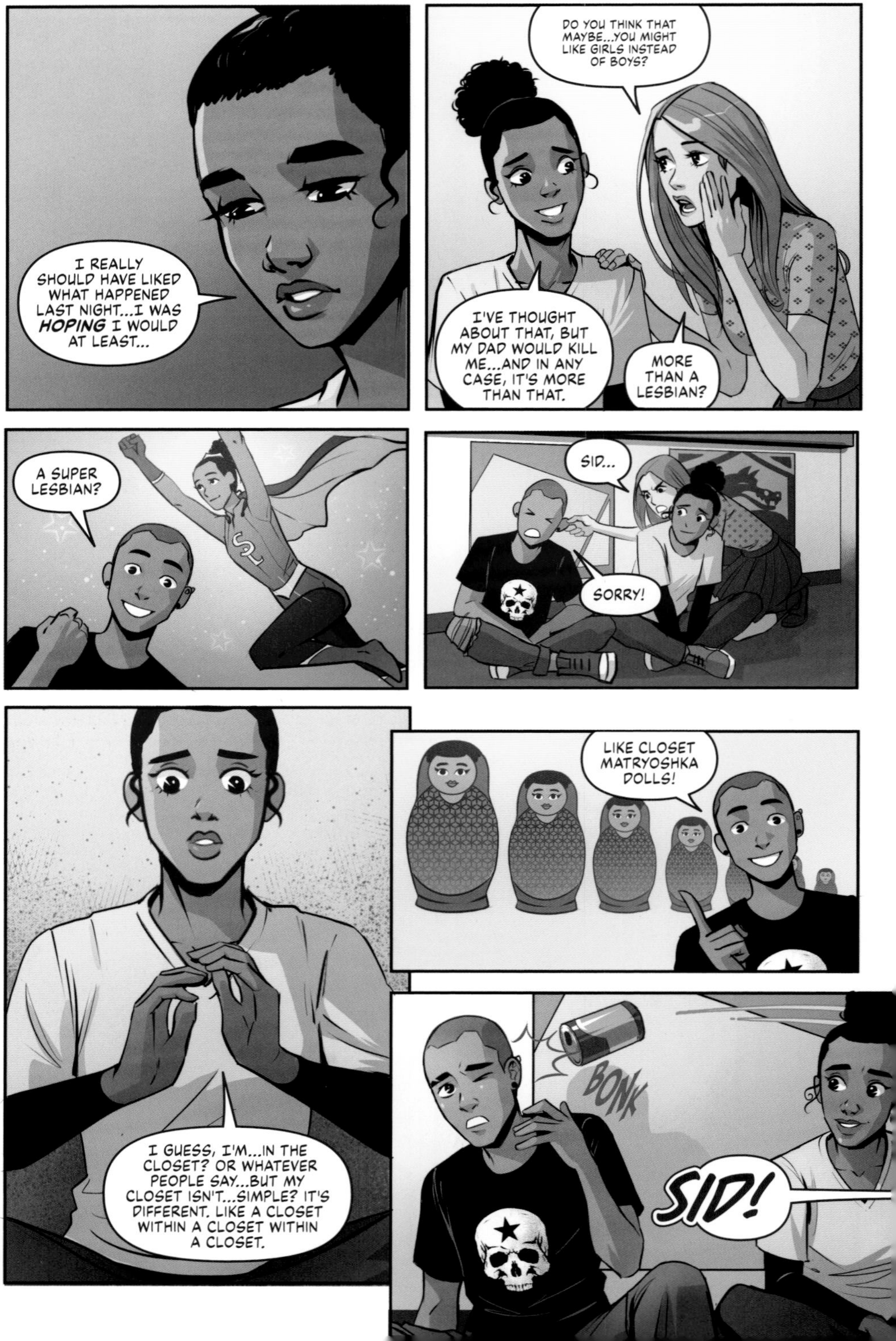
I REALLY SHOULD HAVE LIKED WHAT HAPPENED LAST NIGHT...I WAS *HOPING* I WOULD AT LEAST...
DO YOU THINK THAT MAYBE...YOU MIGHT LIKE GIRLS INSTEAD OF BOYS?
I'VE THOUGHT ABOUT THAT, BUT MY DAD WOULD KILL ME...AND IN ANY CASE, IT'S MORE THAN THAT.
MORE THAN A LESBIAN?
A SUPER LESBIAN?
SID...
SORRY!
I GUESS, I'M...IN THE CLOSET? OR WHATEVER PEOPLE SAY...BUT MY CLOSET ISN'T...SIMPLE? IT'S DIFFERENT. LIKE A CLOSET WITHIN A CLOSET WITHIN A CLOSET.
LIKE CLOSET MATRYOSHKA DOLLS!
BONK
SID!

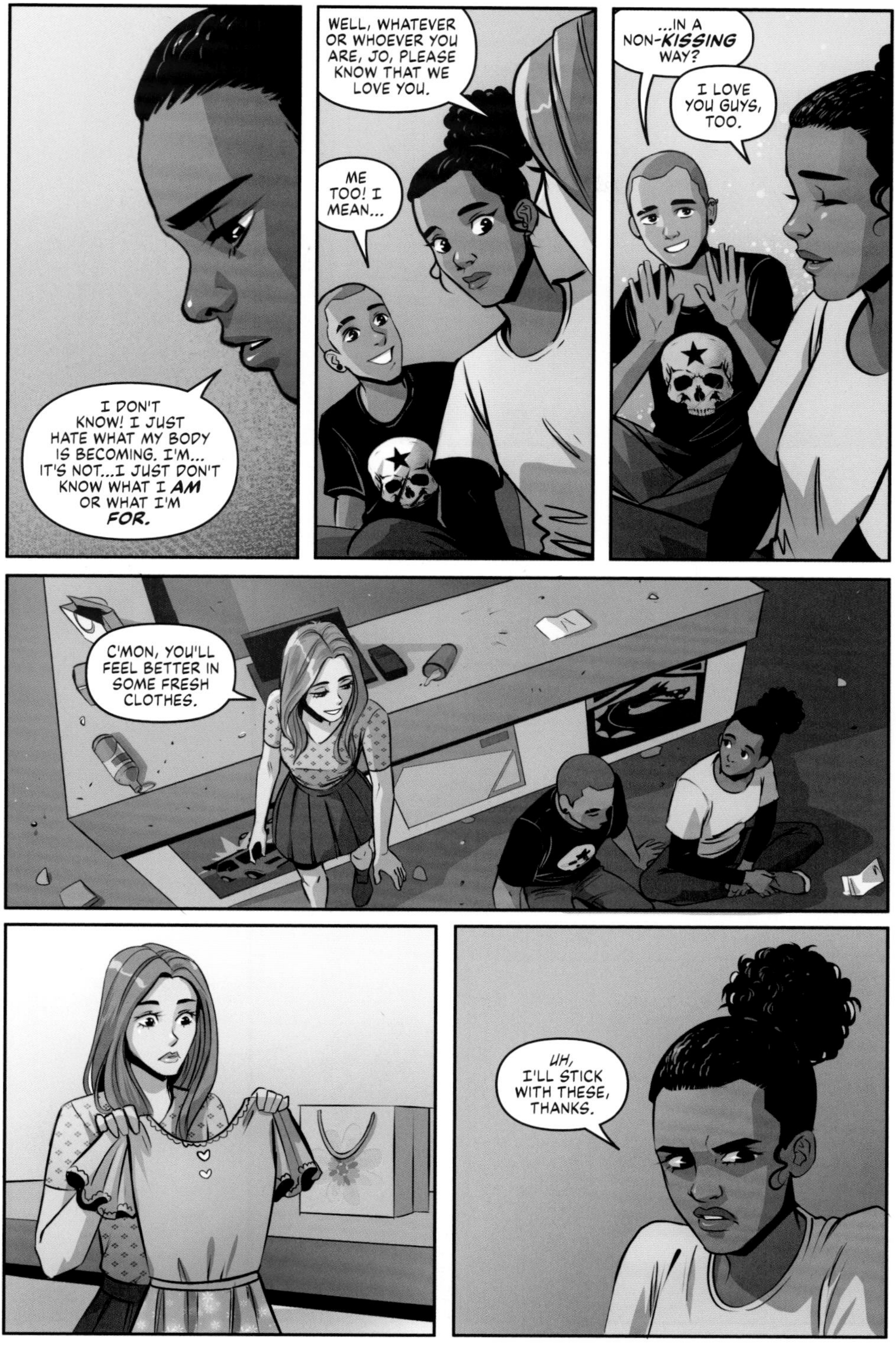
I DON'T KNOW! I JUST HATE WHAT MY BODY IS BECOMING. I'M... IT'S NOT...I JUST DON'T KNOW WHAT I *AM* OR WHAT I'M *FOR.*
WELL, WHATEVER OR WHOEVER YOU ARE, JO, PLEASE KNOW THAT WE LOVE YOU.
ME TOO! I MEAN...
...IN A NON-*KISSING* WAY?
I LOVE YOU GUYS, TOO.
C'MON, YOU'LL FEEL BETTER IN SOME FRESH CLOTHES.
UH, I'LL STICK WITH THESE, THANKS.

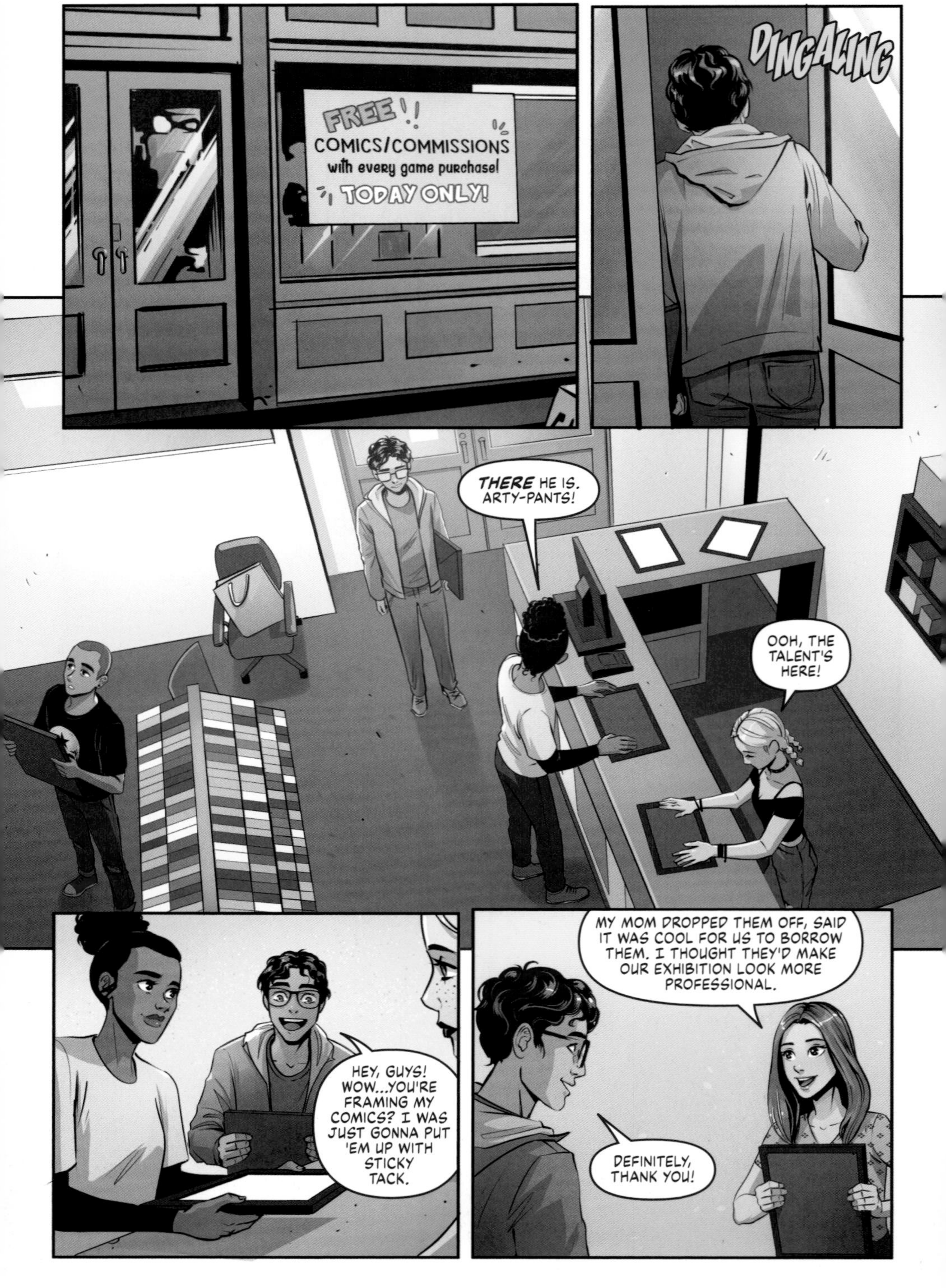
FREE
COMICS/COMMISSIONS
with every game purchase!
TODAY ONLY!
DINGALING
THERE HE IS. ARTY-PANTS!
OOH, THE TALENT'S HERE!
HEY, GUYS! WOW...YOU'RE FRAMING MY COMICS? I WAS JUST GONNA PUT 'EM UP WITH STICKY TACK.
MY MOM DROPPED THEM OFF, SAID IT WAS COOL FOR US TO BORROW THEM. I THOUGHT THEY'D MAKE OUR EXHIBITION LOOK MORE PROFESSIONAL.
DEFINITELY, THANK YOU!

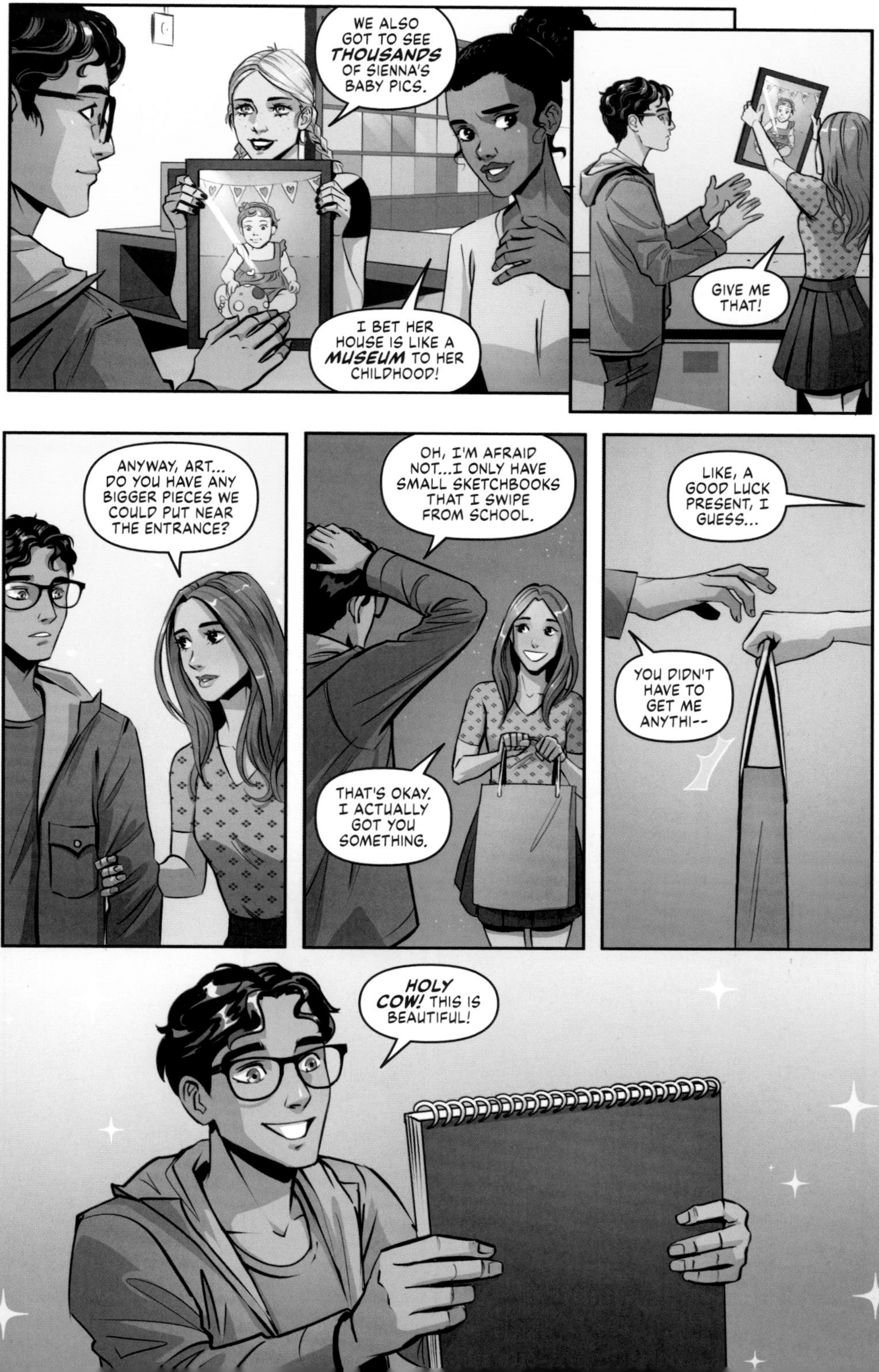
WE ALSO GOT TO SEE THOUSANDS OF SIENNA'S BABY PICS.
I BET HER HOUSE IS LIKE A MUSEUM TO HER CHILDHOOD!
GIVE ME THAT!
ANYWAY, ART... DO YOU HAVE ANY BIGGER PIECES WE COULD PUT NEAR THE ENTRANCE?
OH, I'M AFRAID NOT...I ONLY HAVE SMALL SKETCHBOOKS THAT I SWIPE FROM SCHOOL.
THAT'S OKAY. I ACTUALLY GOT YOU SOMETHING.
LIKE, A GOOD LUCK PRESENT, I GUESS...
YOU DIDN'T HAVE TO GET ME ANYTHI--
HOLY COW! THIS IS BEAUTIFUL!

I THOUGHT IT WOULD BE BETTER FOR DOING THE COMMISSIONS TODAY?

FOR SURE! JEEZ, I DUNNO WHAT TO SAY.

THANK YOU! THIS IS INCREDIBLE!

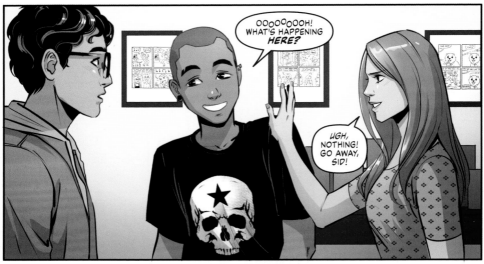

OOOOOOOOH! WHAT'S HAPPENING HERE?

UGH, NOTHING! GO AWAY, SID!

I NEED THE KEY SO WE CAN OPEN!

IS IT THAT TIME ALREADY? ARE ALL THE PICTURES UP?

ALMOST.

ALMOST?! OKAY, YOU OPEN UP, AND I'LL GET THESE ONES HUNG!

GO! GO! GO!

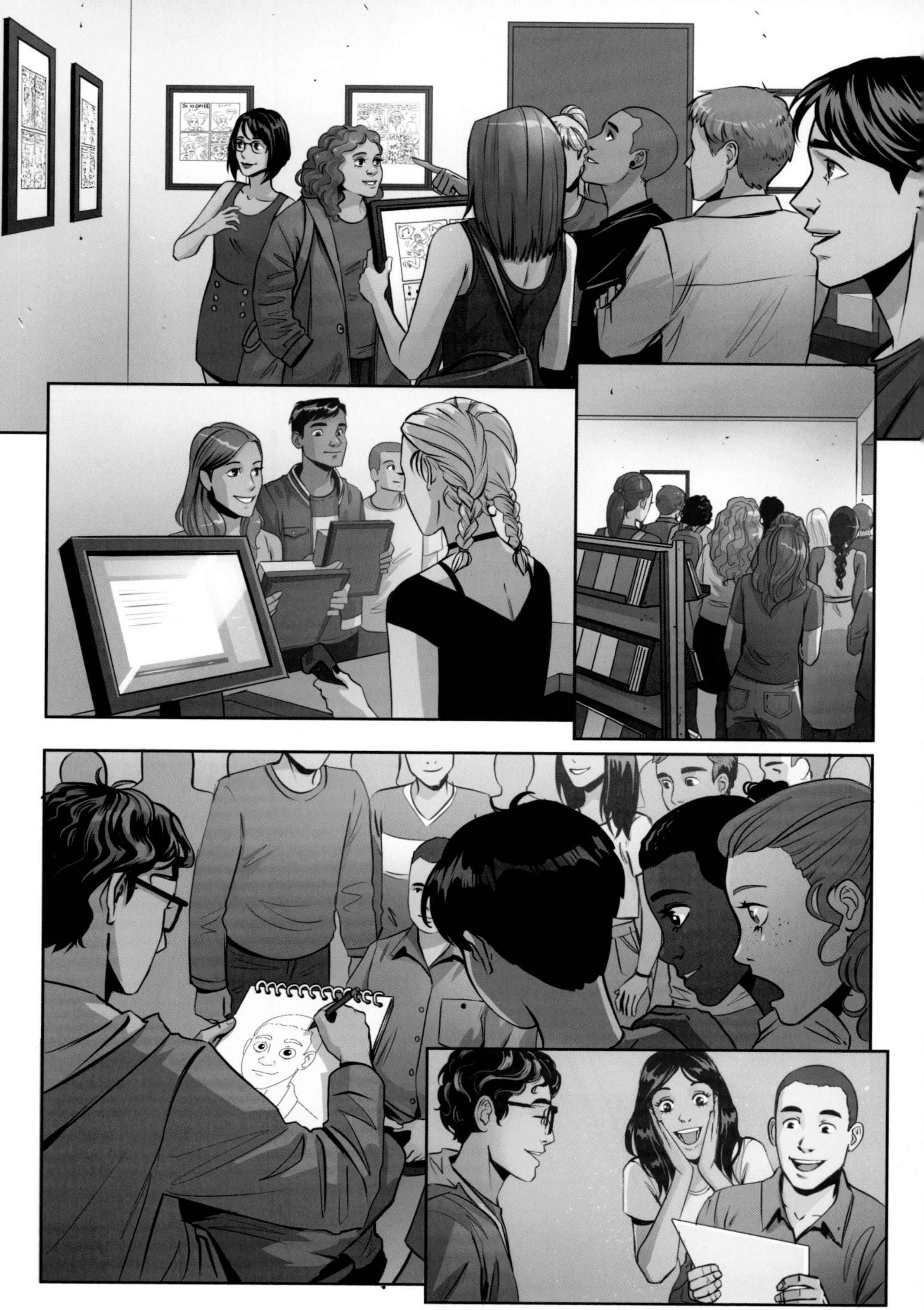

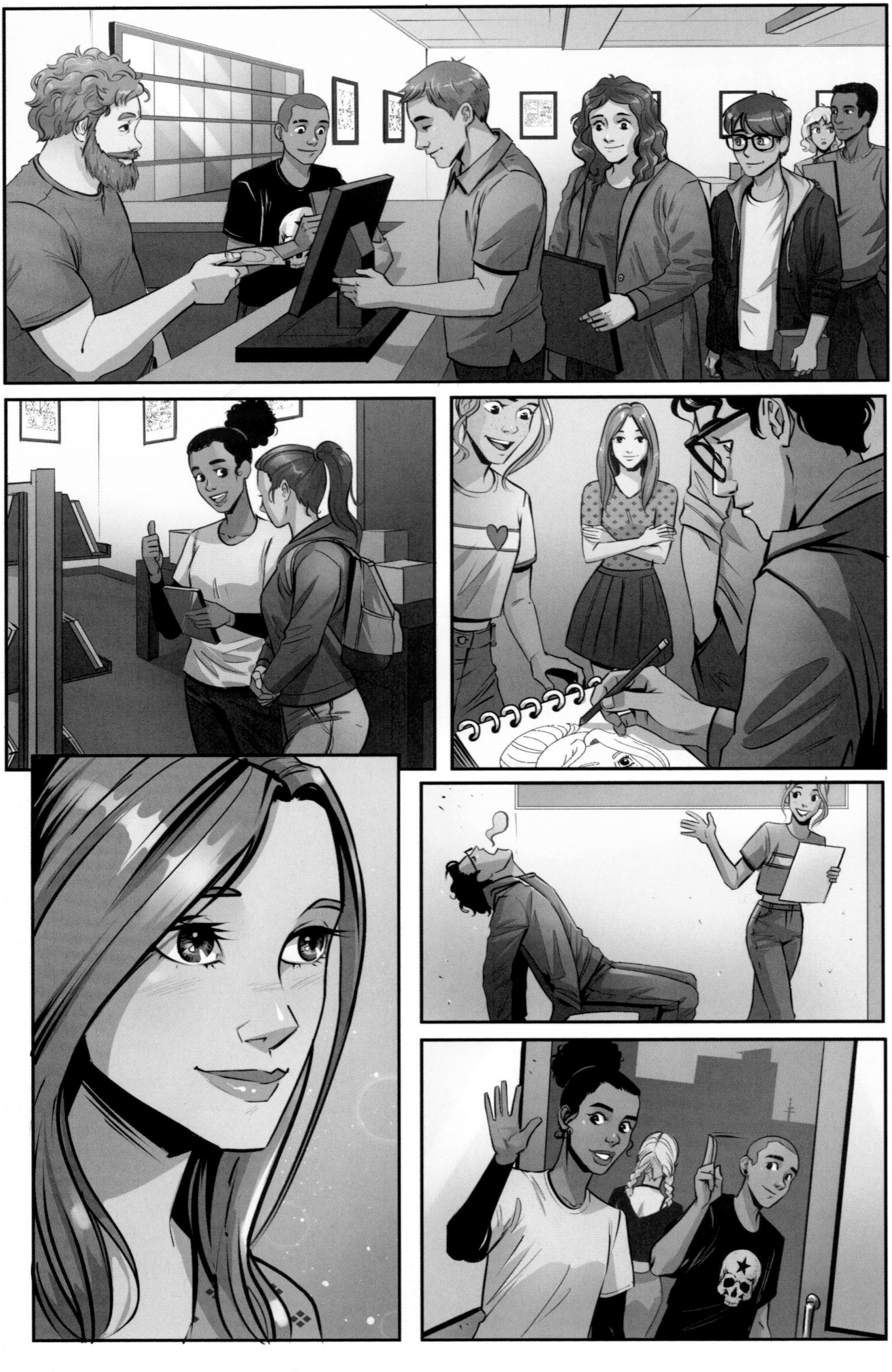

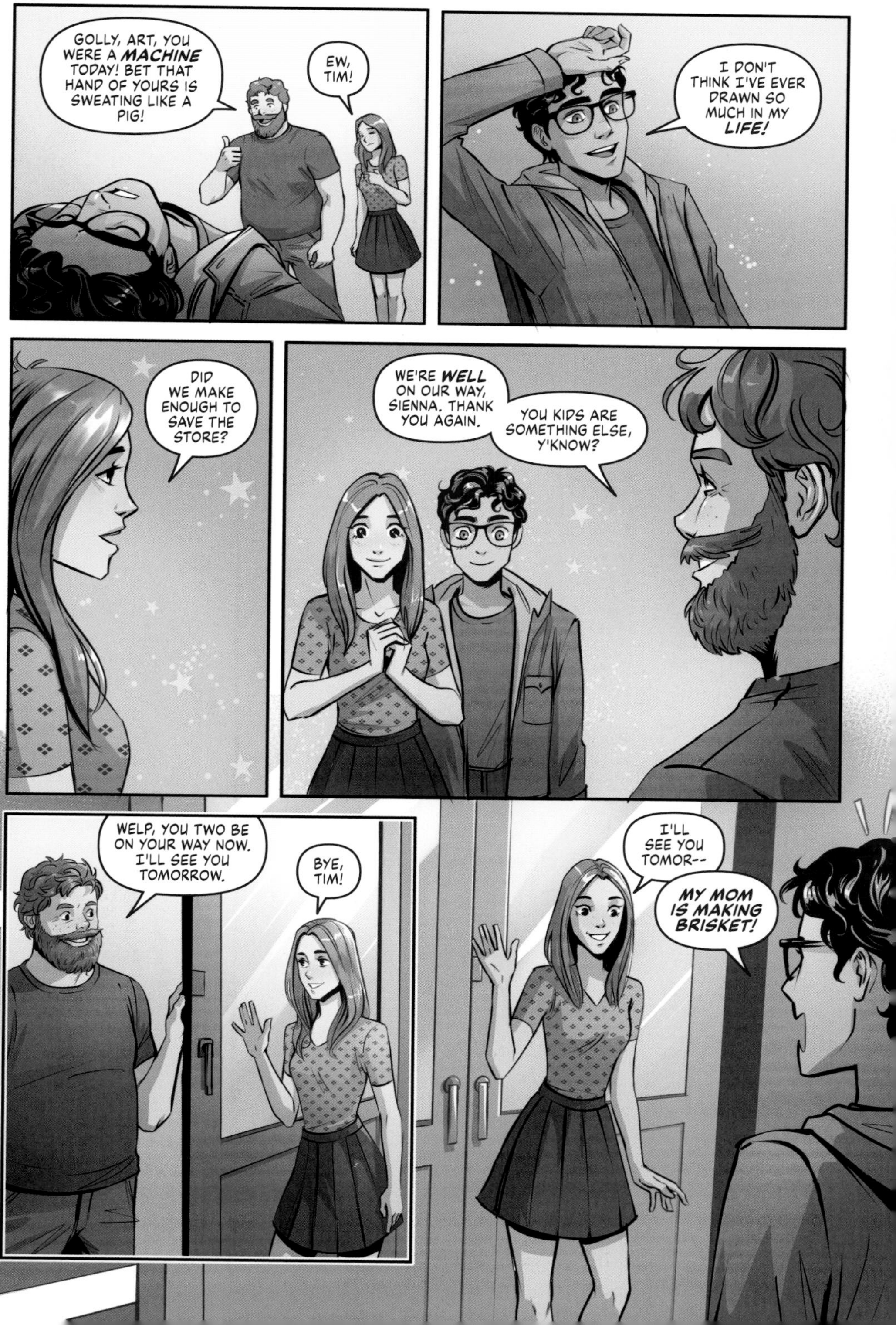
GOLLY, ART, YOU WERE A MACHINE TODAY! BET THAT HAND OF YOURS IS SWEATING LIKE A PIG!
EW, TIM!
I DON'T THINK I'VE EVER DRAWN SO MUCH IN MY LIFE!
DID WE MAKE ENOUGH TO SAVE THE STORE?
WE'RE WELL ON OUR WAY, SIENNA. THANK YOU AGAIN.
YOU KIDS ARE SOMETHING ELSE, Y'KNOW?
WELP, YOU TWO BE ON YOUR WAY NOW. I'LL SEE YOU TOMORROW.
BYE, TIM!
I'LL SEE YOU TOMOR--
MY MOM IS MAKING BRISKET!

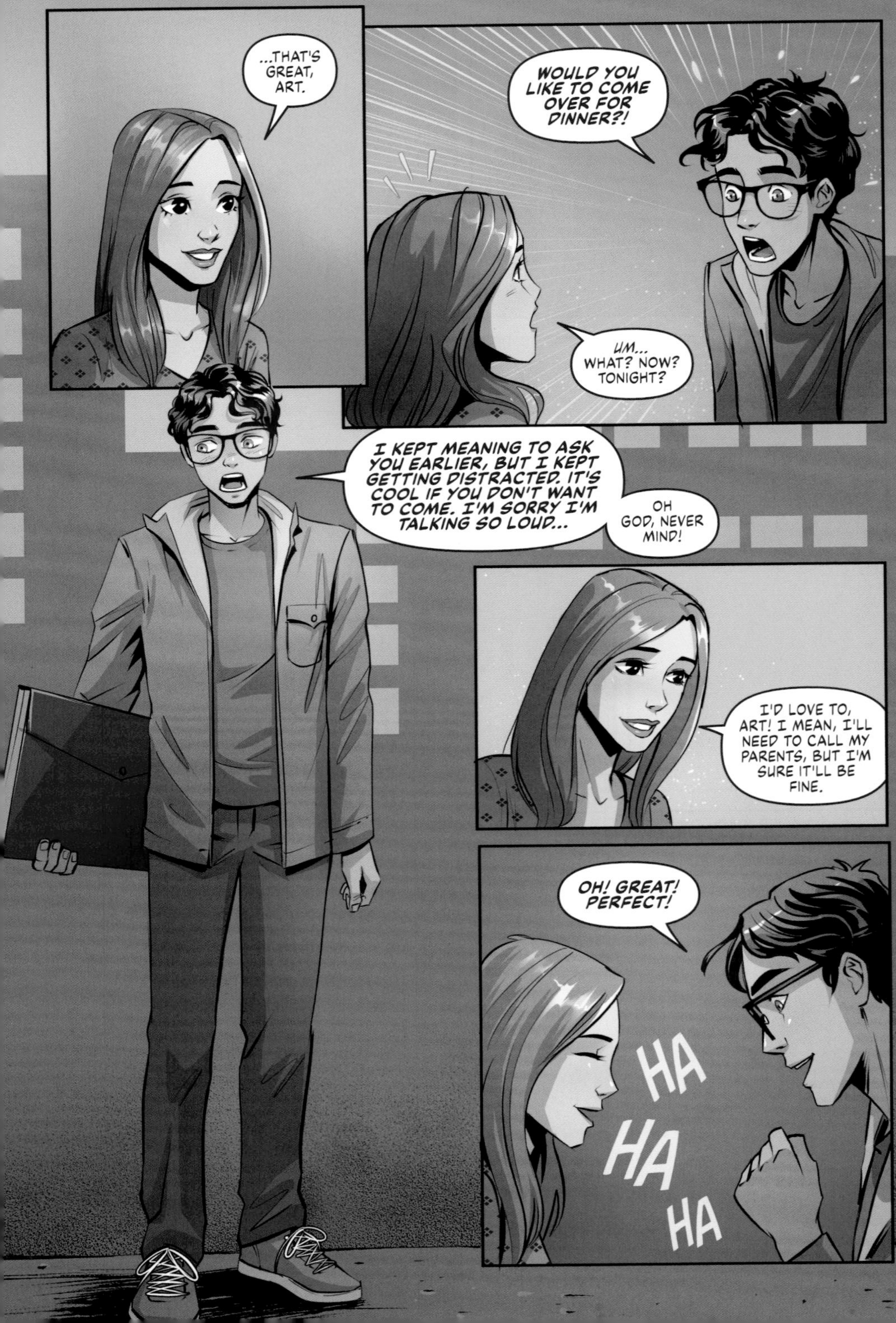
...THAT'S GREAT, ART.
WOULD YOU LIKE TO COME OVER FOR DINNER?!
UM... WHAT? NOW? TONIGHT?
I KEPT MEANING TO ASK YOU EARLIER, BUT I KEPT GETTING DISTRACTED. IT'S COOL IF YOU DON'T WANT TO COME. I'M SORRY I'M TALKING SO LOUD...
OH GOD, NEVER MIND!
I'D LOVE TO, ART! I MEAN, I'LL NEED TO CALL MY PARENTS, BUT I'M SURE IT'LL BE FINE.
OH! GREAT! PERFECT!
HA
HA
HA

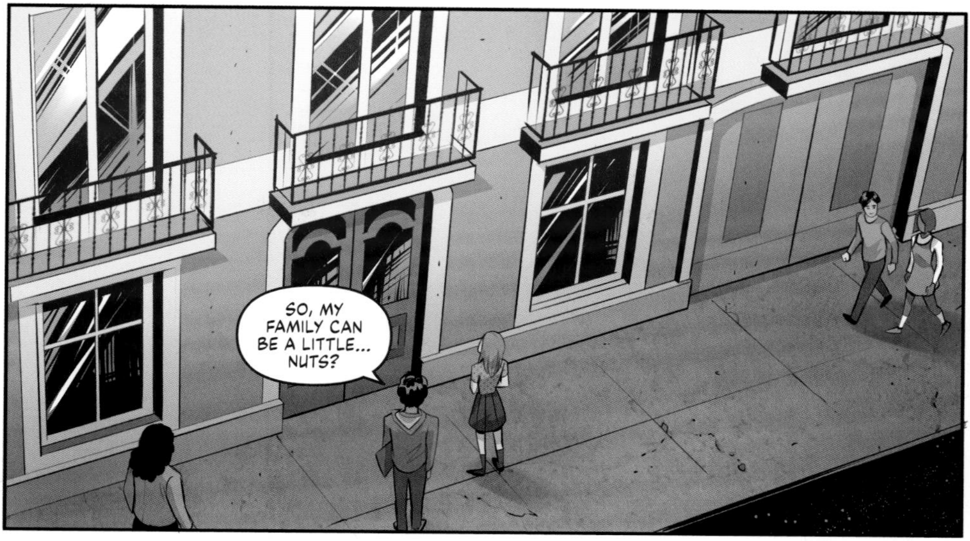
SO, MY FAMILY CAN BE A LITTLE... NUTS?

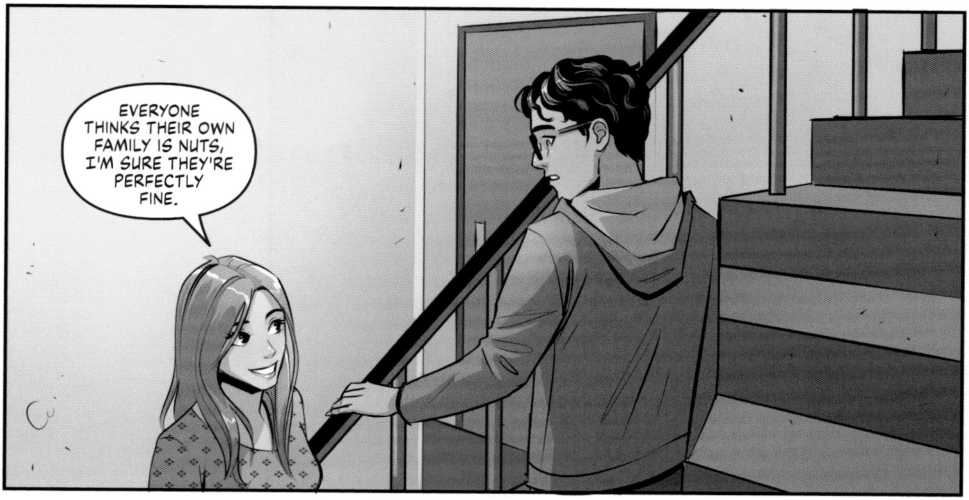
EVERYONE THINKS THEIR OWN FAMILY IS NUTS, I'M SURE THEY'RE PERFECTLY FINE.

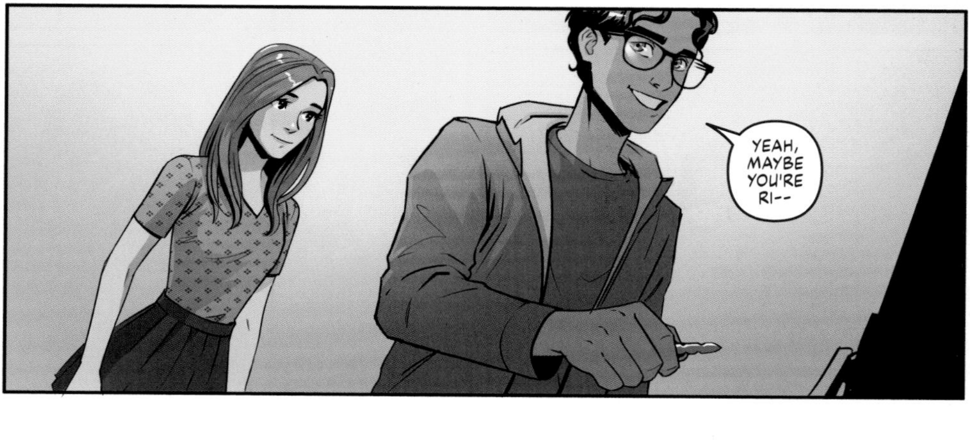
YEAH, MAYBE YOU'RE RI--

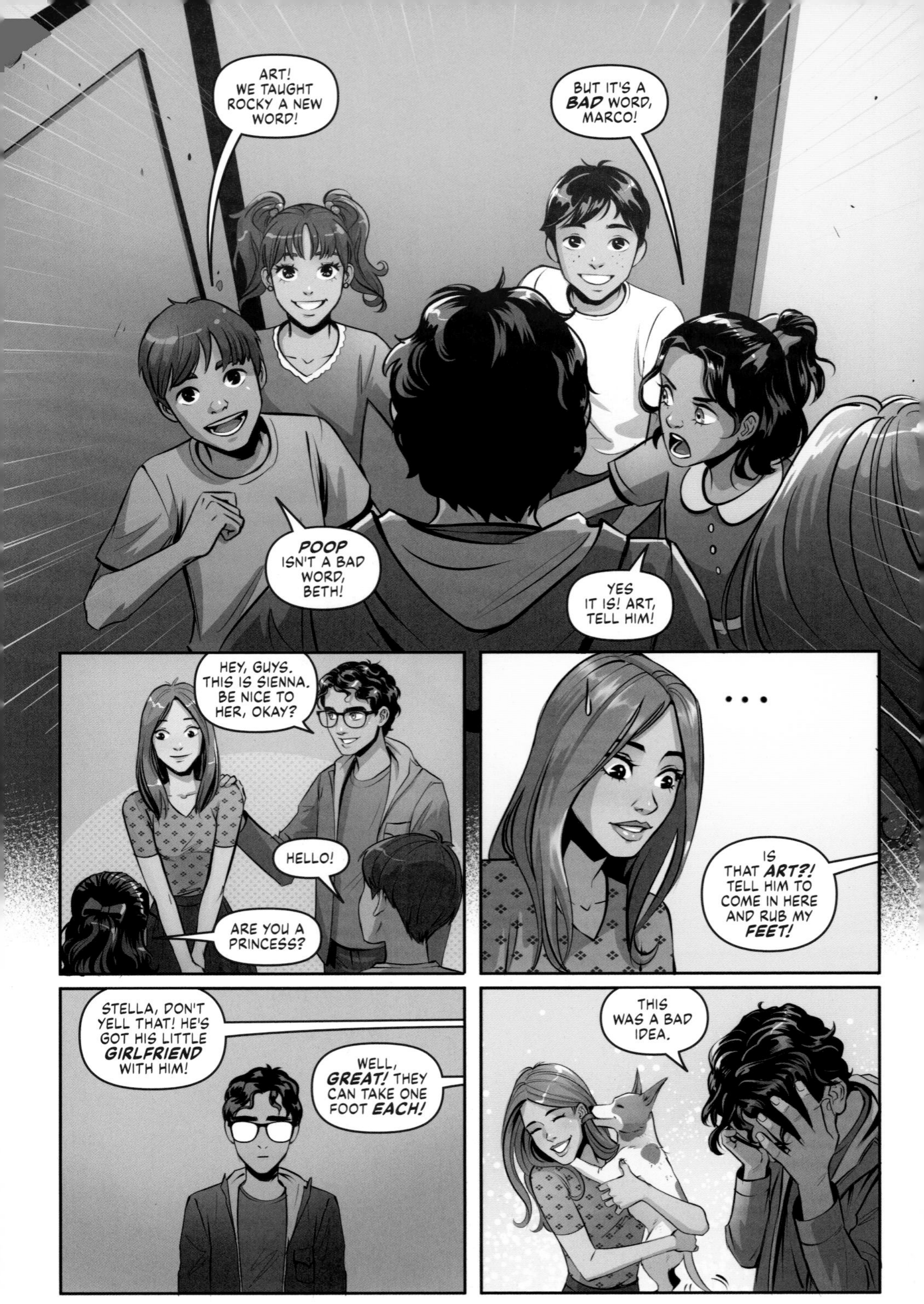

ART! WE TAUGHT ROCKY A NEW WORD!
BUT IT'S A ***BAD*** WORD, MARCO!
POOP ISN'T A BAD WORD, BETH!
YES IT IS! ART, TELL HIM!
HEY, GUYS. THIS IS SIENNA. BE NICE TO HER, OKAY?
HELLO!
ARE YOU A PRINCESS?
...
IS THAT ***ART?!*** TELL HIM TO COME IN HERE AND RUB MY ***FEET!***
STELLA, DON'T YELL THAT! HE'S GOT HIS LITTLE ***GIRLFRIEND*** WITH HIM!
WELL, ***GREAT!*** THEY CAN TAKE ONE FOOT ***EACH!***
THIS WAS A BAD IDEA.

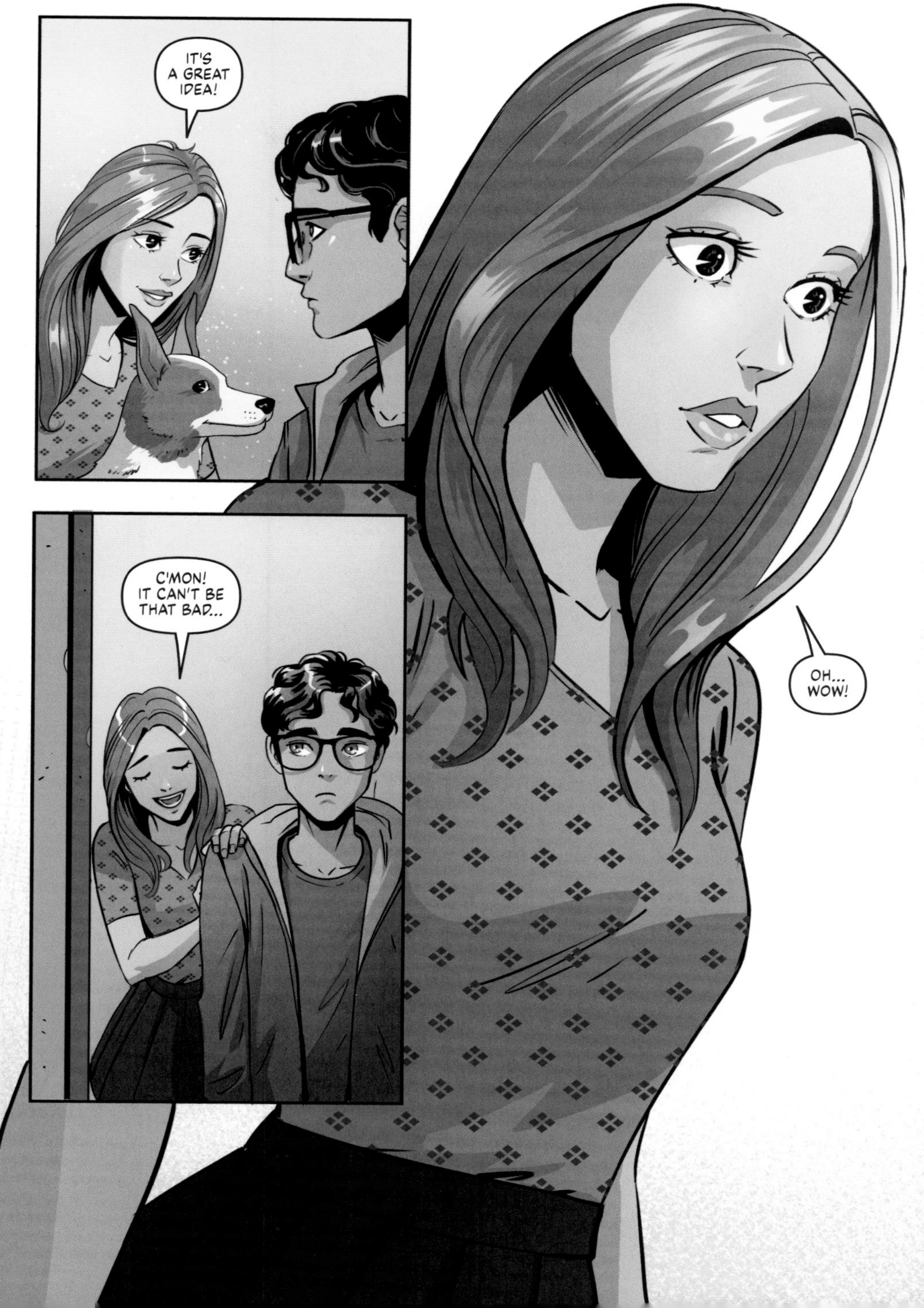
IT'S A GREAT IDEA!
C'MON! IT CAN'T BE THAT BAD...
OH... WOW!

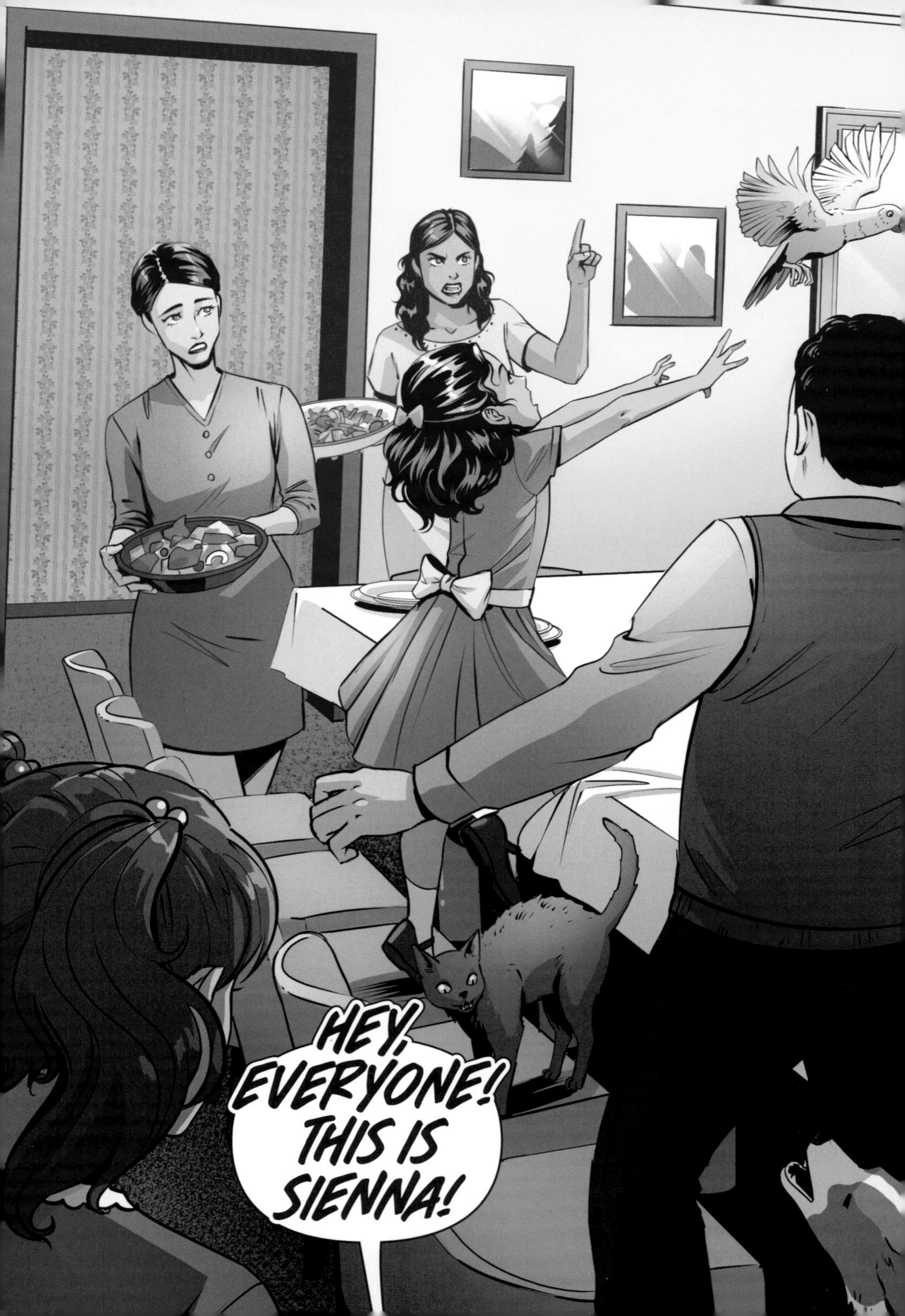
HEY, EVERYONE! THIS IS SIENNA!

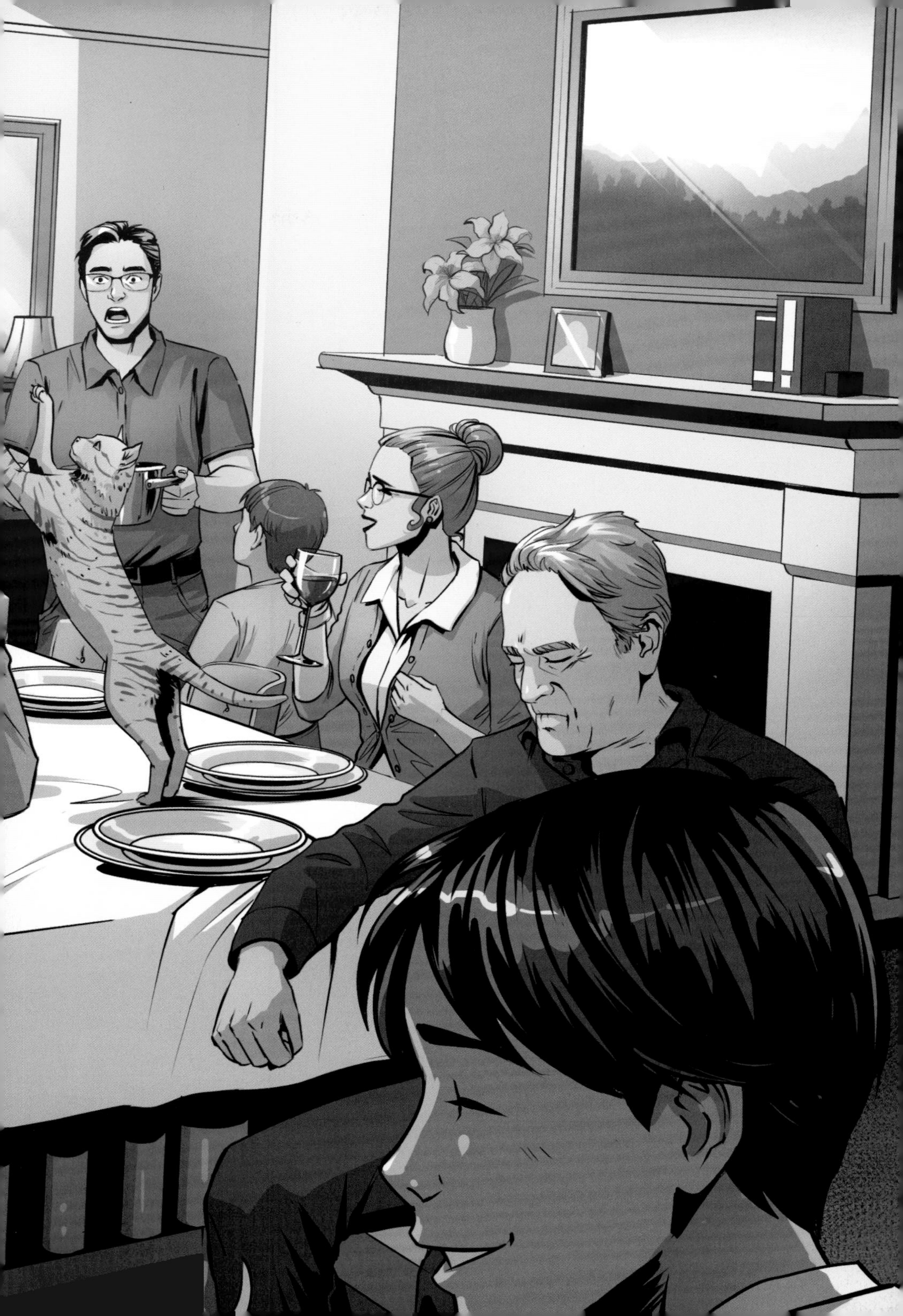

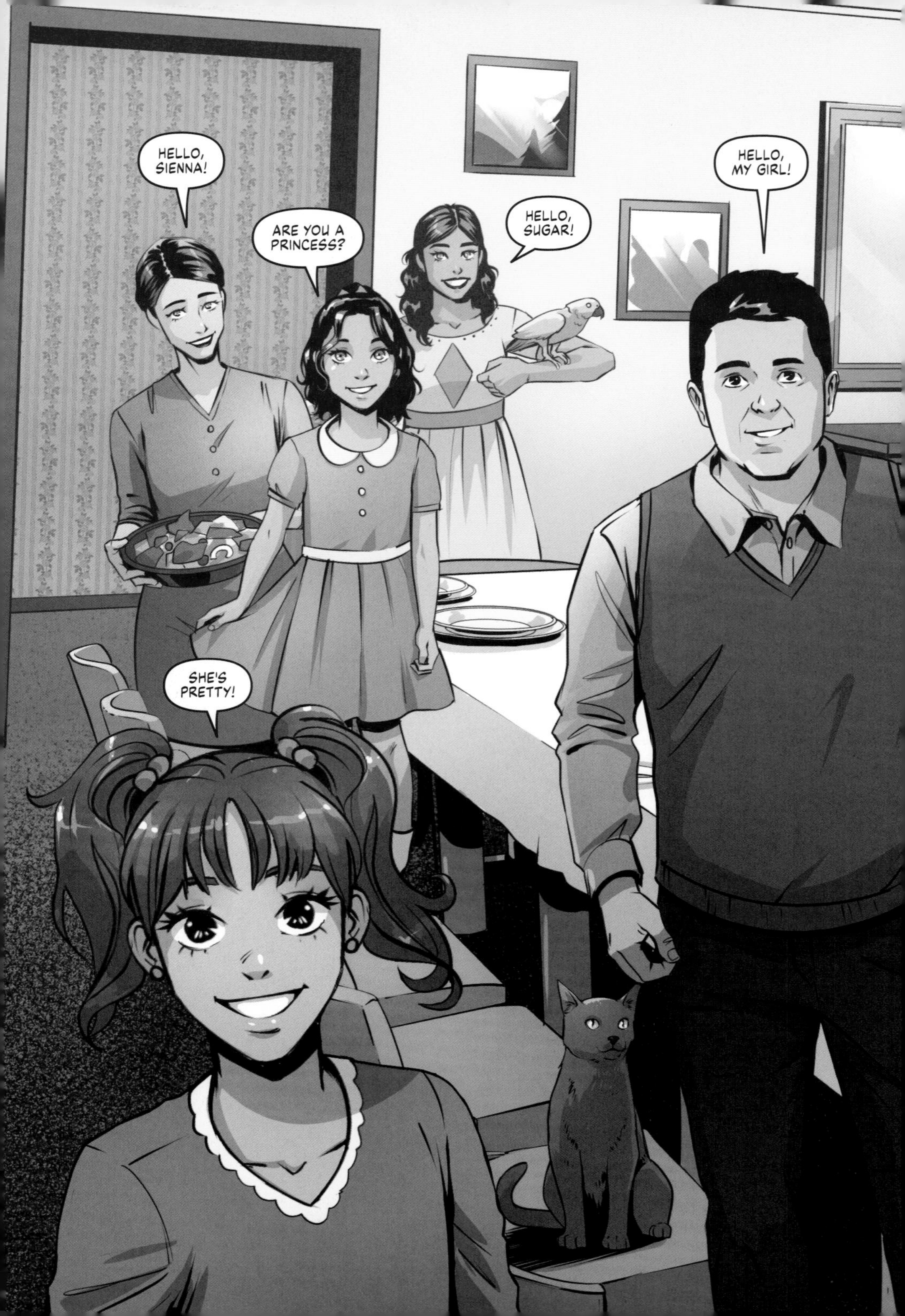
HELLO, SIENNA!
ARE YOU A PRINCESS?
HELLO, SUGAR!
HELLO, MY GIRL!
SHE'S PRETTY!

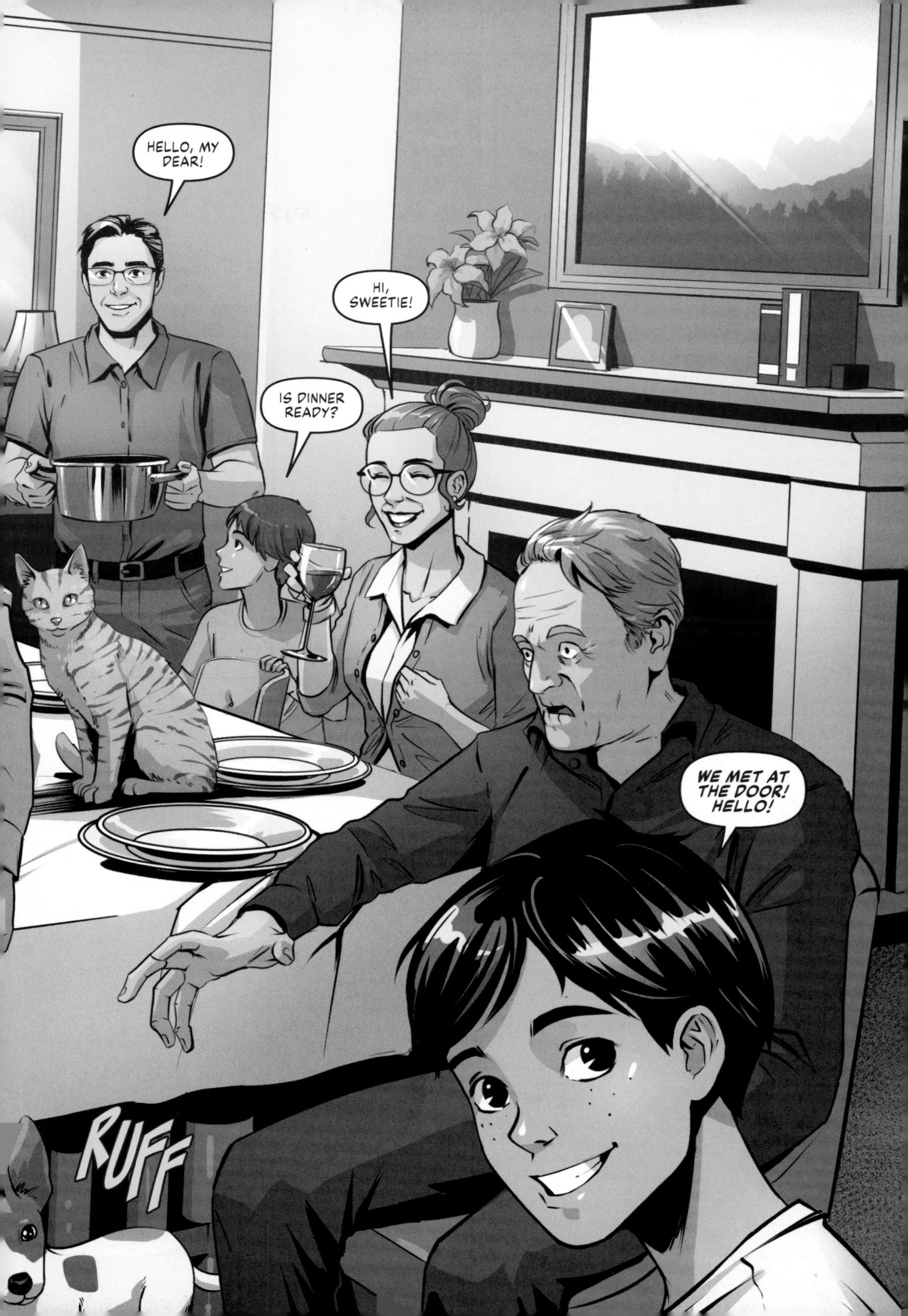
HELLO, MY DEAR!
HI, SWEETIE!
IS DINNER READY?
WE MET AT THE DOOR! HELLO!
RUFF

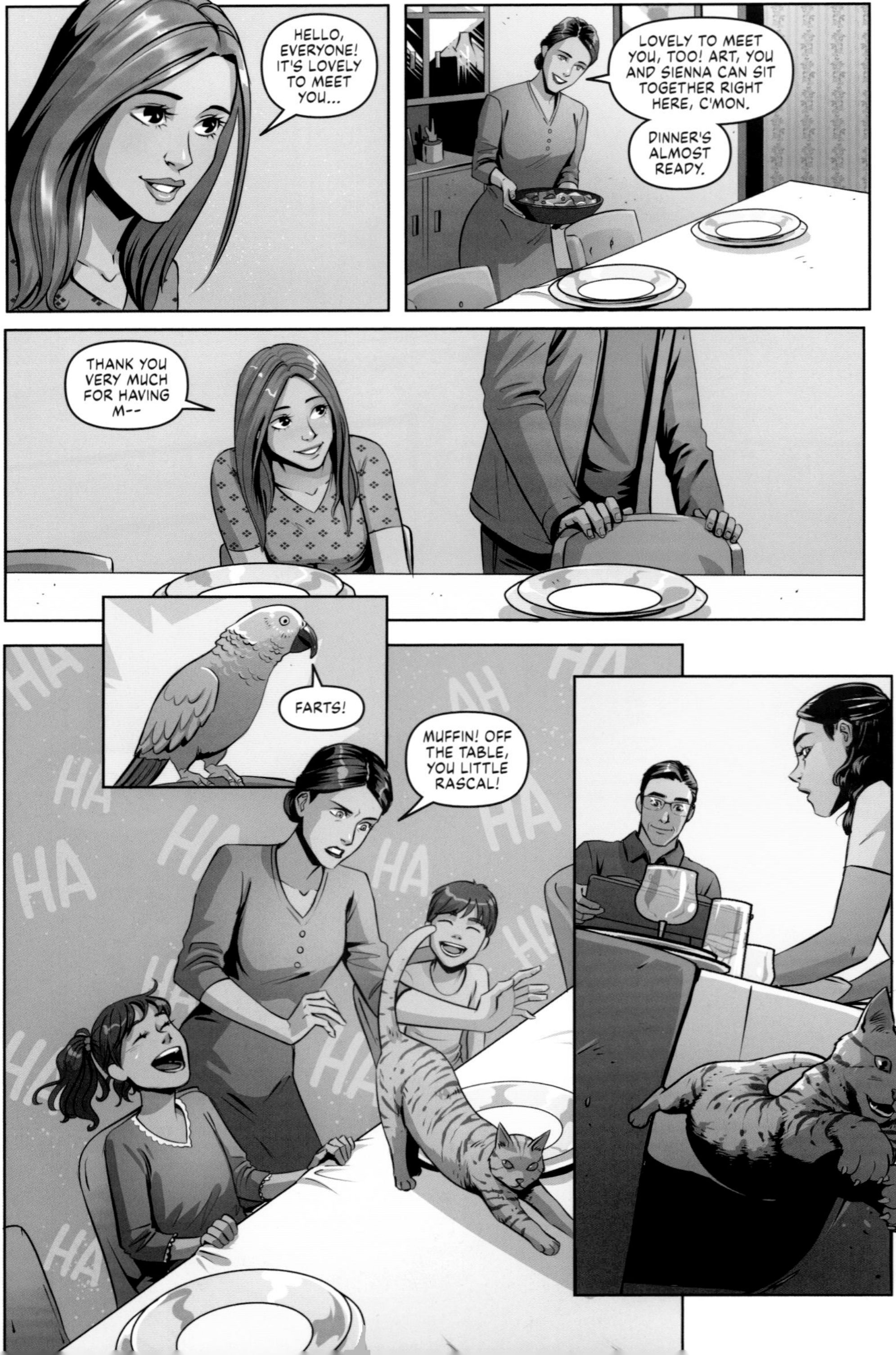
HELLO, EVERYONE! IT'S LOVELY TO MEET YOU...
LOVELY TO MEET YOU, TOO! ART, YOU AND SIENNA CAN SIT TOGETHER RIGHT HERE, C'MON.
DINNER'S ALMOST READY.
THANK YOU VERY MUCH FOR HAVING M--
FARTS!
MUFFIN! OFF THE TABLE, YOU LITTLE RASCAL!
HA HA HA HA HA HA HA HA HA HA HA HA

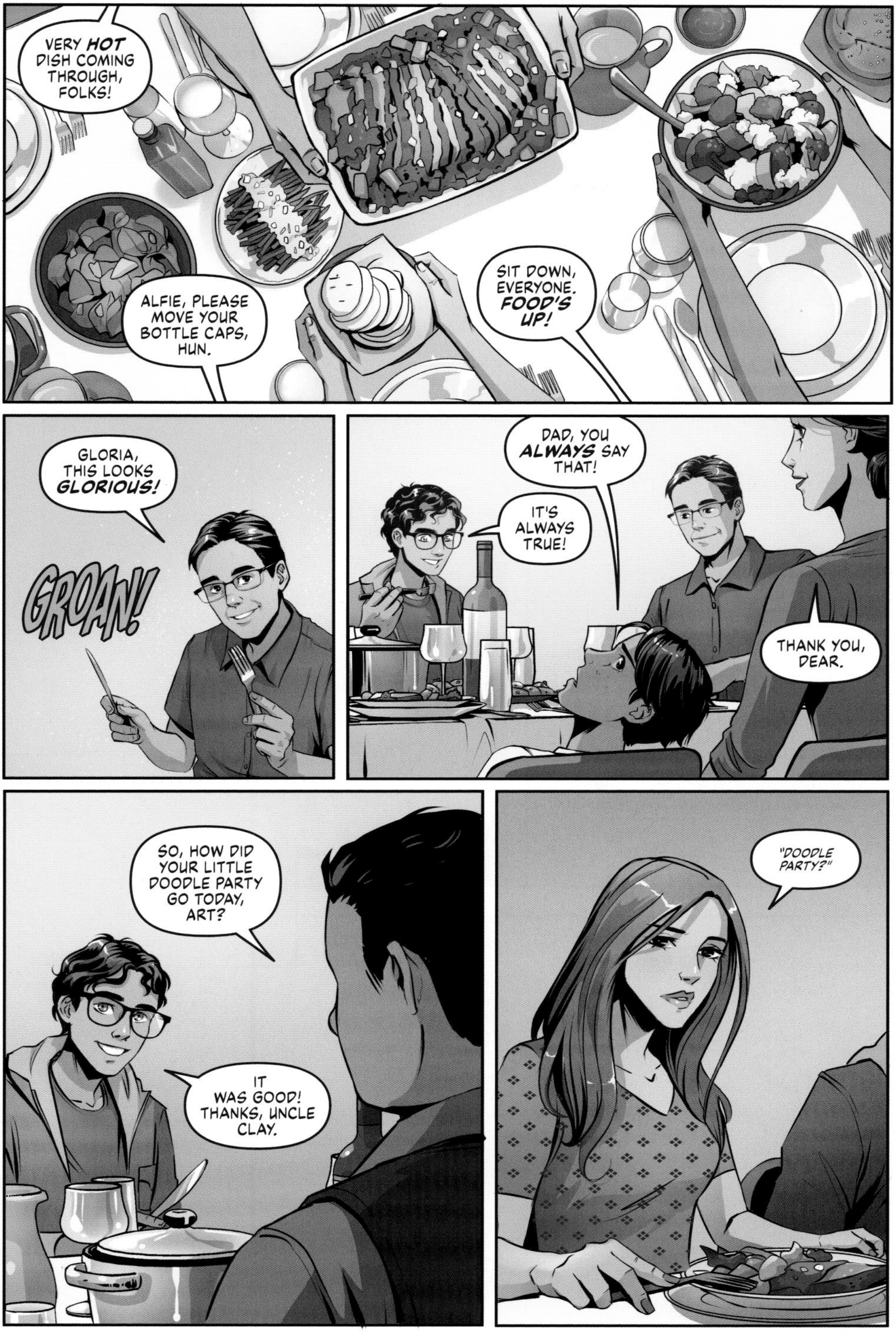
VERY HOT DISH COMING THROUGH, FOLKS!
ALFIE, PLEASE MOVE YOUR BOTTLE CAPS, HUN.
SIT DOWN, EVERYONE. FOOD'S UP!
GLORIA, THIS LOOKS GLORIOUS!
GROAN!
DAD, YOU ALWAYS SAY THAT!
IT'S ALWAYS TRUE!
THANK YOU, DEAR.
SO, HOW DID YOUR LITTLE DOODLE PARTY GO TODAY, ART?
IT WAS GOOD! THANKS, UNCLE CLAY.
"DOODLE PARTY?"

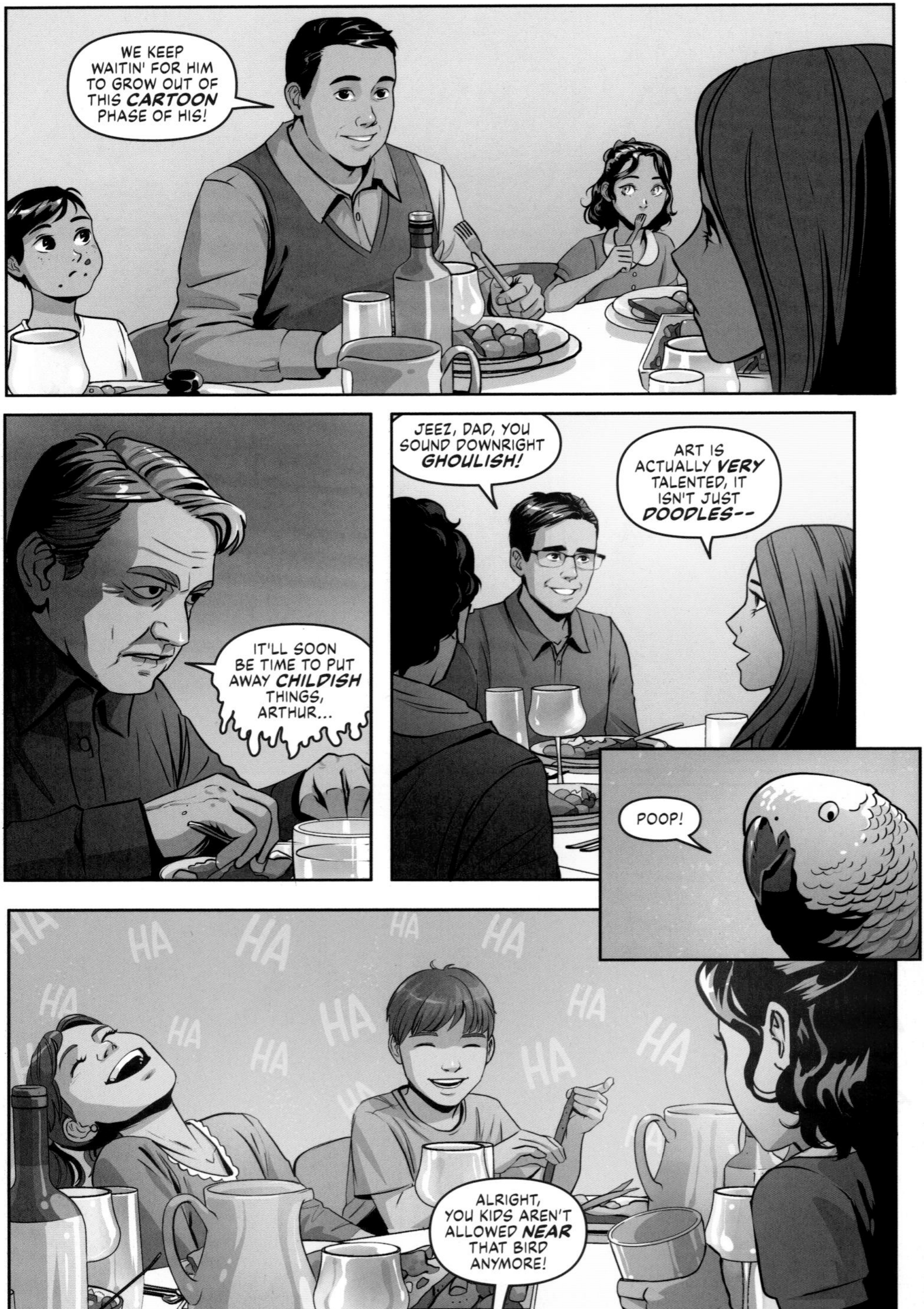
WE KEEP WAITIN' FOR HIM TO GROW OUT OF THIS CARTOON PHASE OF HIS!
IT'LL SOON BE TIME TO PUT AWAY CHILDISH THINGS, ARTHUR...
JEEZ, DAD, YOU SOUND DOWNRIGHT GHOULISH!
ART IS ACTUALLY VERY TALENTED, IT ISN'T JUST DOODLES--
POOP!
HA HA HA HA HA HA HA HA HA HA HA HA
ALRIGHT, YOU KIDS AREN'T ALLOWED NEAR THAT BIRD ANYMORE!

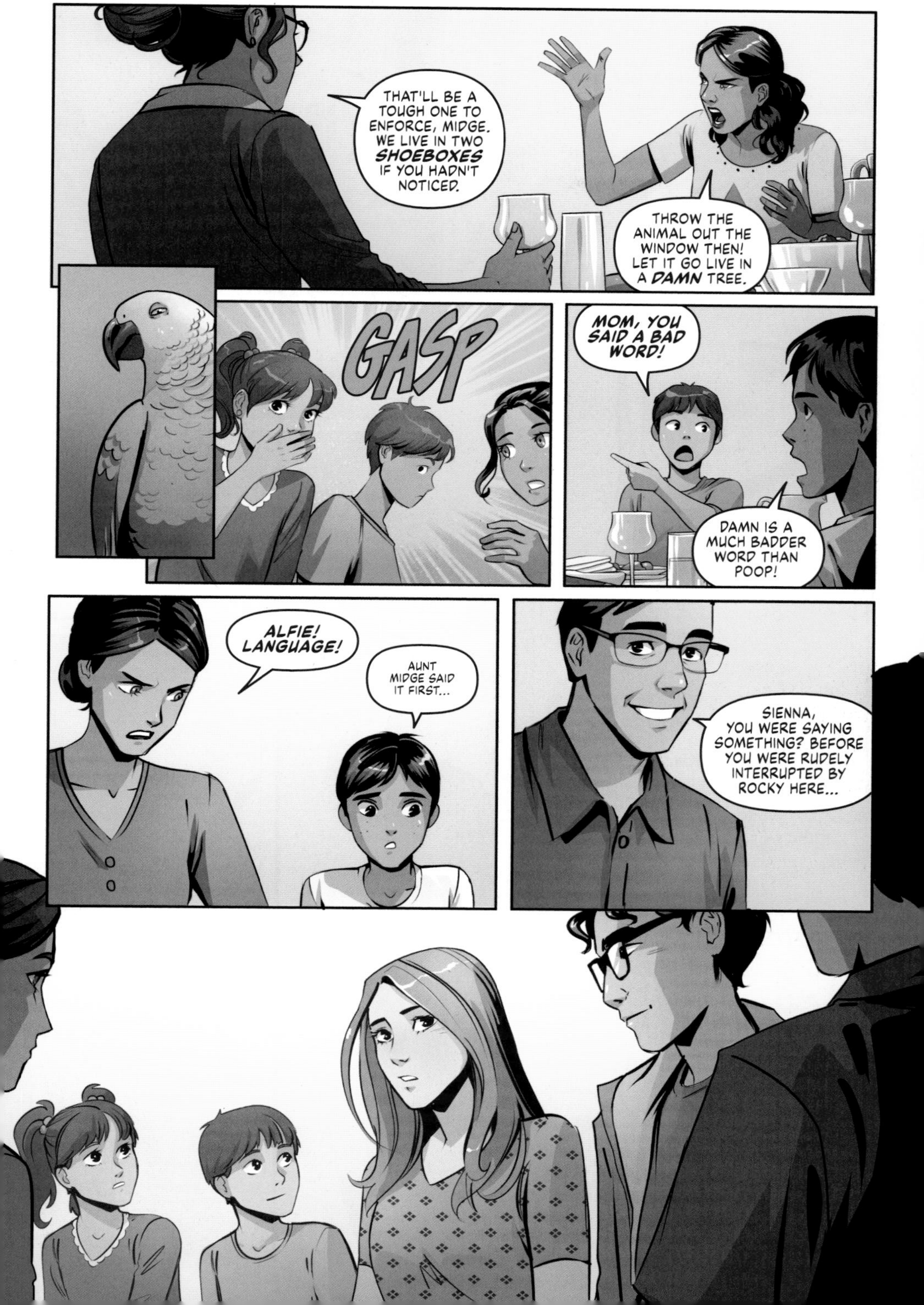
THAT'LL BE A TOUGH ONE TO ENFORCE, MIDGE. WE LIVE IN TWO ***SHOEBOXES*** IF YOU HADN'T NOTICED.
THROW THE ANIMAL OUT THE WINDOW THEN! LET IT GO LIVE IN A ***DAMN*** TREE.
GASP
MOM, YOU SAID A BAD WORD!
DAMN IS A MUCH BADDER WORD THAN POOP!
ALFIE! LANGUAGE!
AUNT MIDGE SAID IT FIRST...
SIENNA, YOU WERE SAYING SOMETHING? BEFORE YOU WERE RUDELY INTERRUPTED BY ROCKY HERE...

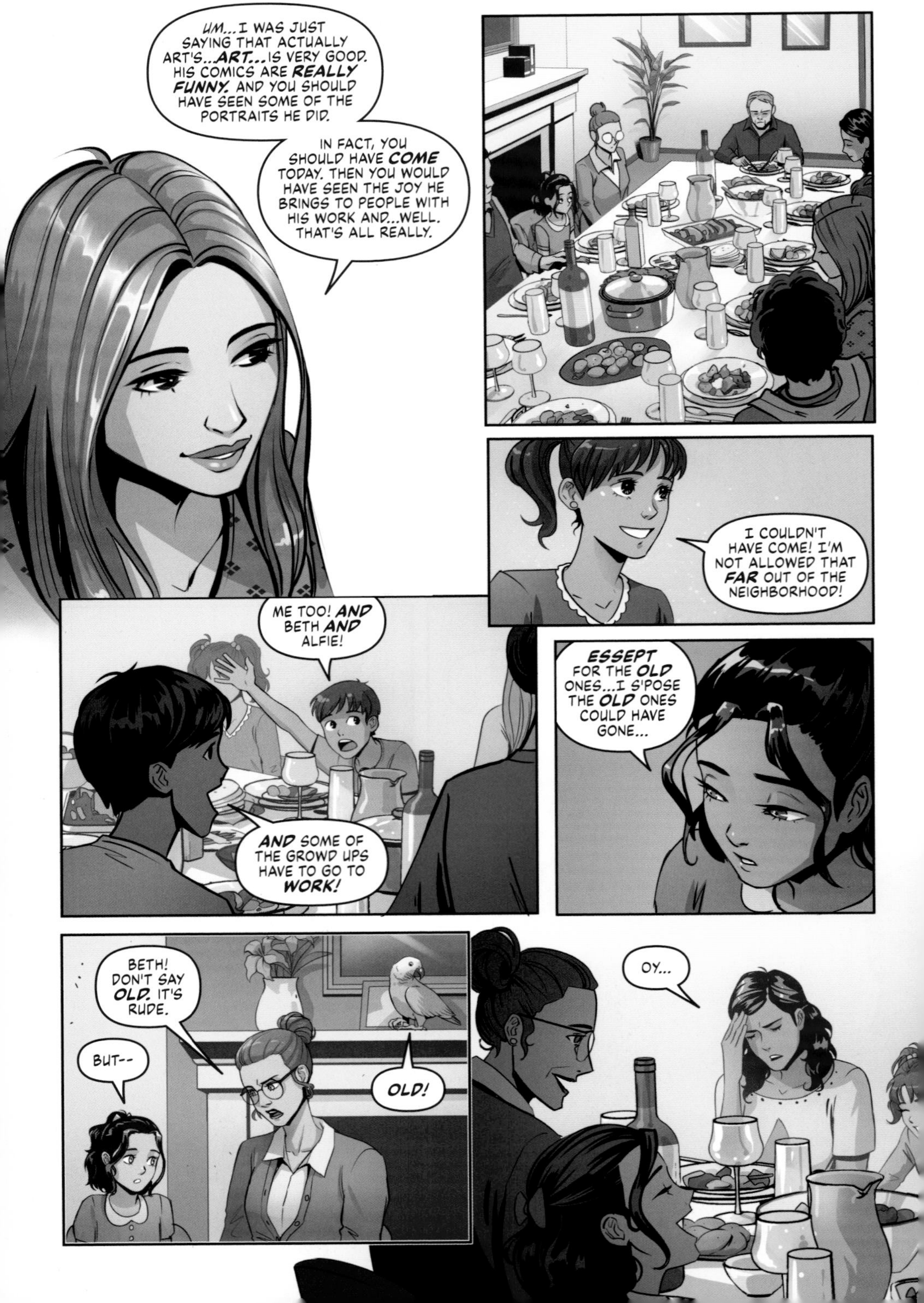
UM...I WAS JUST SAYING THAT ACTUALLY ART'S...ART...IS VERY GOOD. HIS COMICS ARE REALLY FUNNY. AND YOU SHOULD HAVE SEEN SOME OF THE PORTRAITS HE DID.
IN FACT, YOU SHOULD HAVE COME TODAY. THEN YOU WOULD HAVE SEEN THE JOY HE BRINGS TO PEOPLE WITH HIS WORK AND...WELL. THAT'S ALL REALLY.
I COULDN'T HAVE COME! I'M NOT ALLOWED THAT FAR OUT OF THE NEIGHBORHOOD!
ME TOO! AND BETH AND ALFIE!
AND SOME OF THE GROWD UPS HAVE TO GO TO WORK!
ESSEPT FOR THE OLD ONES...I S'POSE THE OLD ONES COULD HAVE GONE...
BETH! DON'T SAY OLD. IT'S RUDE.
BUT--
OLD!
OY...

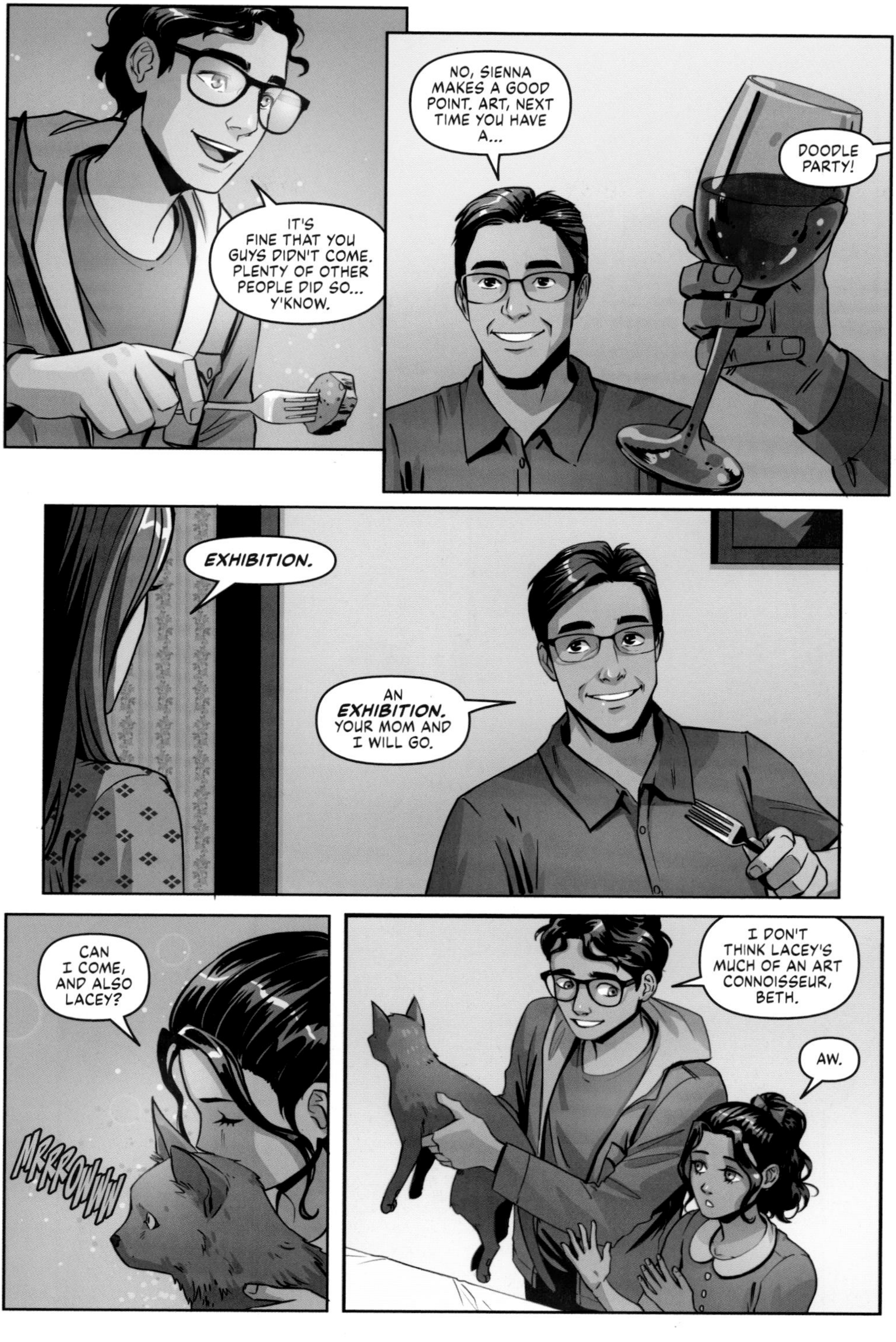

IT'S FINE THAT YOU GUYS DIDN'T COME. PLENTY OF OTHER PEOPLE DID SO... Y'KNOW.
NO, SIENNA MAKES A GOOD POINT. ART, NEXT TIME YOU HAVE A...
DOODLE PARTY!
EXHIBITION.
AN EXHIBITION. YOUR MOM AND I WILL GO.
CAN I COME, AND ALSO LACEY?
MRROWWW
I DON'T THINK LACEY'S MUCH OF AN ART CONNOISSEUR, BETH.
AW.

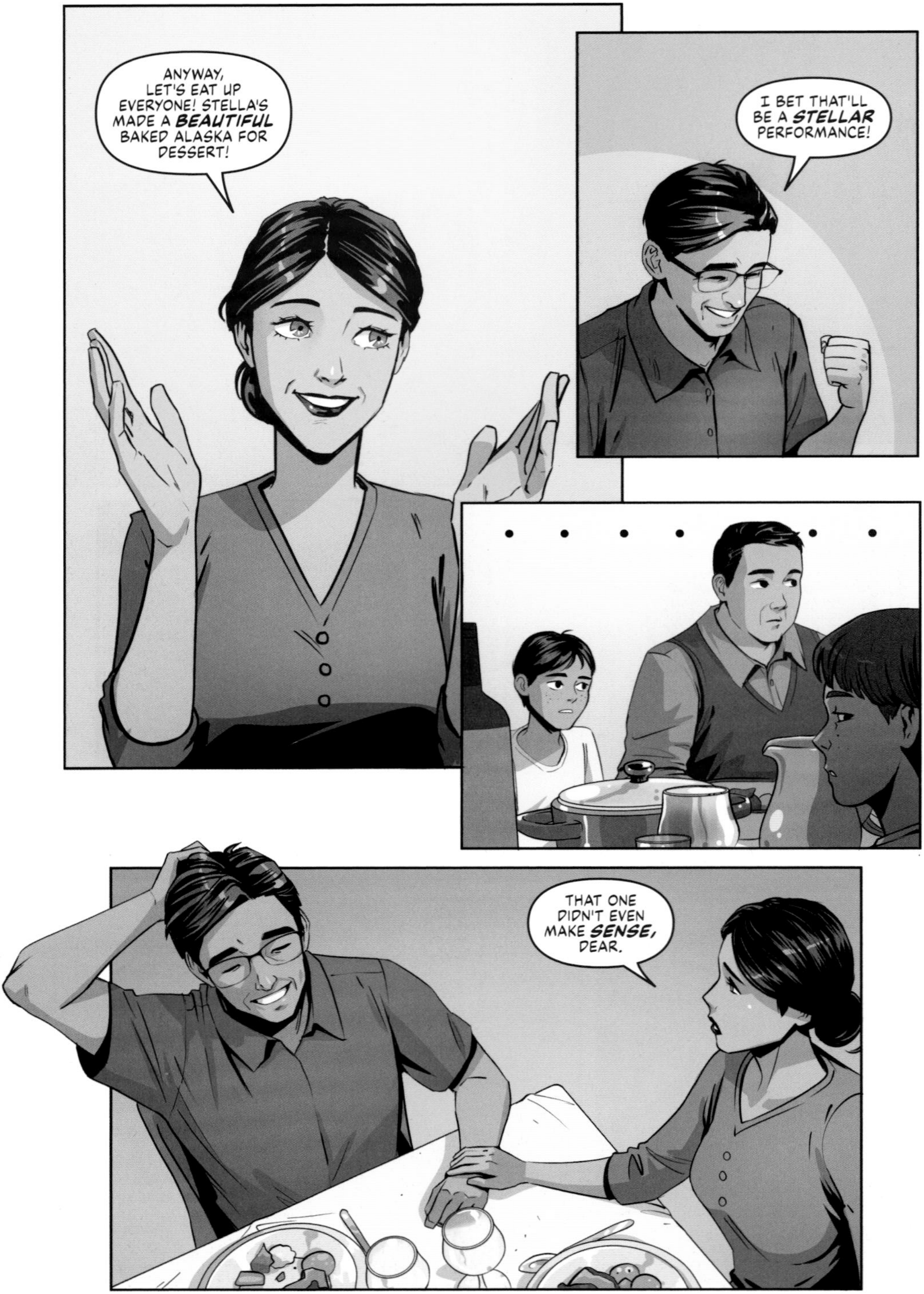
ANYWAY, LET'S EAT UP EVERYONE! STELLA'S MADE A BEAUTIFUL BAKED ALASKA FOR DESSERT!
I BET THAT'LL BE A STELLAR PERFORMANCE!
• • • • • • •
THAT ONE DIDN'T EVEN MAKE SENSE, DEAR.

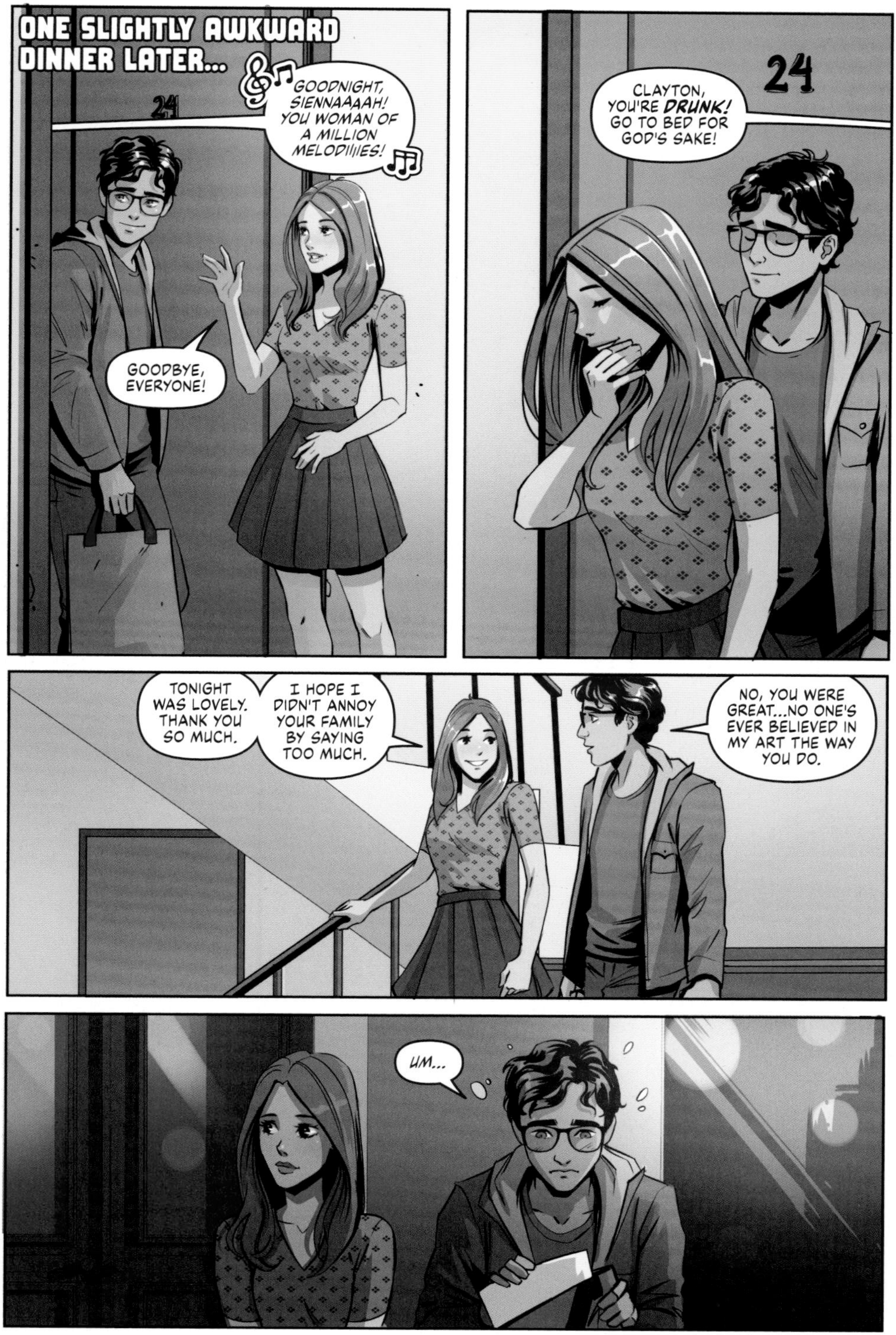
ONE SLIGHTLY AWKWARD DINNER LATER...
GOODNIGHT, SIENNAAAAH! YOU WOMAN OF A MILLION MELODIIIIES!
GOODBYE, EVERYONE!
24
CLAYTON, YOU'RE DRUNK! GO TO BED FOR GOD'S SAKE!
TONIGHT WAS LOVELY. THANK YOU SO MUCH.
I HOPE I DIDN'T ANNOY YOUR FAMILY BY SAYING TOO MUCH.
NO, YOU WERE GREAT...NO ONE'S EVER BELIEVED IN MY ART THE WAY YOU DO.
UM...

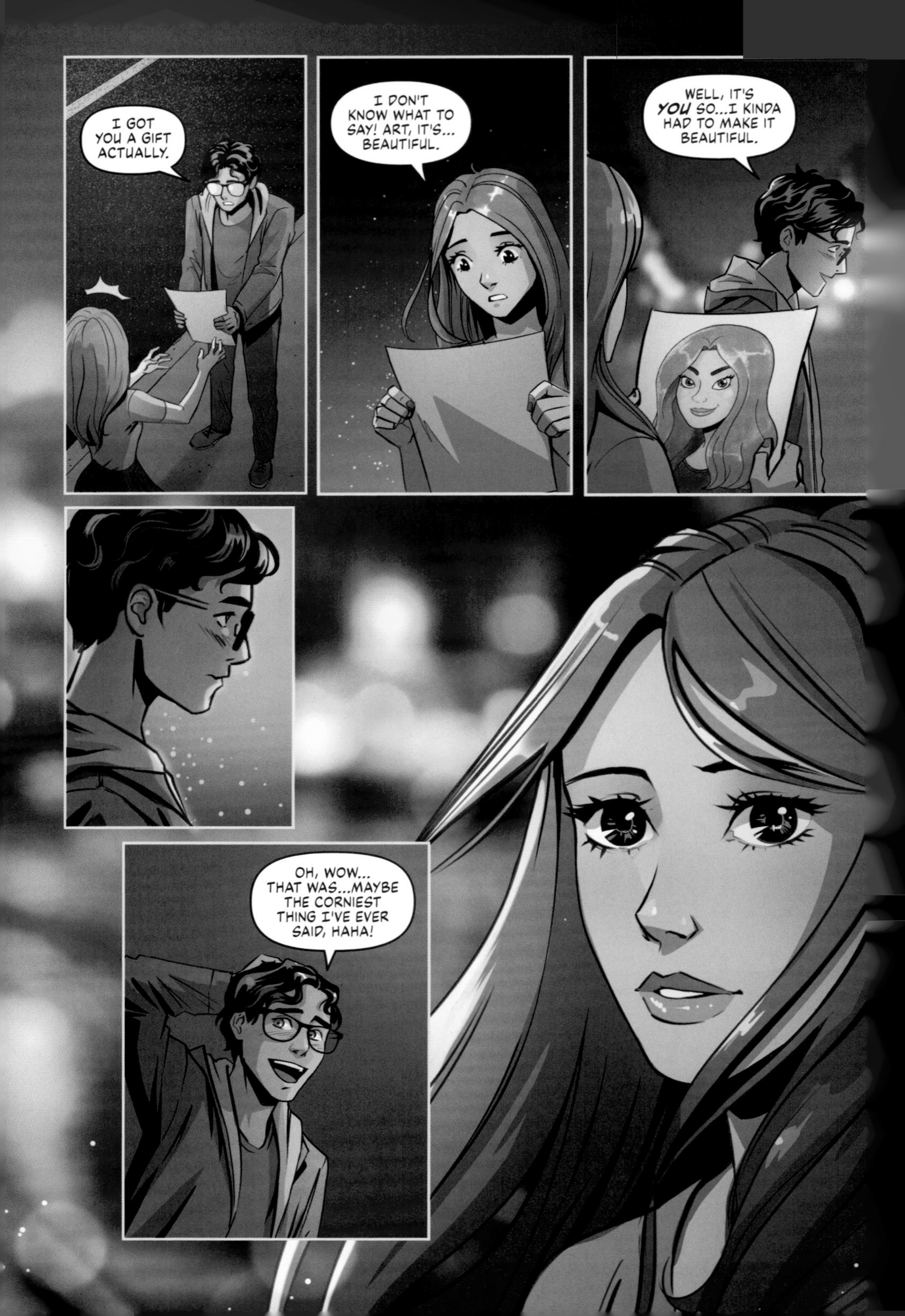
I GOT YOU A GIFT ACTUALLY.
I DON'T KNOW WHAT TO SAY! ART, IT'S... BEAUTIFUL.
WELL, IT'S *YOU* SO...I KINDA HAD TO MAKE IT BEAUTIFUL.
OH, WOW... THAT WAS...MAYBE THE CORNIEST THING I'VE EVER SAID, HAHA!

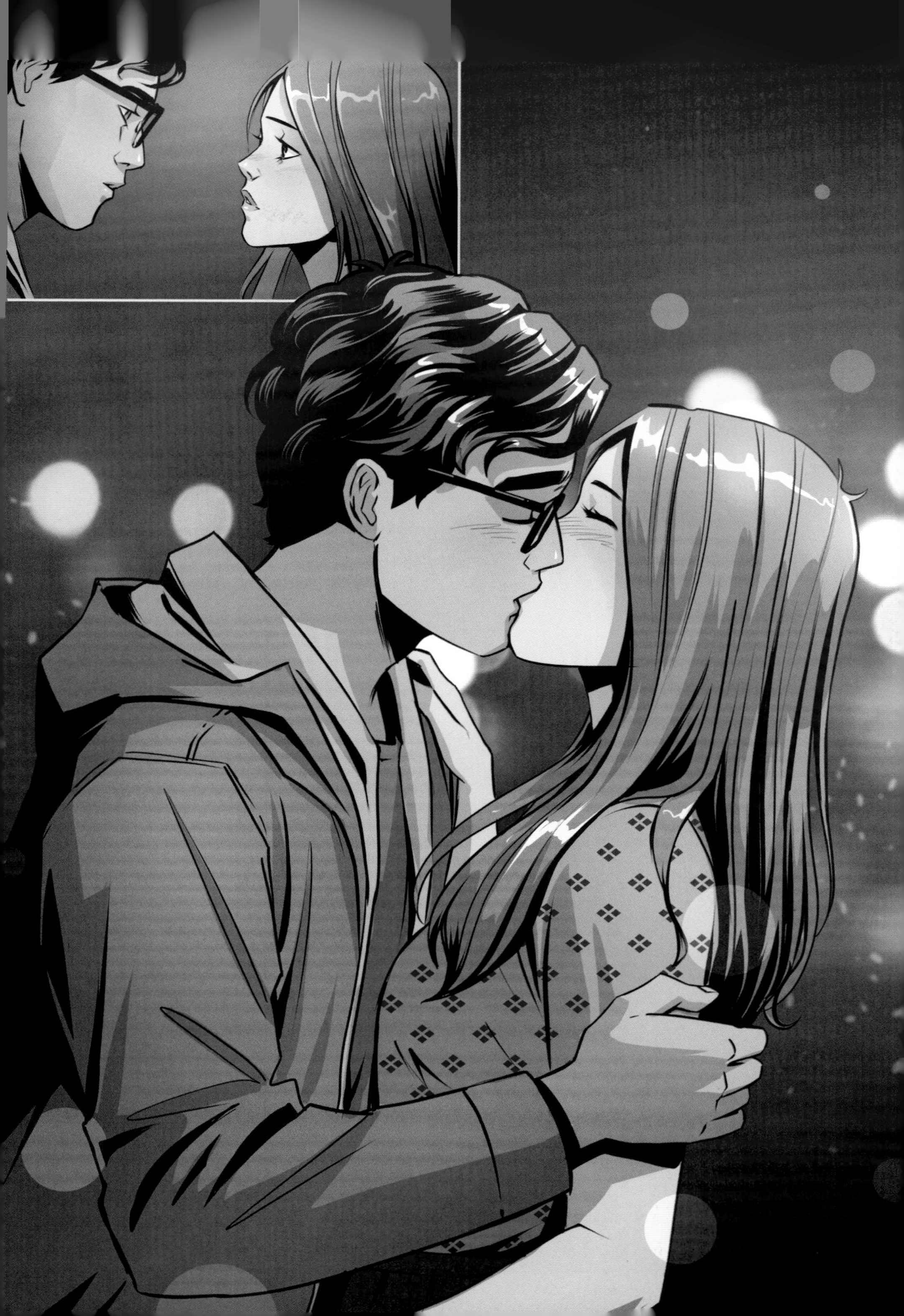

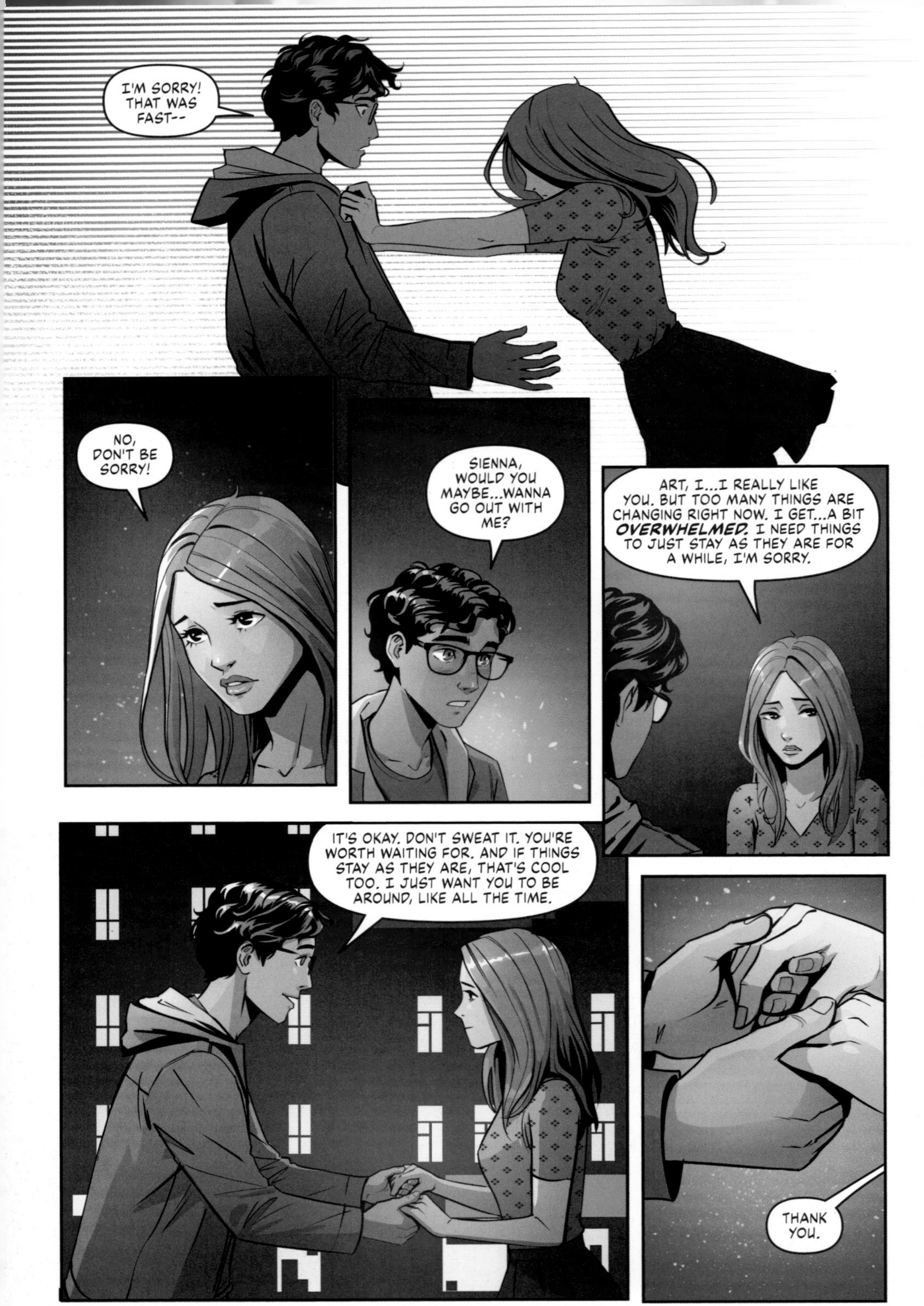
I'M SORRY! THAT WAS FAST--
NO, DON'T BE SORRY!
SIENNA, WOULD YOU MAYBE...WANNA GO OUT WITH ME?
ART, I...I REALLY LIKE YOU. BUT TOO MANY THINGS ARE CHANGING RIGHT NOW. I GET...A BIT ***OVERWHELMED.*** I NEED THINGS TO JUST STAY AS THEY ARE FOR A WHILE, I'M SORRY.
IT'S OKAY. DON'T SWEAT IT. YOU'RE WORTH WAITING FOR. AND IF THINGS STAY AS THEY ARE, THAT'S COOL TOO. I JUST WANT YOU TO BE AROUND, LIKE ALL THE TIME.
THANK YOU.

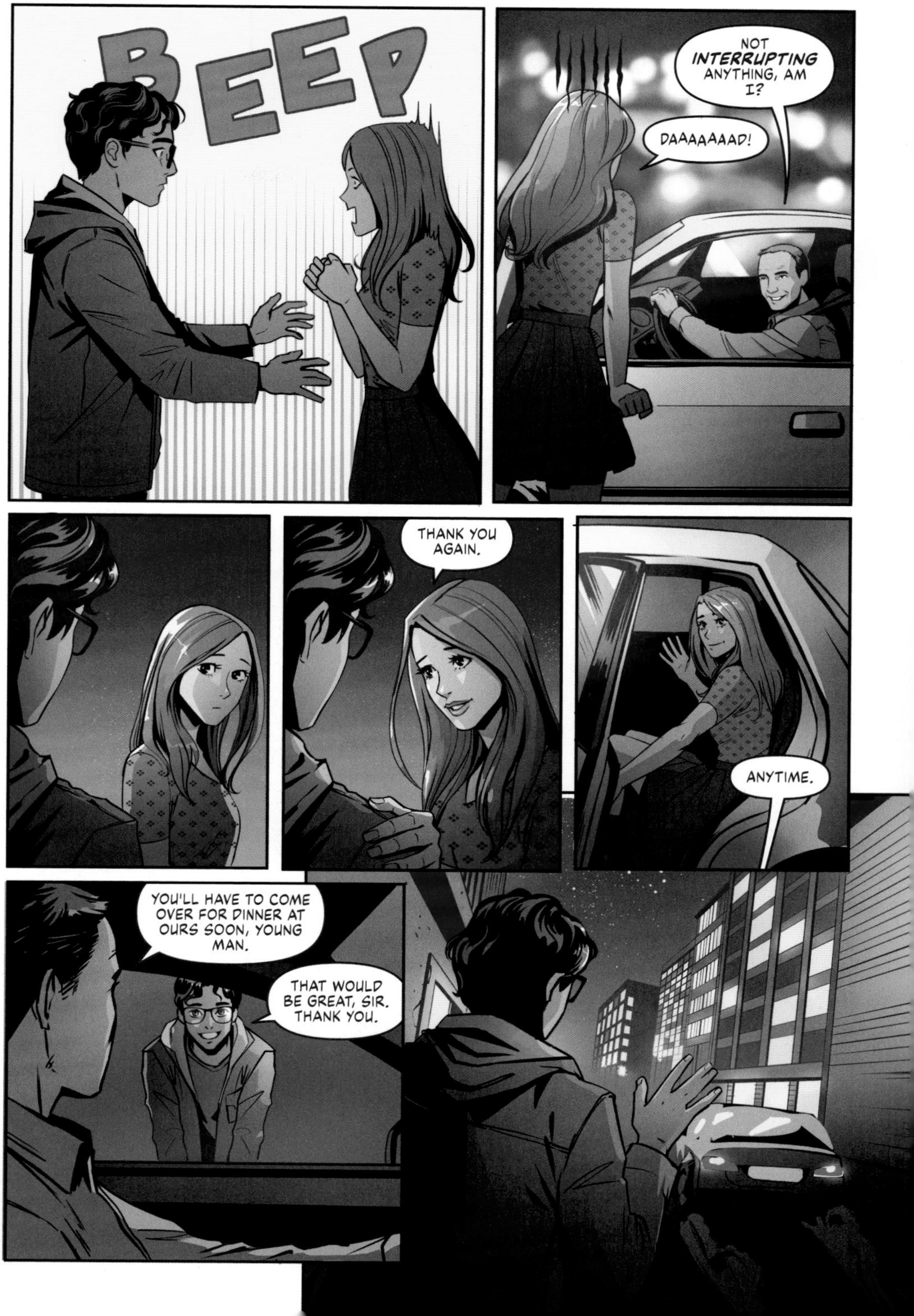
BEEP
NOT INTERRUPTING ANYTHING, AM I?
DAAAAAAAD!
THANK YOU AGAIN.
ANYTIME.
YOU'LL HAVE TO COME OVER FOR DINNER AT OURS SOON, YOUNG MAN.
THAT WOULD BE GREAT, SIR. THANK YOU.

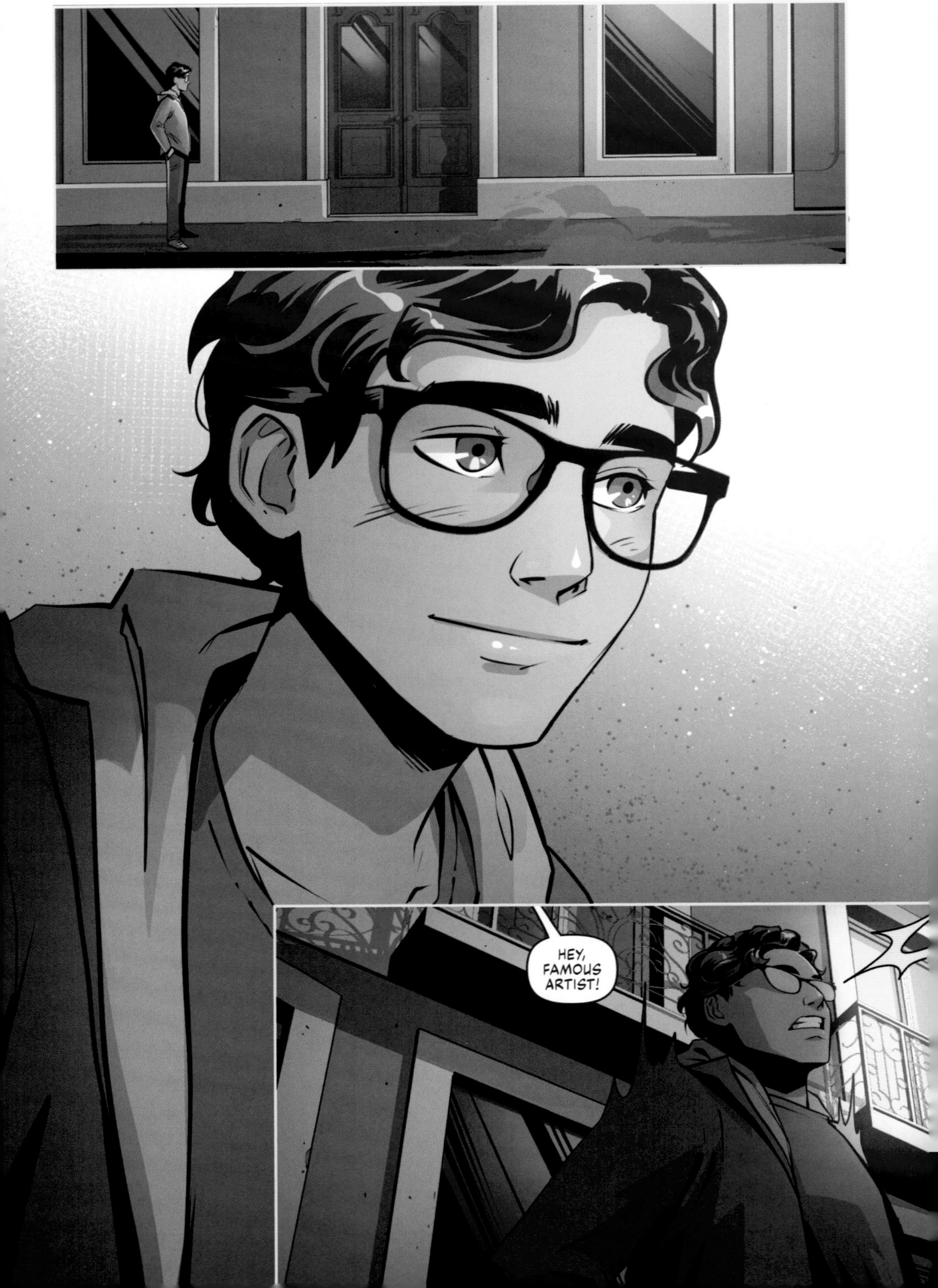
HEY, FAMOUS ARTIST!

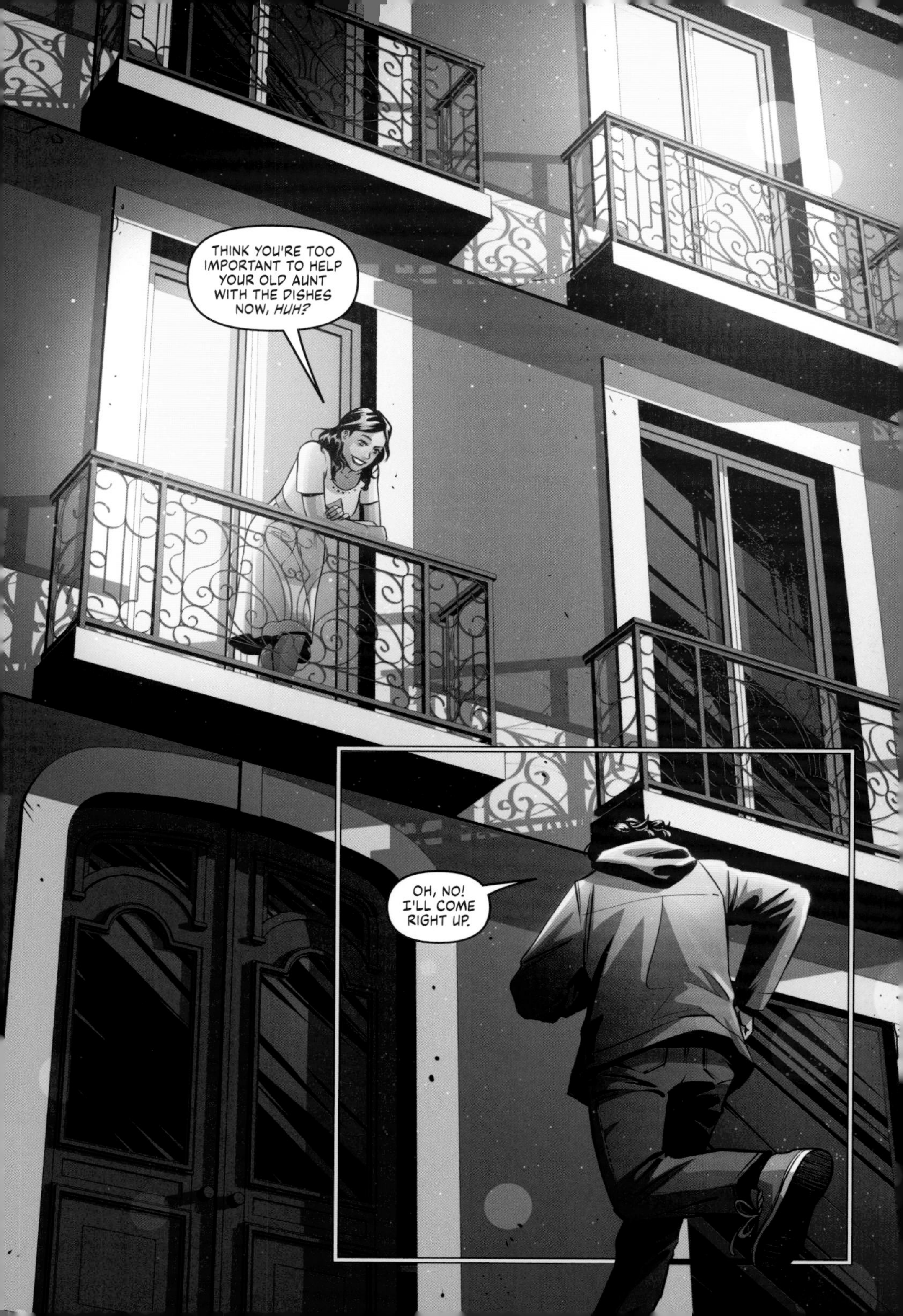
THINK YOU'RE TOO IMPORTANT TO HELP YOUR OLD AUNT WITH THE DISHES NOW, *HUH?*
OH, NO! I'LL COME RIGHT UP.

24 DAYS

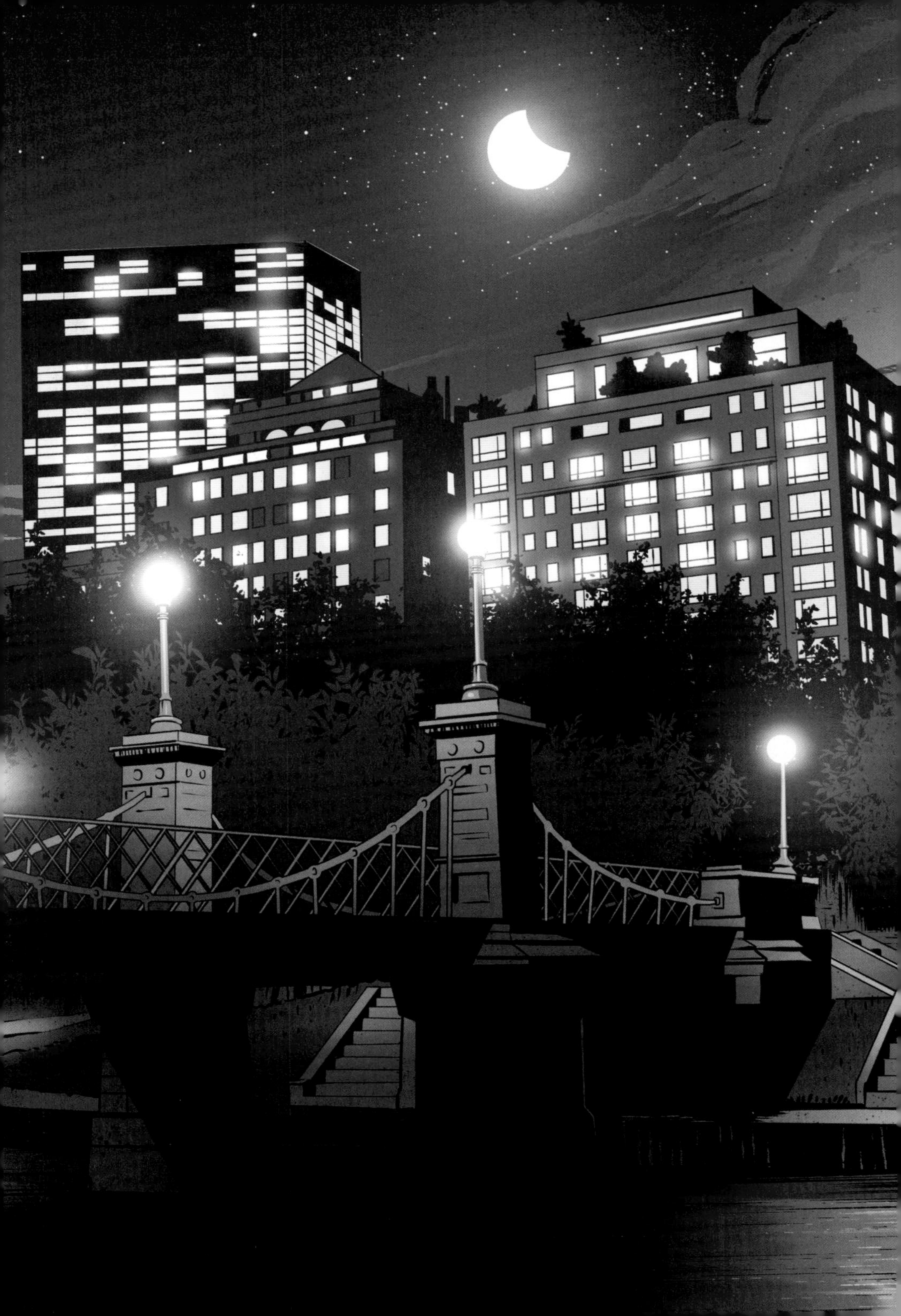

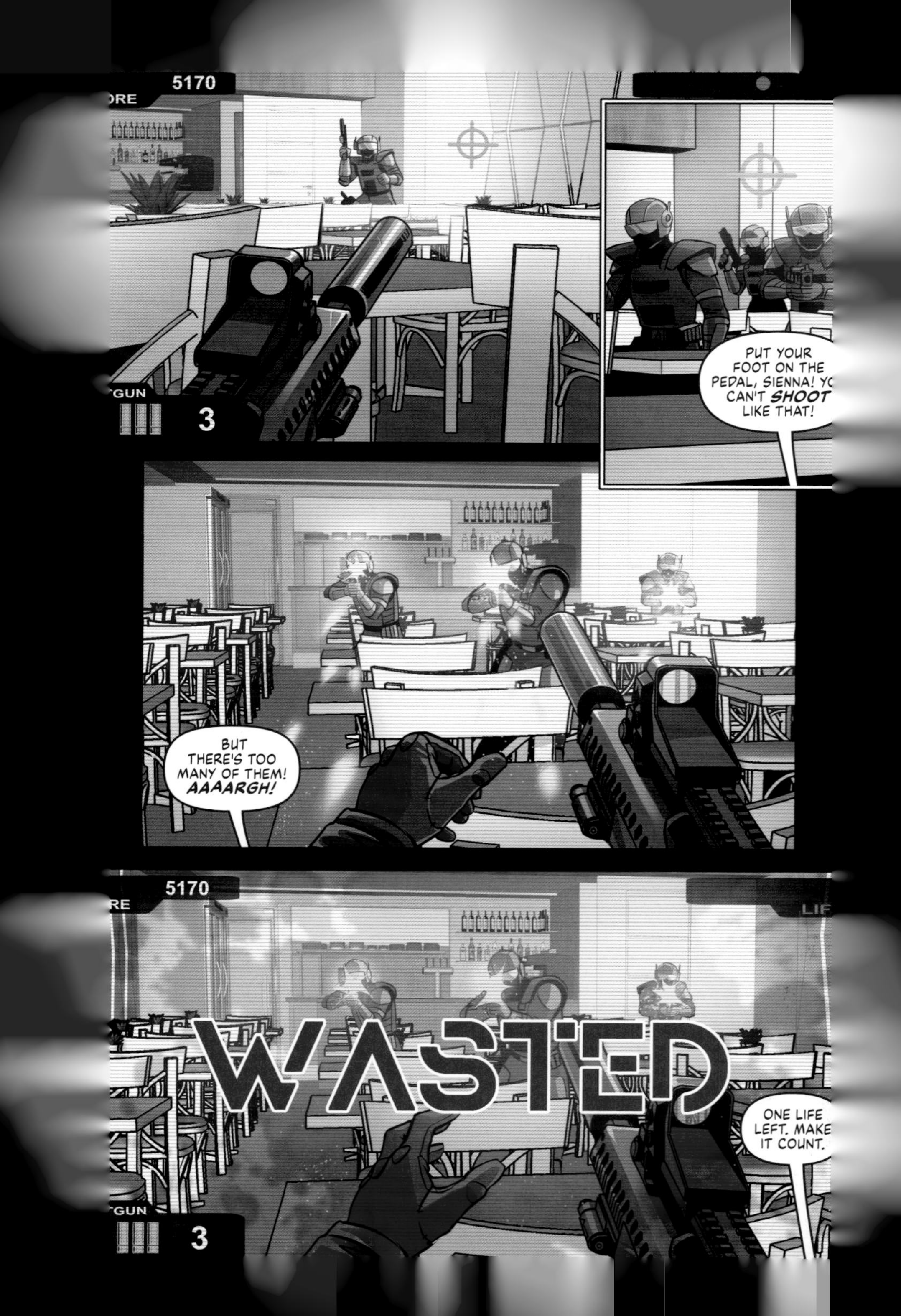
5170
3
PUT YOUR FOOT ON THE PEDAL, SIENNA! YO
CAN'T **SHOOT** LIKE THAT!
BUT THERE'S TOO MANY OF THEM! ***AAAARGH!***
5170
WASTED
ONE LIFE LEFT. MAKE IT COUNT.
3

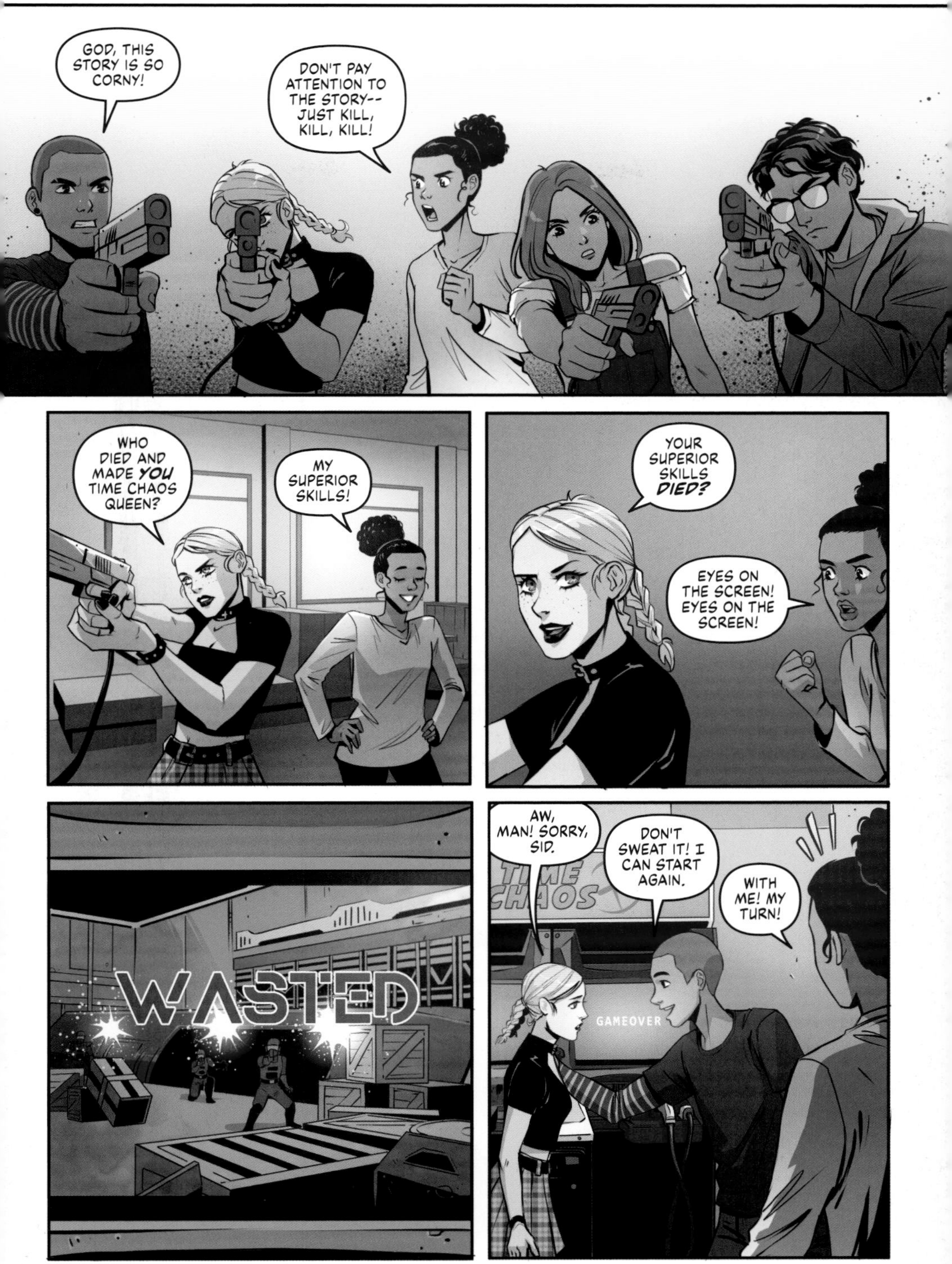
GOD, THIS STORY IS SO CORNY!
DON'T PAY ATTENTION TO THE STORY-- JUST KILL, KILL, KILL!
WHO DIED AND MADE *YOU* TIME CHAOS QUEEN?
MY SUPERIOR SKILLS!
YOUR SUPERIOR SKILLS *DIED?*
EYES ON THE SCREEN! EYES ON THE SCREEN!
WASTED
AW, MAN! SORRY, SID.
DON'T SWEAT IT! I CAN START AGAIN.
WITH ME! MY TURN!
TIME CHAOS
GAMEOVER

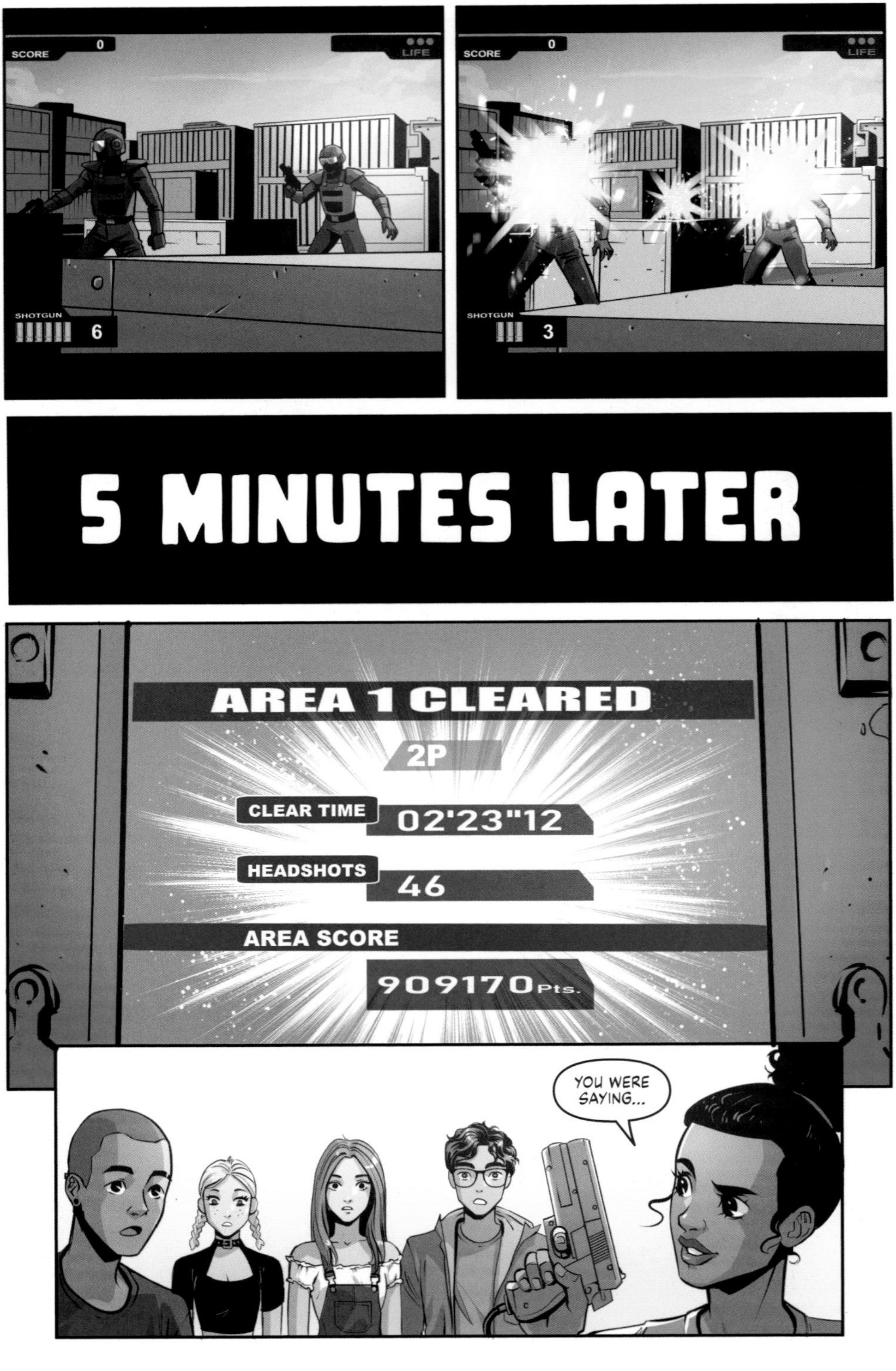
SCORE 0
LIFE
SHOTGUN 6
SCORE 0
LIFE
SHOTGUN 3
5 MINUTES LATER
AREA 1 CLEARED
2P
CLEAR TIME 02'23"12
HEADSHOTS 46
AREA SCORE
909170 Pts.
YOU WERE SAYING...

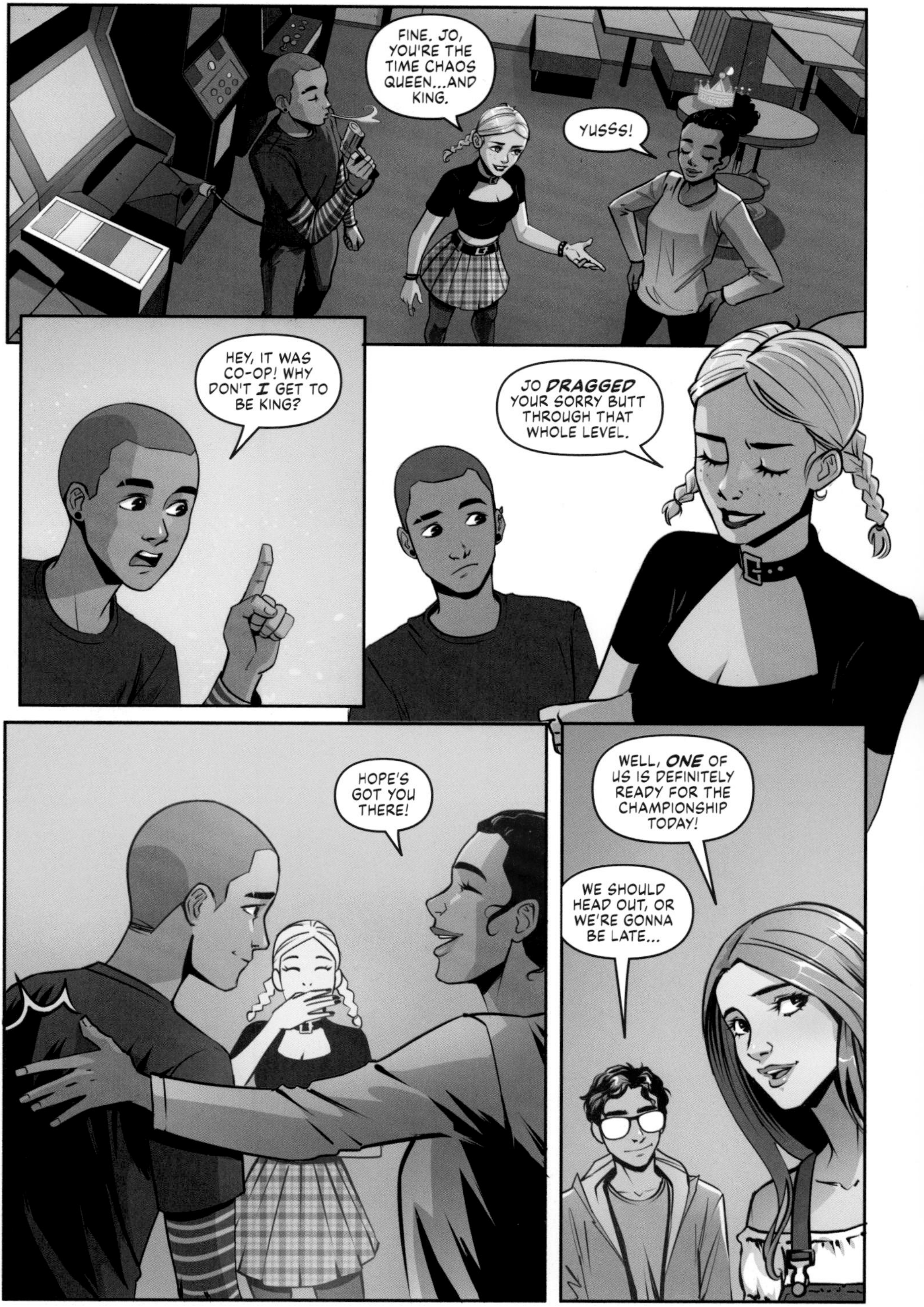
FINE. JO, YOU'RE THE TIME CHAOS QUEEN...AND KING.
YUSSS!
HEY, IT WAS CO-OP! WHY DON'T I GET TO BE KING?
JO DRAGGED YOUR SORRY BUTT THROUGH THAT WHOLE LEVEL.
HOPE'S GOT YOU THERE!
WELL, ONE OF US IS DEFINITELY READY FOR THE CHAMPIONSHIP TODAY!
WE SHOULD HEAD OUT, OR WE'RE GONNA BE LATE...

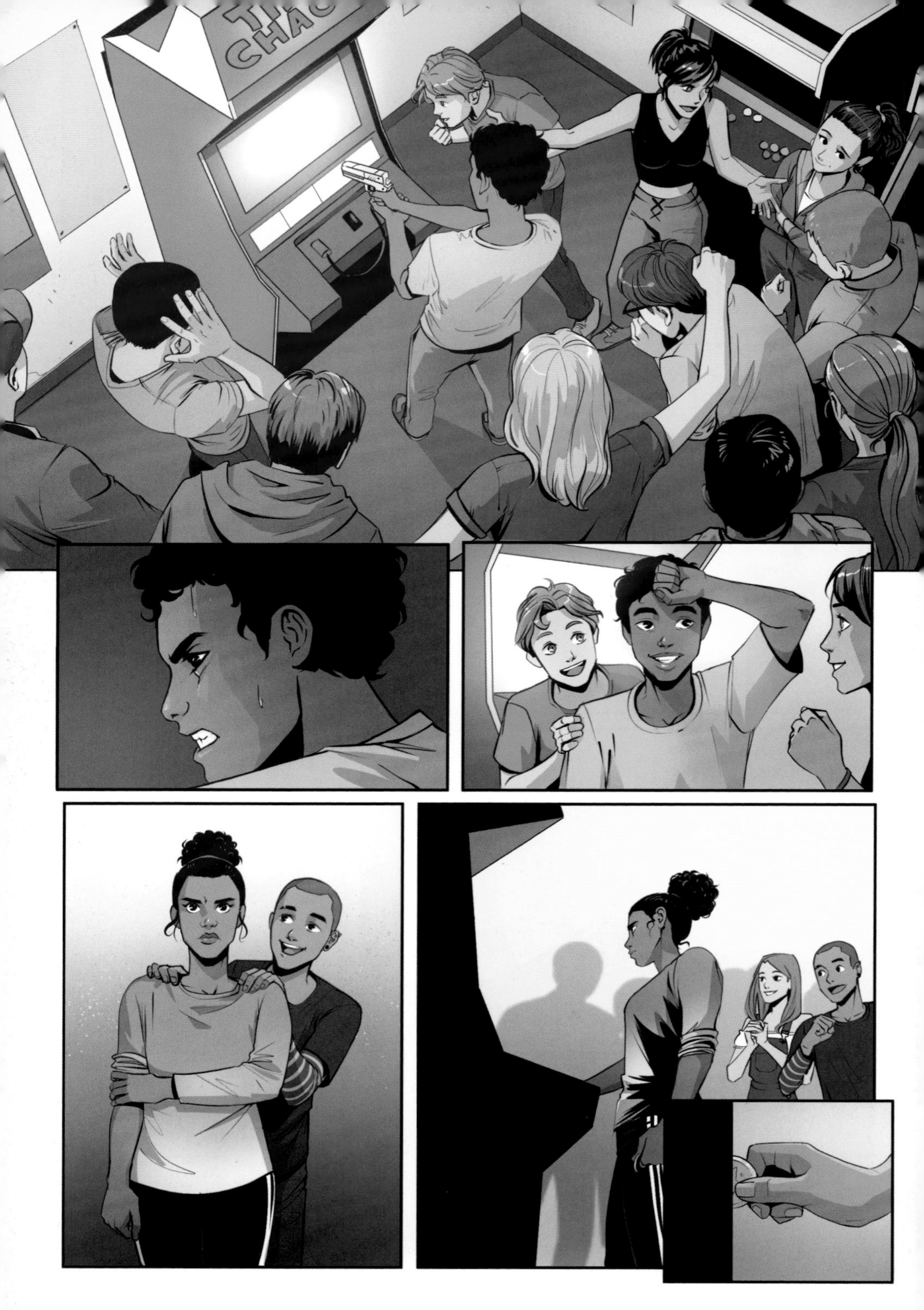

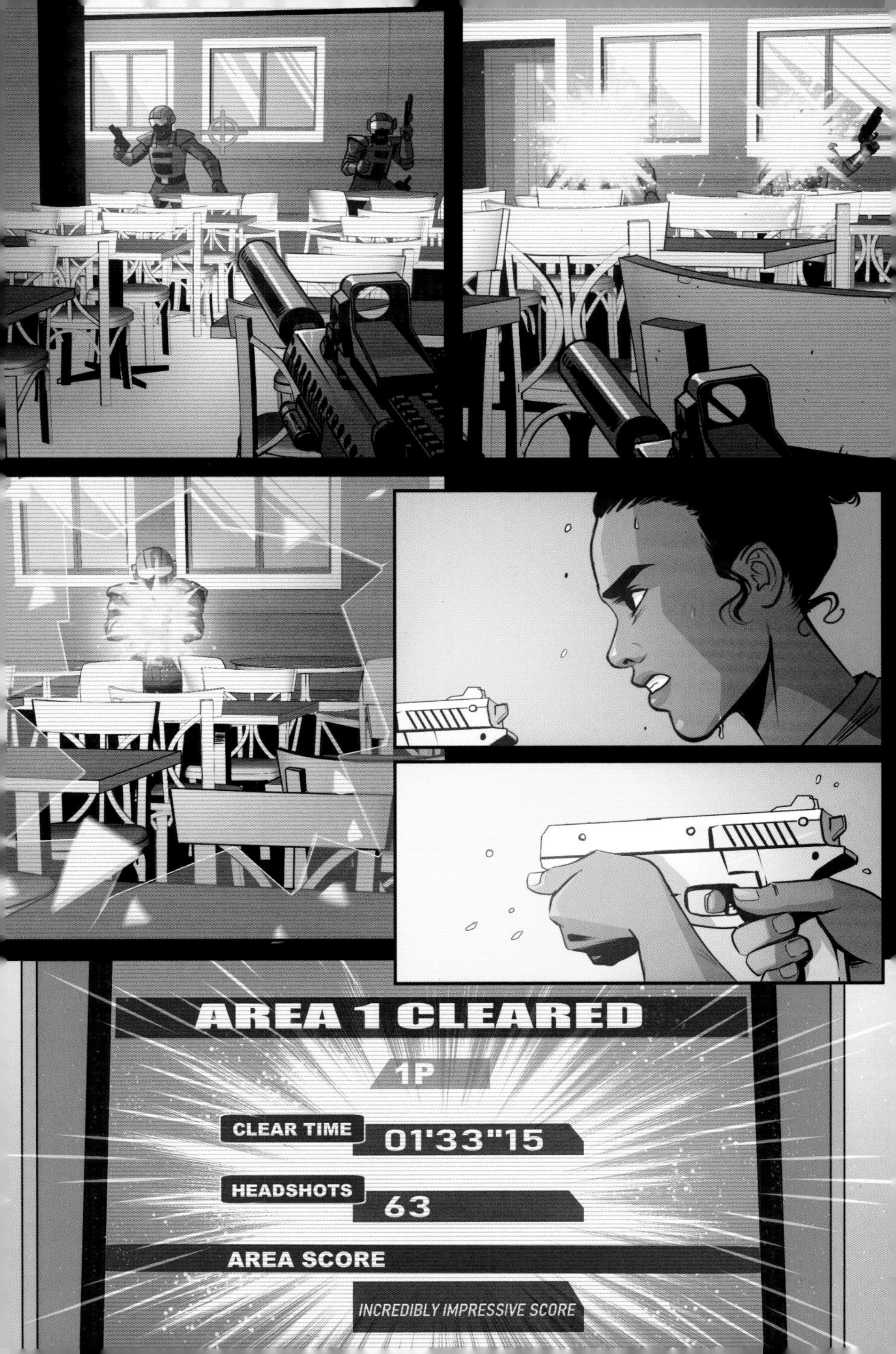
AREA 1 CLEARED
1P
CLEAR TIME
01'33"15
HEADSHOTS
63
AREA SCORE
INCREDIBLY IMPRESSIVE SCORE

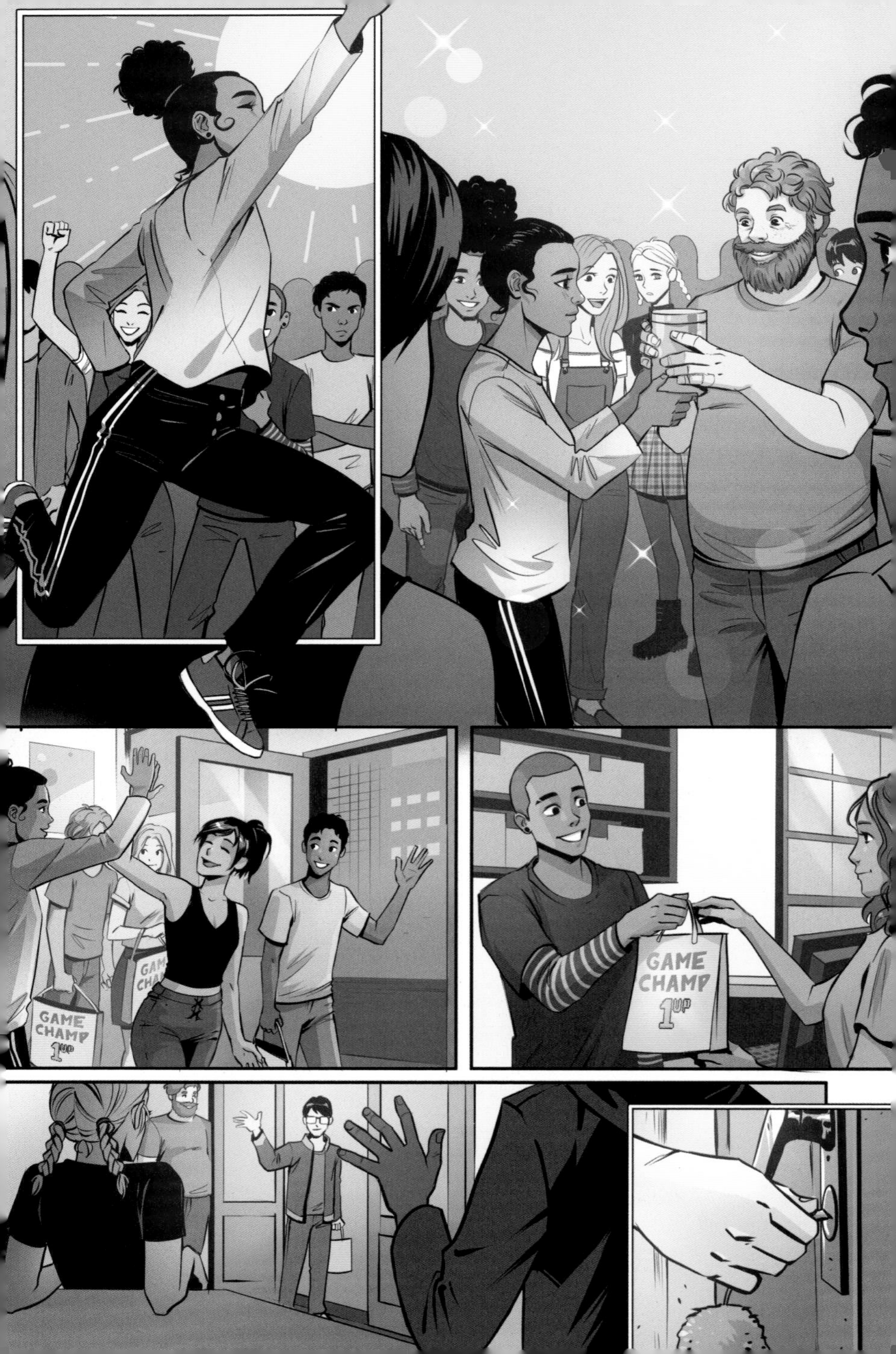
GAME CHAMP 1UP
GAME CHAMP 1UP

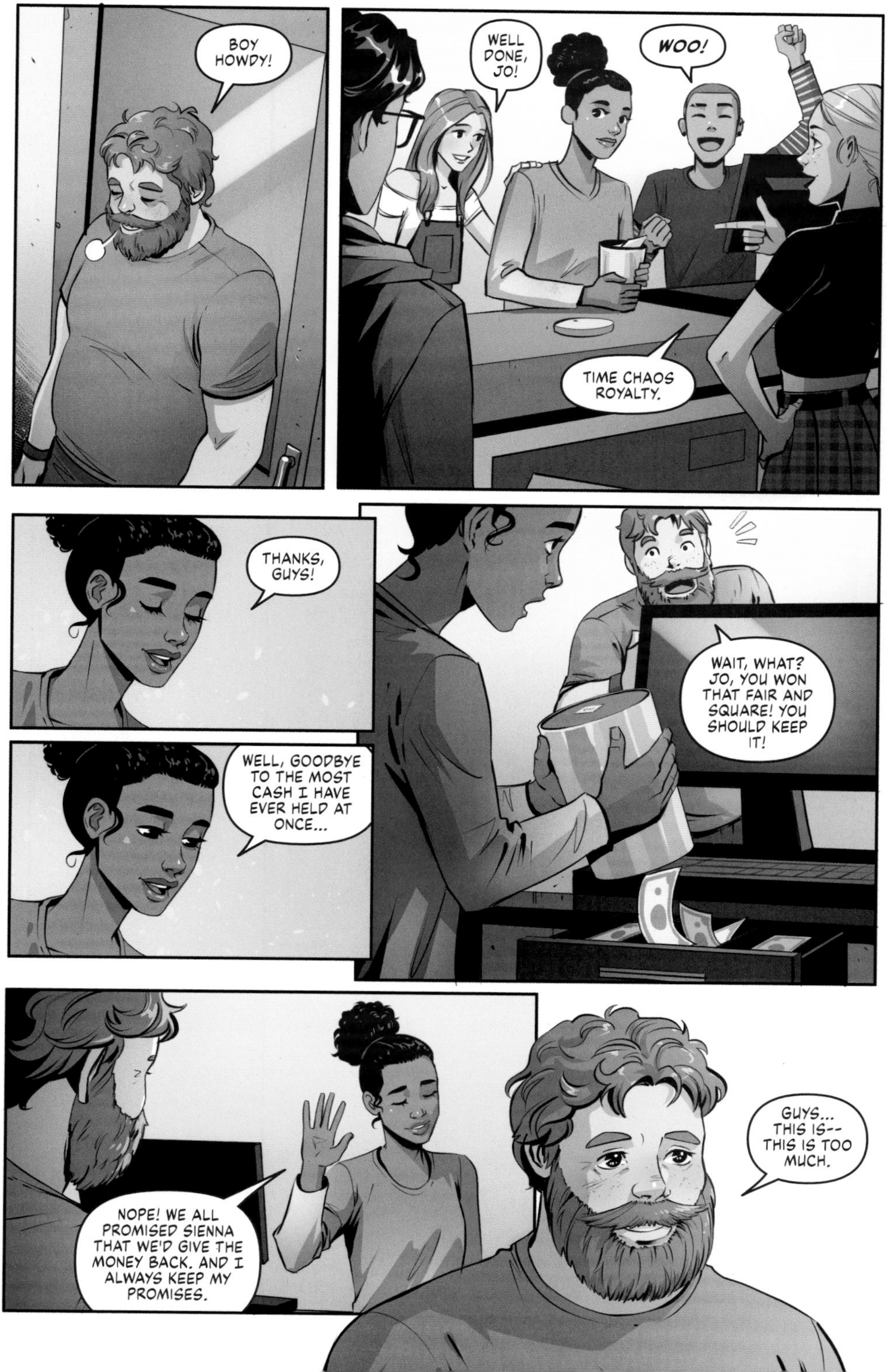
BOY HOWDY!
WELL DONE, JO!
WOO!
TIME CHAOS ROYALTY.
THANKS, GUYS!
WELL, GOODBYE TO THE MOST CASH I HAVE EVER HELD AT ONCE...
WAIT, WHAT? JO, YOU WON THAT FAIR AND SQUARE! YOU SHOULD KEEP IT!
GUYS... THIS IS-- THIS IS TOO MUCH.
NOPE! WE ALL PROMISED SIENNA THAT WE'D GIVE THE MONEY BACK. AND I ALWAYS KEEP MY PROMISES.

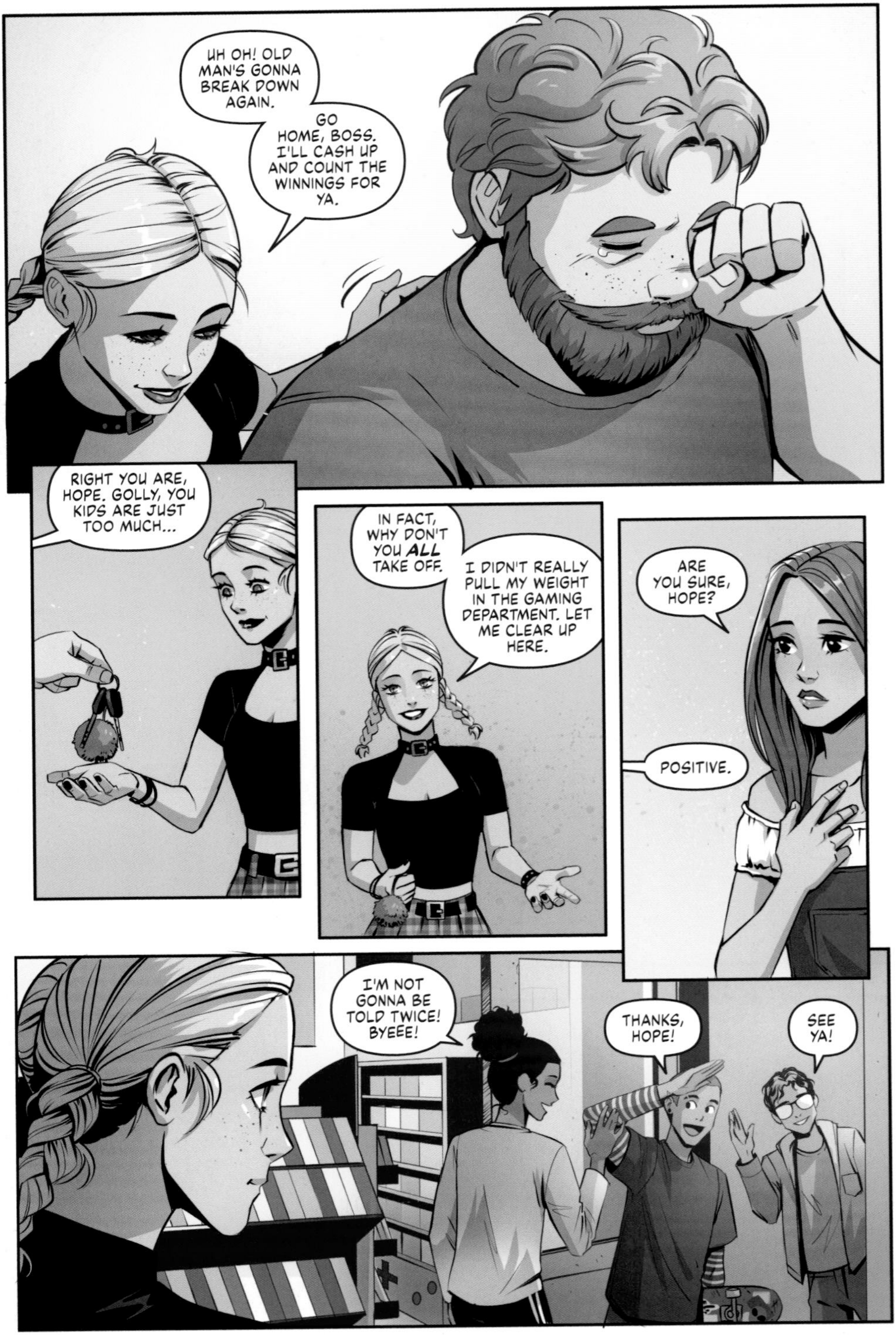
UH OH! OLD MAN'S GONNA BREAK DOWN AGAIN.
GO HOME, BOSS. I'LL CASH UP AND COUNT THE WINNINGS FOR YA.
RIGHT YOU ARE, HOPE. GOLLY, YOU KIDS ARE JUST TOO MUCH...
IN FACT, WHY DON'T YOU **ALL** TAKE OFF.
I DIDN'T REALLY PULL MY WEIGHT IN THE GAMING DEPARTMENT. LET ME CLEAR UP HERE.
ARE YOU SURE, HOPE?
POSITIVE.
I'M NOT GONNA BE TOLD TWICE! BYEEE!
THANKS, HOPE!
SEE YA!

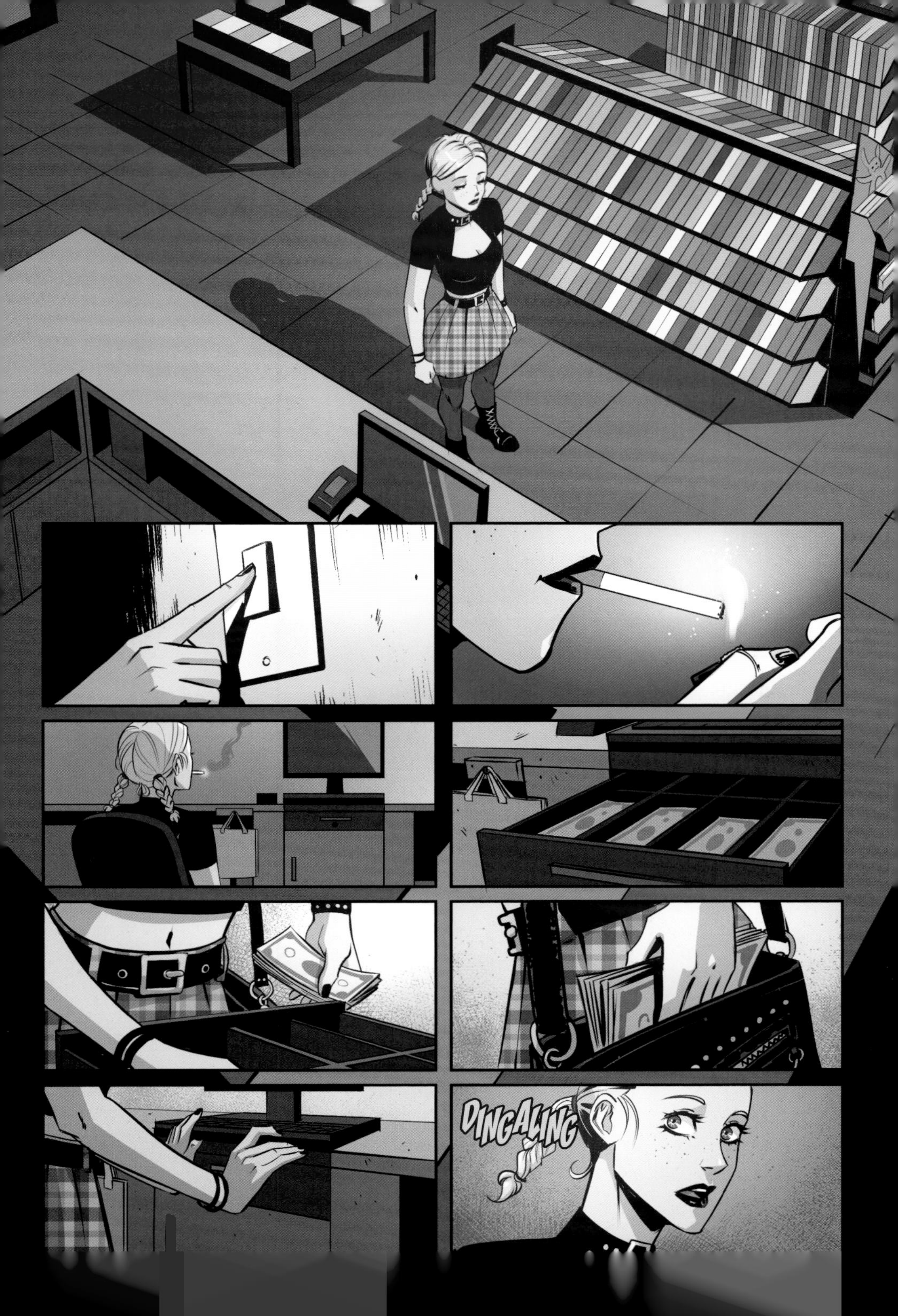
DINGALING

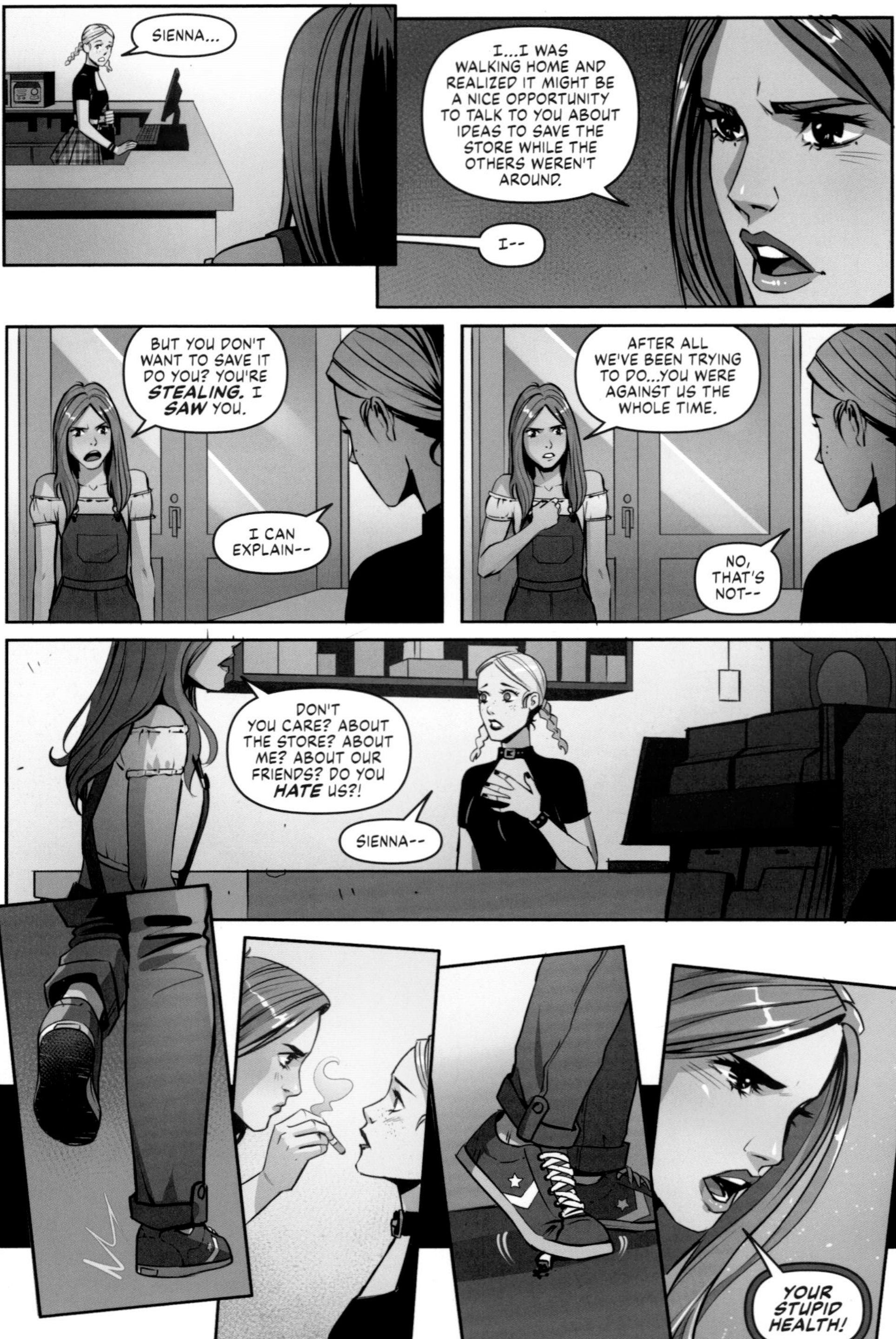
SIENNA...
I...I WAS WALKING HOME AND REALIZED IT MIGHT BE A NICE OPPORTUNITY TO TALK TO YOU ABOUT IDEAS TO SAVE THE STORE WHILE THE OTHERS WEREN'T AROUND.
I--
BUT YOU DON'T WANT TO SAVE IT DO YOU? YOU'RE **STEALING.** I **SAW** YOU.
I CAN EXPLAIN--
AFTER ALL WE'VE BEEN TRYING TO DO...YOU WERE AGAINST US THE WHOLE TIME.
NO, THAT'S NOT--
DON'T YOU CARE? ABOUT THE STORE? ABOUT ME? ABOUT OUR FRIENDS? DO YOU **HATE** US?!
SIENNA--
YOUR STUPID HEALTH!

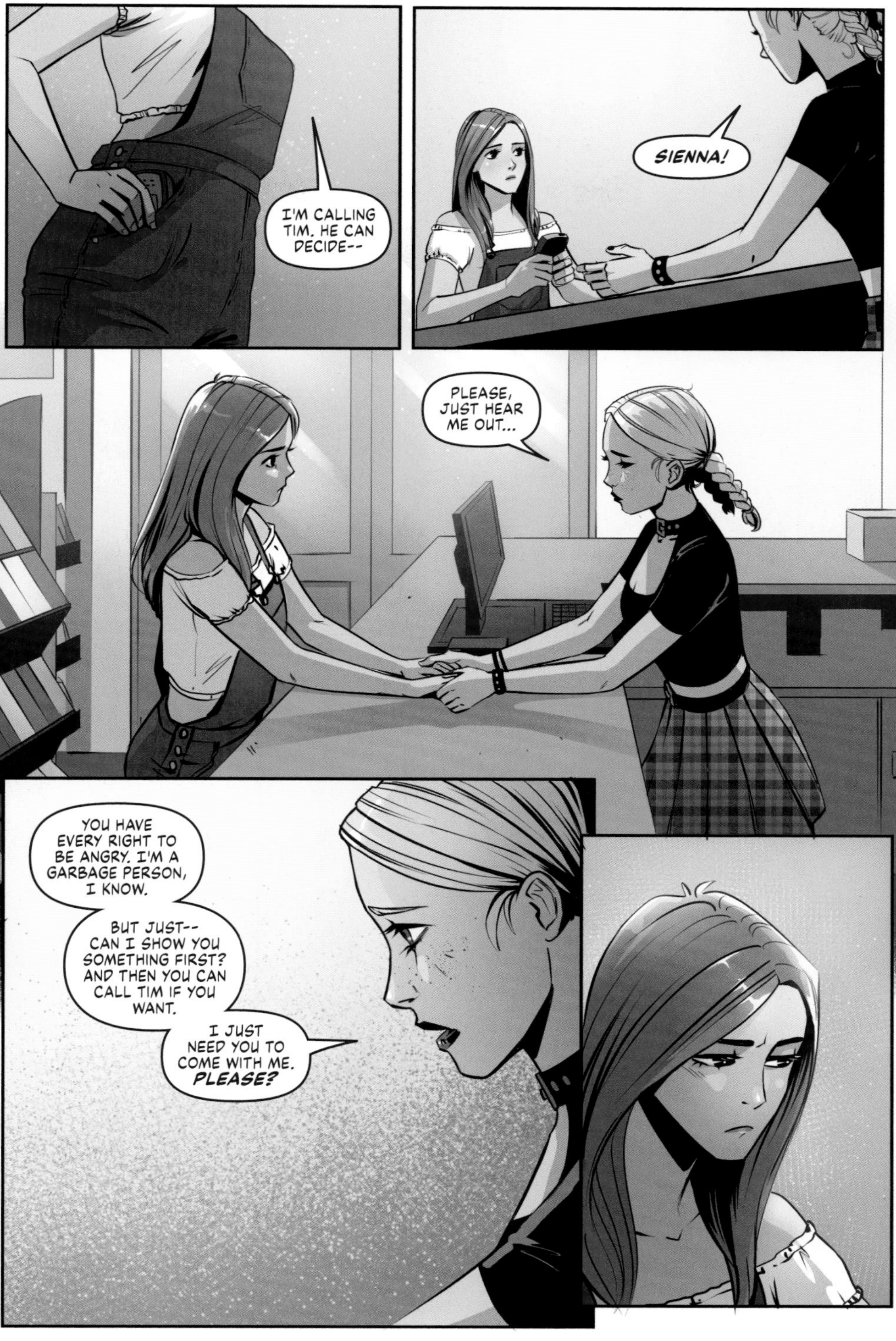
I'M CALLING TIM. HE CAN DECIDE--
SIENNA!
PLEASE, JUST HEAR ME OUT...
YOU HAVE EVERY RIGHT TO BE ANGRY. I'M A GARBAGE PERSON, I KNOW.
BUT JUST-- CAN I SHOW YOU SOMETHING FIRST? AND THEN YOU CAN CALL TIM IF YOU WANT.
I JUST NEED YOU TO COME WITH ME. *PLEASE?*

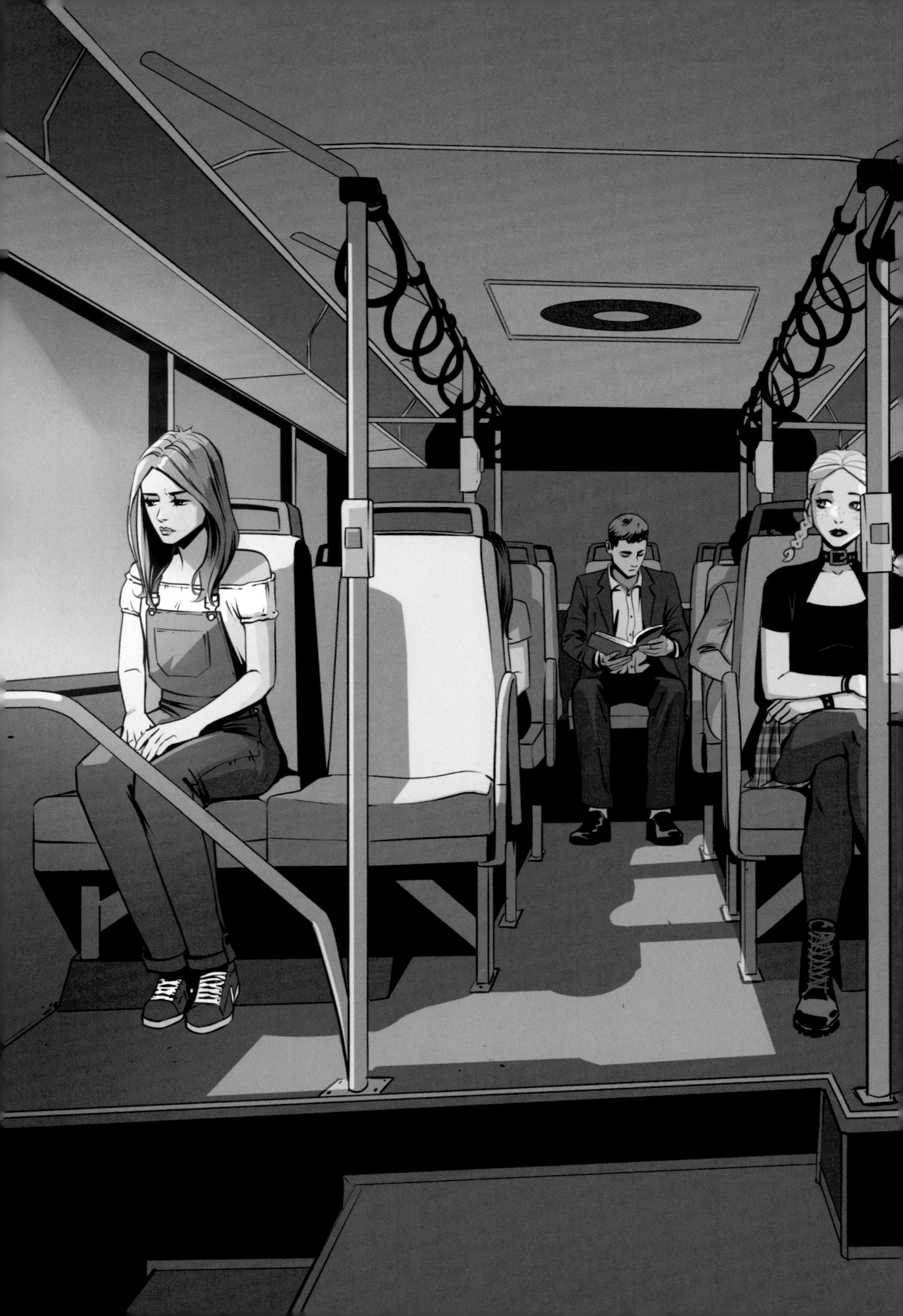

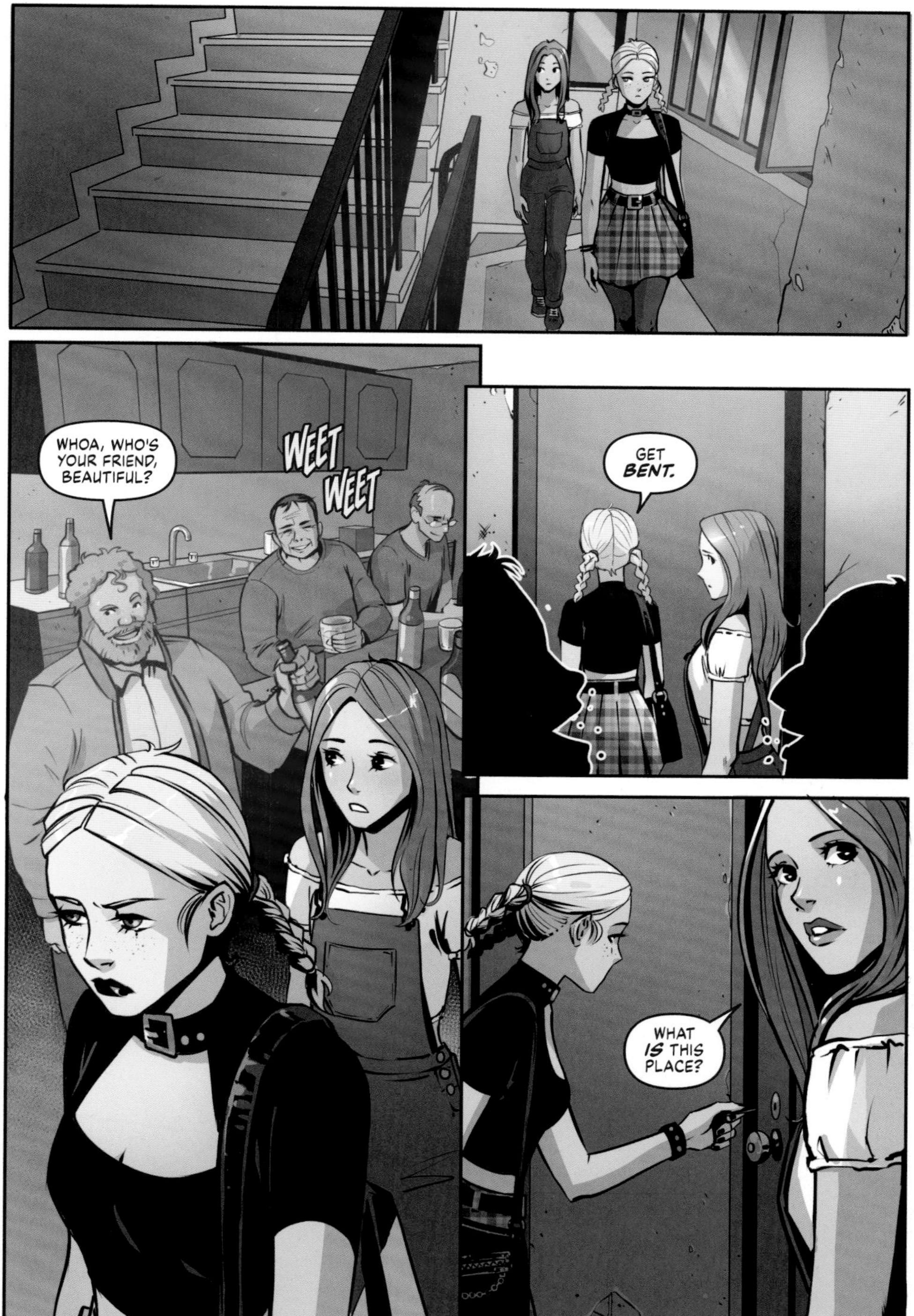
WHOA, WHO'S YOUR FRIEND, BEAUTIFUL?
WEET WEET
GET *BENT.*
WHAT *IS* THIS PLACE?

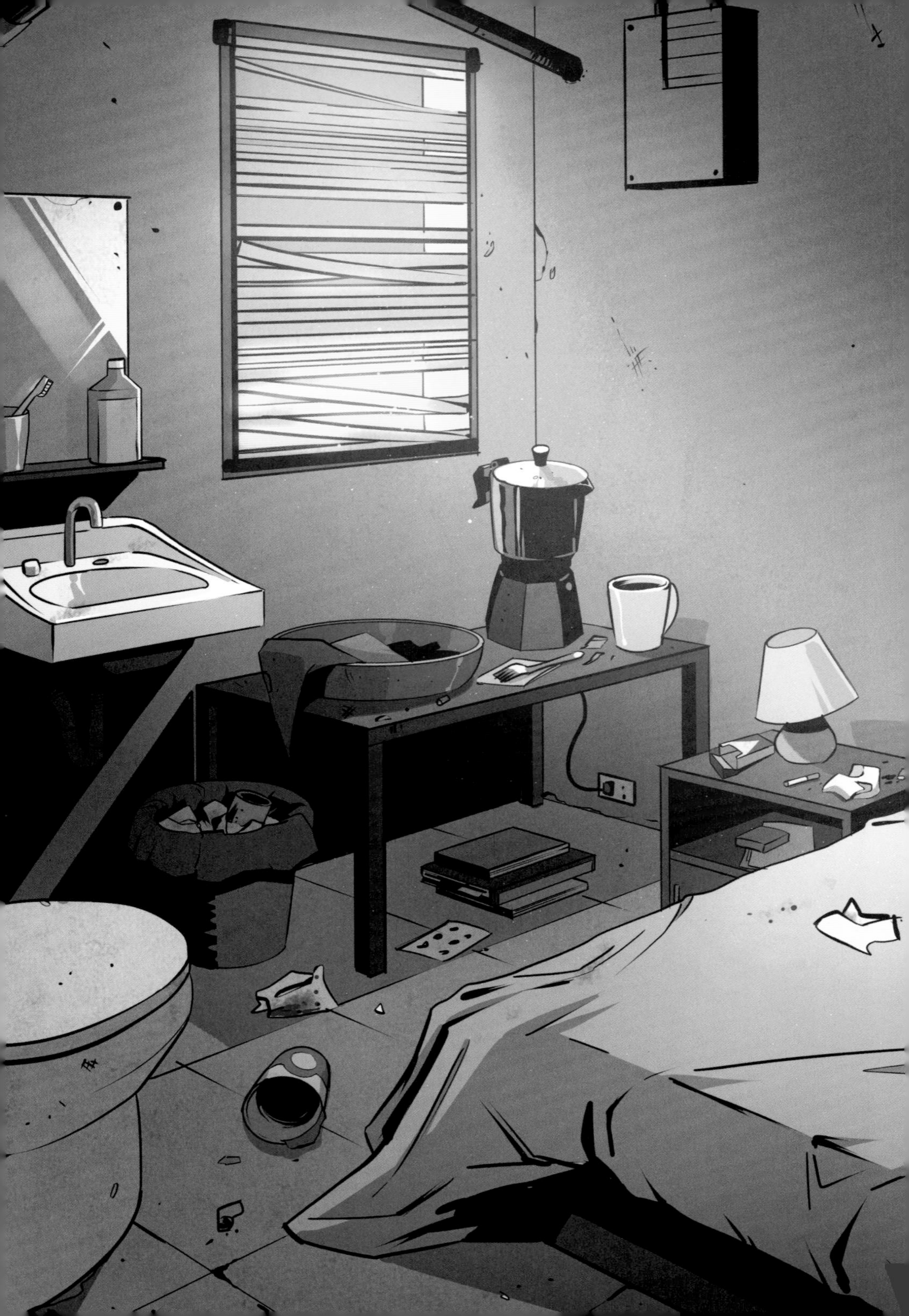

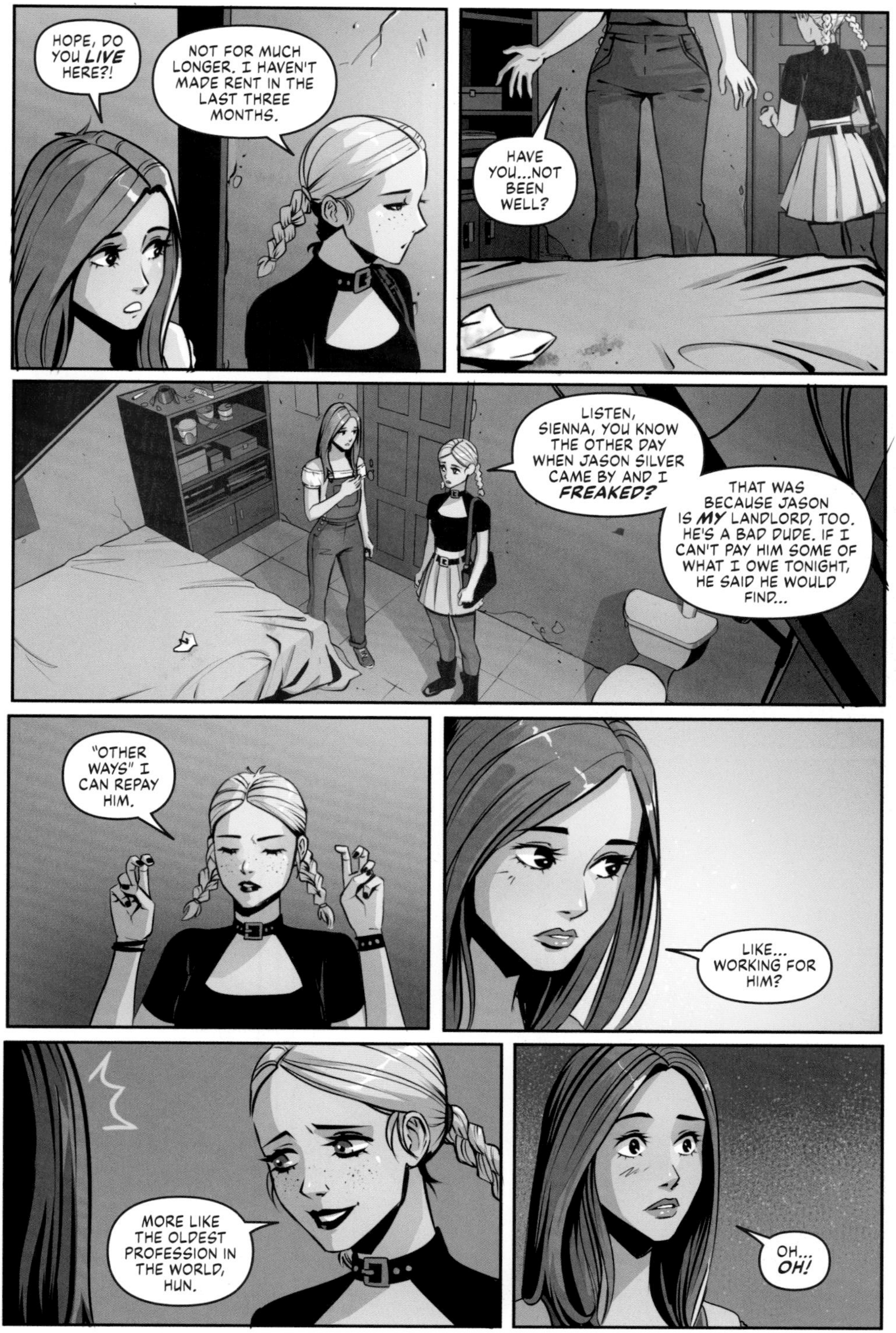
HOPE, DO YOU LIVE HERE?!
NOT FOR MUCH LONGER. I HAVEN'T MADE RENT IN THE LAST THREE MONTHS.
HAVE YOU...NOT BEEN WELL?
LISTEN, SIENNA, YOU KNOW THE OTHER DAY WHEN JASON SILVER CAME BY AND I FREAKED?
THAT WAS BECAUSE JASON IS MY LANDLORD, TOO. HE'S A BAD DUDE. IF I CAN'T PAY HIM SOME OF WHAT I OWE TONIGHT, HE SAID HE WOULD FIND...
"OTHER WAYS" I CAN REPAY HIM.
LIKE... WORKING FOR HIM?
MORE LIKE THE OLDEST PROFESSION IN THE WORLD, HUN.
OH... OH!

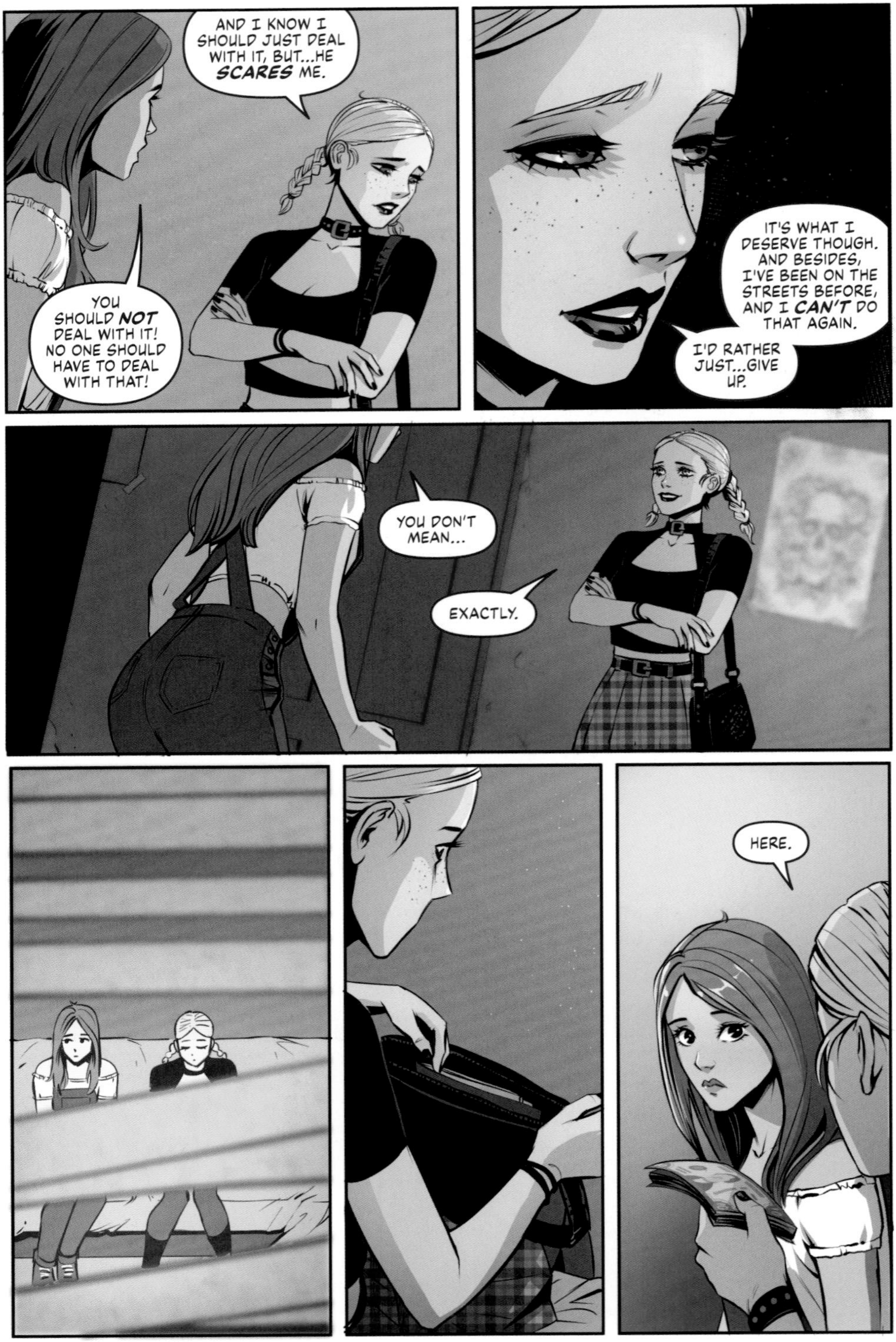
AND I KNOW I SHOULD JUST DEAL WITH IT, BUT...HE *SCARES* ME.
YOU SHOULD *NOT* DEAL WITH IT! NO ONE SHOULD HAVE TO DEAL WITH THAT!
IT'S WHAT I DESERVE THOUGH. AND BESIDES, I'VE BEEN ON THE STREETS BEFORE, AND I *CAN'T* DO THAT AGAIN.
I'D RATHER JUST...GIVE UP.
YOU DON'T MEAN...
EXACTLY.
HERE.

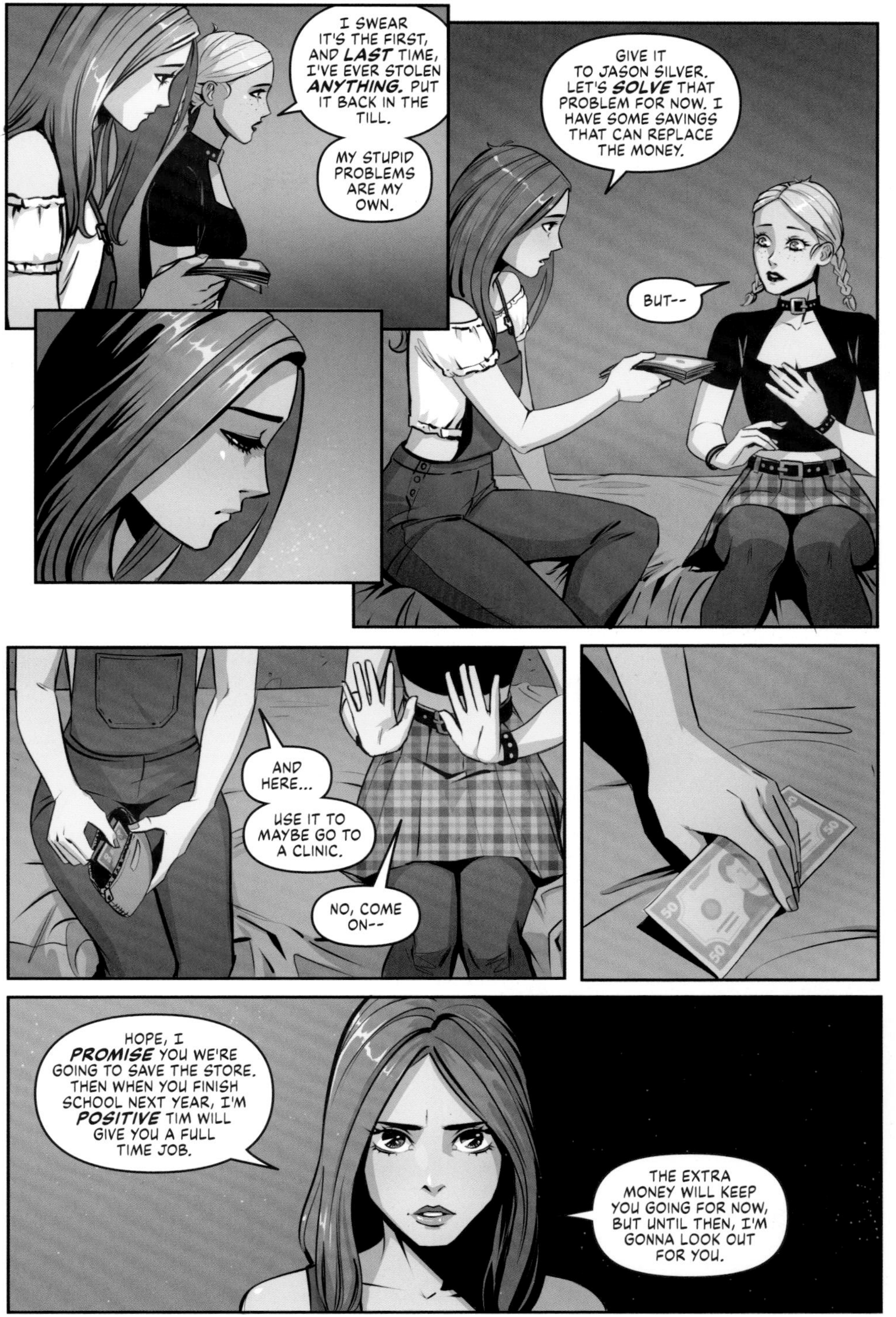
I SWEAR IT'S THE FIRST, AND **LAST** TIME, I'VE EVER STOLEN **ANYTHING.** PUT IT BACK IN THE TILL.
MY STUPID PROBLEMS ARE MY OWN.
GIVE IT TO JASON SILVER. LET'S **SOLVE** THAT PROBLEM FOR NOW. I HAVE SOME SAVINGS THAT CAN REPLACE THE MONEY.
BUT--
AND HERE...
USE IT TO MAYBE GO TO A CLINIC.
NO, COME ON--
50
HOPE, I **PROMISE** YOU WE'RE GOING TO SAVE THE STORE. THEN WHEN YOU FINISH SCHOOL NEXT YEAR, I'M **POSITIVE** TIM WILL GIVE YOU A FULL TIME JOB.
THE EXTRA MONEY WILL KEEP YOU GOING FOR NOW, BUT UNTIL THEN, I'M GONNA LOOK OUT FOR YOU.

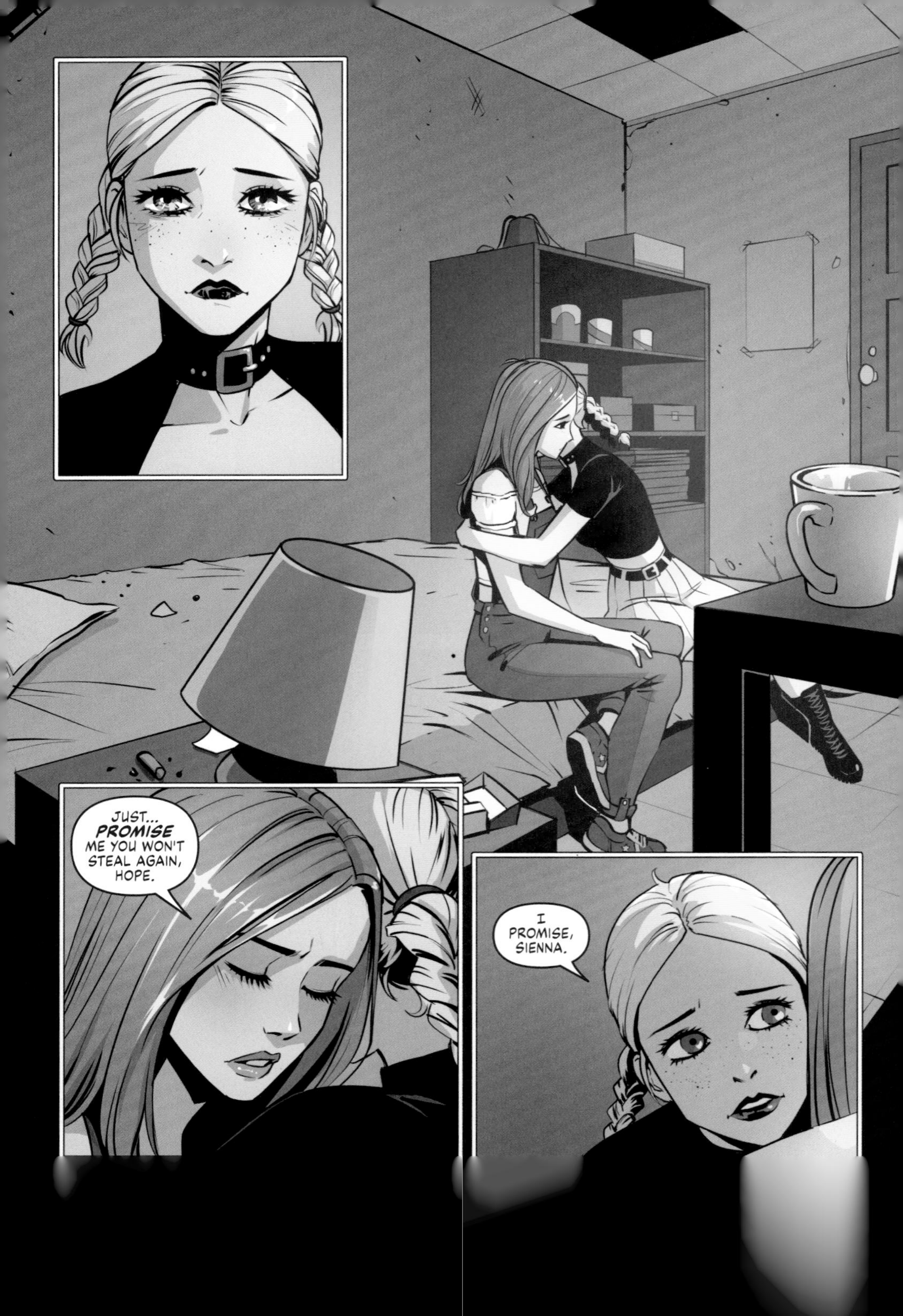
JUST... **PROMISE** ME YOU WON'T STEAL AGAIN, HOPE.
I PROMISE, SIENNA.

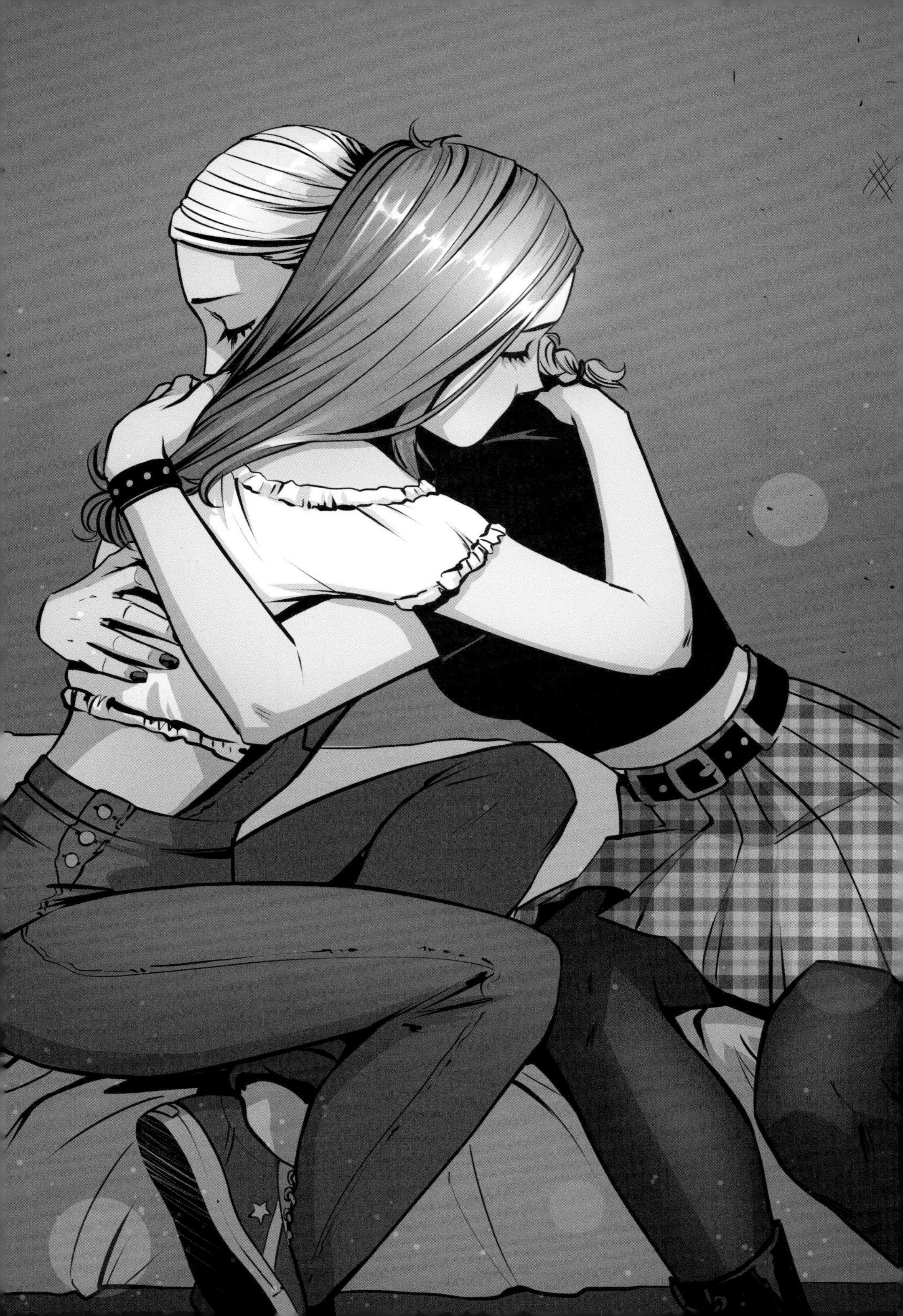

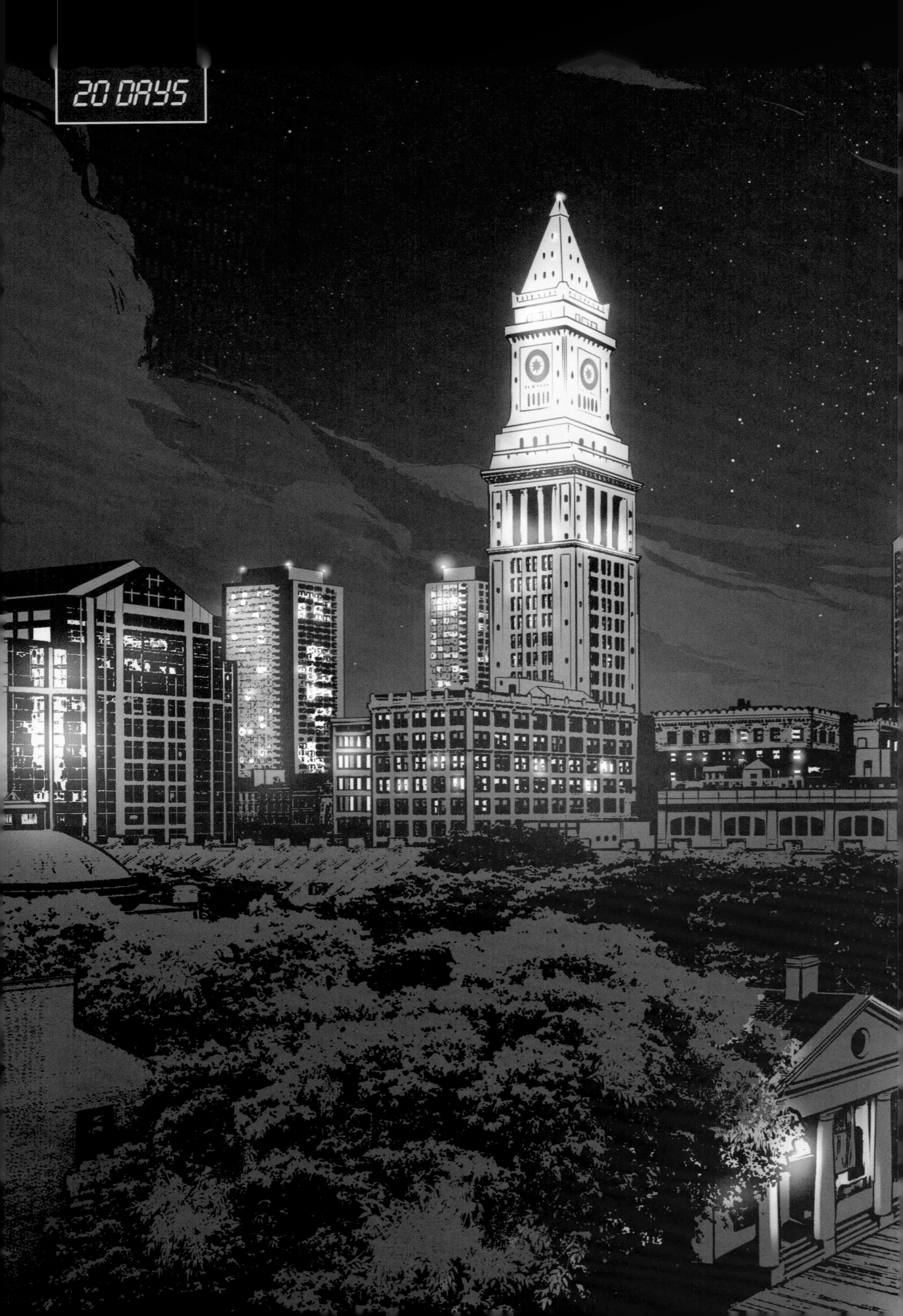
20 DAYS

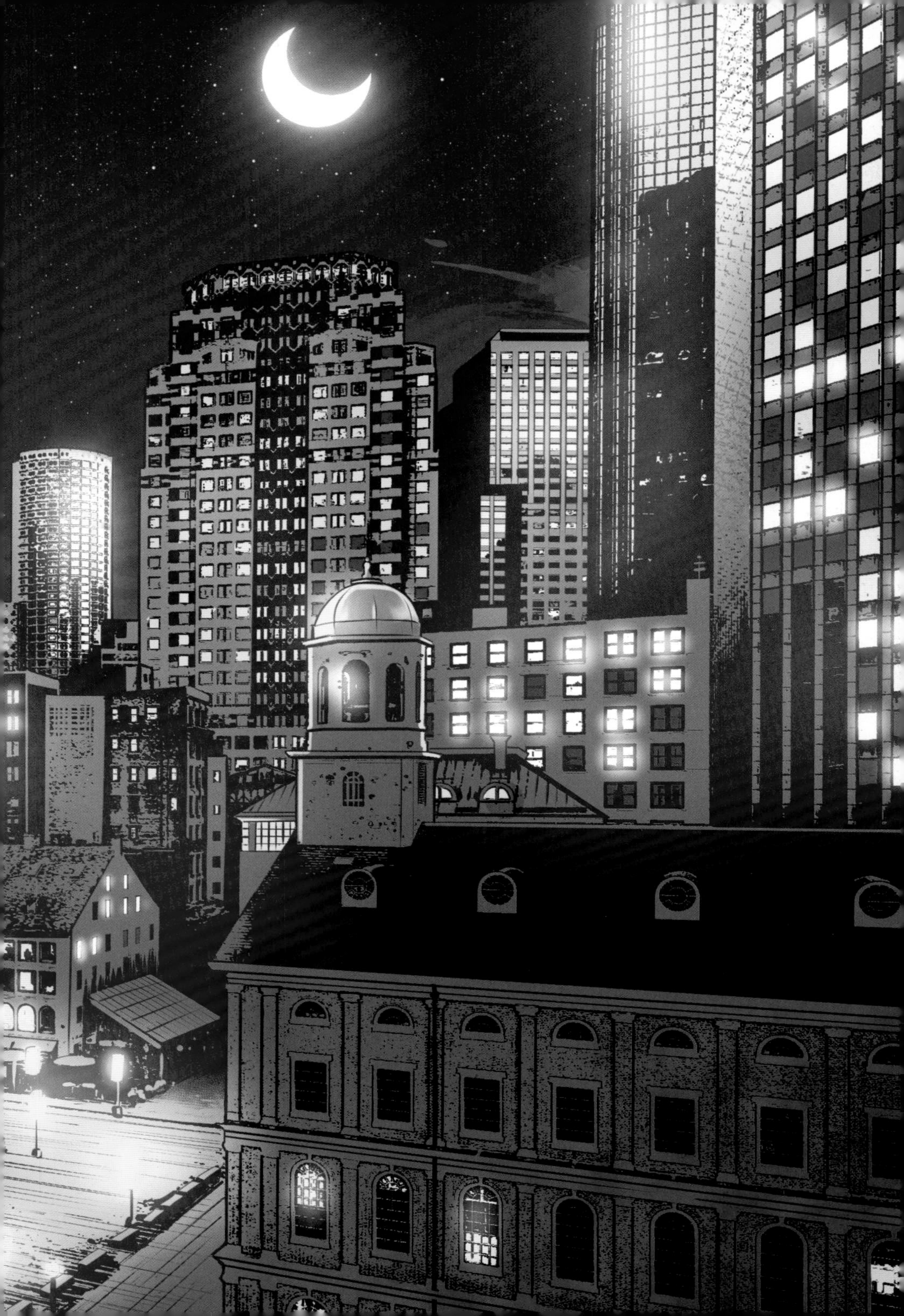

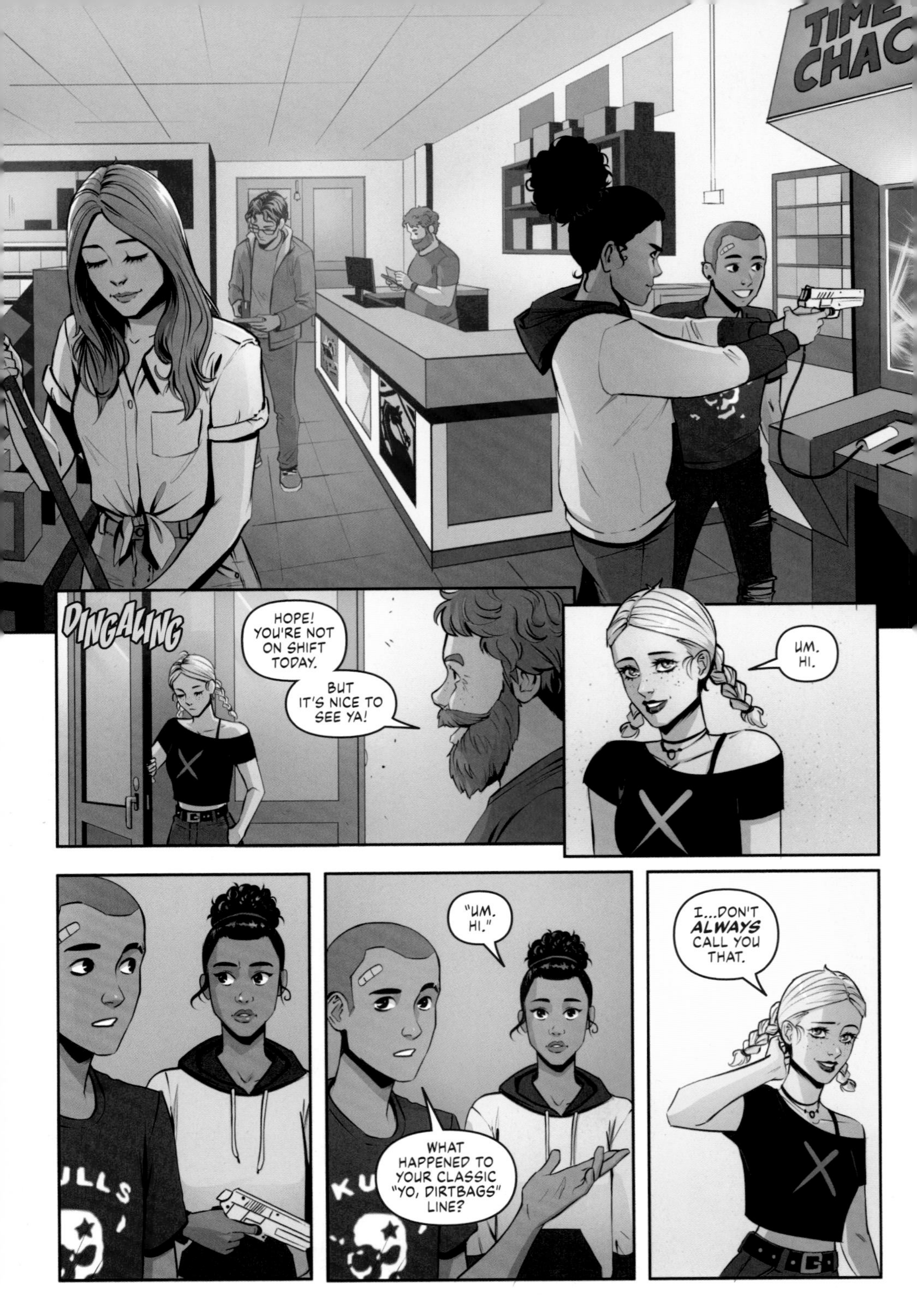
TIME CHAC
DINGALING
HOPE! YOU'RE NOT ON SHIFT TODAY.
BUT IT'S NICE TO SEE YA!
UM. HI.
"UM. HI."
WHAT HAPPENED TO YOUR CLASSIC "YO, DIRTBAGS" LINE?
I...DON'T ***ALWAYS*** CALL YOU THAT.

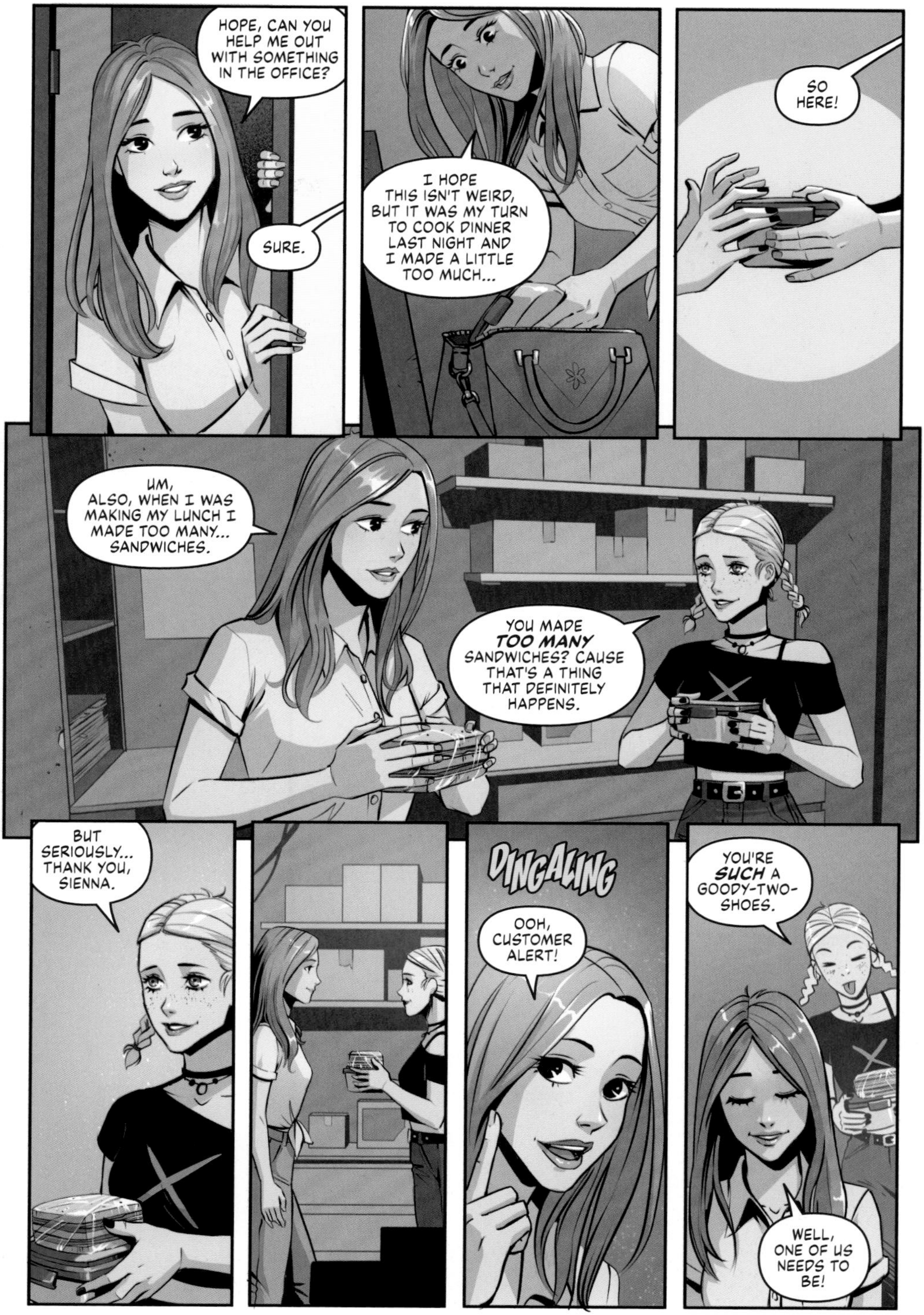
HOPE, CAN YOU HELP ME OUT WITH SOMETHING IN THE OFFICE?
SURE.
I HOPE THIS ISN'T WEIRD, BUT IT WAS MY TURN TO COOK DINNER LAST NIGHT AND I MADE A LITTLE TOO MUCH...
SO HERE!
UM, ALSO, WHEN I WAS MAKING MY LUNCH I MADE TOO MANY... SANDWICHES.
YOU MADE *TOO MANY* SANDWICHES? CAUSE THAT'S A THING THAT DEFINITELY HAPPENS.
BUT SERIOUSLY... THANK YOU, SIENNA.
DINGALING
OOH, CUSTOMER ALERT!
YOU'RE *SUCH* A GOODY-TWO-SHOES.
WELL, ONE OF US NEEDS TO BE!

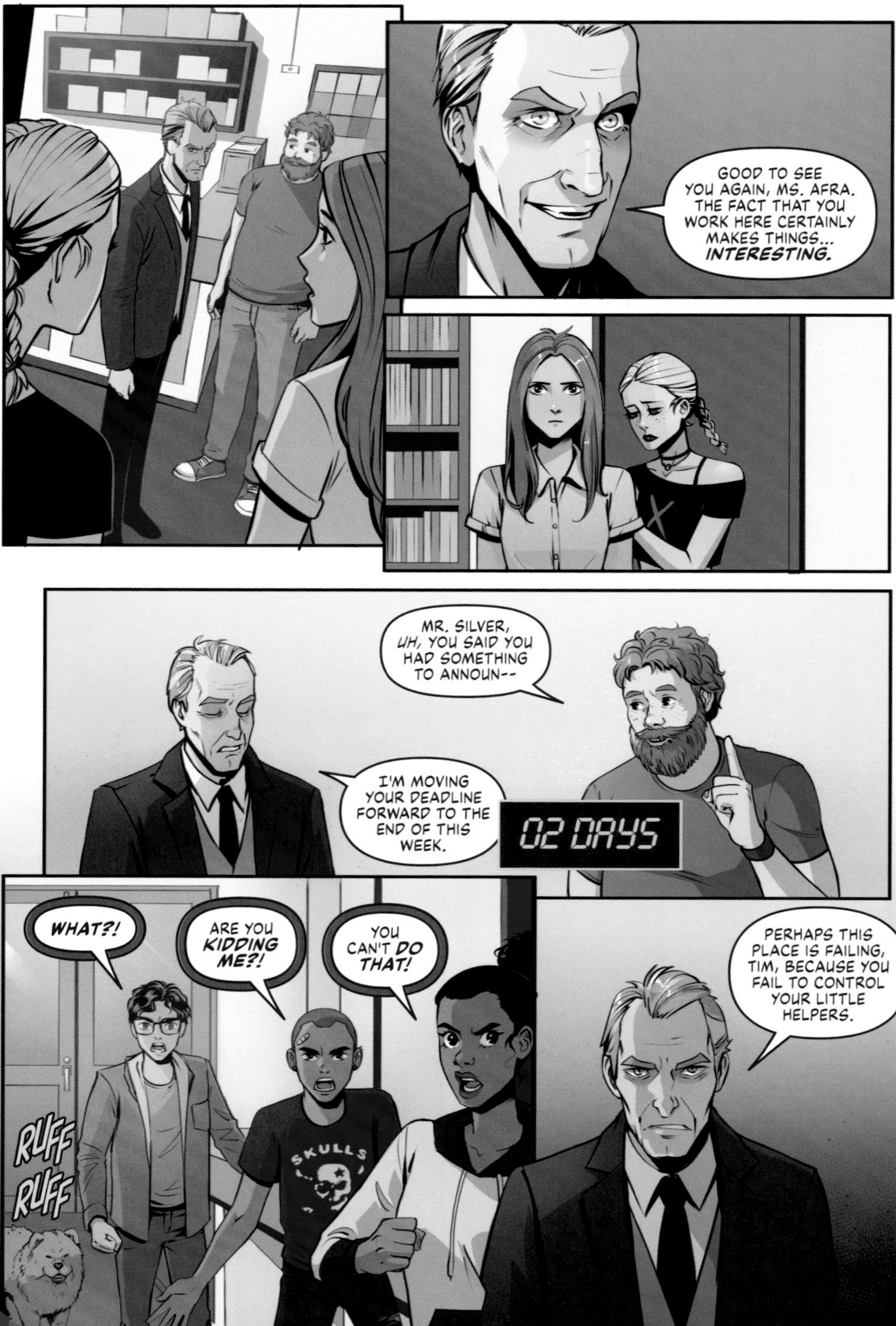
GOOD TO SEE YOU AGAIN, MS. AFRA. THE FACT THAT YOU WORK HERE CERTAINLY MAKES THINGS... INTERESTING.
MR. SILVER, UH, YOU SAID YOU HAD SOMETHING TO ANNOUN--
I'M MOVING YOUR DEADLINE FORWARD TO THE END OF THIS WEEK.
02 DAYS
WHAT?!
ARE YOU KIDDING ME?!
YOU CAN'T DO THAT!
RUFF RUFF
PERHAPS THIS PLACE IS FAILING, TIM, BECAUSE YOU FAIL TO CONTROL YOUR LITTLE HELPERS.

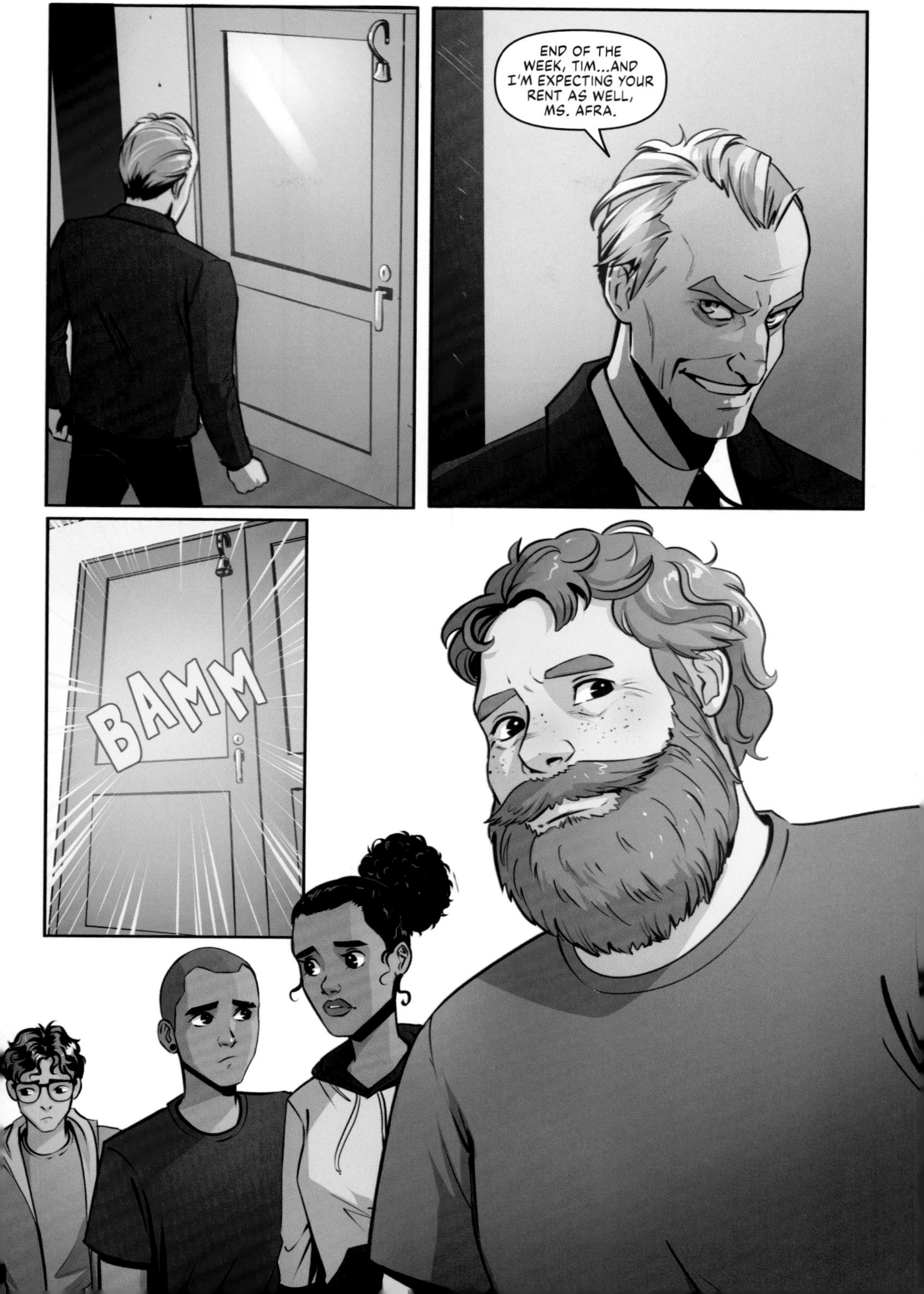
END OF THE WEEK, TIM...AND I'M EXPECTING YOUR RENT AS WELL, MS. AFRA.
BAMM

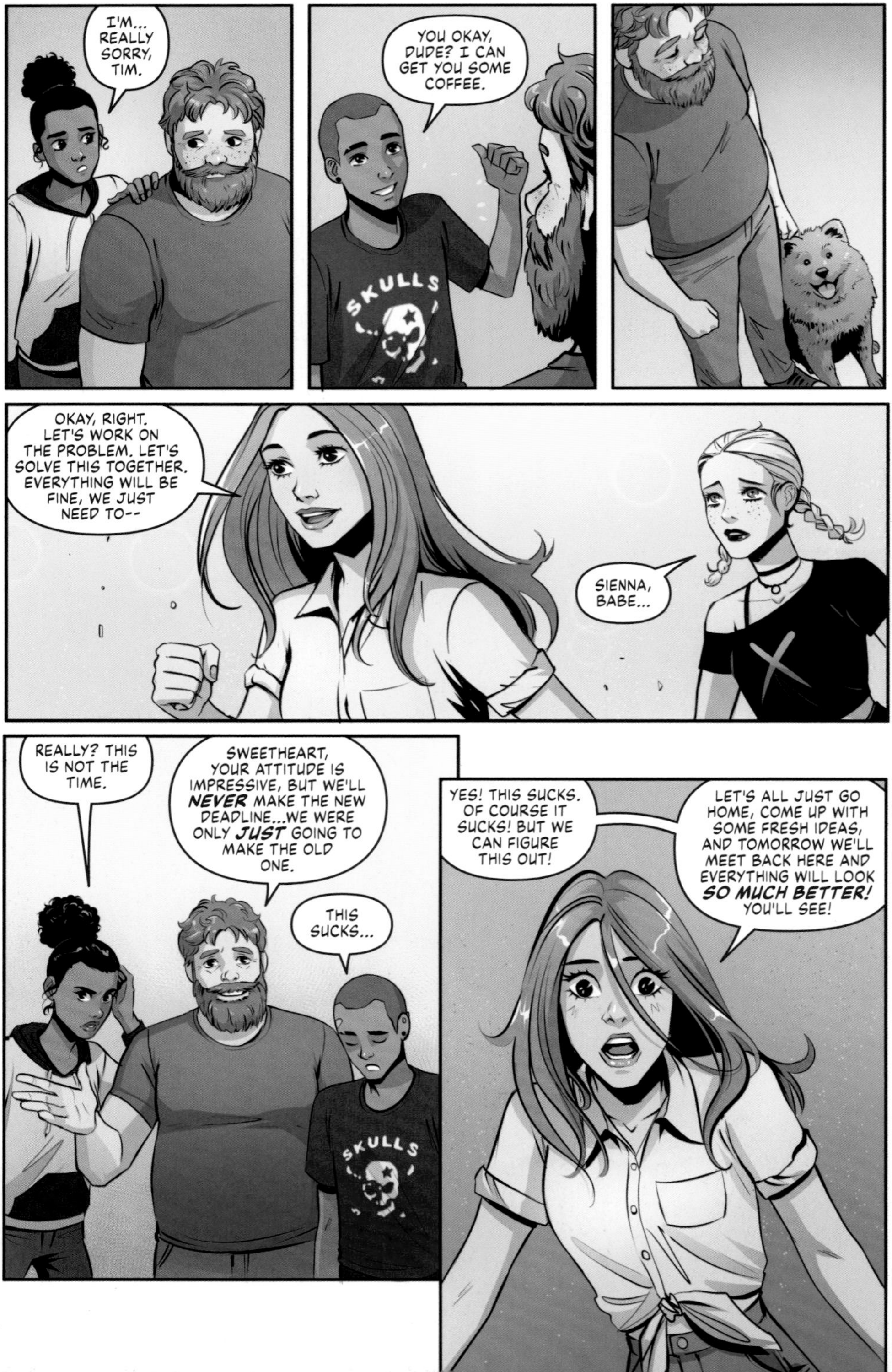
I'M... REALLY SORRY, TIM.
YOU OKAY, DUDE? I CAN GET YOU SOME COFFEE.
SKULLS
OKAY, RIGHT. LET'S WORK ON THE PROBLEM. LET'S SOLVE THIS TOGETHER. EVERYTHING WILL BE FINE, WE JUST NEED TO--
SIENNA, BABE...
REALLY? THIS IS NOT THE TIME.
SWEETHEART, YOUR ATTITUDE IS IMPRESSIVE, BUT WE'LL ***NEVER*** MAKE THE NEW DEADLINE...WE WERE ONLY ***JUST*** GOING TO MAKE THE OLD ONE.
THIS SUCKS...
SKULLS
YES! THIS SUCKS. OF COURSE IT SUCKS! BUT WE CAN FIGURE THIS OUT!
LET'S ALL JUST GO HOME, COME UP WITH SOME FRESH IDEAS, AND TOMORROW WE'LL MEET BACK HERE AND EVERYTHING WILL LOOK ***SO MUCH BETTER!*** YOU'LL SEE!

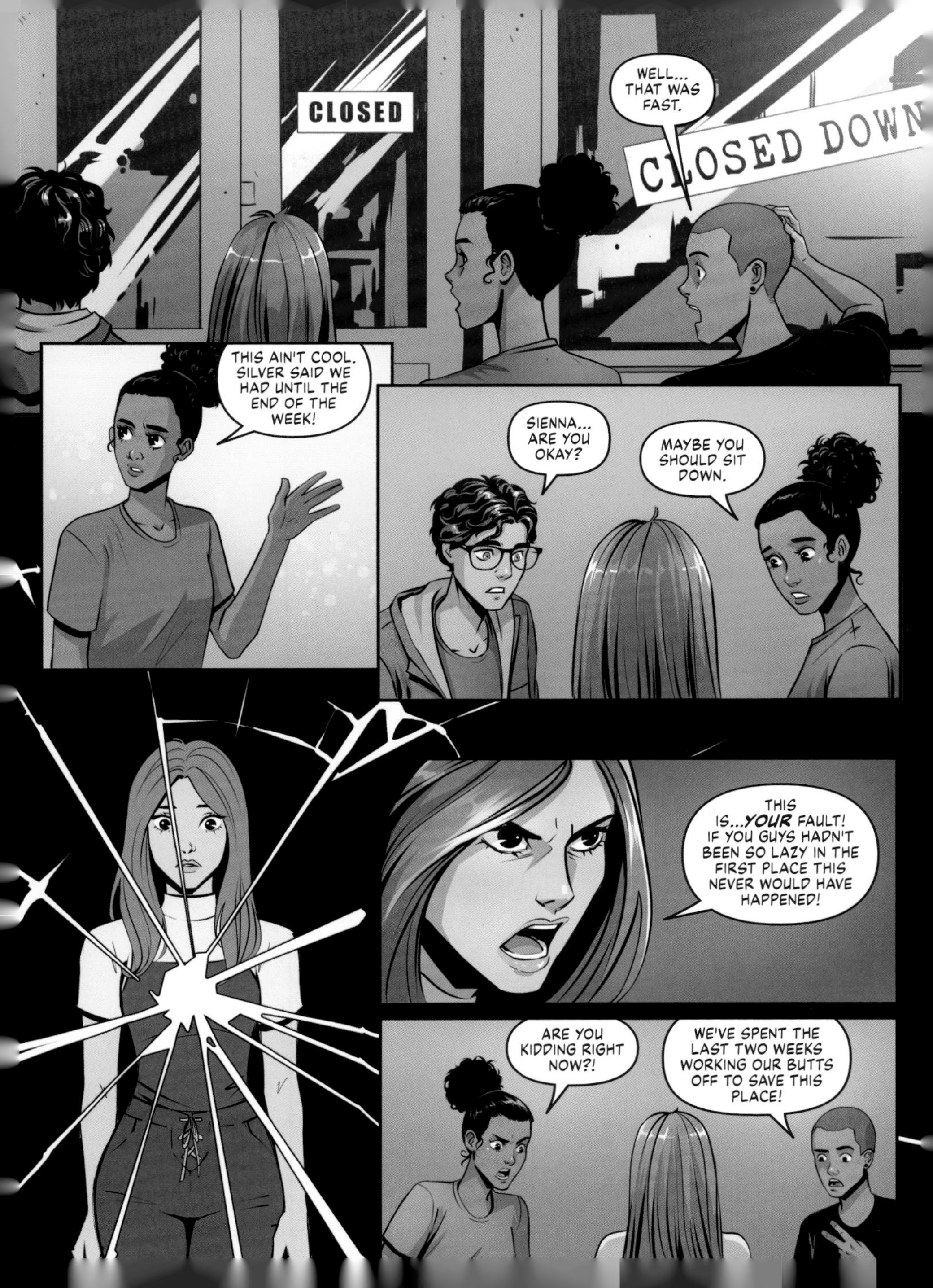
CLOSED
WELL... THAT WAS FAST.
CLOSED DOWN
THIS AIN'T COOL. SILVER SAID WE HAD UNTIL THE END OF THE WEEK!
SIENNA... ARE YOU OKAY?
MAYBE YOU SHOULD SIT DOWN.
THIS IS...YOUR FAULT! IF YOU GUYS HADN'T BEEN SO LAZY IN THE FIRST PLACE THIS NEVER WOULD HAVE HAPPENED!
ARE YOU KIDDING RIGHT NOW?!
WE'VE SPENT THE LAST TWO WEEKS WORKING OUR BUTTS OFF TO SAVE THIS PLACE!

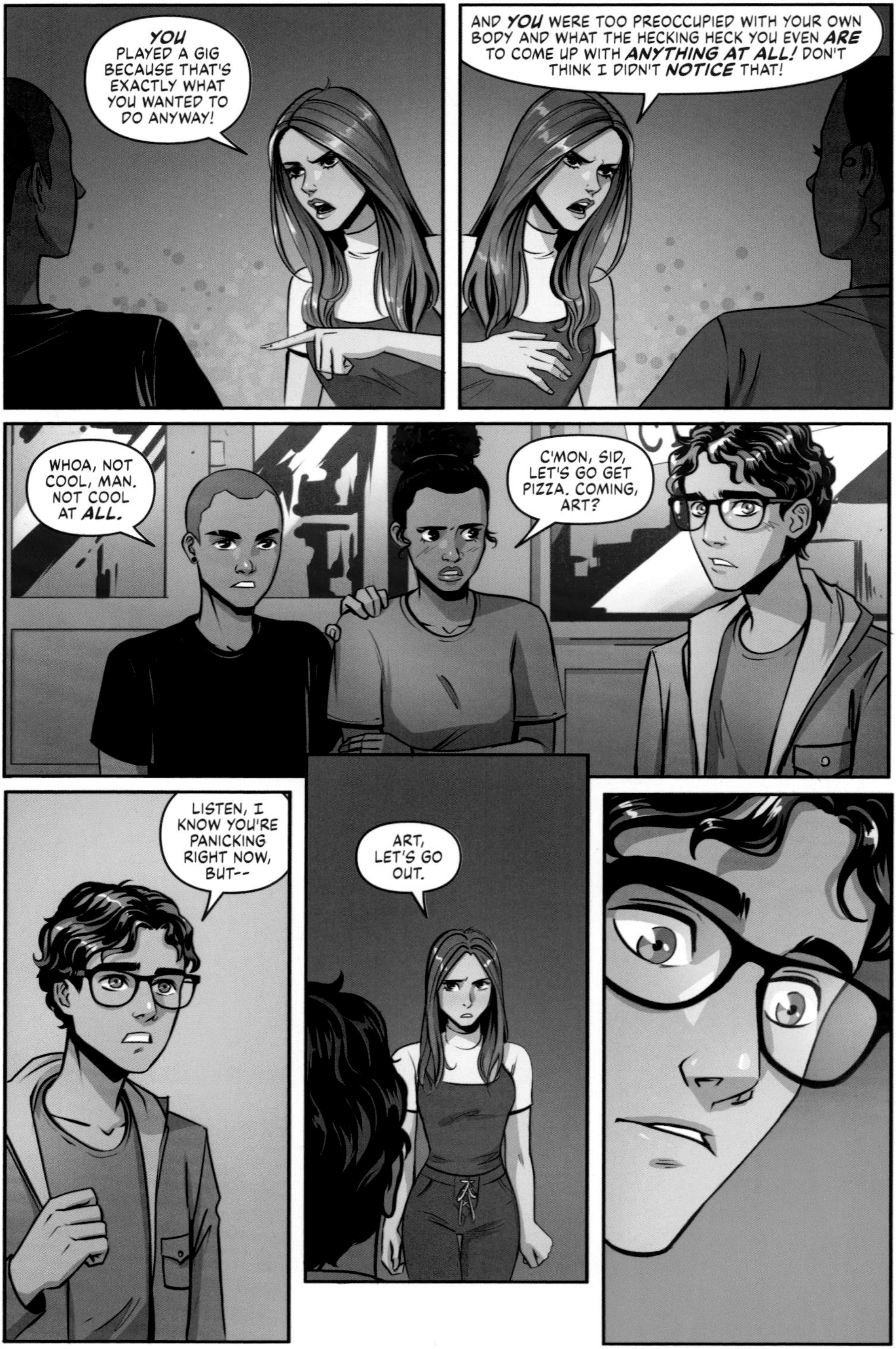
YOU PLAYED A GIG BECAUSE THAT'S EXACTLY WHAT YOU WANTED TO DO ANYWAY!
AND YOU WERE TOO PREOCCUPIED WITH YOUR OWN BODY AND WHAT THE HECKING HECK YOU EVEN ARE TO COME UP WITH ANYTHING AT ALL! DON'T THINK I DIDN'T NOTICE THAT!
WHOA, NOT COOL, MAN. NOT COOL AT ALL.
C'MON, SID, LET'S GO GET PIZZA. COMING, ART?
LISTEN, I KNOW YOU'RE PANICKING RIGHT NOW, BUT--
ART, LET'S GO OUT.

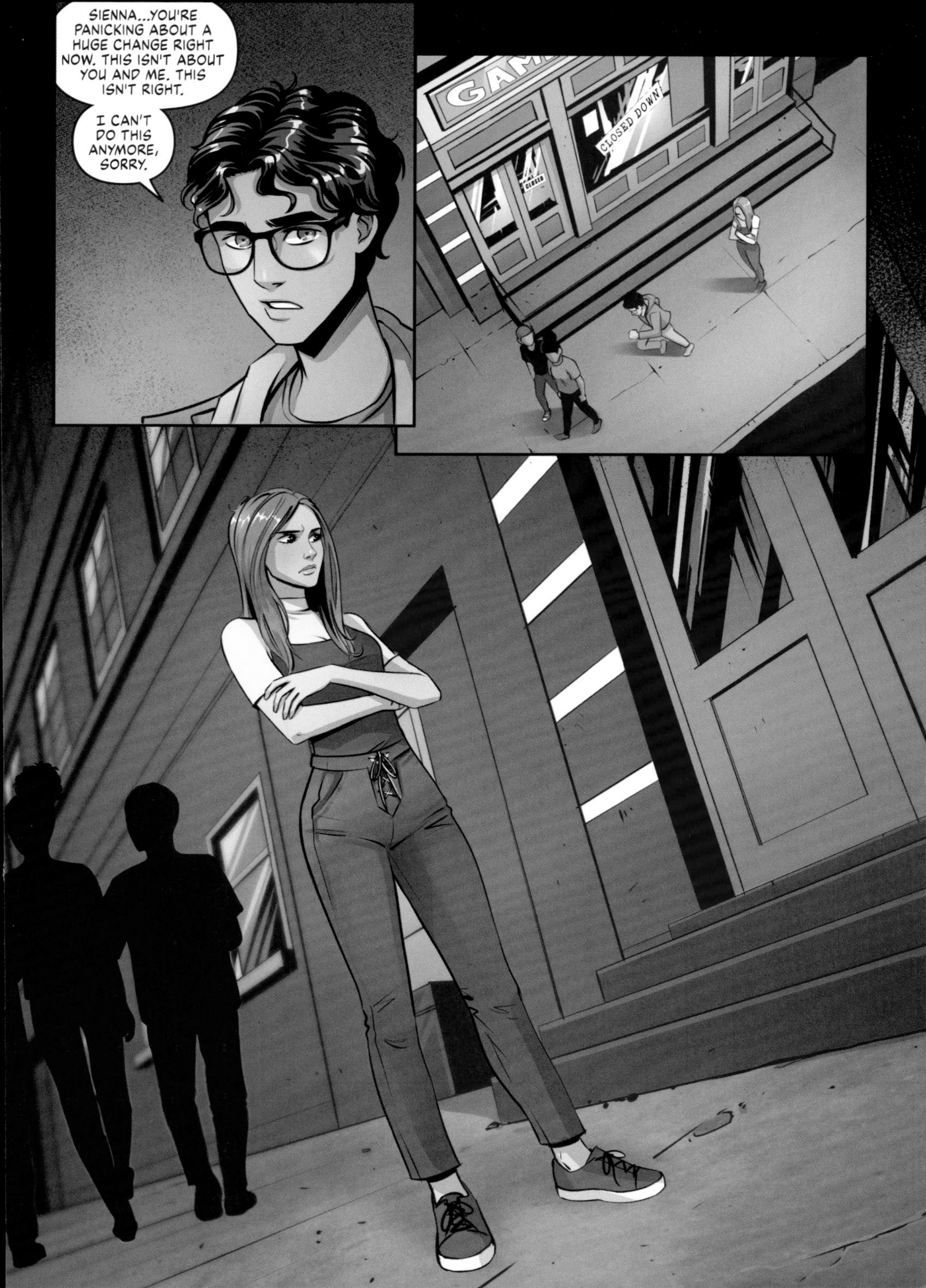
SIENNA...YOU'RE PANICKING ABOUT A HUGE CHANGE RIGHT NOW. THIS ISN'T ABOUT YOU AND ME. THIS ISN'T RIGHT.
I CAN'T DO THIS ANYMORE, SORRY.
CLOSED DOWN!
CLOSED

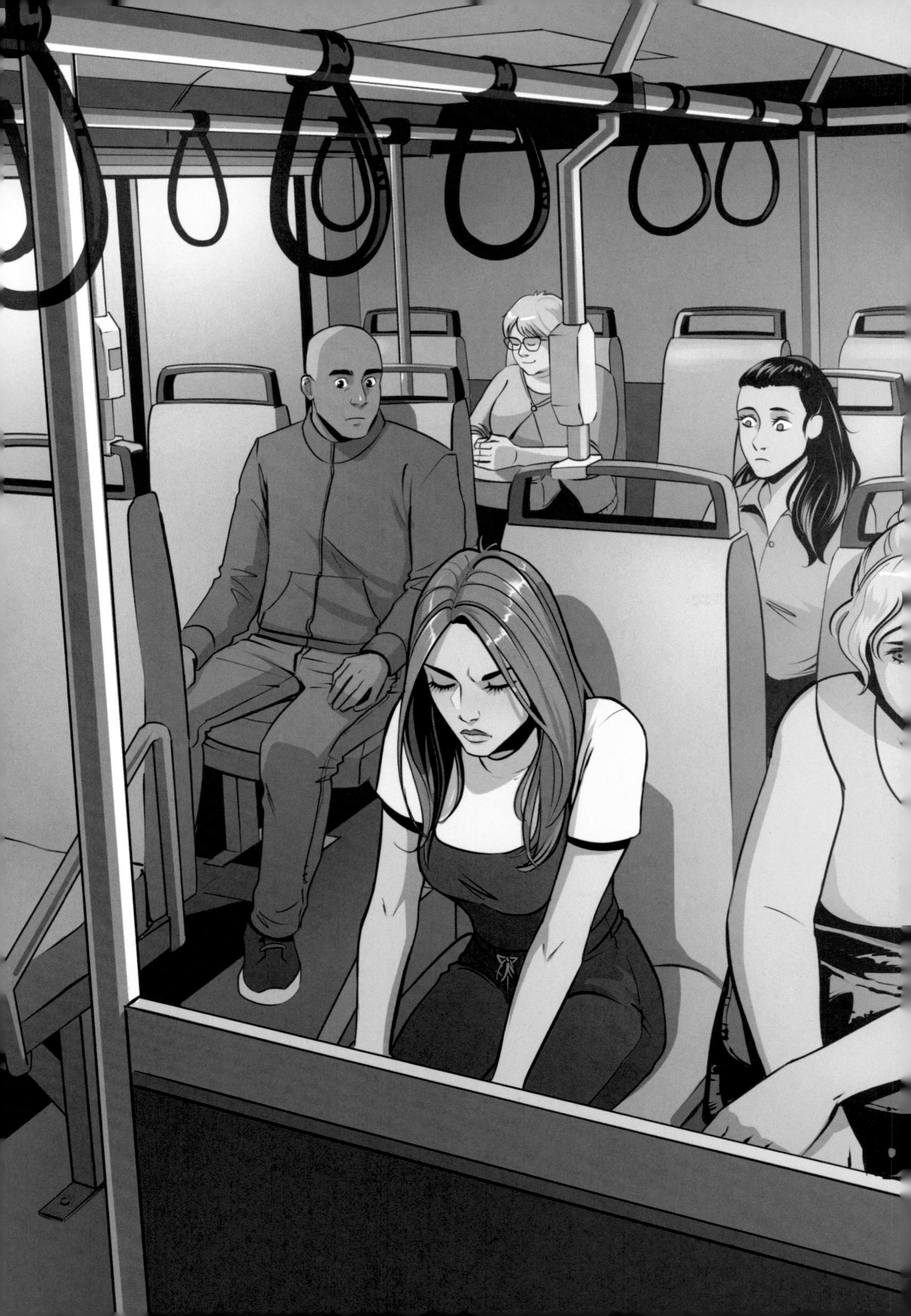

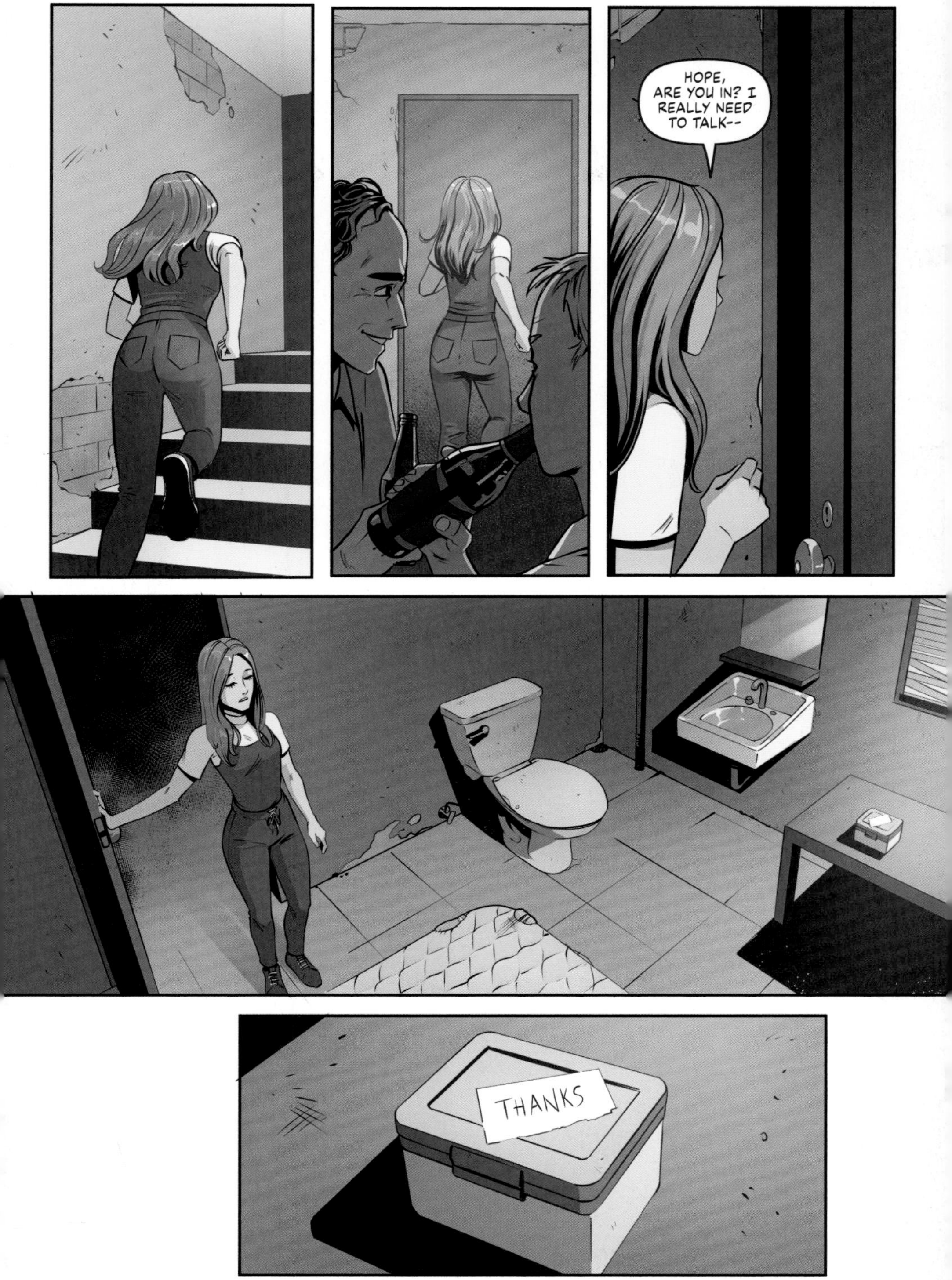
HOPE, ARE YOU IN? I REALLY NEED TO TALK--
THANKS

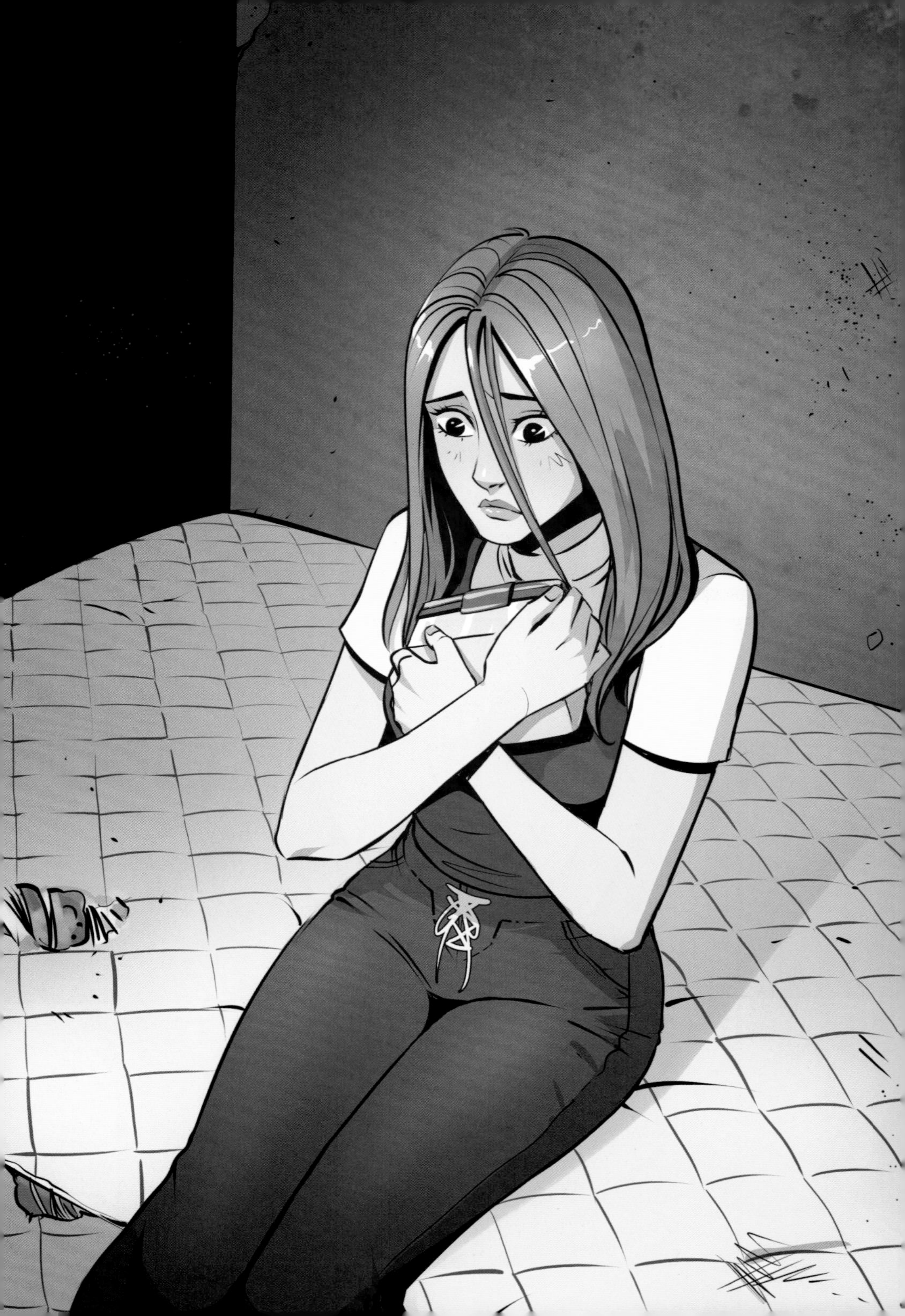

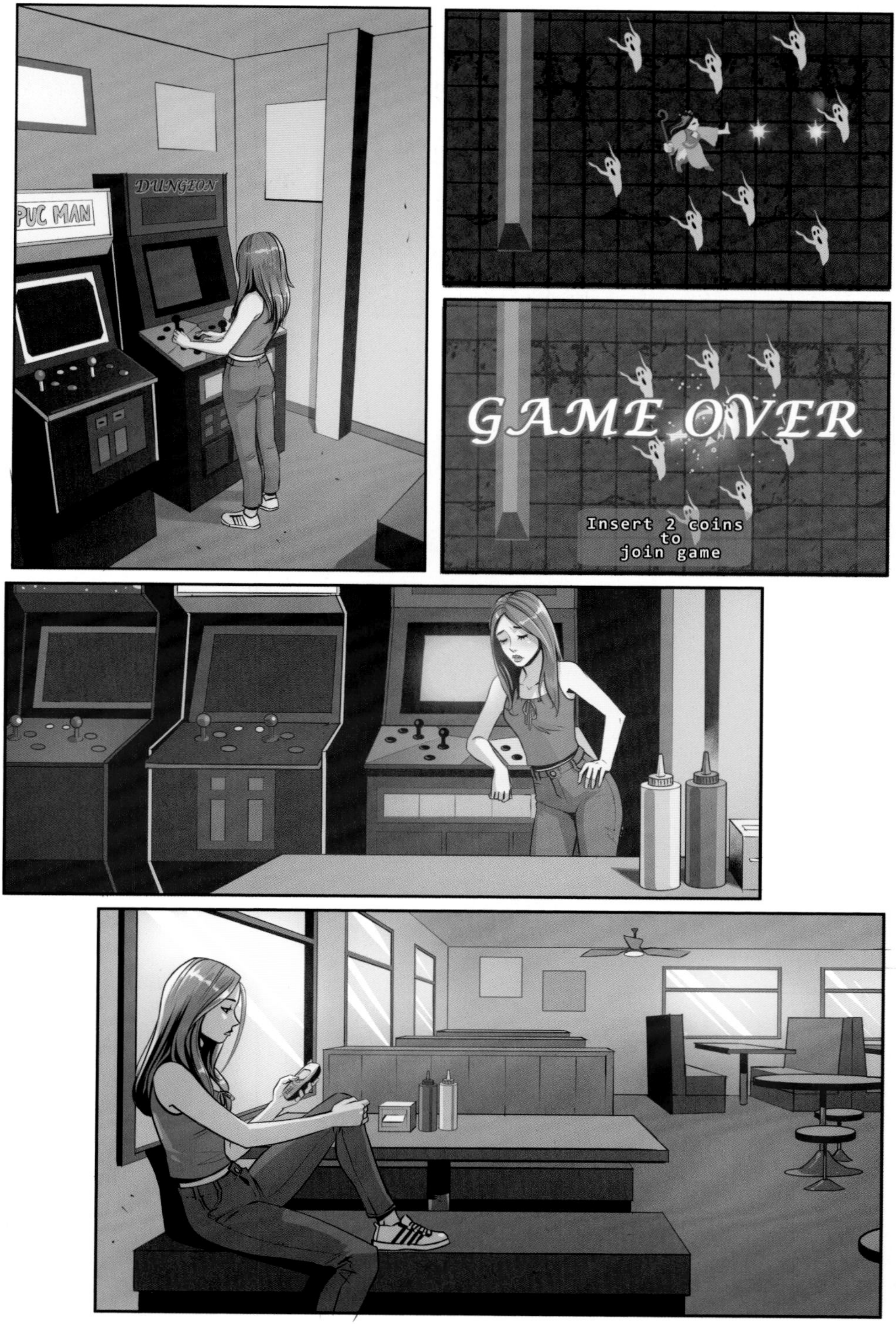
DUNGEON
PUC MAN
GAME OVER
Insert 2 coins
to
join game

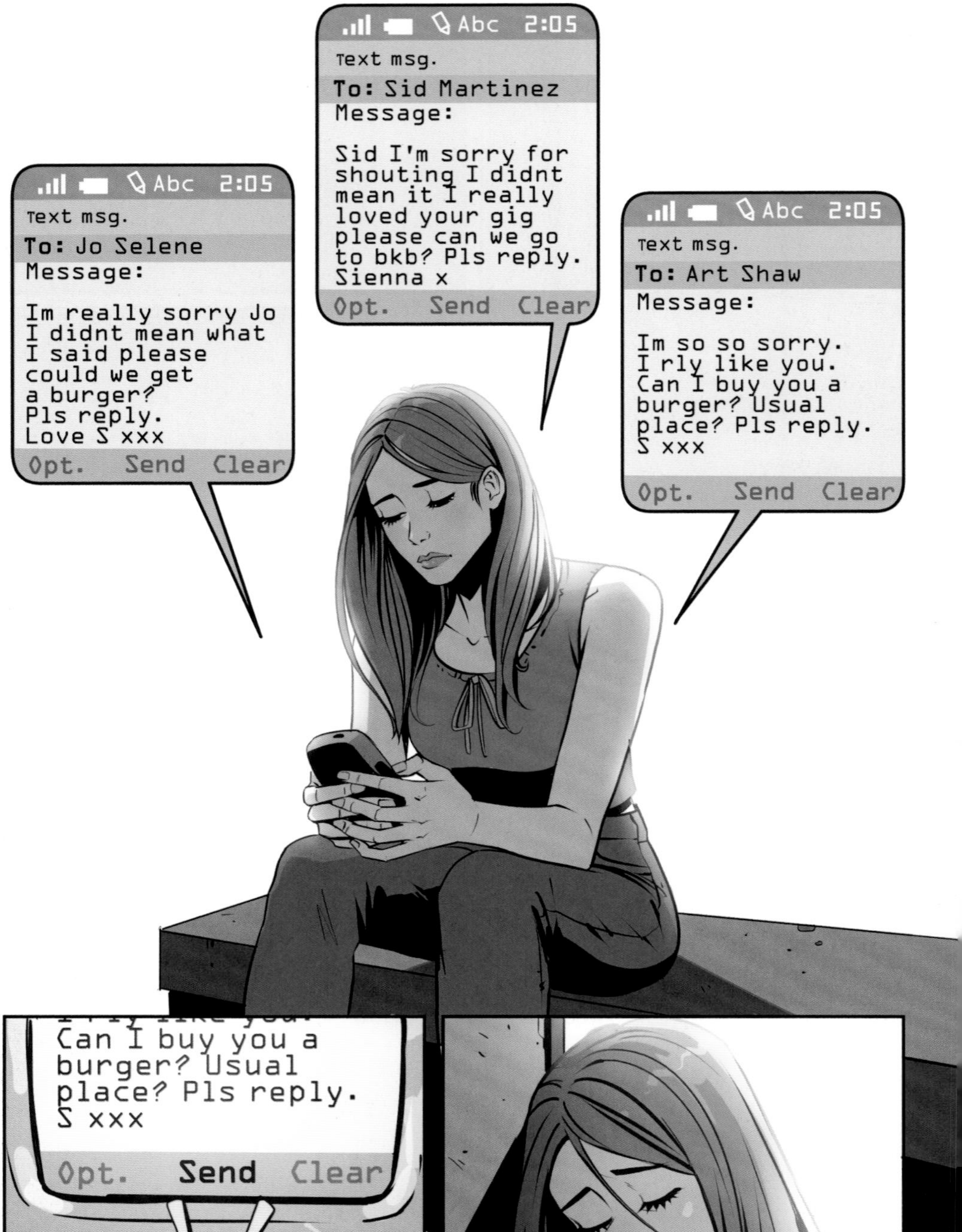

2:05
Text msg.
To: Jo Selene
Message:
Im really sorry Jo I didnt mean what I said please could we get a burger? Pls reply. Love S xxx
Opt. Send Clear
2:05
Text msg.
To: Sid Martinez
Message:
Sid I'm sorry for shouting I didnt mean it I really loved your gig please can we go to bkb? Pls reply. Sienna x
Opt. Send Clear
2:05
Text msg.
To: Art Shaw
Message:
Im so so sorry. I rly like you. Can I buy you a burger? Usual place? Pls reply. S xxx
Opt. Send Clear
Can I buy you a burger? Usual place? Pls reply. S xxx
Opt. Send Clear
C

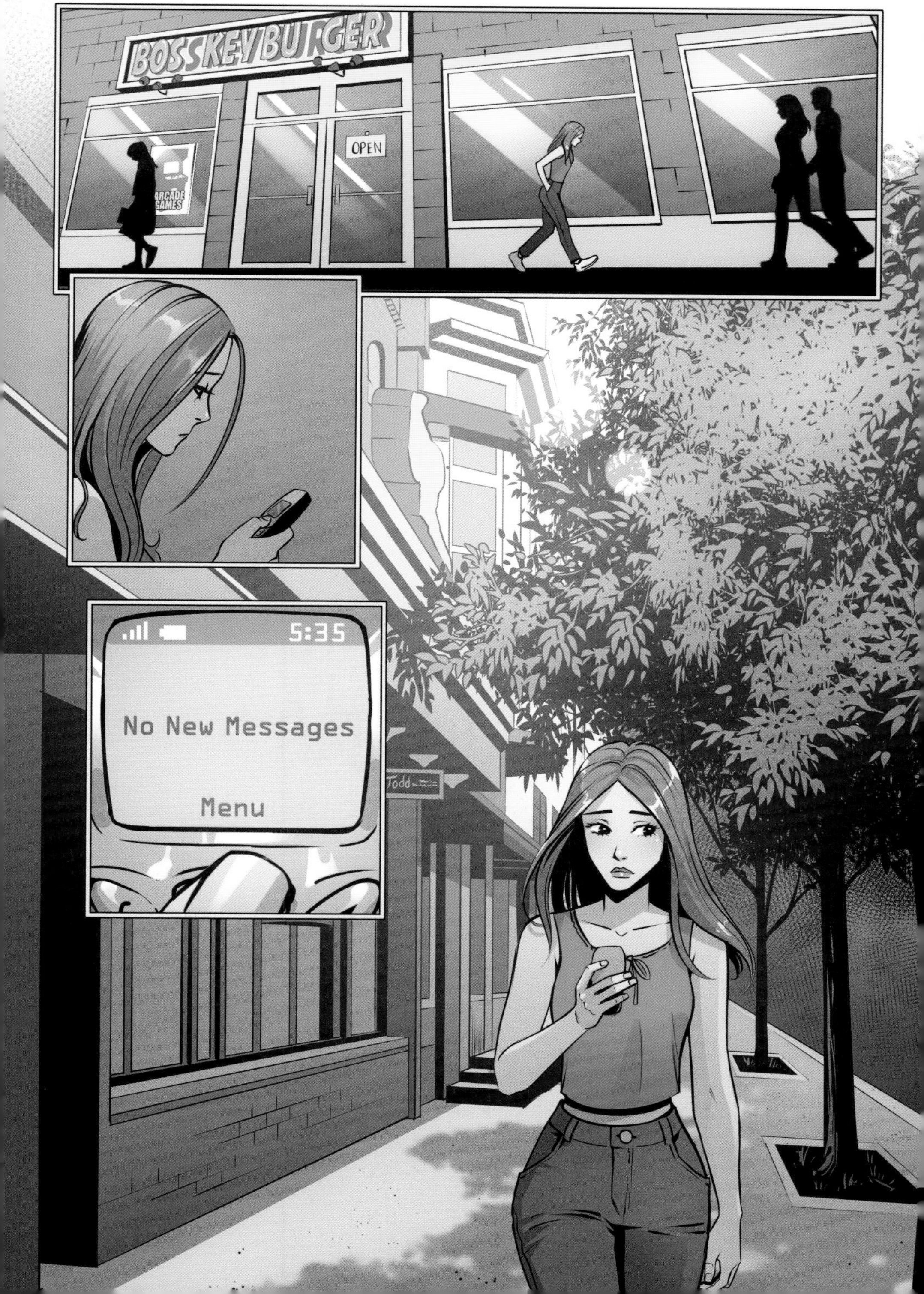
BOSS KEY BURGER
OPEN
ARCADE GAMES
5:35
No New Messages
Menu

AUTUMN 2009
BOSTON, MA

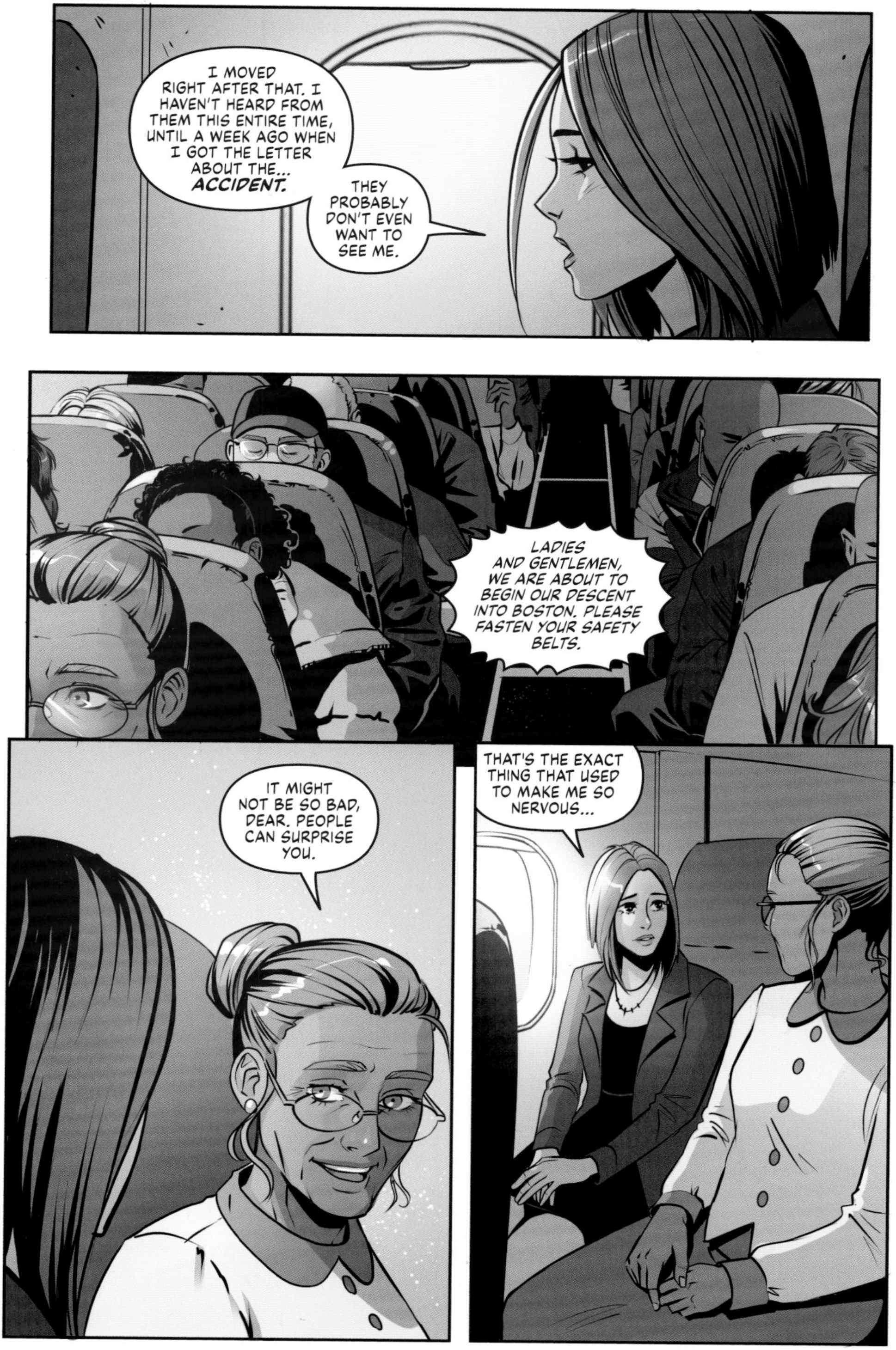
I MOVED RIGHT AFTER THAT. I HAVEN'T HEARD FROM THEM THIS ENTIRE TIME, UNTIL A WEEK AGO WHEN I GOT THE LETTER ABOUT THE... **ACCIDENT.**
THEY PROBABLY DON'T EVEN WANT TO SEE ME.
LADIES AND GENTLEMEN, WE ARE ABOUT TO BEGIN OUR DESCENT INTO BOSTON. PLEASE FASTEN YOUR SAFETY BELTS.
IT MIGHT NOT BE SO BAD, DEAR. PEOPLE CAN SURPRISE YOU.
THAT'S THE EXACT THING THAT USED TO MAKE ME SO NERVOUS...

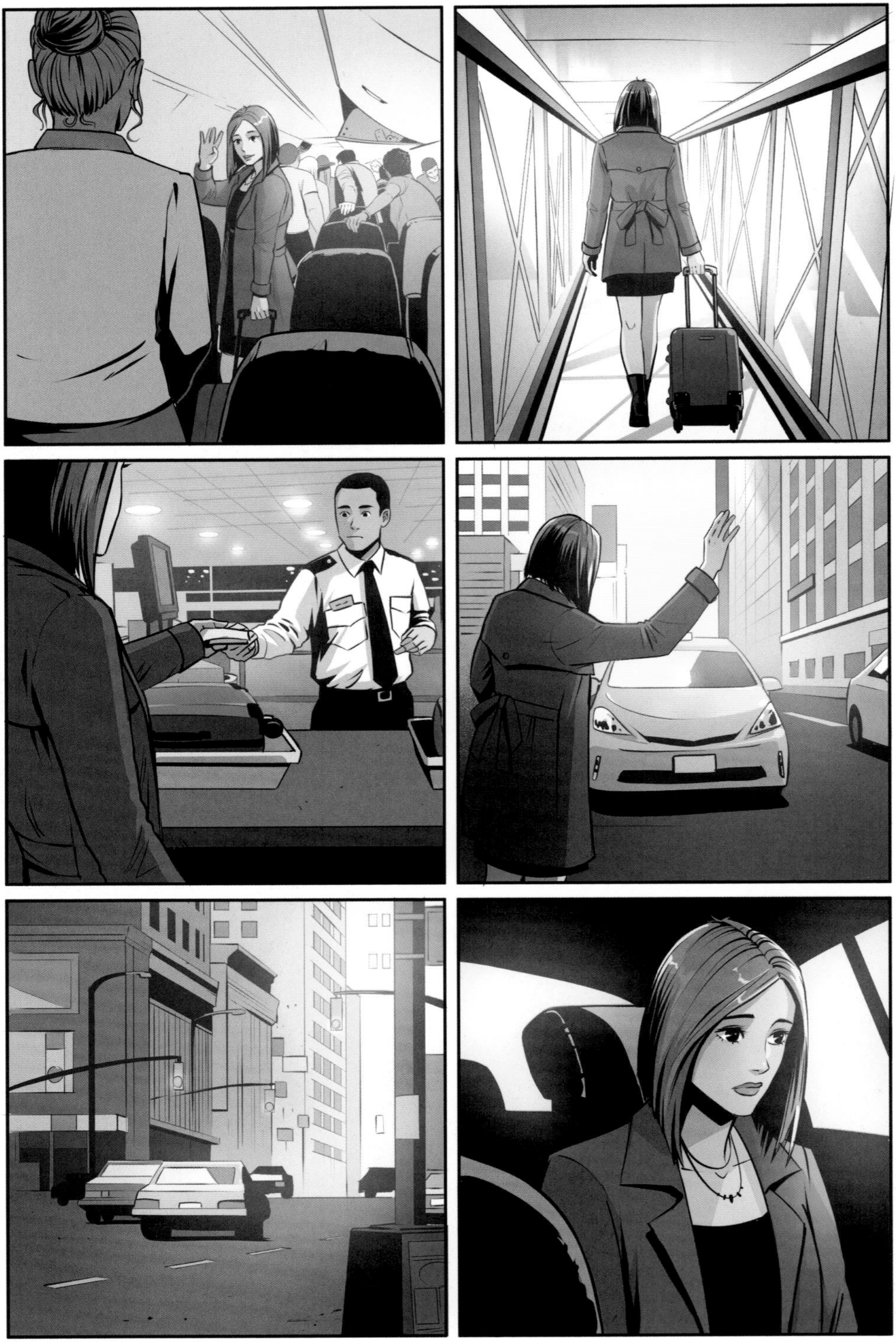

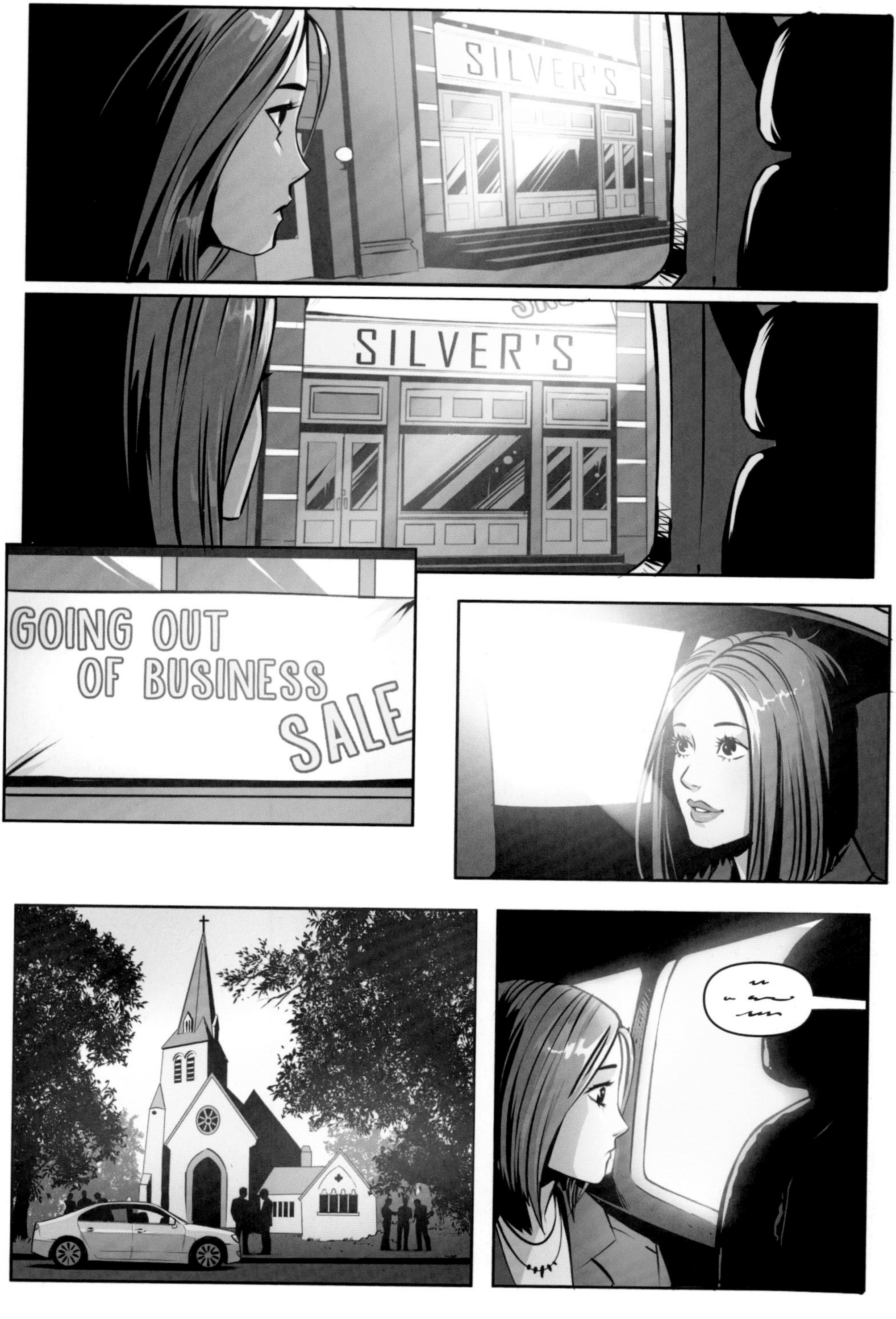

SILVER'S
SILVER'S
GOING OUT OF BUSINESS SALE

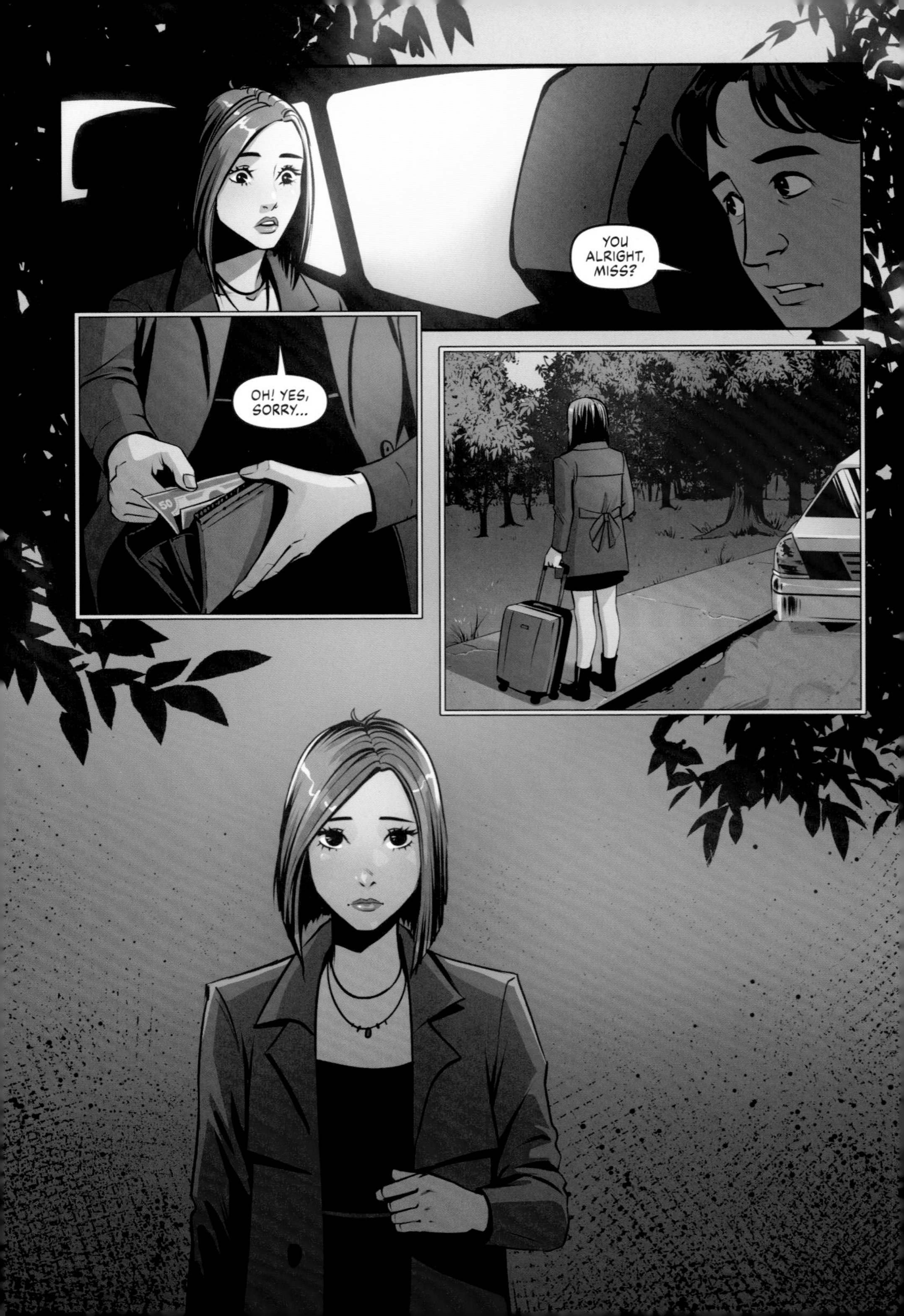
YOU ALRIGHT, MISS?
OH! YES, SORRY...

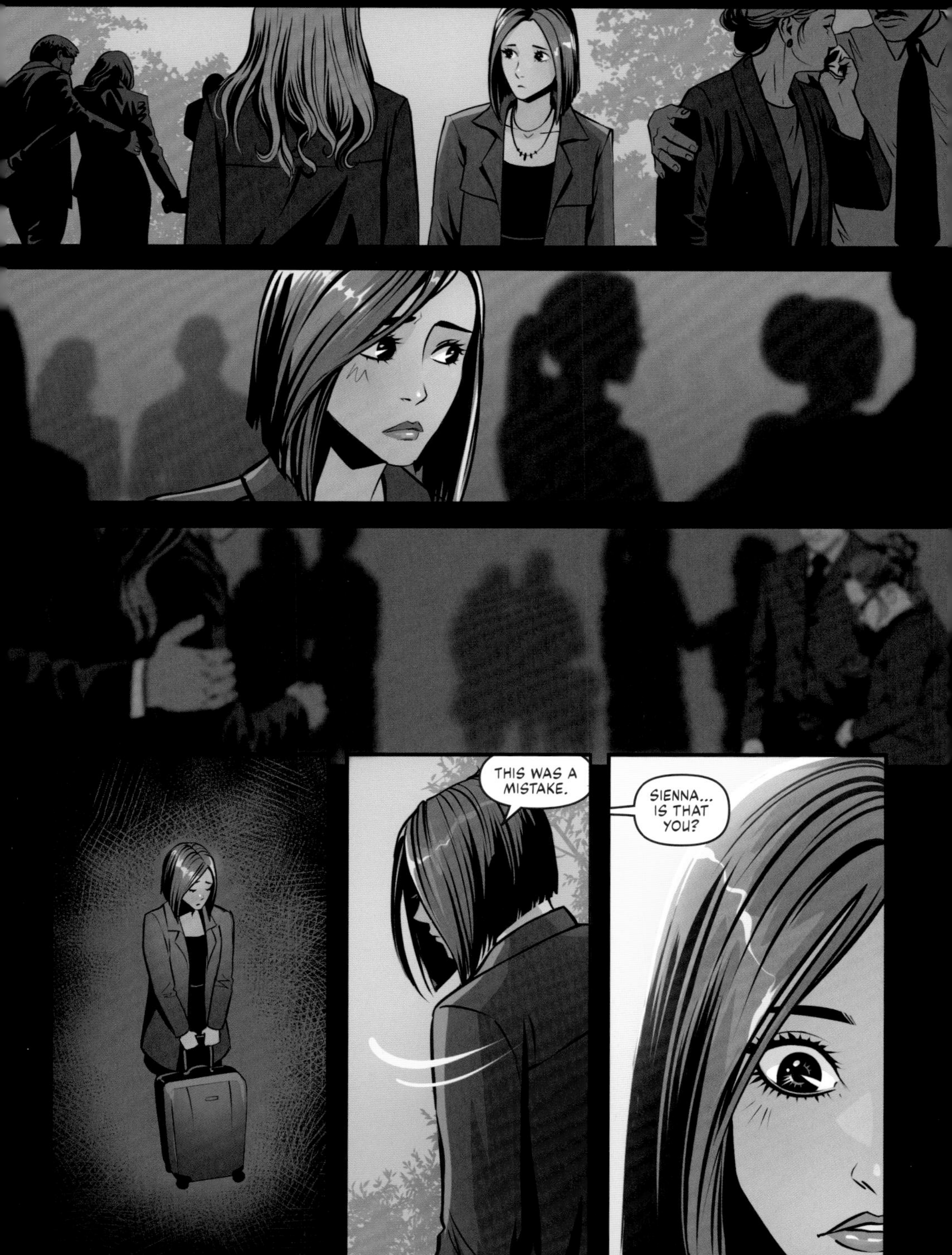
THIS WAS A MISTAKE.
SIENNA... IS THAT YOU?

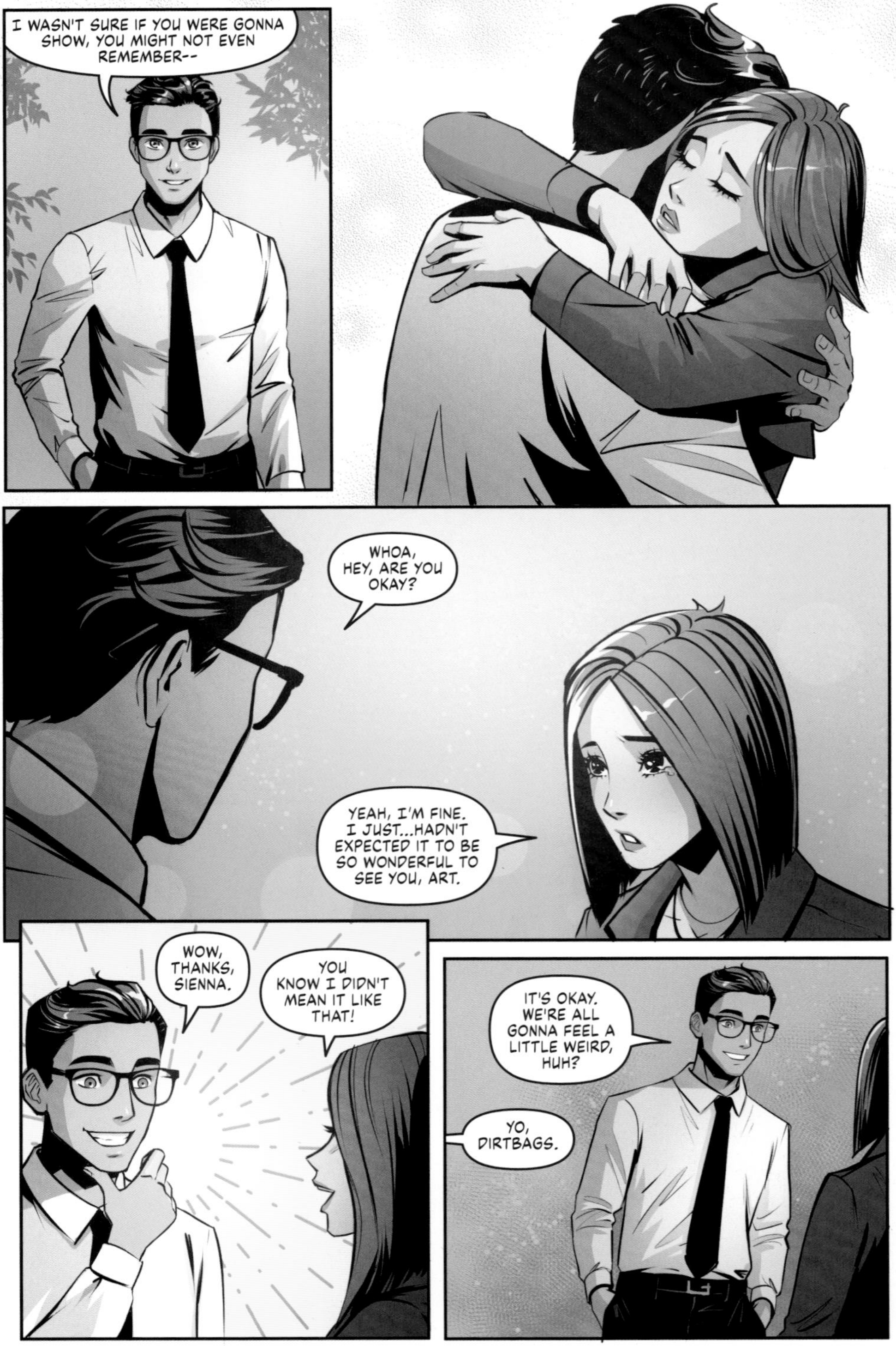
I WASN'T SURE IF YOU WERE GONNA SHOW, YOU MIGHT NOT EVEN REMEMBER--
WHOA, HEY, ARE YOU OKAY?
YEAH, I'M FINE. I JUST...HADN'T EXPECTED IT TO BE SO WONDERFUL TO SEE YOU, ART.
WOW, THANKS, SIENNA.
YOU KNOW I DIDN'T MEAN IT LIKE THAT!
IT'S OKAY. WE'RE ALL GONNA FEEL A LITTLE WEIRD, HUH?
YO, DIRTBAGS.

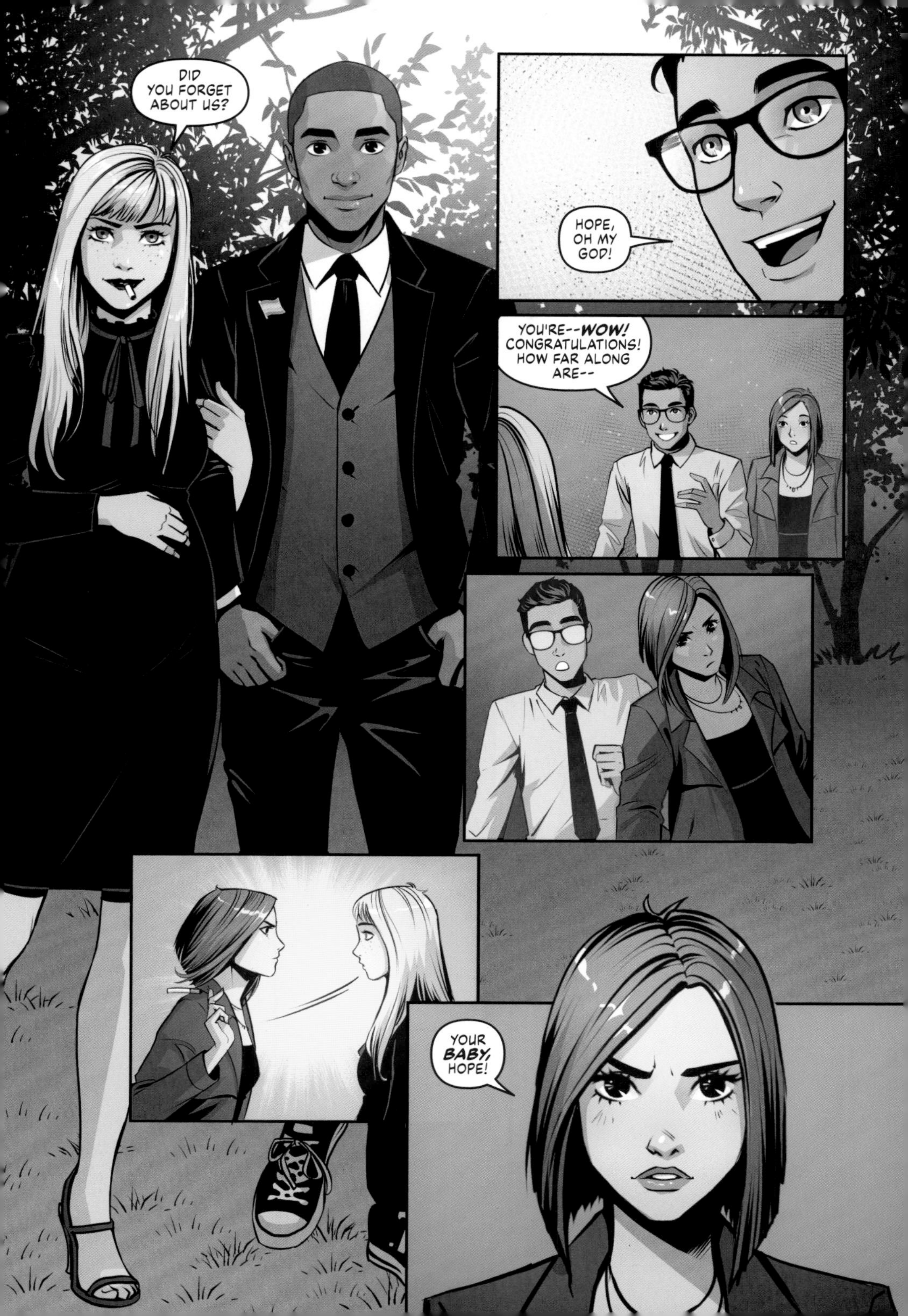
DID YOU FORGET ABOUT US?
HOPE, OH MY GOD!
YOU'RE--*WOW!* CONGRATULATIONS! HOW FAR ALONG ARE--
YOUR *BABY,* HOPE!

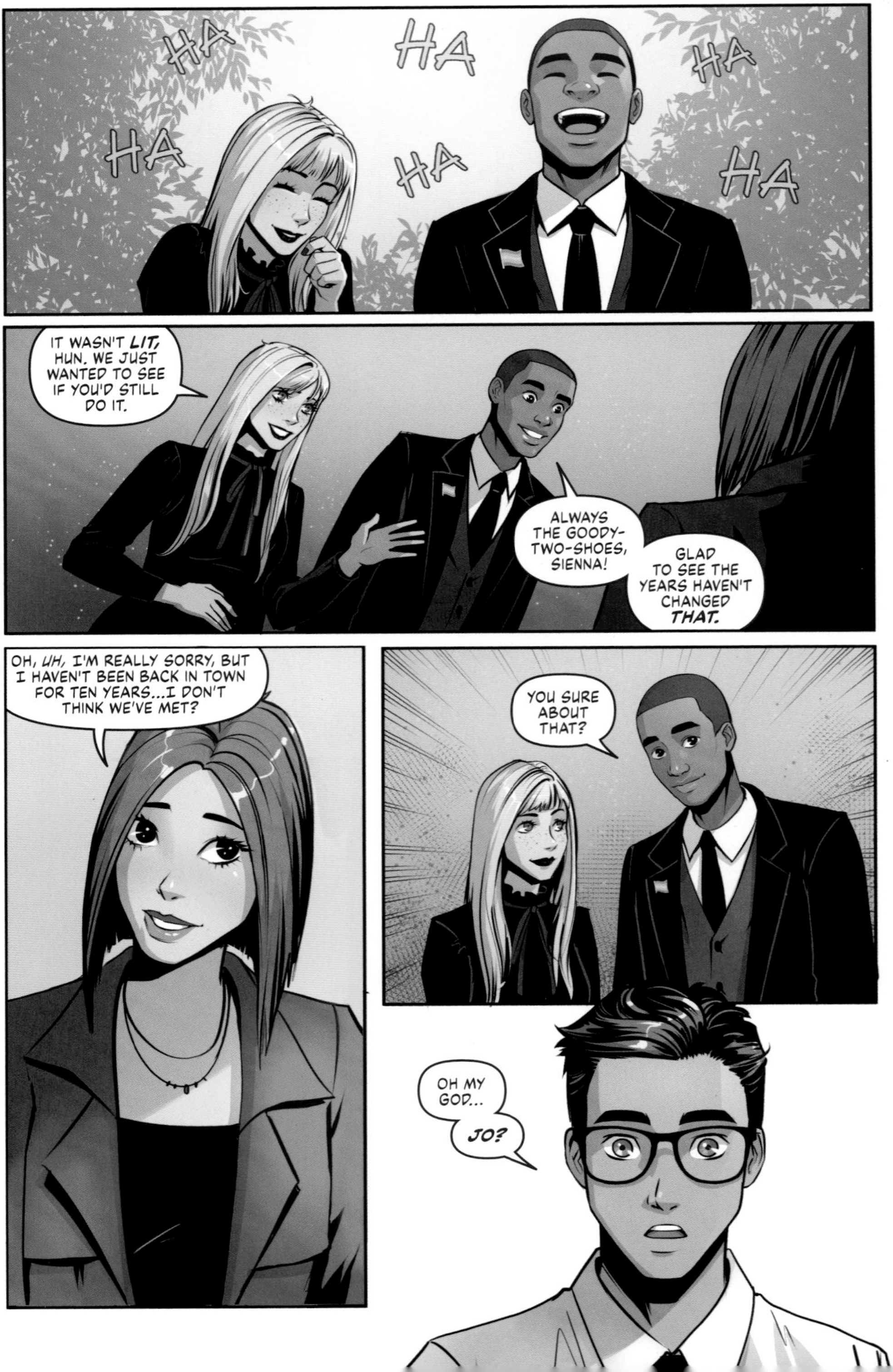
HA
HA
HA
HA
HA
HA
IT WASN'T *LIT,* HUN. WE JUST WANTED TO SEE IF YOU'D STILL DO IT.
ALWAYS THE GOODY-TWO-SHOES, SIENNA!
GLAD TO SEE THE YEARS HAVEN'T CHANGED *THAT.*
OH, *UH,* I'M REALLY SORRY, BUT I HAVEN'T BEEN BACK IN TOWN FOR TEN YEARS...I DON'T THINK WE'VE MET?
YOU SURE ABOUT THAT?
OH MY GOD...
JO?

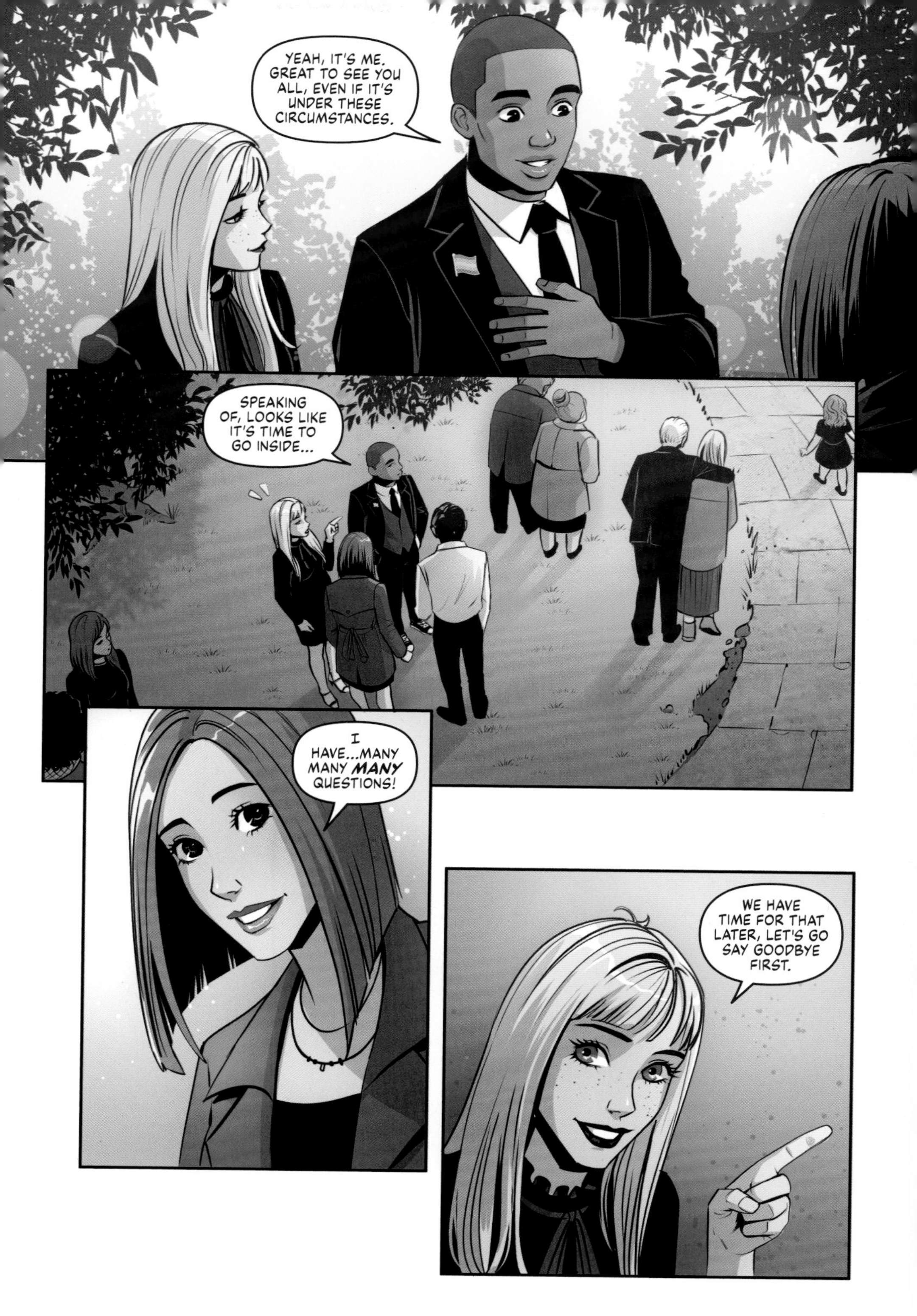
YEAH, IT'S ME. GREAT TO SEE YOU ALL, EVEN IF IT'S UNDER THESE CIRCUMSTANCES.
SPEAKING OF, LOOKS LIKE IT'S TIME TO GO INSIDE...
I HAVE...MANY MANY ***MANY*** QUESTIONS!
WE HAVE TIME FOR THAT LATER, LET'S GO SAY GOODBYE FIRST.

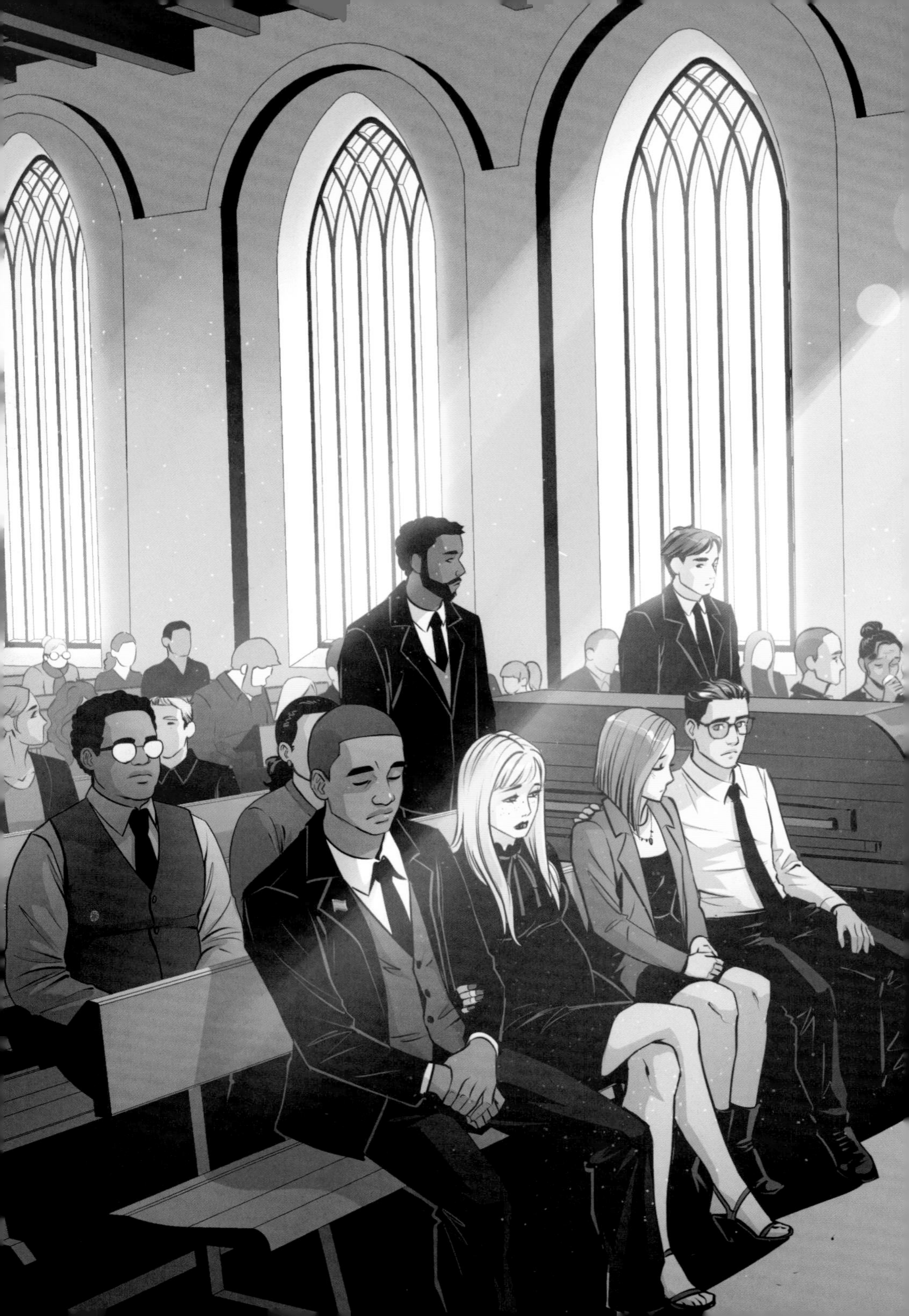

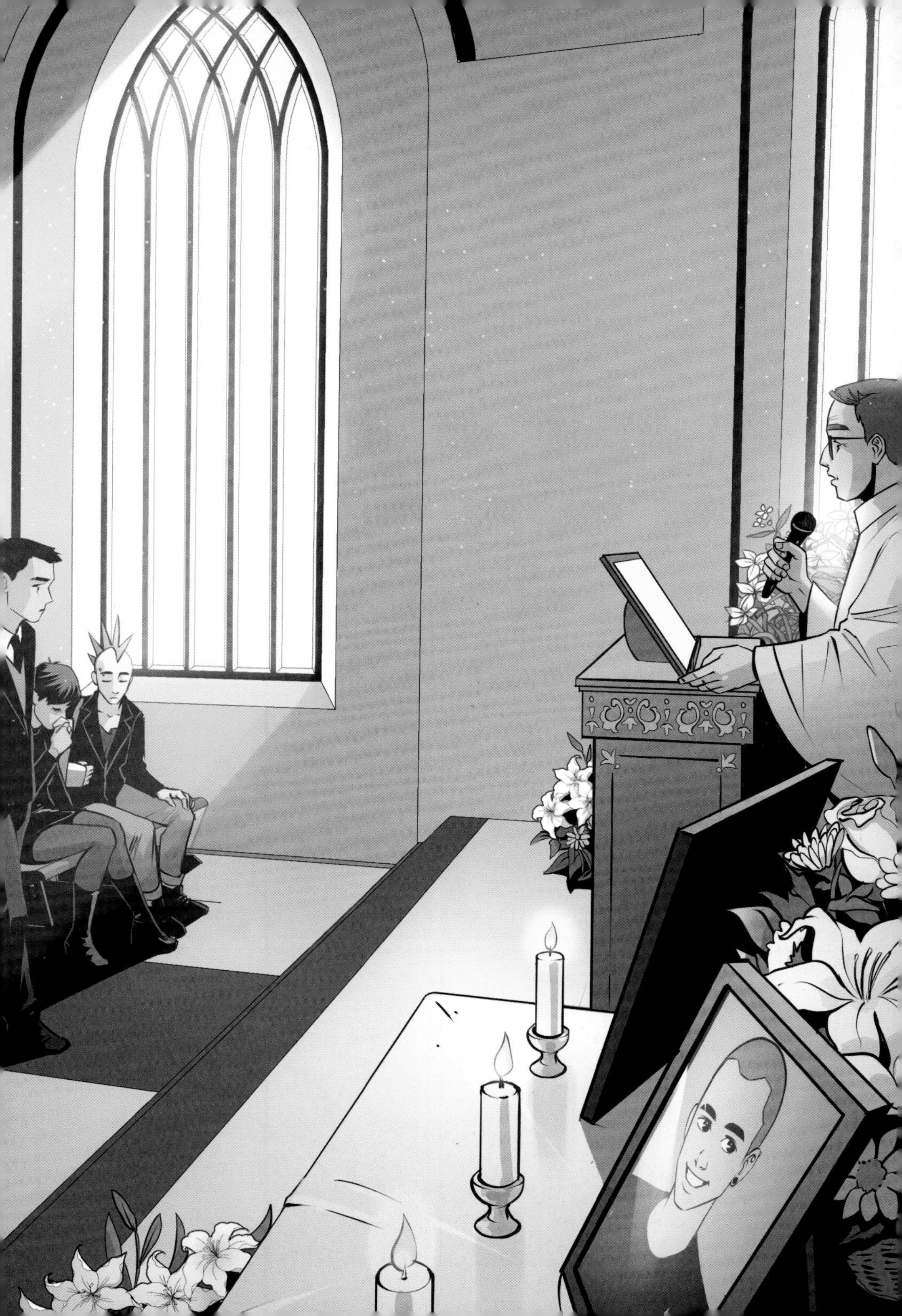

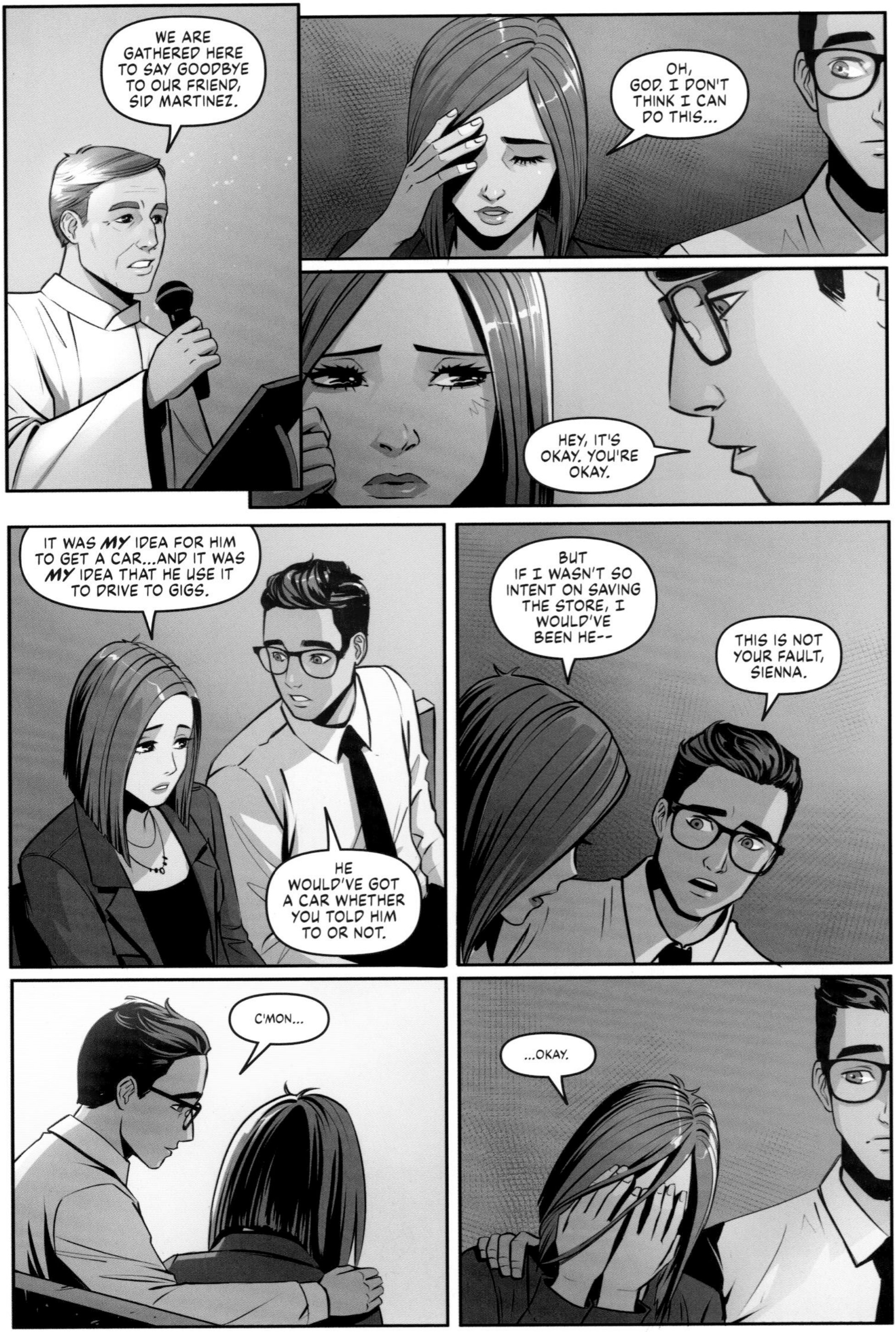
WE ARE GATHERED HERE TO SAY GOODBYE TO OUR FRIEND, SID MARTINEZ.
OH, GOD. I DON'T THINK I CAN DO THIS...
HEY, IT'S OKAY. YOU'RE OKAY.
IT WAS *MY* IDEA FOR HIM TO GET A CAR...AND IT WAS *MY* IDEA THAT HE USE IT TO DRIVE TO GIGS.
HE WOULD'VE GOT A CAR WHETHER YOU TOLD HIM TO OR NOT.
BUT IF I WASN'T SO INTENT ON SAVING THE STORE, I WOULD'VE BEEN HE--
THIS IS NOT YOUR FAULT, SIENNA.
C'MON...
...OKAY.

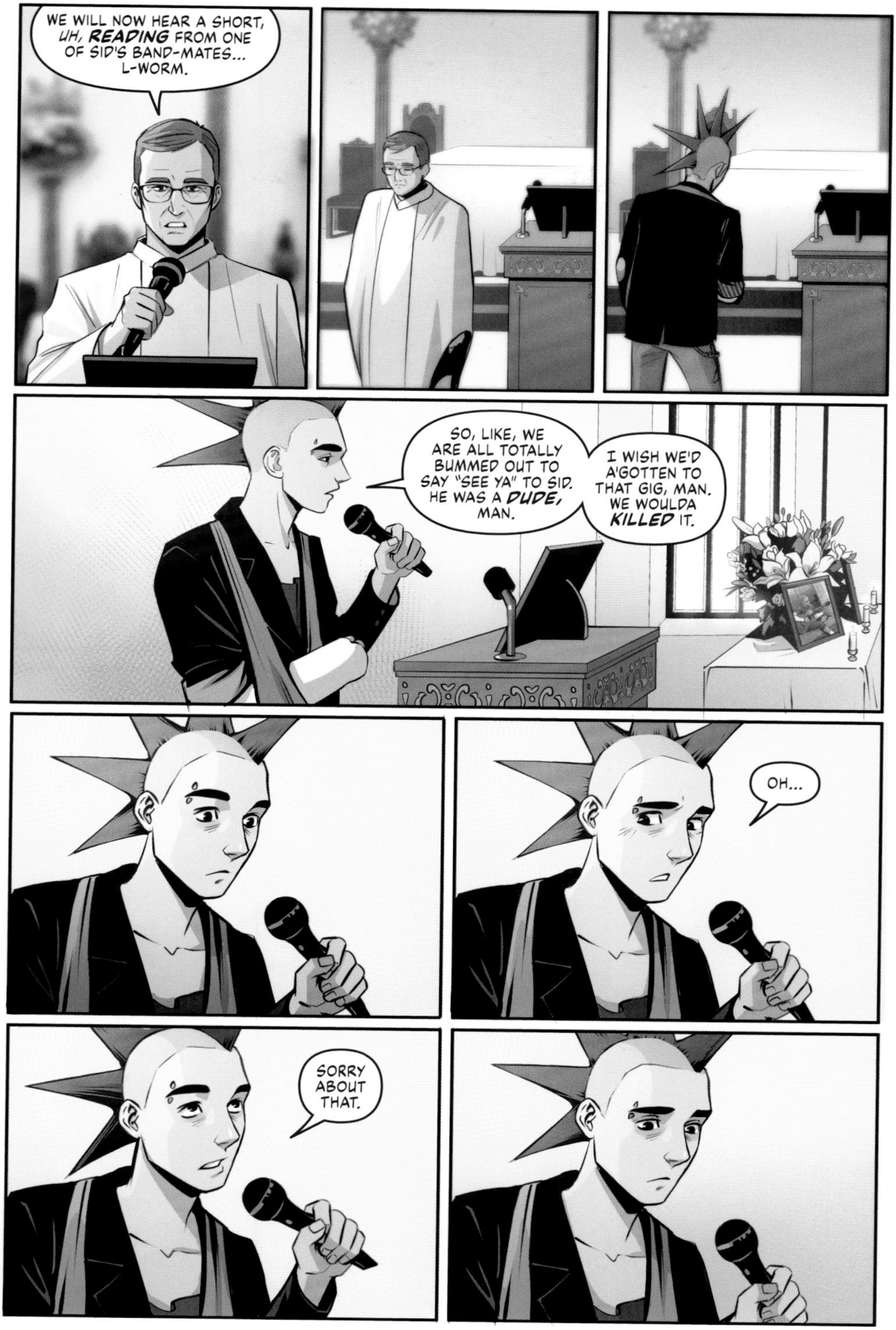
WE WILL NOW HEAR A SHORT, UH, READING FROM ONE OF SID'S BAND-MATES... L-WORM.
SO, LIKE, WE ARE ALL TOTALLY BUMMED OUT TO SAY "SEE YA" TO SID. HE WAS A DUDE, MAN.
I WISH WE'D A'GOTTEN TO THAT GIG, MAN. WE WOULDA KILLED IT.
OH...
SORRY ABOUT THAT.

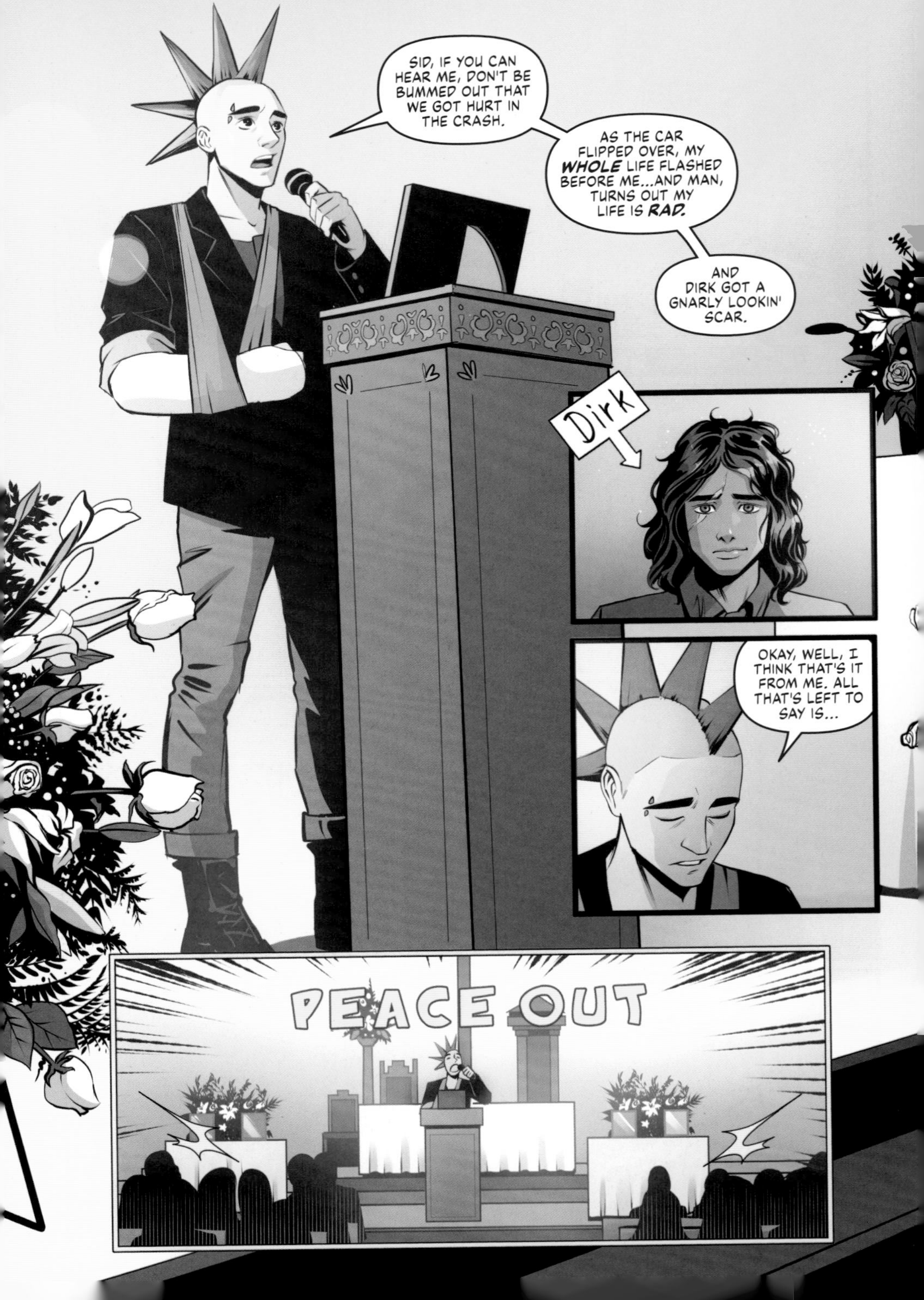
SID, IF YOU CAN HEAR ME, DON'T BE BUMMED OUT THAT WE GOT HURT IN THE CRASH.
AS THE CAR FLIPPED OVER, MY ***WHOLE*** LIFE FLASHED BEFORE ME...AND MAN, TURNS OUT MY LIFE IS ***RAD.***
AND DIRK GOT A GNARLY LOOKIN' SCAR.
Dirk
OKAY, WELL, I THINK THAT'S IT FROM ME. ALL THAT'S LEFT TO SAY IS...
PEACE OUT

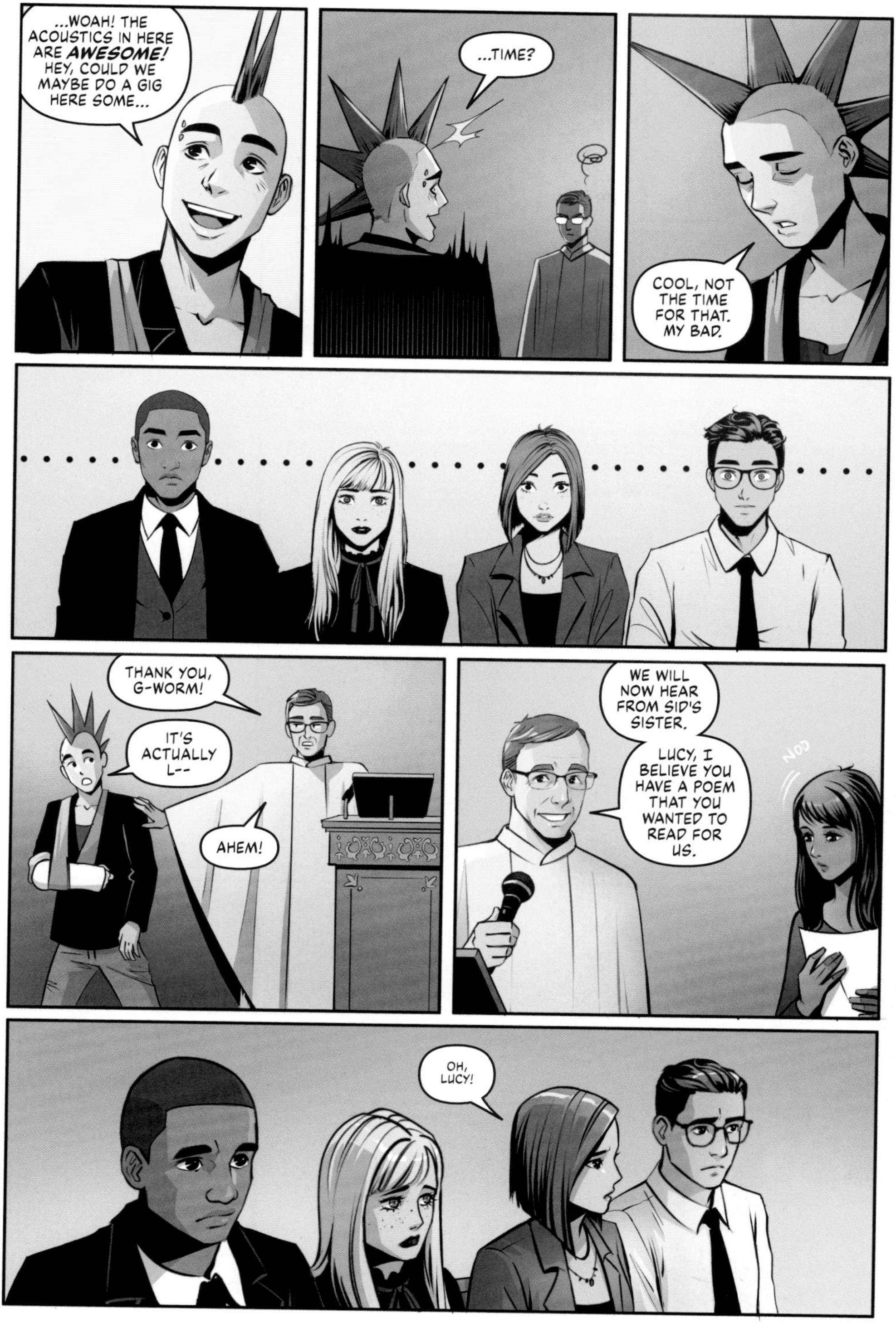
...WOAH! THE ACOUSTICS IN HERE ARE AWESOME! HEY, COULD WE MAYBE DO A GIG HERE SOME...
...TIME?
COOL, NOT THE TIME FOR THAT. MY BAD.
THANK YOU, G-WORM!
IT'S ACTUALLY L--
AHEM!
WE WILL NOW HEAR FROM SID'S SISTER.
LUCY, I BELIEVE YOU HAVE A POEM THAT YOU WANTED TO READ FOR US.
NOD
OH, LUCY!

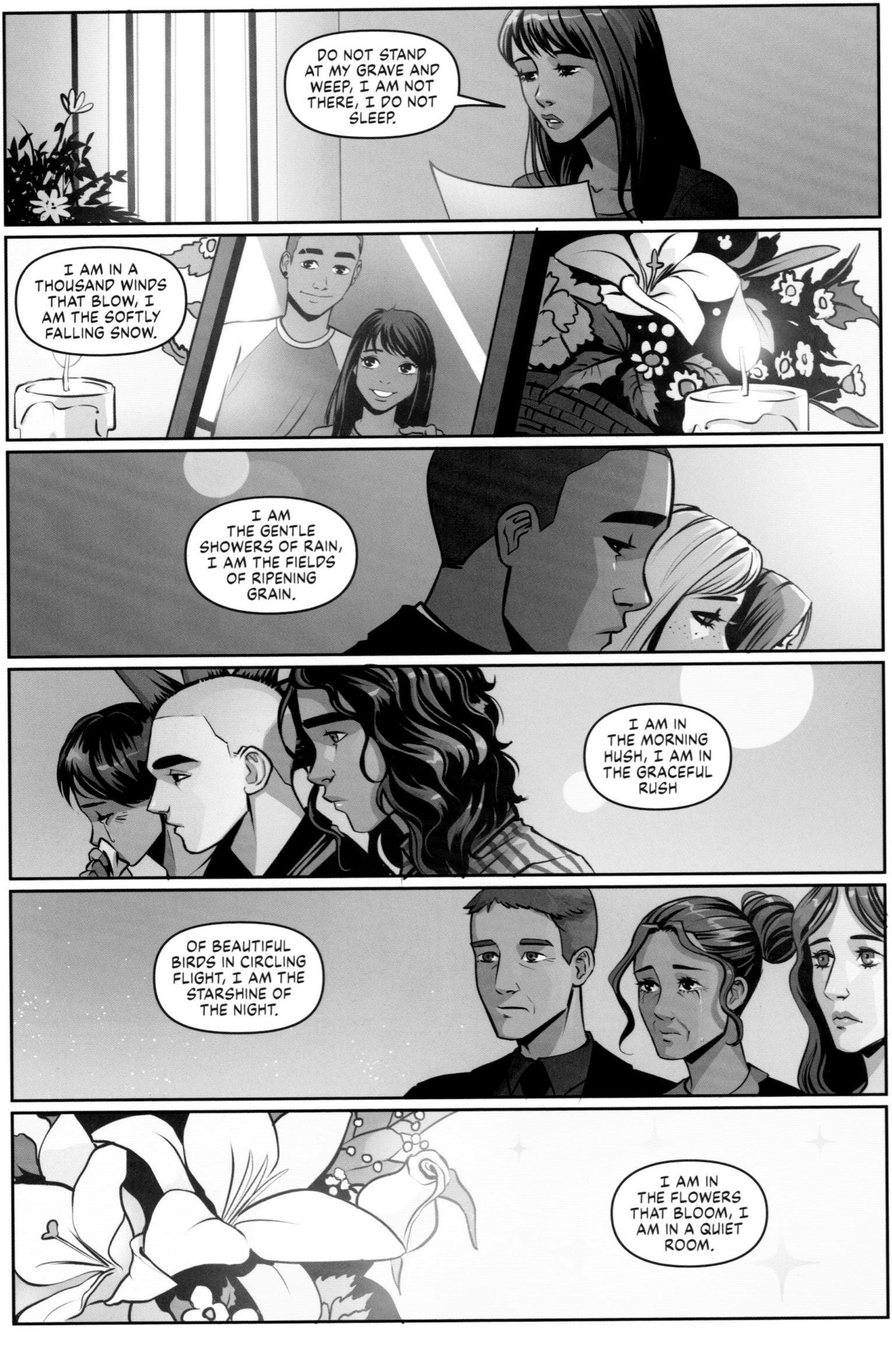
DO NOT STAND AT MY GRAVE AND WEEP, I AM NOT THERE, I DO NOT SLEEP.
I AM IN A THOUSAND WINDS THAT BLOW, I AM THE SOFTLY FALLING SNOW.
I AM THE GENTLE SHOWERS OF RAIN, I AM THE FIELDS OF RIPENING GRAIN.
I AM IN THE MORNING HUSH, I AM IN THE GRACEFUL RUSH
OF BEAUTIFUL BIRDS IN CIRCLING FLIGHT, I AM THE STARSHINE OF THE NIGHT.
I AM IN THE FLOWERS THAT BLOOM, I AM IN A QUIET ROOM.

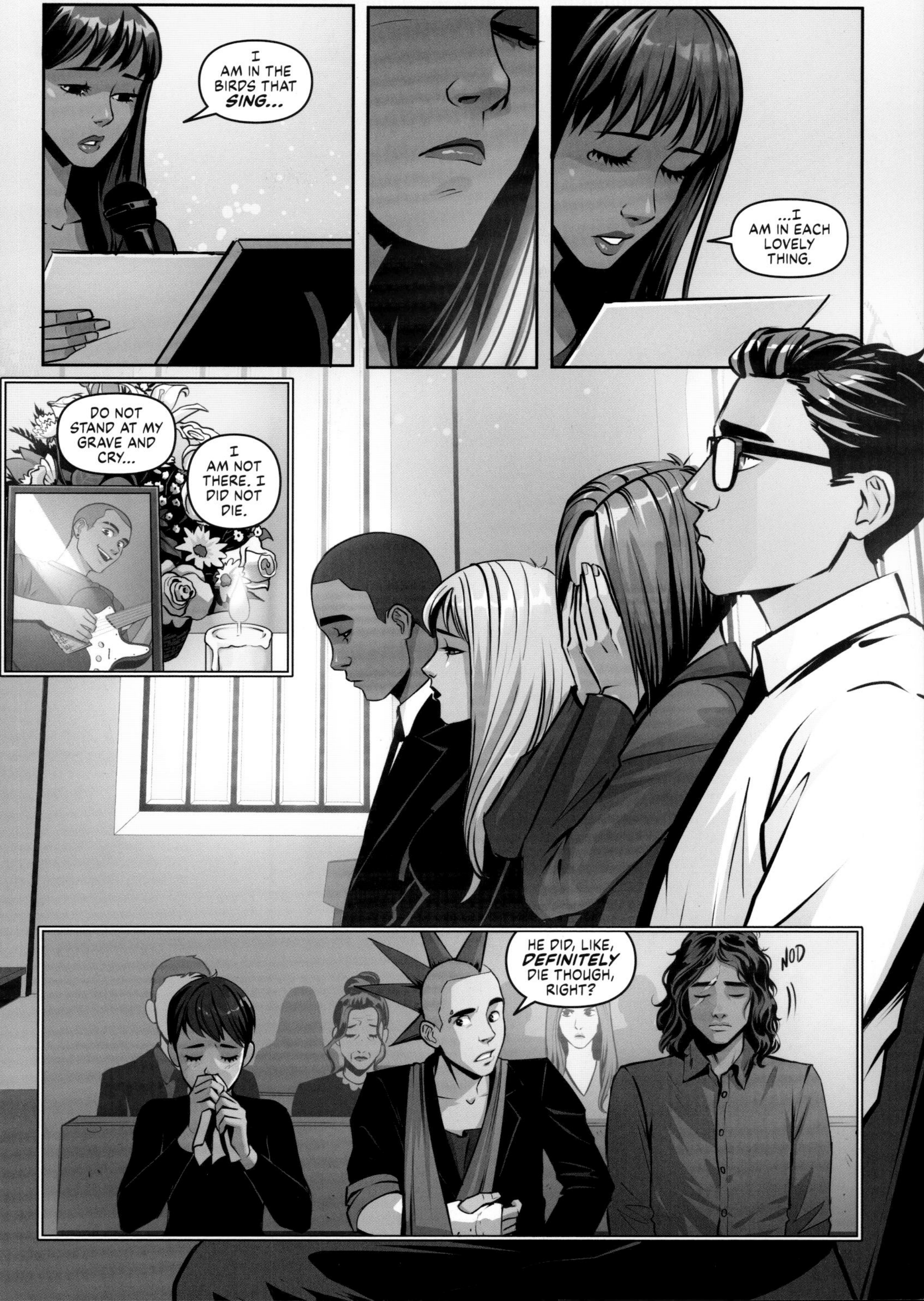
I AM IN THE BIRDS THAT SING...
...I AM IN EACH LOVELY THING.
DO NOT STAND AT MY GRAVE AND CRY...
I AM NOT THERE. I DID NOT DIE.
HE DID, LIKE, DEFINITELY DIE THOUGH, RIGHT?
NOD

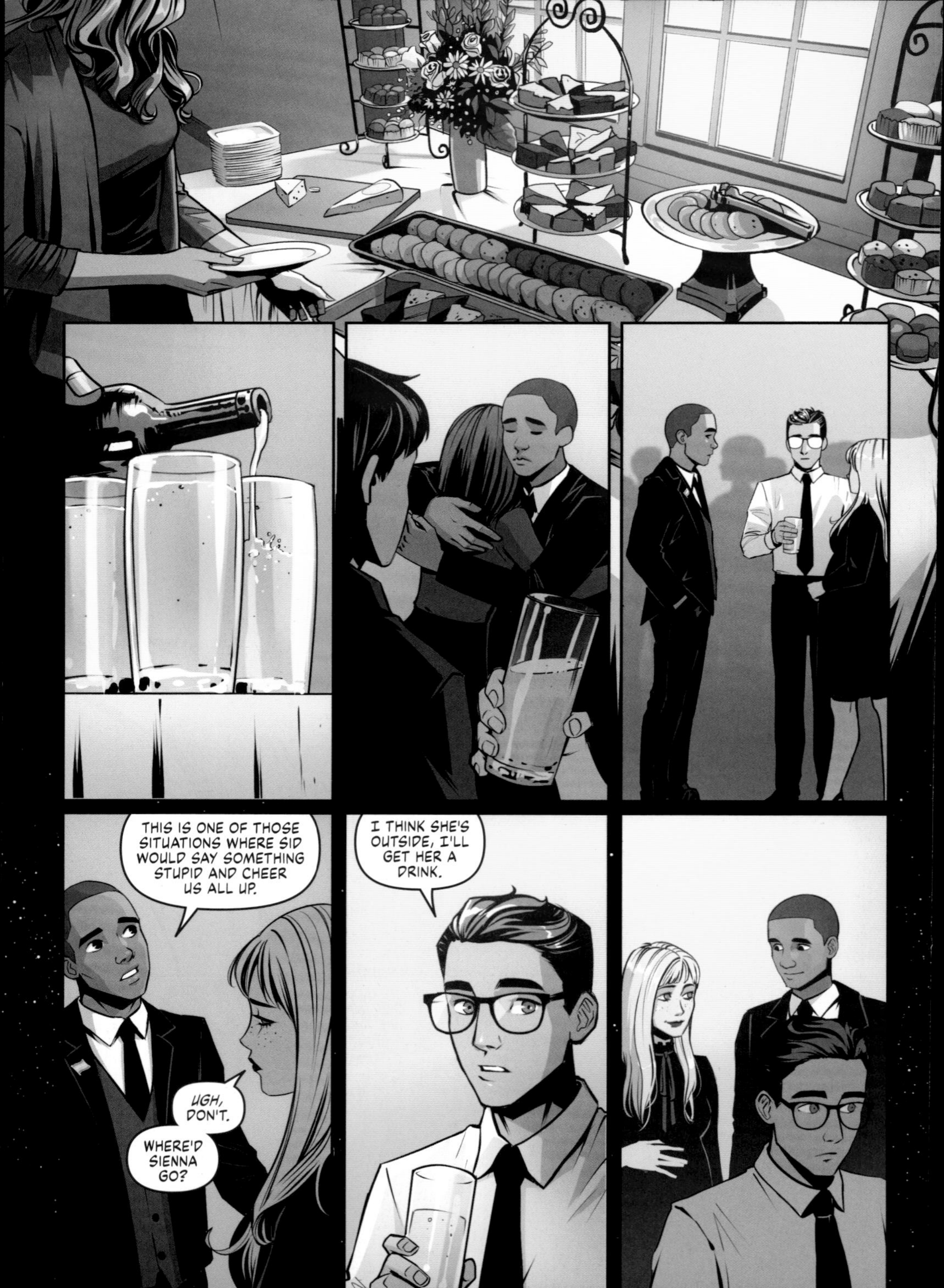
THIS IS ONE OF THOSE SITUATIONS WHERE SID WOULD SAY SOMETHING STUPID AND CHEER US ALL UP.
UGH, DON'T.
WHERE'D SIENNA GO?
I THINK SHE'S OUTSIDE, I'LL GET HER A DRINK.

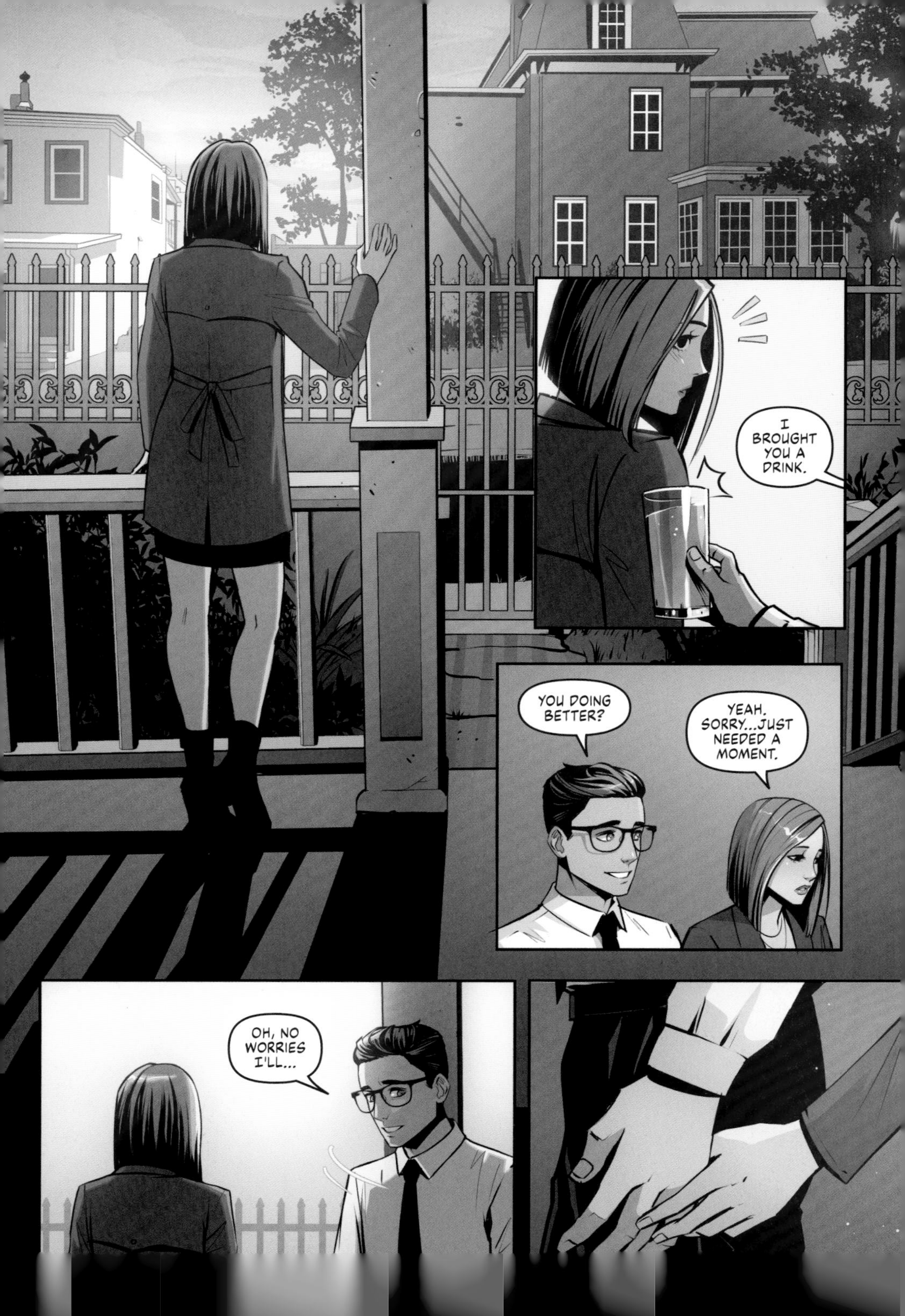
I BROUGHT YOU A DRINK.
YOU DOING BETTER?
YEAH. SORRY...JUST NEEDED A MOMENT.
OH, NO WORRIES I'LL...

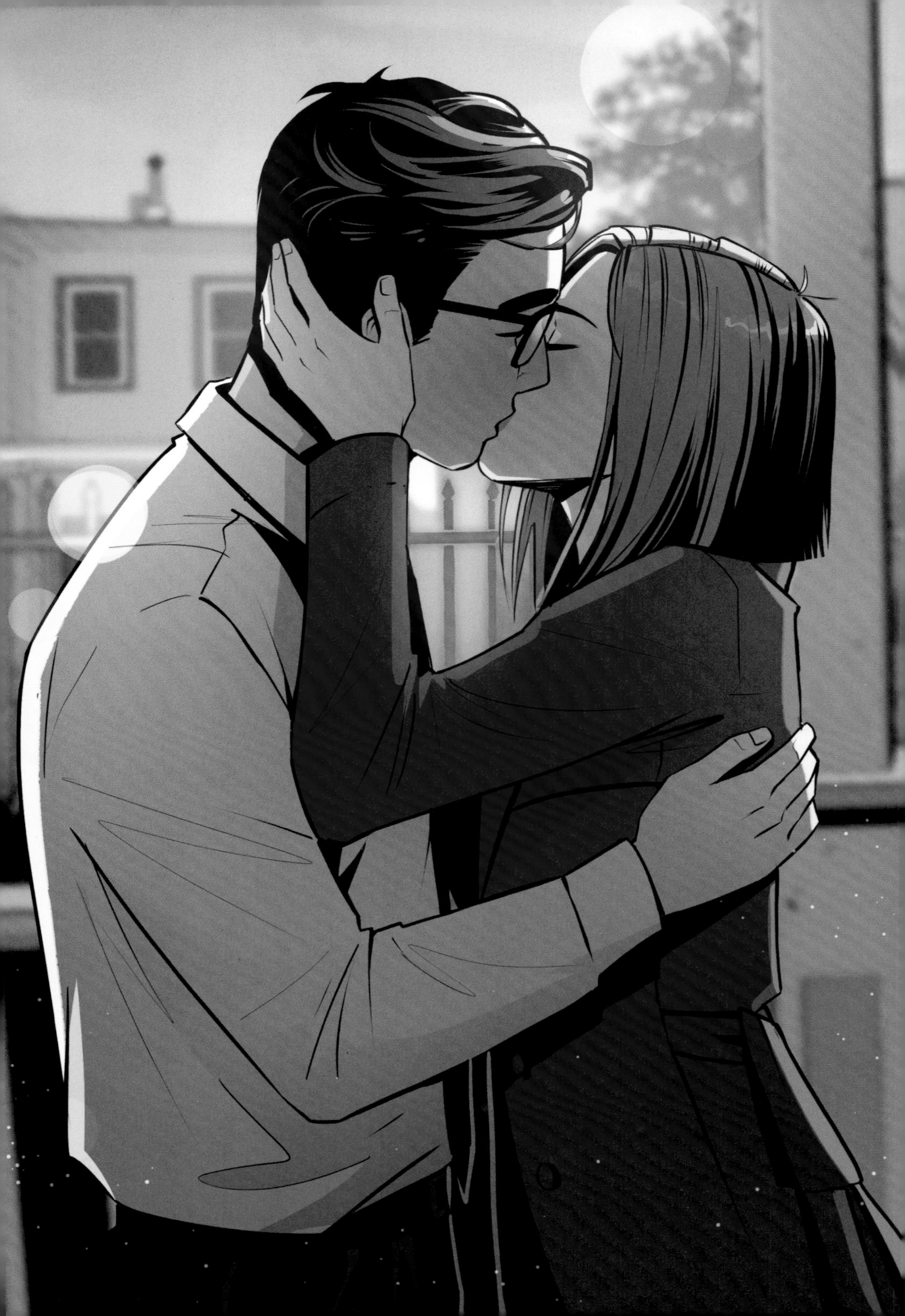

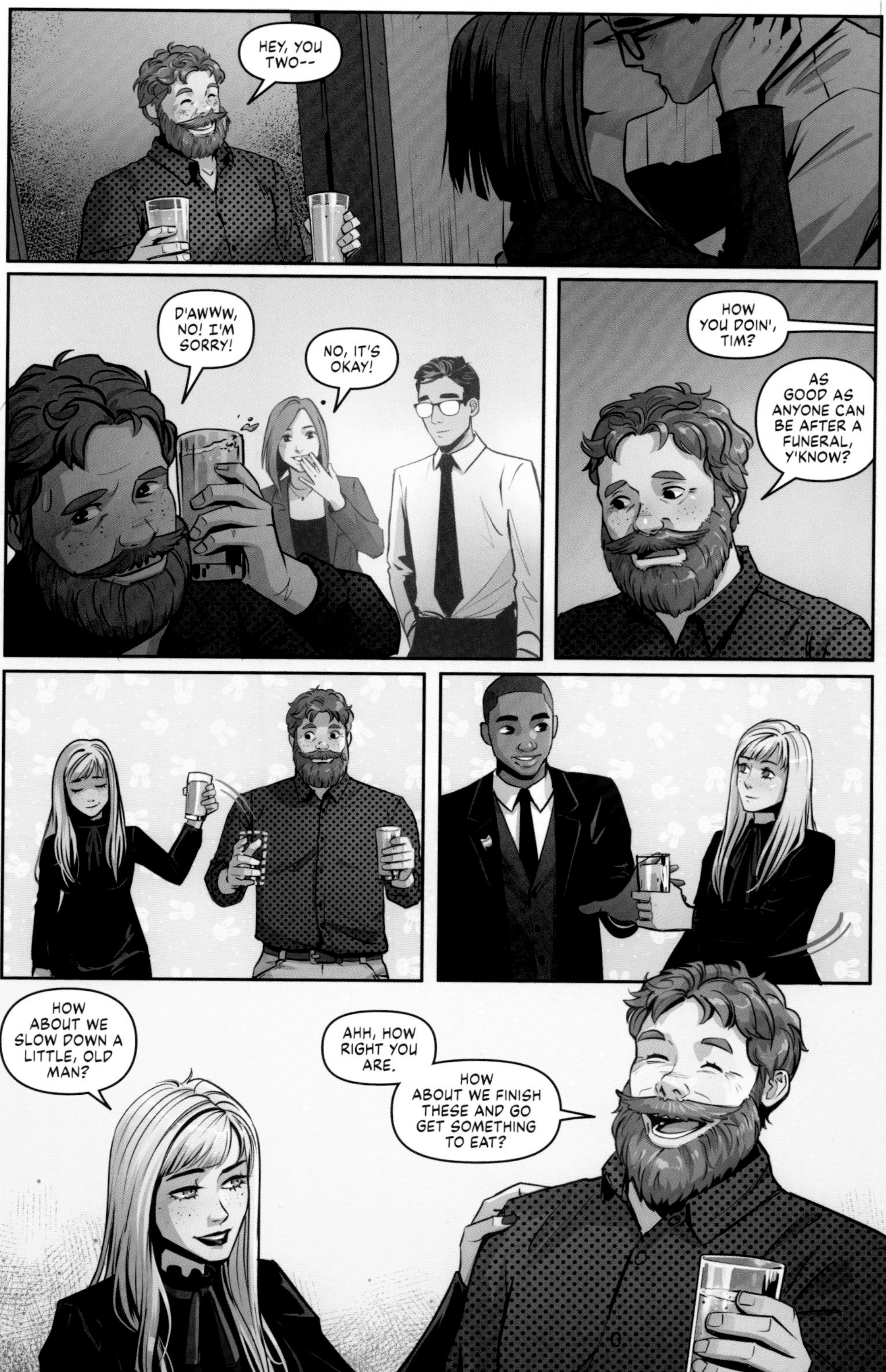
HEY, YOU TWO--
D'AWWW, NO! I'M SORRY!
NO, IT'S OKAY!
HOW YOU DOIN', TIM?
AS GOOD AS ANYONE CAN BE AFTER A FUNERAL, Y'KNOW?
HOW ABOUT WE SLOW DOWN A LITTLE, OLD MAN?
AHH, HOW RIGHT YOU ARE.
HOW ABOUT WE FINISH THESE AND GO GET SOMETHING TO EAT?

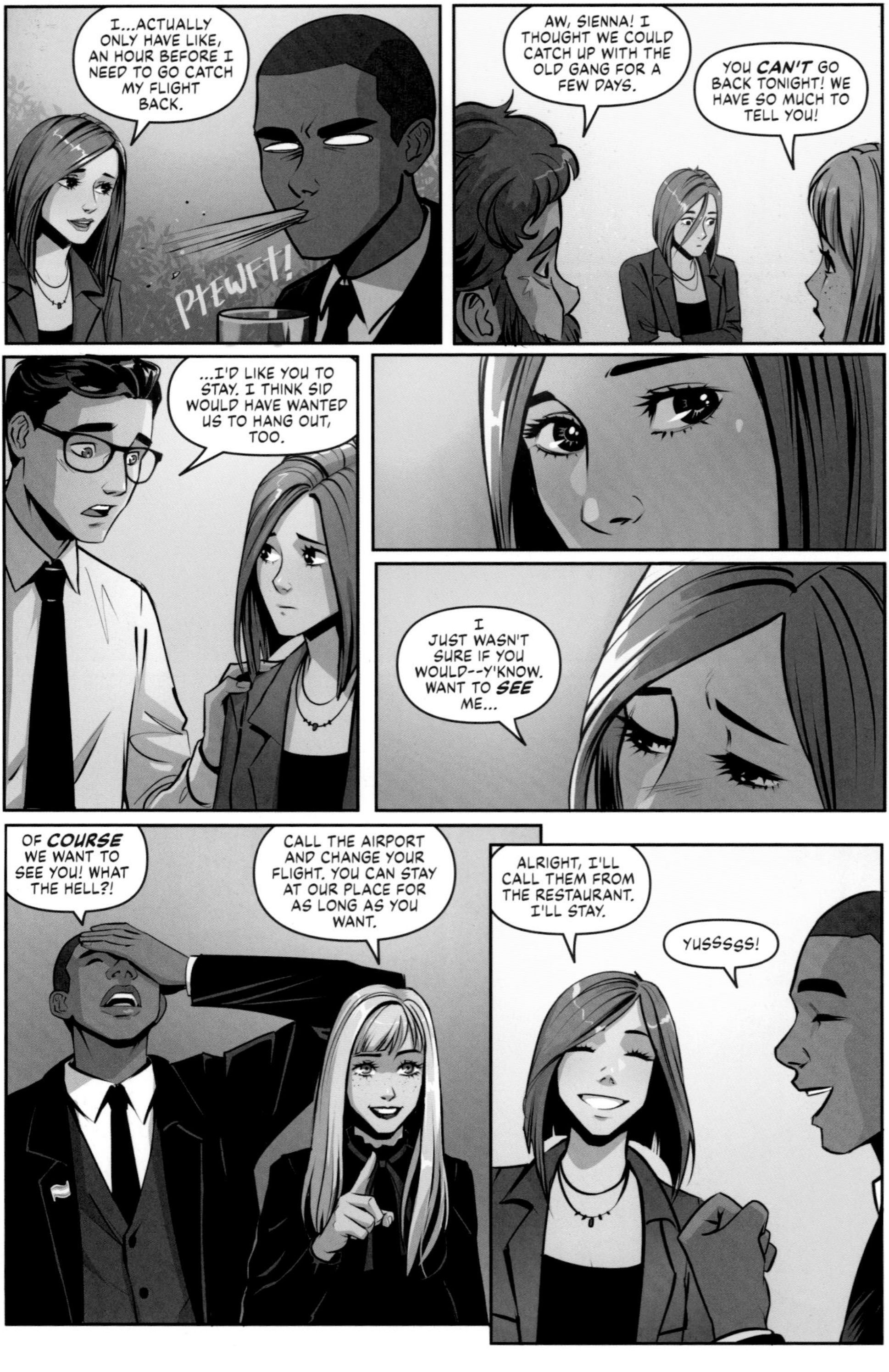
I...ACTUALLY ONLY HAVE LIKE, AN HOUR BEFORE I NEED TO GO CATCH MY FLIGHT BACK.
PFEWFT!
AW, SIENNA! I THOUGHT WE COULD CATCH UP WITH THE OLD GANG FOR A FEW DAYS.
YOU CAN'T GO BACK TONIGHT! WE HAVE SO MUCH TO TELL YOU!
...I'D LIKE YOU TO STAY. I THINK SID WOULD HAVE WANTED US TO HANG OUT, TOO.
I JUST WASN'T SURE IF YOU WOULD--Y'KNOW. WANT TO SEE ME...
OF COURSE WE WANT TO SEE YOU! WHAT THE HELL?!
CALL THE AIRPORT AND CHANGE YOUR FLIGHT. YOU CAN STAY AT OUR PLACE FOR AS LONG AS YOU WANT.
ALRIGHT, I'LL CALL THEM FROM THE RESTAURANT. I'LL STAY.
YUSSSSS!

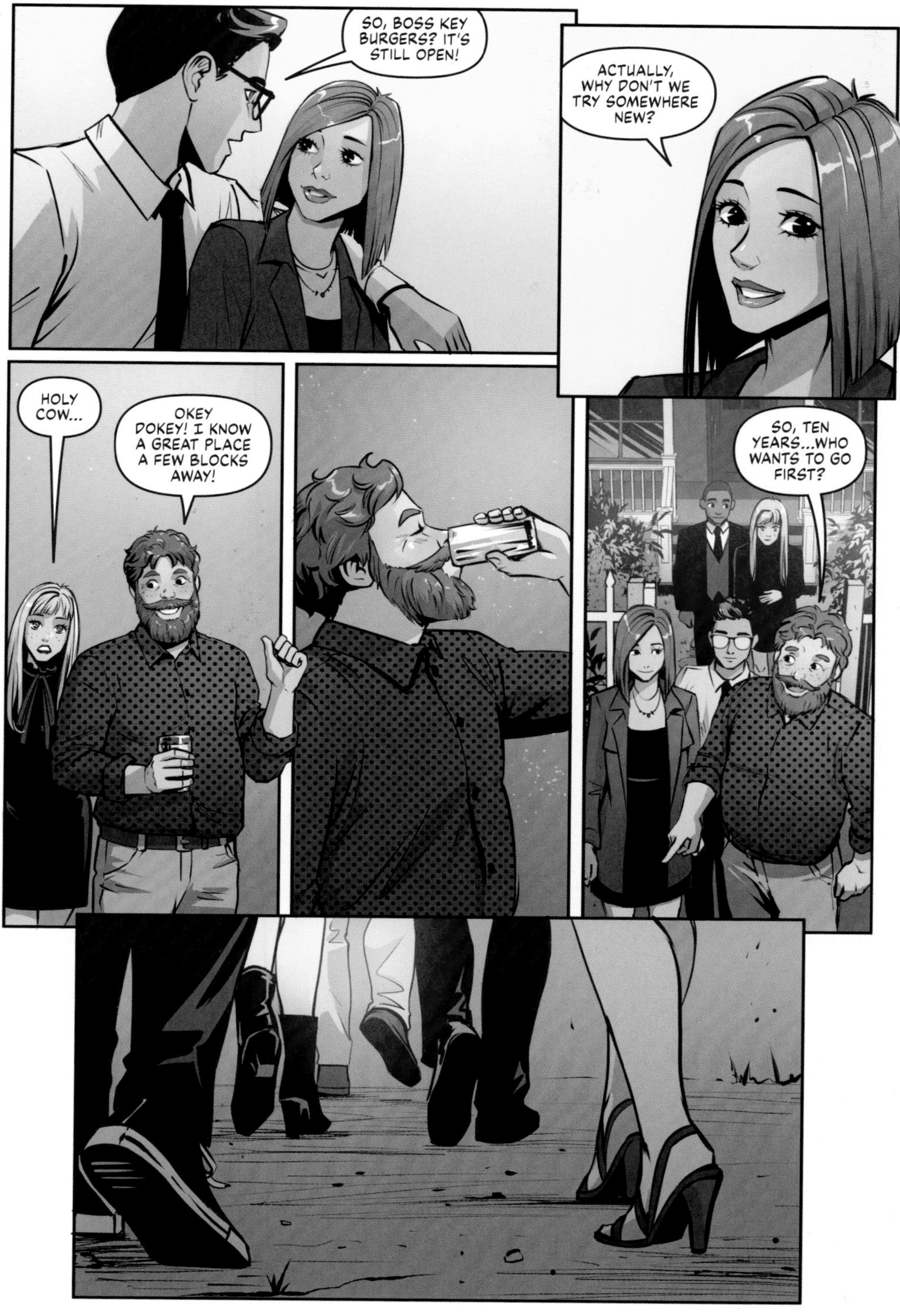
SO, BOSS KEY BURGERS? IT'S STILL OPEN!
ACTUALLY, WHY DON'T WE TRY SOMEWHERE NEW?
HOLY COW...
OKEY DOKEY! I KNOW A GREAT PLACE A FEW BLOCKS AWAY!
SO, TEN YEARS...WHO WANTS TO GO FIRST?

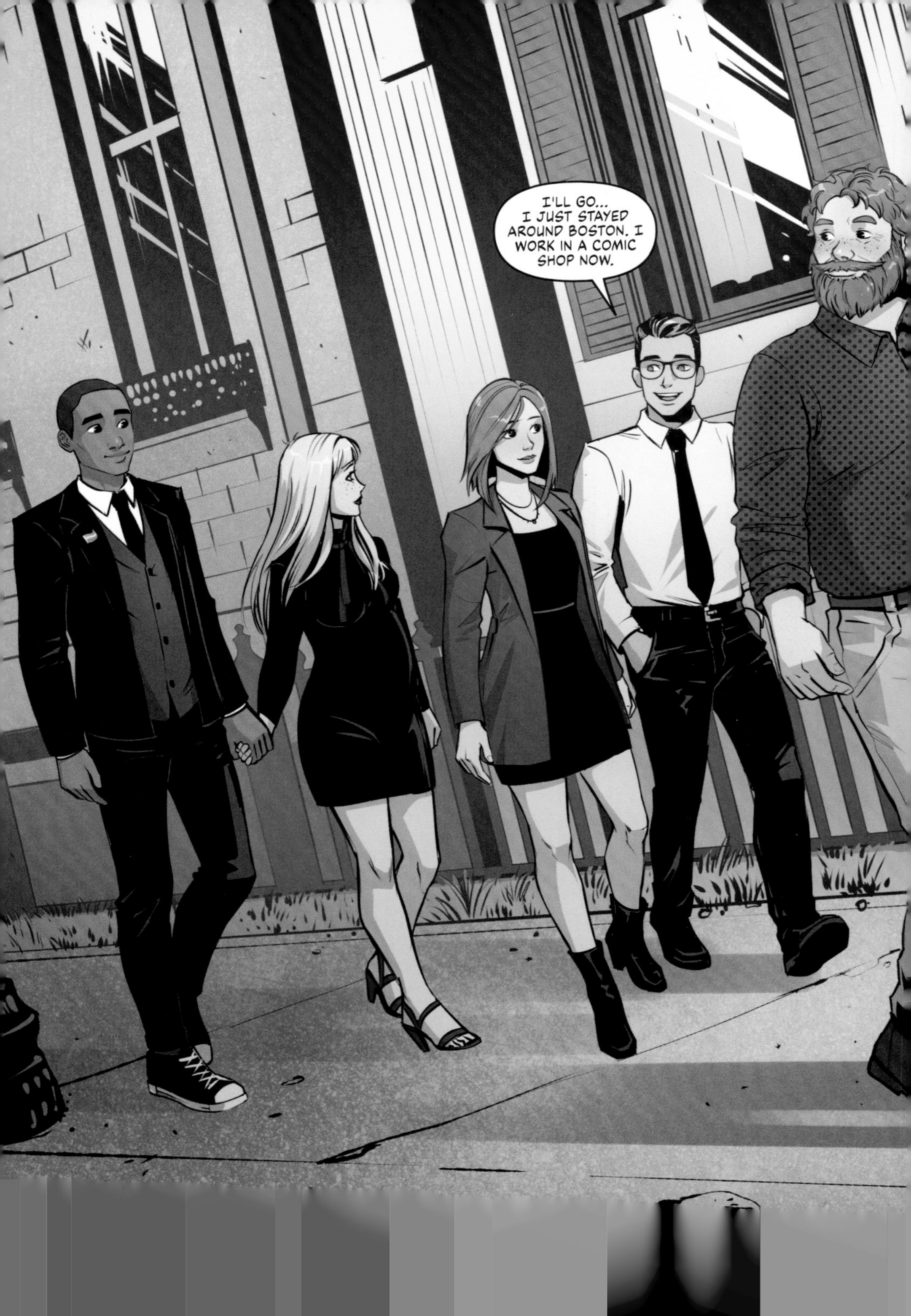
I'LL GO... I JUST STAYED AROUND BOSTON. I WORK IN A COMIC SHOP NOW.

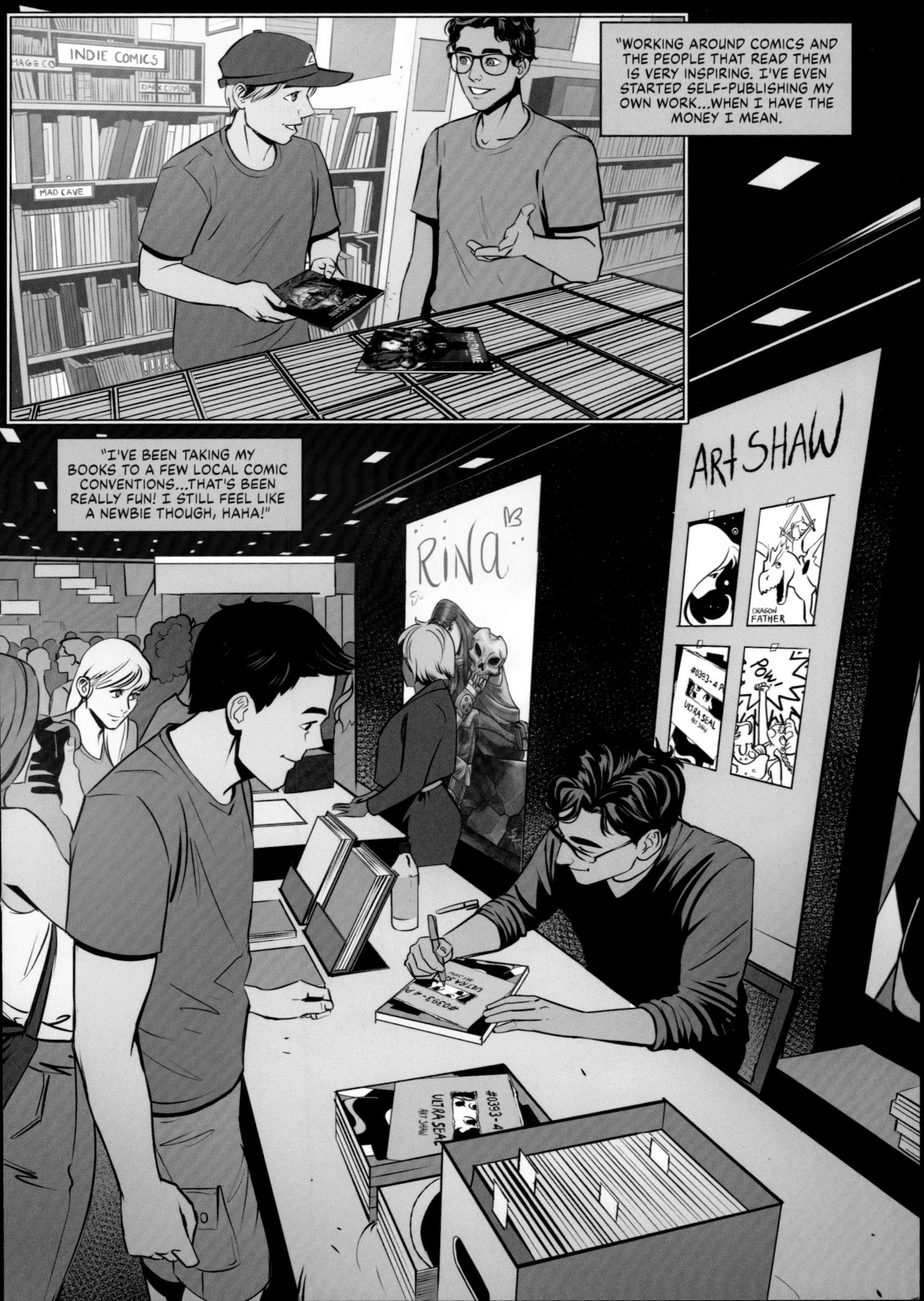
"WORKING AROUND COMICS AND THE PEOPLE THAT READ THEM IS VERY INSPIRING. I'VE EVEN STARTED SELF-PUBLISHING MY OWN WORK...WHEN I HAVE THE MONEY I MEAN.
INDIE COMICS
MAD CAVE
"I'VE BEEN TAKING MY BOOKS TO A FEW LOCAL COMIC CONVENTIONS...THAT'S BEEN REALLY FUN! I STILL FEEL LIKE A NEWBIE THOUGH, HAHA!"
ART SHAW
RINA
DRAGON FATHER
#0393-4
ULTRA SEAL
ART SHAW
POW!

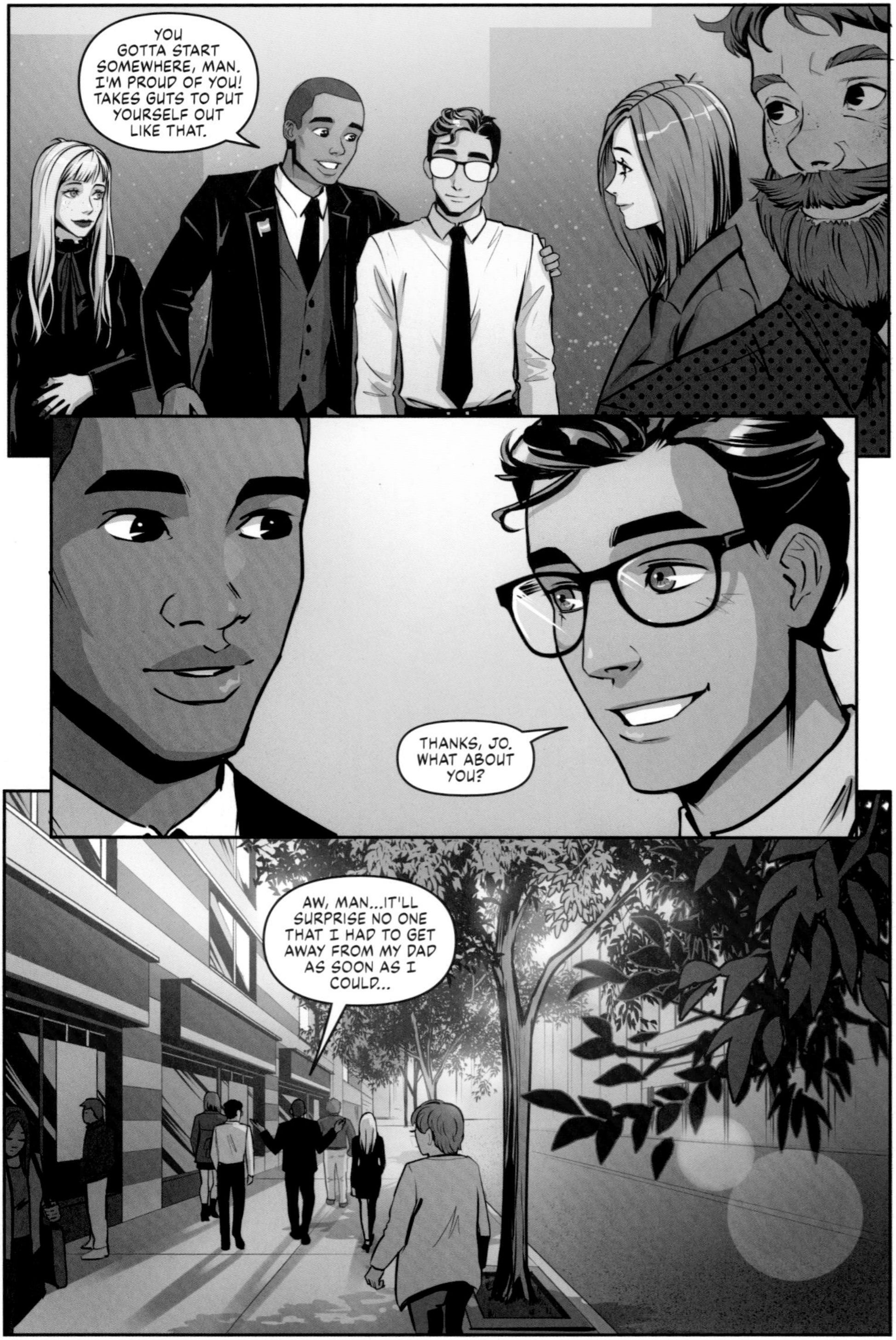
YOU GOTTA START SOMEWHERE, MAN. I'M PROUD OF YOU! TAKES GUTS TO PUT YOURSELF OUT LIKE THAT.
THANKS, JO. WHAT ABOUT YOU?
AW, MAN...IT'LL SURPRISE NO ONE THAT I HAD TO GET AWAY FROM MY DAD AS SOON AS I COULD...

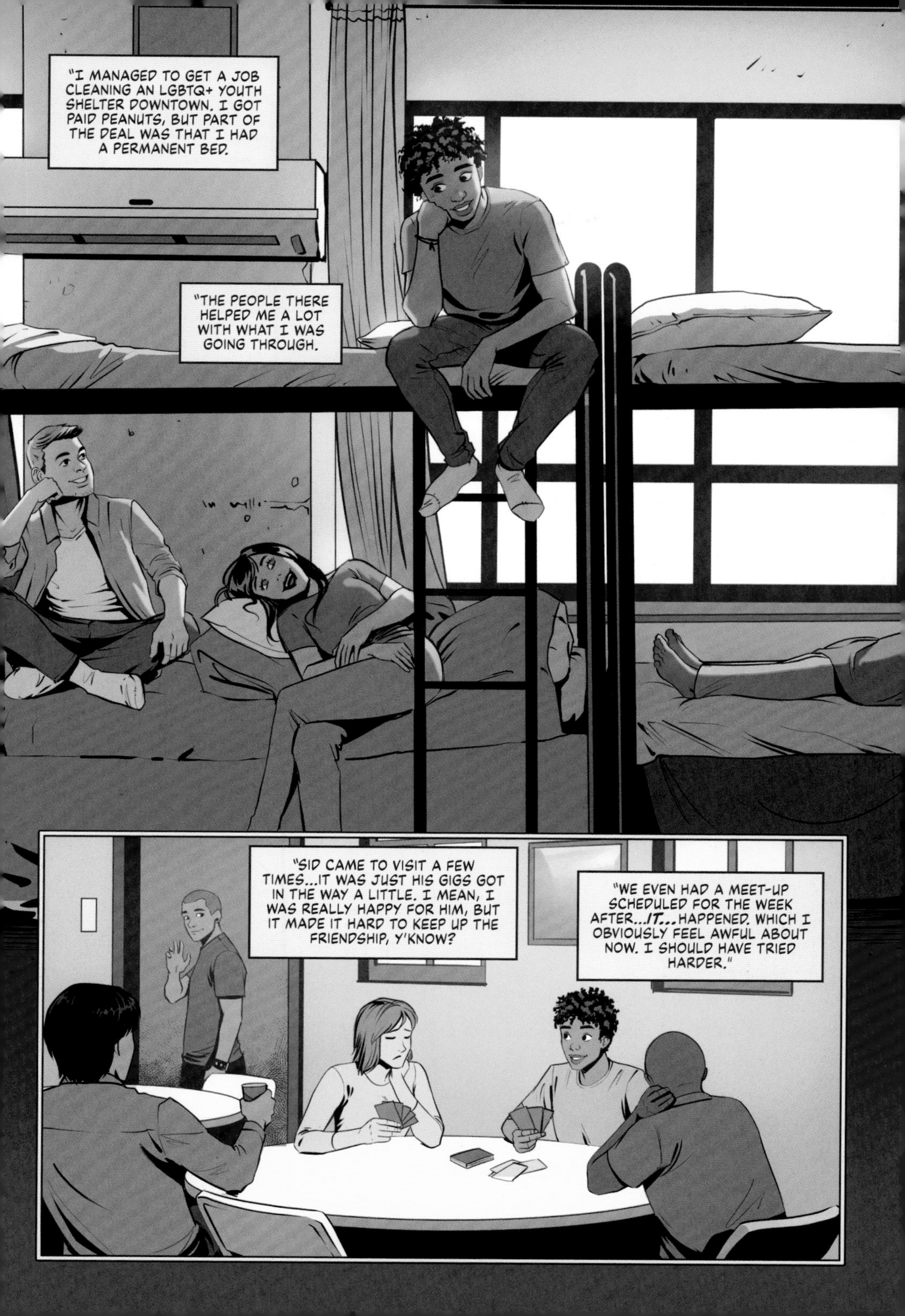
"I MANAGED TO GET A JOB CLEANING AN LGBTQ+ YOUTH SHELTER DOWNTOWN. I GOT PAID PEANUTS, BUT PART OF THE DEAL WAS THAT I HAD A PERMANENT BED.
"THE PEOPLE THERE HELPED ME A LOT WITH WHAT I WAS GOING THROUGH.
"SID CAME TO VISIT A FEW TIMES...IT WAS JUST HIS GIGS GOT IN THE WAY A LITTLE. I MEAN, I WAS REALLY HAPPY FOR HIM, BUT IT MADE IT HARD TO KEEP UP THE FRIENDSHIP, Y'KNOW?
"WE EVEN HAD A MEET-UP SCHEDULED FOR THE WEEK AFTER...*IT*...HAPPENED. WHICH I OBVIOUSLY FEEL AWFUL ABOUT NOW. I SHOULD HAVE TRIED HARDER."

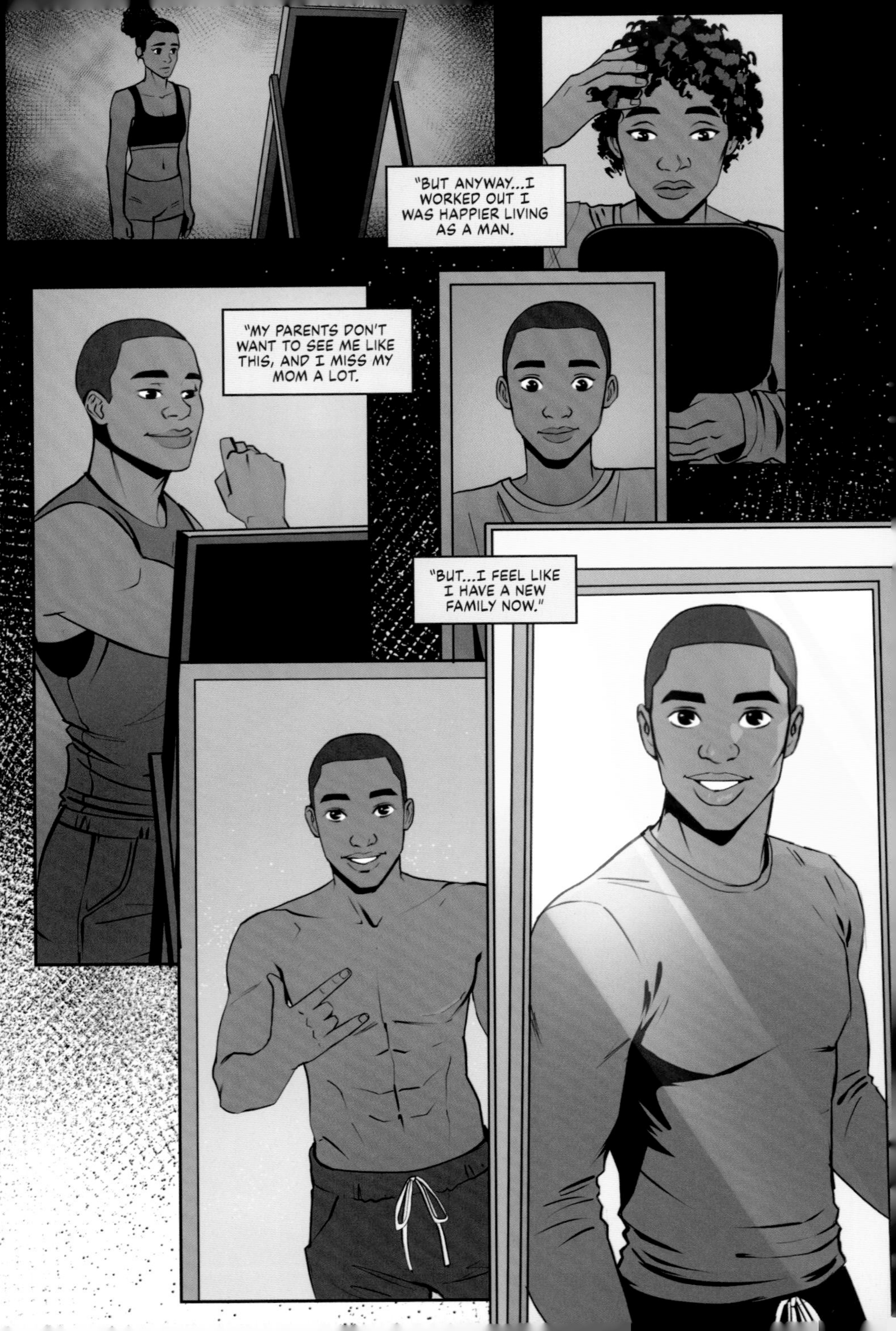
"BUT ANYWAY...I WORKED OUT I WAS HAPPIER LIVING AS A MAN.
"MY PARENTS DON'T WANT TO SEE ME LIKE THIS, AND I MISS MY MOM A LOT.
"BUT...I FEEL LIKE I HAVE A NEW FAMILY NOW."

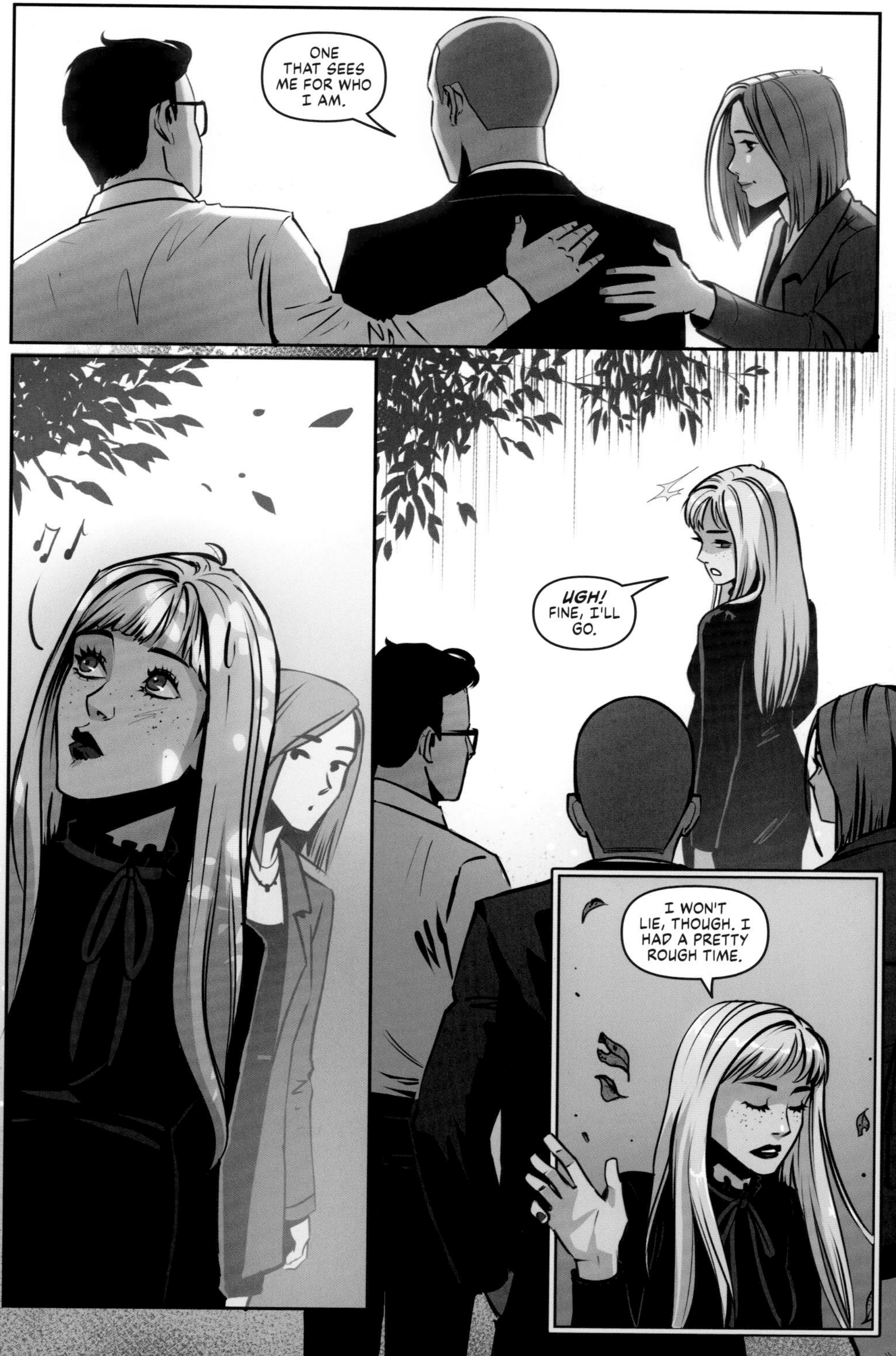
ONE THAT SEES ME FOR WHO I AM.
UGH! FINE, I'LL GO.
I WON'T LIE, THOUGH. I HAD A PRETTY ROUGH TIME.

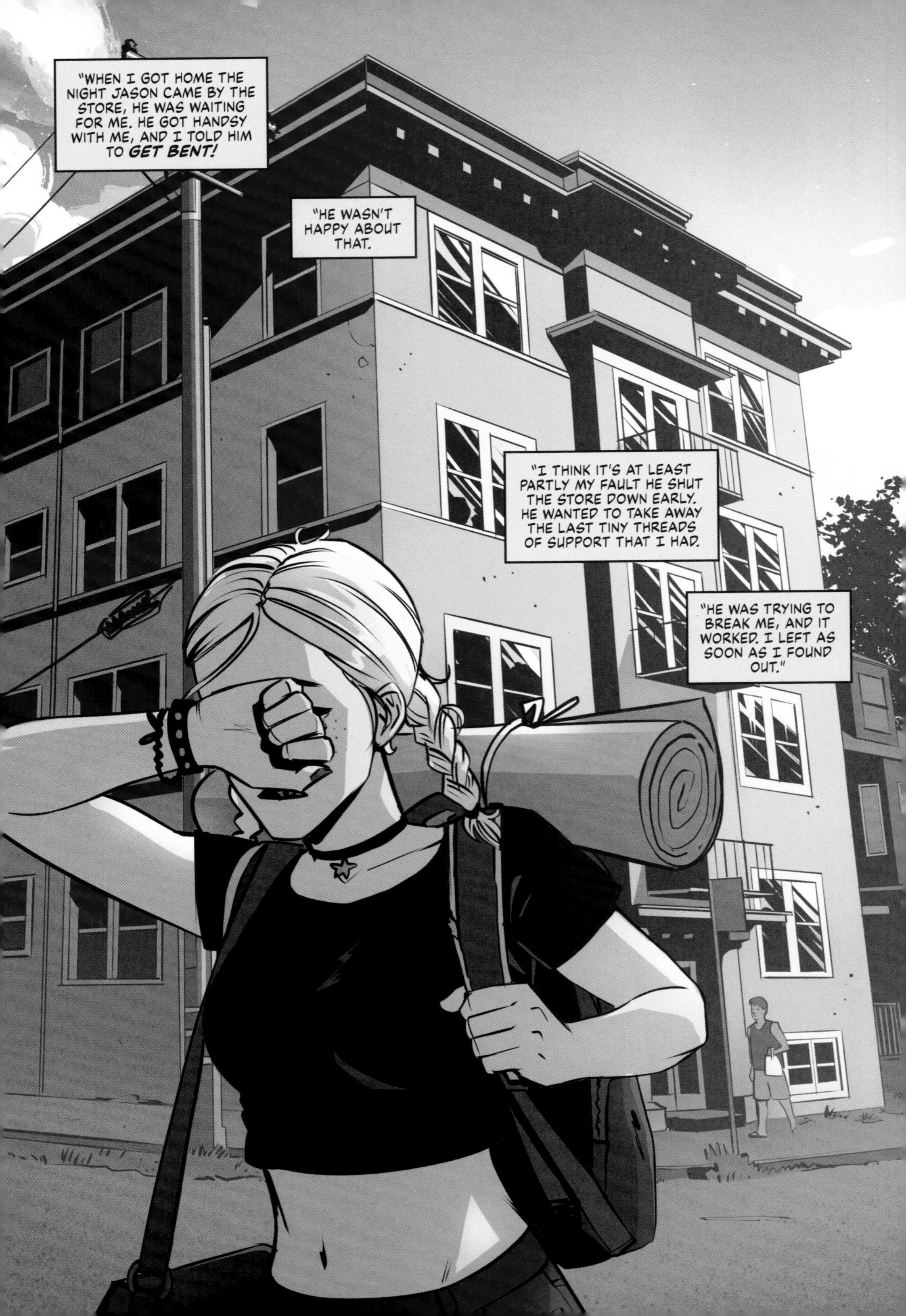
"WHEN I GOT HOME THE NIGHT JASON CAME BY THE STORE, HE WAS WAITING FOR ME. HE GOT HANDSY WITH ME, AND I TOLD HIM TO **GET BENT!**
"HE WASN'T HAPPY ABOUT THAT.
"I THINK IT'S AT LEAST PARTLY MY FAULT HE SHUT THE STORE DOWN EARLY. HE WANTED TO TAKE AWAY THE LAST TINY THREADS OF SUPPORT THAT I HAD.
"HE WAS TRYING TO BREAK ME, AND IT WORKED. I LEFT AS SOON AS I FOUND OUT."

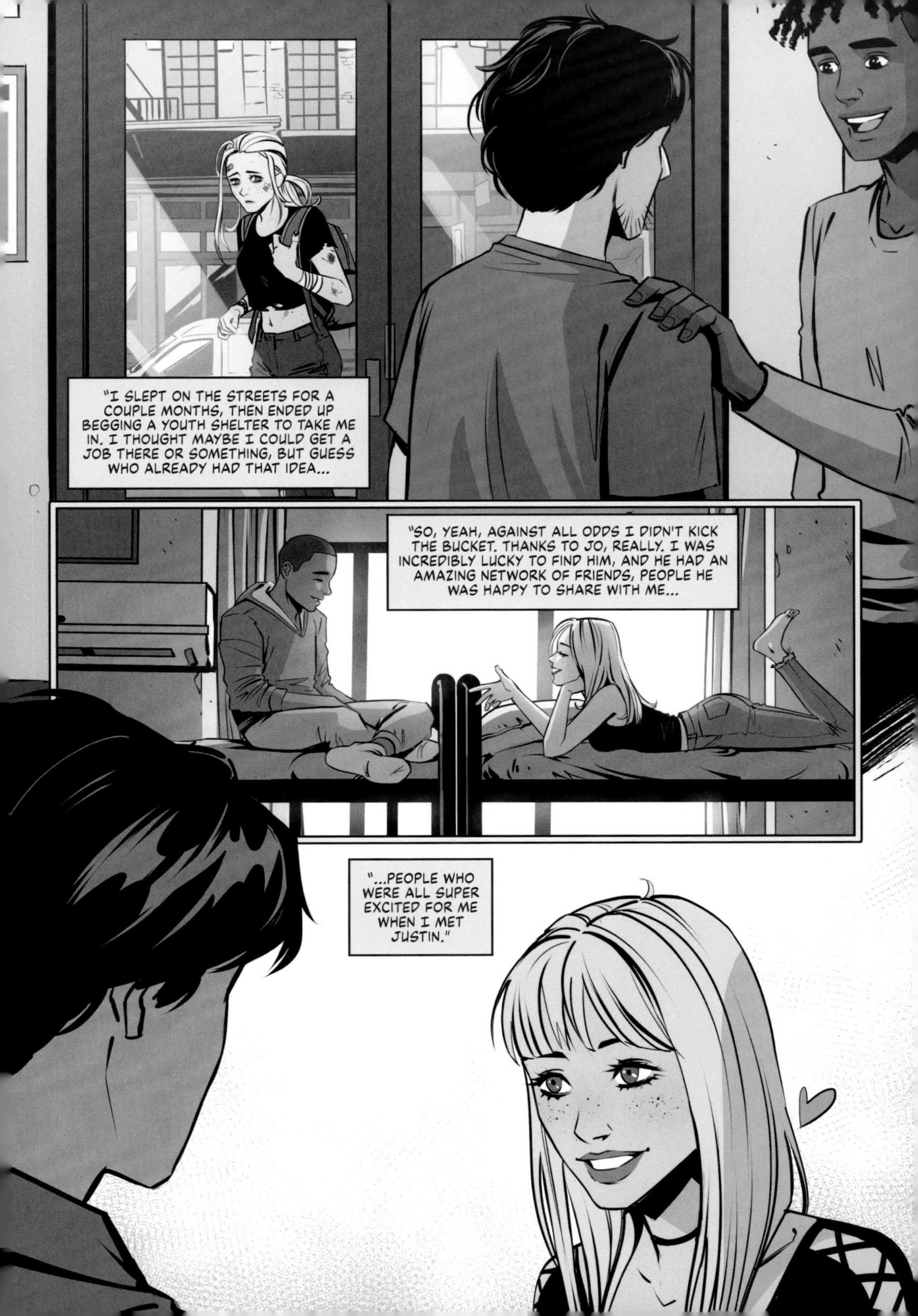
"I SLEPT ON THE STREETS FOR A COUPLE MONTHS, THEN ENDED UP BEGGING A YOUTH SHELTER TO TAKE ME IN. I THOUGHT MAYBE I COULD GET A JOB THERE OR SOMETHING, BUT GUESS WHO ALREADY HAD THAT IDEA...
"SO, YEAH, AGAINST ALL ODDS I DIDN'T KICK THE BUCKET. THANKS TO JO, REALLY. I WAS INCREDIBLY LUCKY TO FIND HIM, AND HE HAD AN AMAZING NETWORK OF FRIENDS, PEOPLE HE WAS HAPPY TO SHARE WITH ME...
"...PEOPLE WHO WERE ALL SUPER EXCITED FOR ME WHEN I MET JUSTIN."

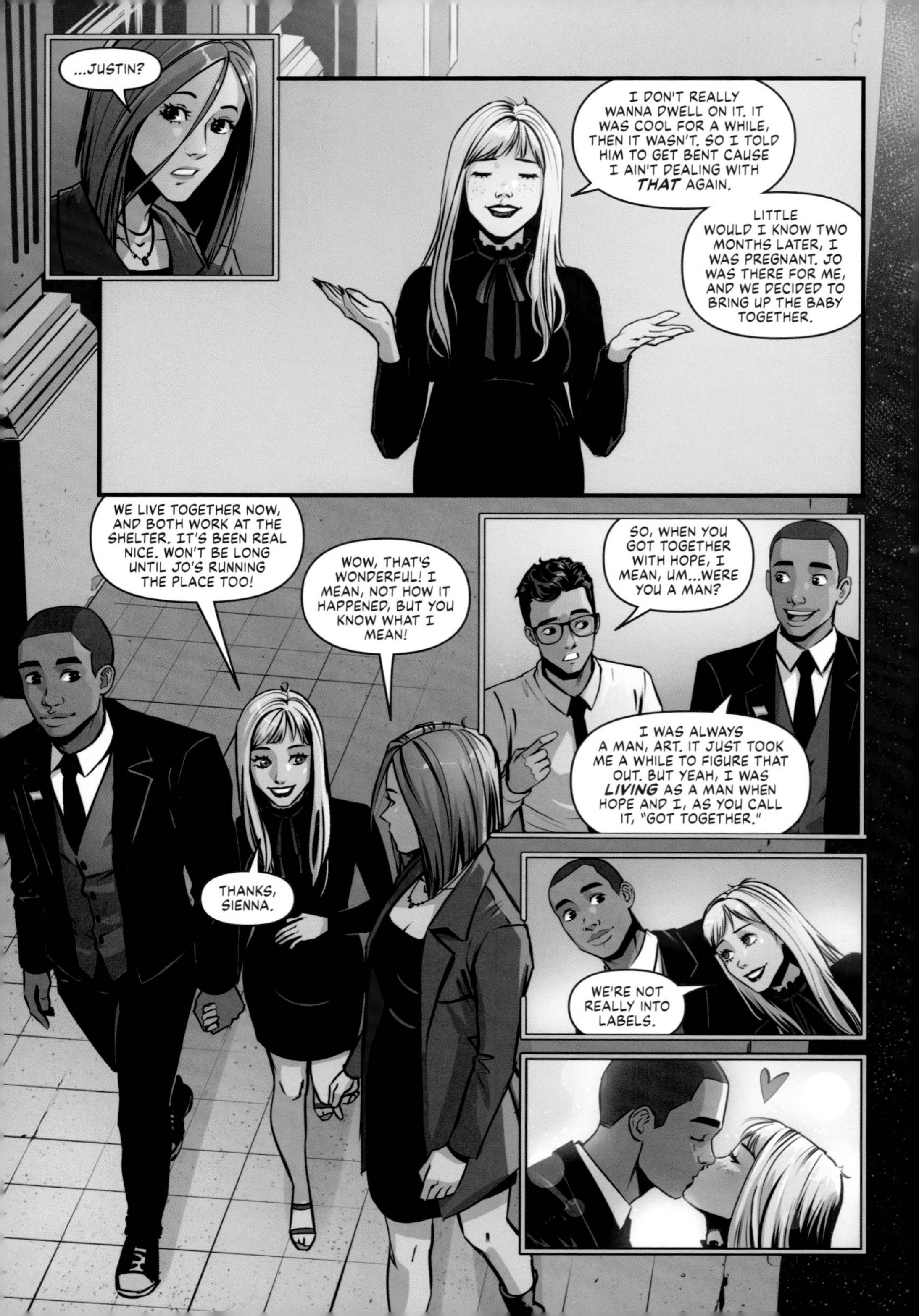
...JUSTIN?
I DON'T REALLY WANNA DWELL ON IT. IT WAS COOL FOR A WHILE, THEN IT WASN'T. SO I TOLD HIM TO GET BENT CAUSE I AIN'T DEALING WITH *THAT* AGAIN.
LITTLE WOULD I KNOW TWO MONTHS LATER, I WAS PREGNANT. JO WAS THERE FOR ME, AND WE DECIDED TO BRING UP THE BABY TOGETHER.
WE LIVE TOGETHER NOW, AND BOTH WORK AT THE SHELTER. IT'S BEEN REAL NICE. WON'T BE LONG UNTIL JO'S RUNNING THE PLACE TOO!
WOW, THAT'S WONDERFUL! I MEAN, NOT HOW IT HAPPENED, BUT YOU KNOW WHAT I MEAN!
THANKS, SIENNA.
SO, WHEN YOU GOT TOGETHER WITH HOPE, I MEAN, UM...WERE YOU A MAN?
I WAS ALWAYS A MAN, ART. IT JUST TOOK ME A WHILE TO FIGURE THAT OUT. BUT YEAH, I WAS *LIVING* AS A MAN WHEN HOPE AND I, AS YOU CALL IT, "GOT TOGETHER."
WE'RE NOT REALLY INTO LABELS.

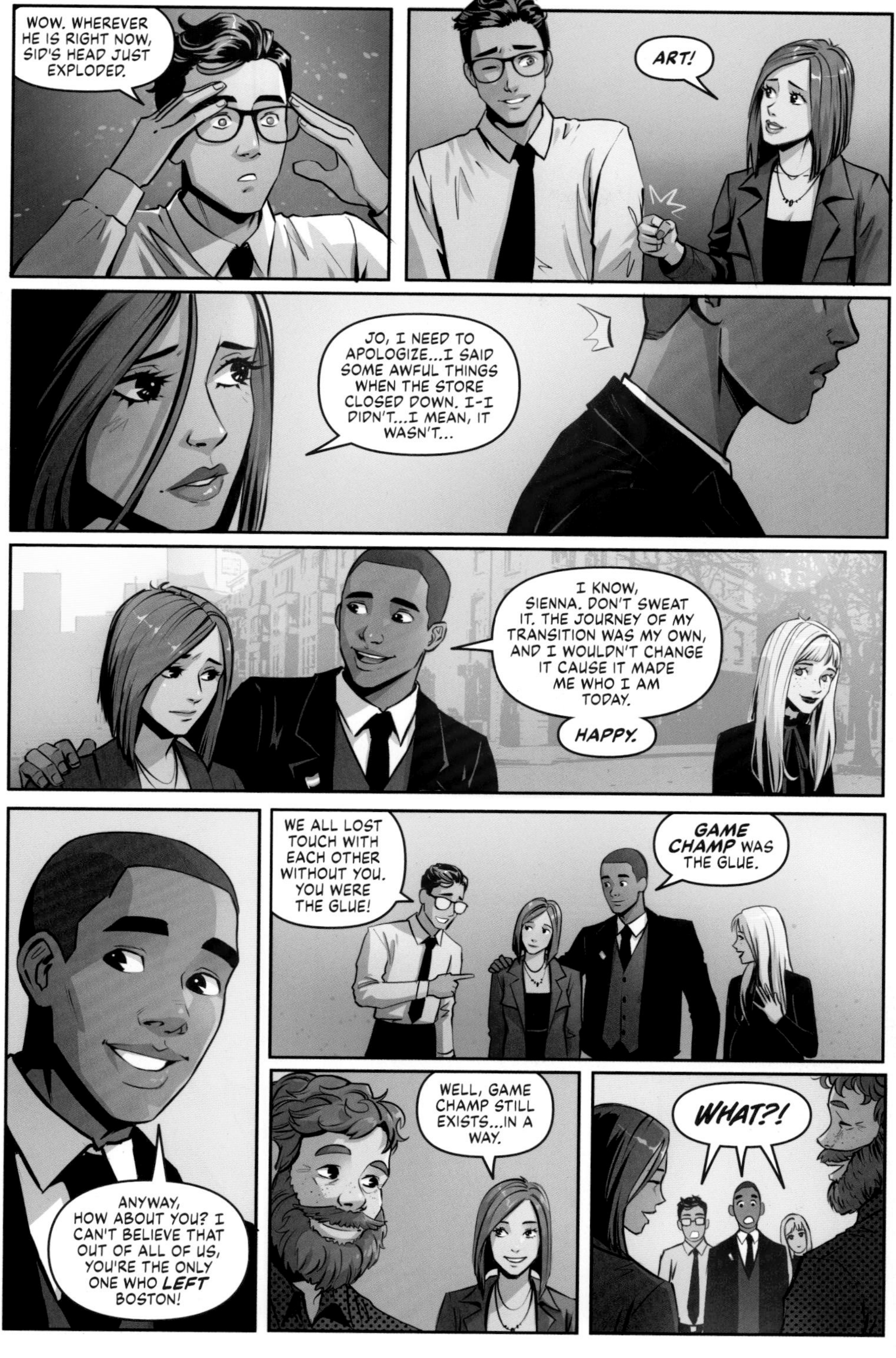
WOW. WHEREVER HE IS RIGHT NOW, SID'S HEAD JUST EXPLODED.
ART!
JO, I NEED TO APOLOGIZE...I SAID SOME AWFUL THINGS WHEN THE STORE CLOSED DOWN. I-I DIDN'T...I MEAN, IT WASN'T...
I KNOW, SIENNA. DON'T SWEAT IT. THE JOURNEY OF MY TRANSITION WAS MY OWN, AND I WOULDN'T CHANGE IT CAUSE IT MADE ME WHO I AM TODAY.
HAPPY.
ANYWAY, HOW ABOUT YOU? I CAN'T BELIEVE THAT OUT OF ALL OF US, YOU'RE THE ONLY ONE WHO LEFT BOSTON!
WE ALL LOST TOUCH WITH EACH OTHER WITHOUT YOU. YOU WERE THE GLUE!
GAME CHAMP WAS THE GLUE.
WELL, GAME CHAMP STILL EXISTS...IN A WAY.
WHAT?!

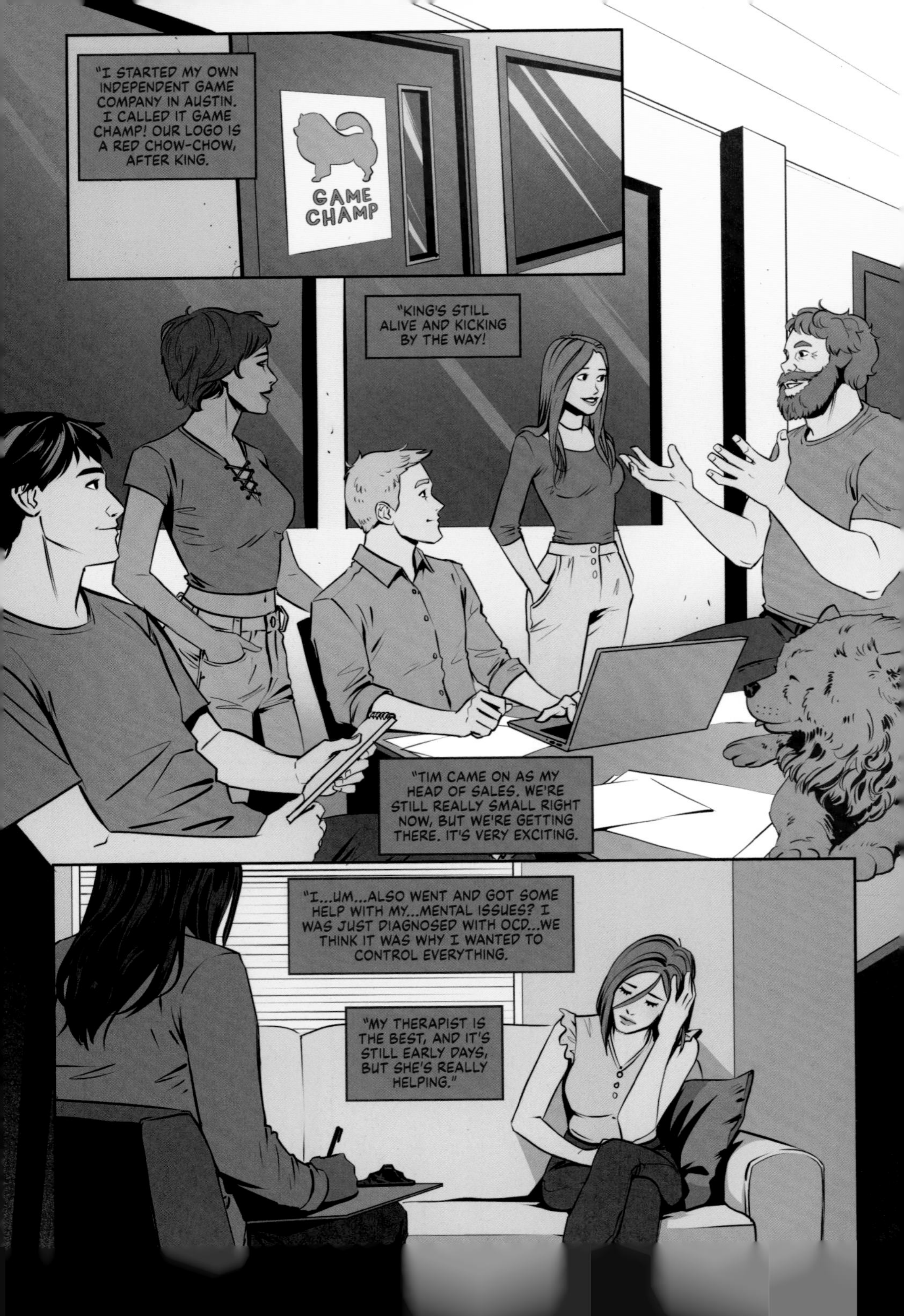
"I STARTED MY OWN INDEPENDENT GAME COMPANY IN AUSTIN. I CALLED IT GAME CHAMP! OUR LOGO IS A RED CHOW-CHOW, AFTER KING.
GAME CHAMP
"KING'S STILL ALIVE AND KICKING BY THE WAY!
"TIM CAME ON AS MY HEAD OF SALES. WE'RE STILL REALLY SMALL RIGHT NOW, BUT WE'RE GETTING THERE. IT'S VERY EXCITING.
"I...UM...ALSO WENT AND GOT SOME HELP WITH MY...MENTAL ISSUES? I WAS JUST DIAGNOSED WITH OCD...WE THINK IT WAS WHY I WANTED TO CONTROL EVERYTHING.
"MY THERAPIST IS THE BEST, AND IT'S STILL EARLY DAYS, BUT SHE'S REALLY HELPING."

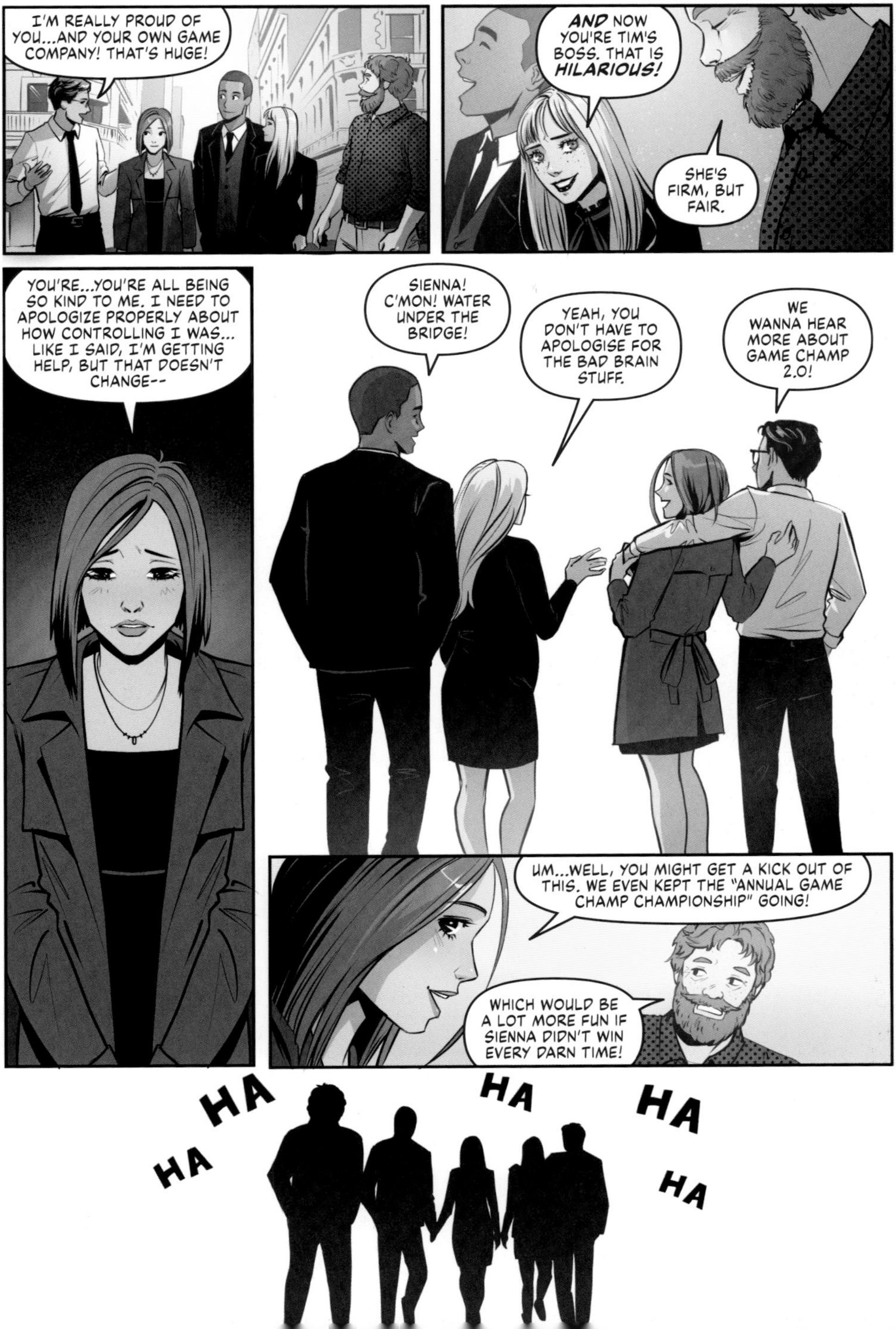
I'M REALLY PROUD OF YOU...AND YOUR OWN GAME COMPANY! THAT'S HUGE!
AND NOW YOU'RE TIM'S BOSS. THAT IS HILARIOUS!
SHE'S FIRM, BUT FAIR.
YOU'RE...YOU'RE ALL BEING SO KIND TO ME. I NEED TO APOLOGIZE PROPERLY ABOUT HOW CONTROLLING I WAS... LIKE I SAID, I'M GETTING HELP, BUT THAT DOESN'T CHANGE--
SIENNA! C'MON! WATER UNDER THE BRIDGE!
YEAH, YOU DON'T HAVE TO APOLOGISE FOR THE BAD BRAIN STUFF.
WE WANNA HEAR MORE ABOUT GAME CHAMP 2.0!
UM...WELL, YOU MIGHT GET A KICK OUT OF THIS. WE EVEN KEPT THE "ANNUAL GAME CHAMP CHAMPIONSHIP" GOING!
WHICH WOULD BE A LOT MORE FUN IF SIENNA DIDN'T WIN EVERY DARN TIME!
HA
HA
HA
HA
HA

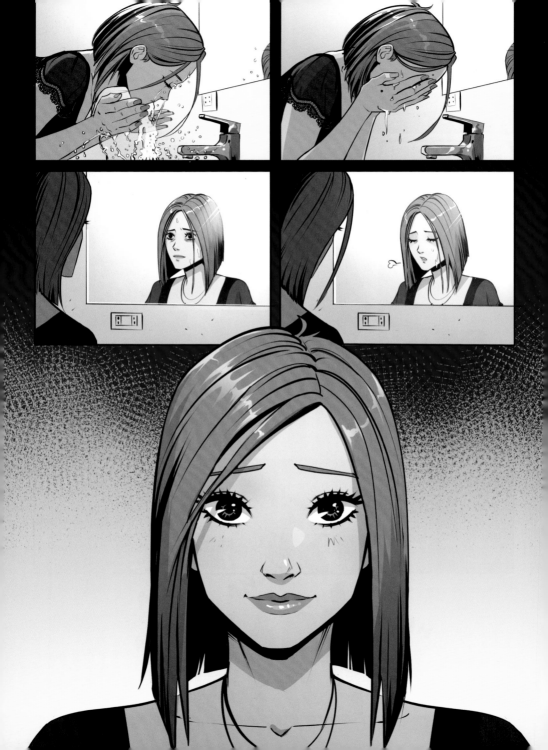

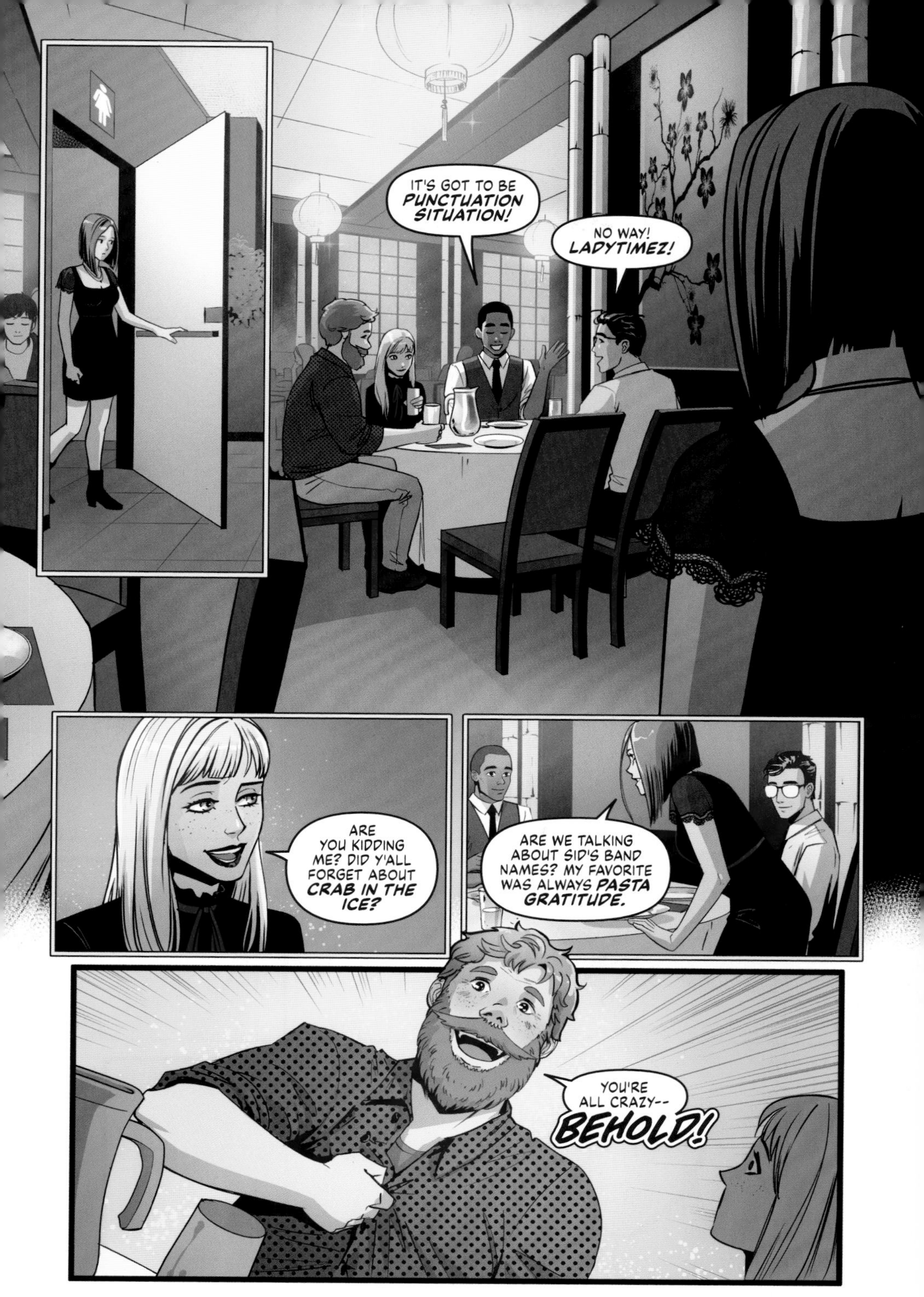
IT'S GOT TO BE PUNCTUATION SITUATION!
NO WAY! LADYTIMEZ!
ARE YOU KIDDING ME? DID Y'ALL FORGET ABOUT CRAB IN THE ICE?
ARE WE TALKING ABOUT SID'S BAND NAMES? MY FAVORITE WAS ALWAYS PASTA GRATITUDE.
YOU'RE ALL CRAZY--
BEHOLD!

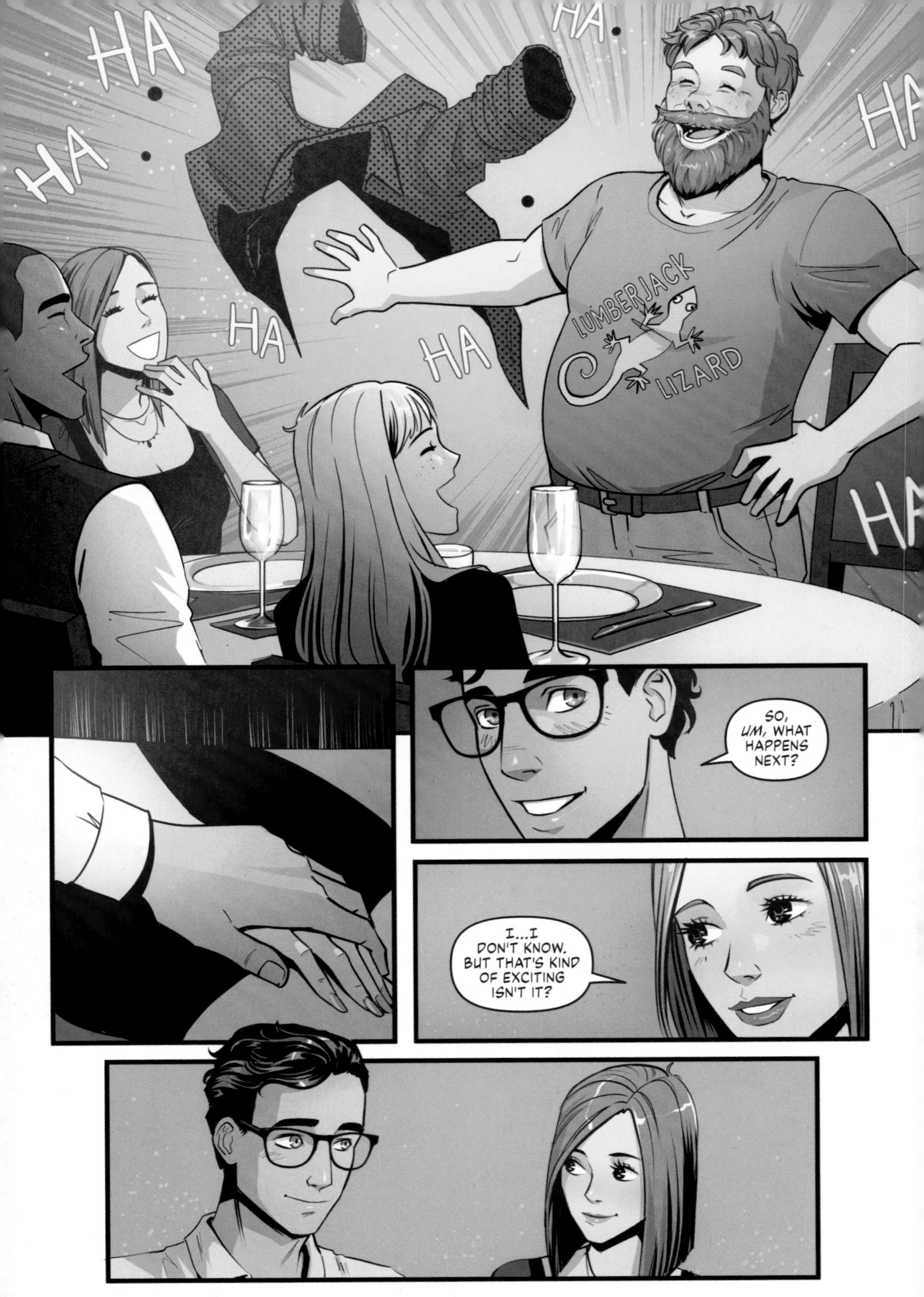
HA HA
HA
HA
HA
HA
HA
HA
LUMBERJACK LIZARD
SO, UM, WHAT HAPPENS NEXT?
I...I DON'T KNOW. BUT THAT'S KIND OF EXCITING ISN'T IT?

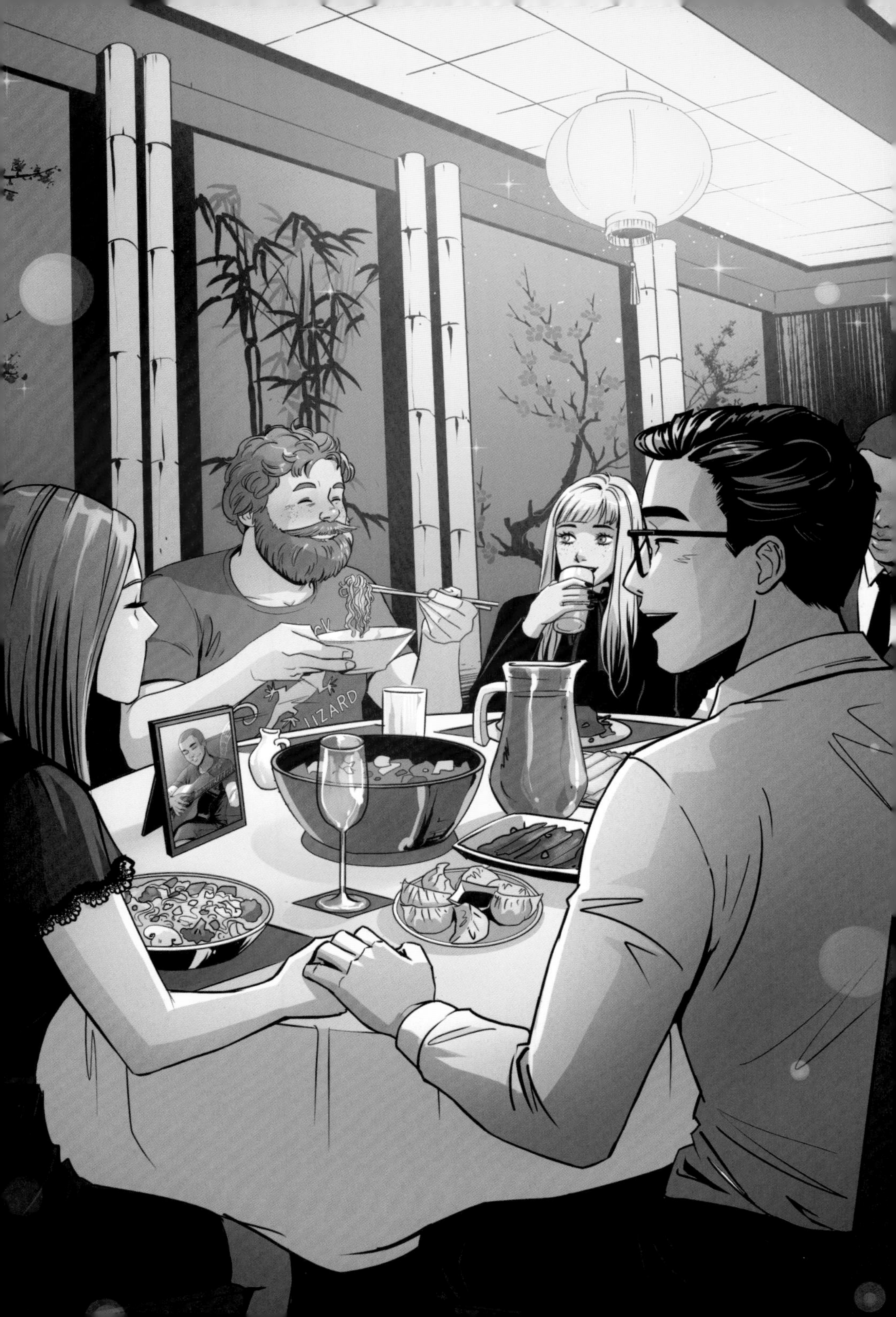

ONE YEAR LATER

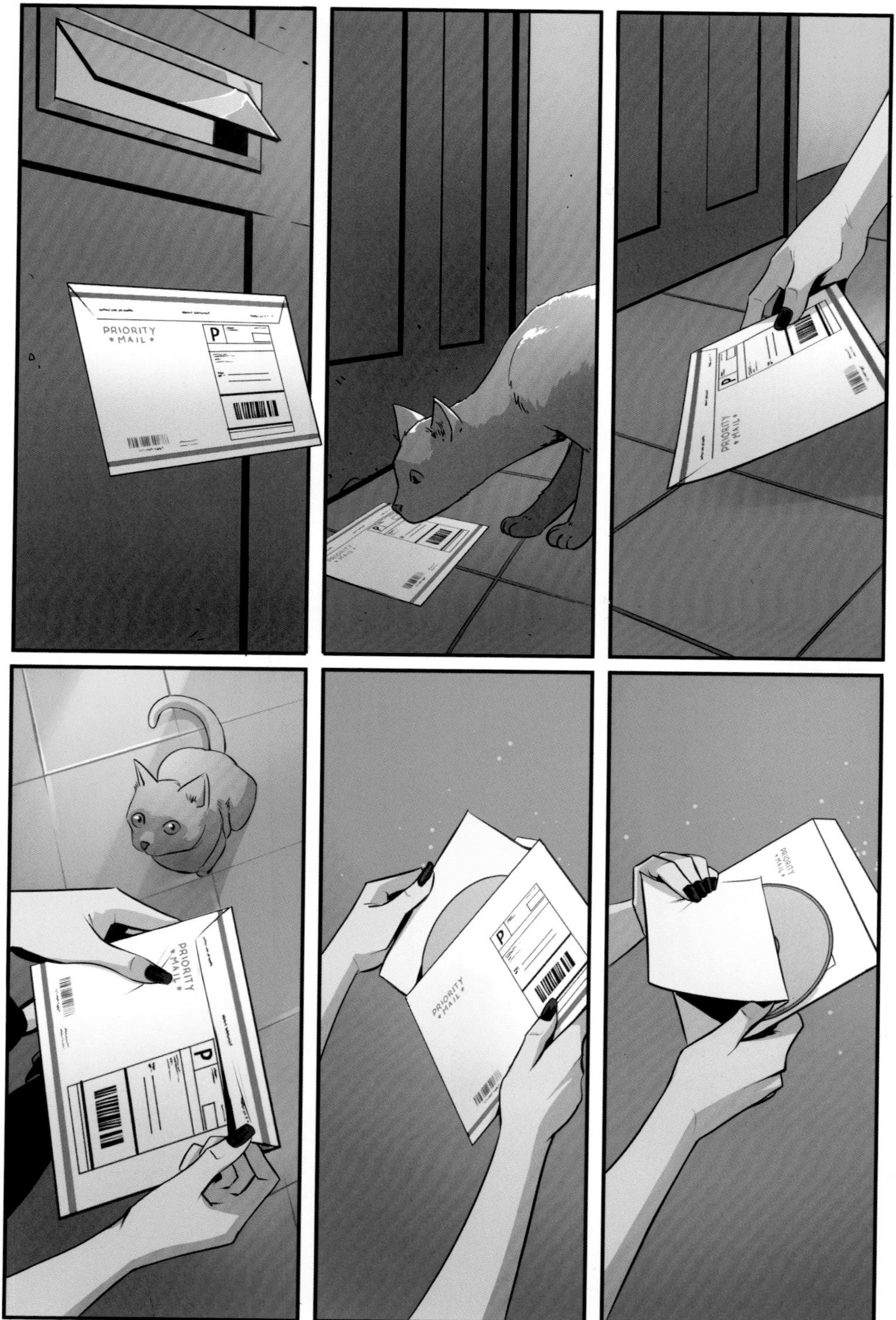
PRIORITY
MAIL
P

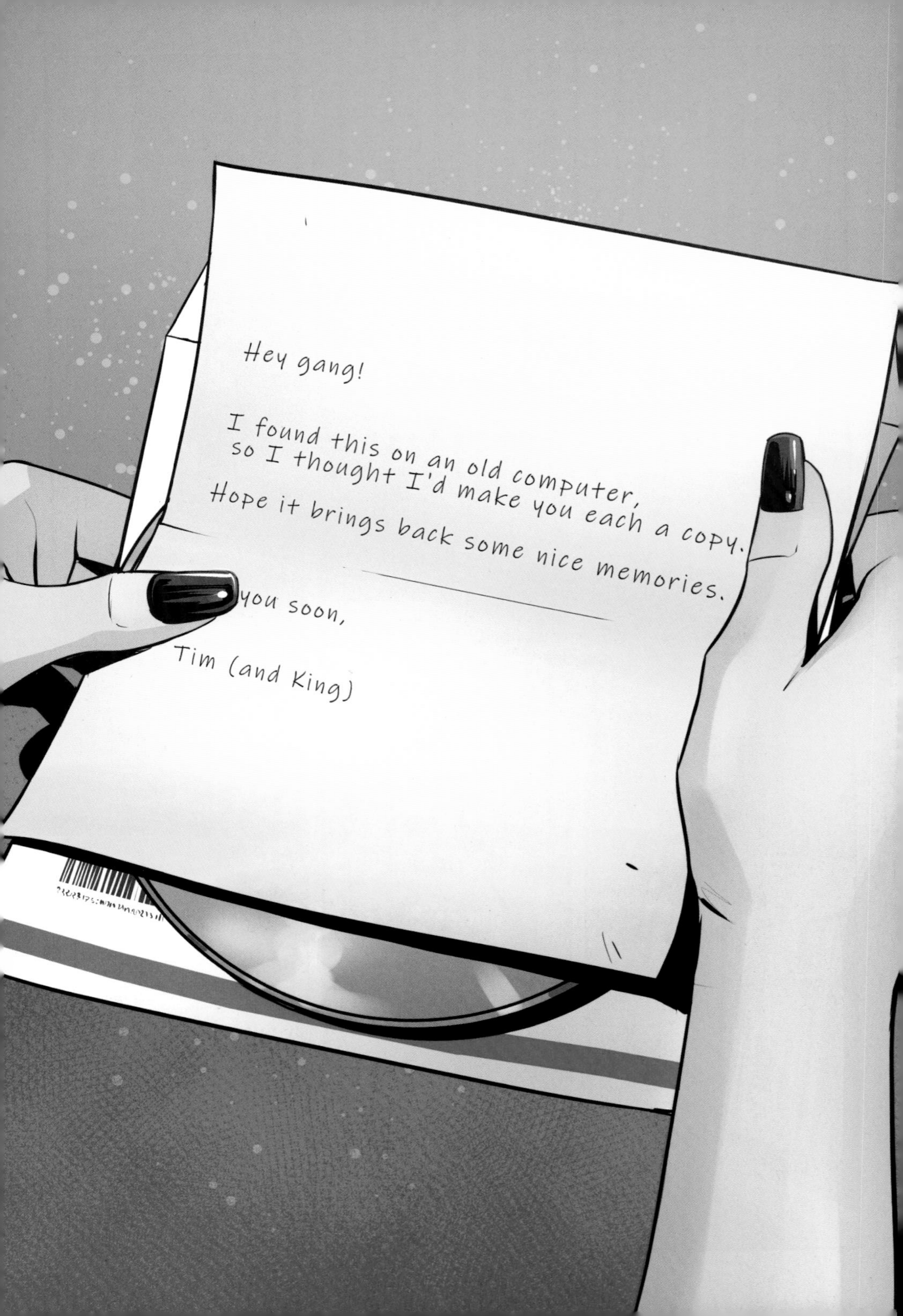

Hey gang!
I found this on an old computer, so I thought I'd make you each a copy.
Hope it brings back some nice memories.
you soon,
Tim (and King)

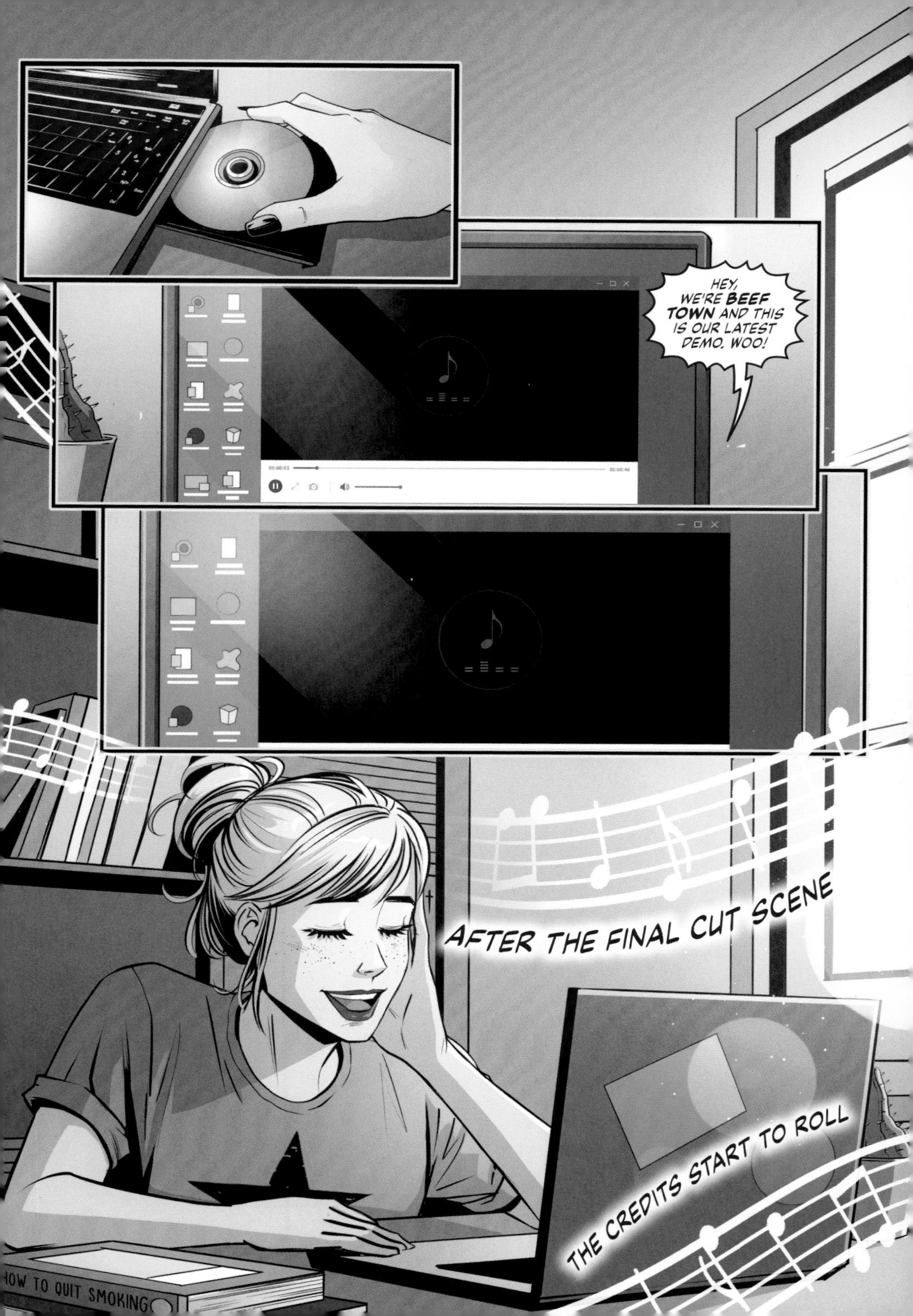
HEY, WE'RE BEEF TOWN AND THIS IS OUR LATEST DEMO. WOO!
00:00:03
00:00:46
AFTER THE FINAL CUT SCENE
THE CREDITS START TO ROLL
HOW TO QUIT SMOKING

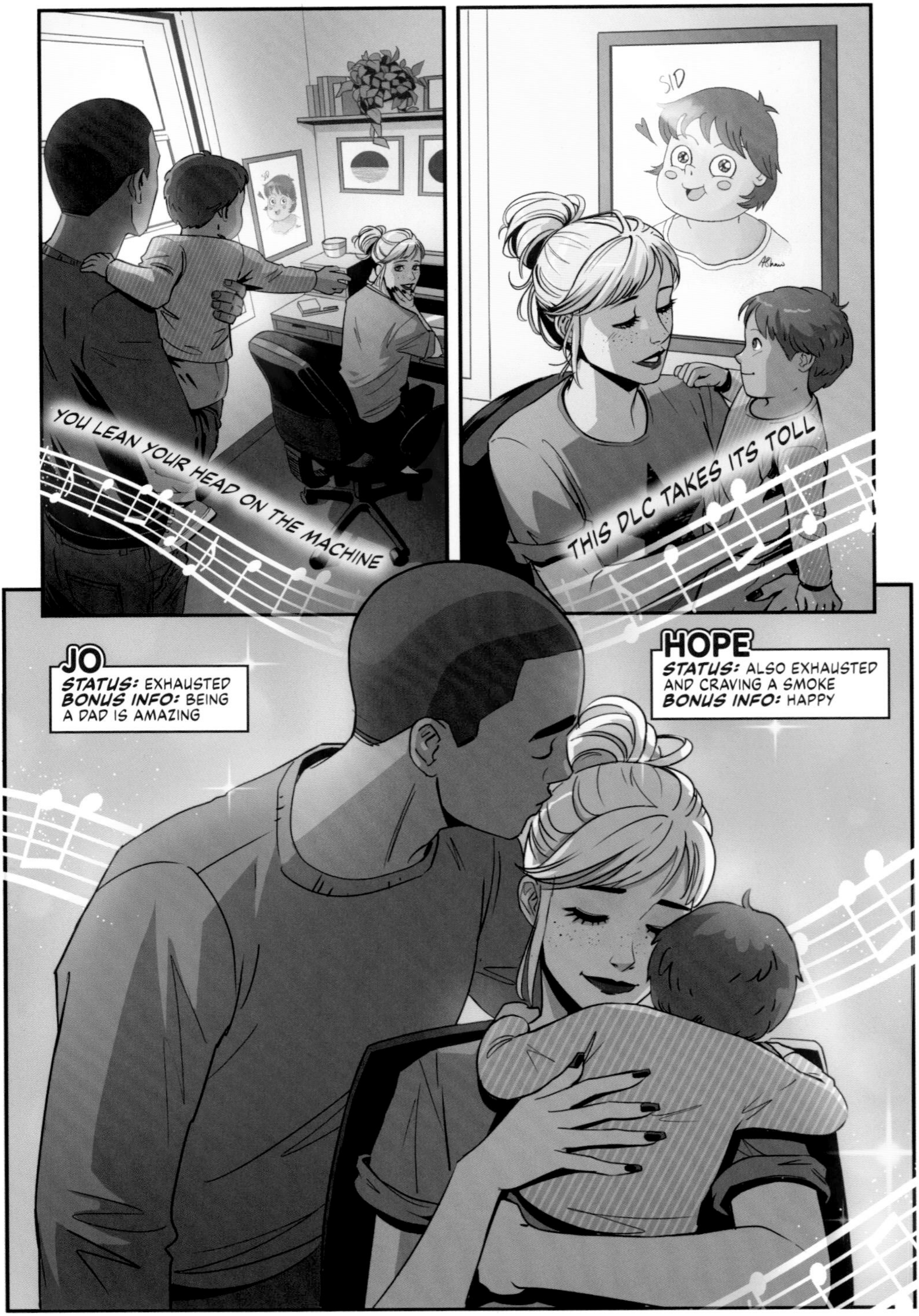
SID
YOU LEAN YOUR HEAD ON THE MACHINE
THIS DLC TAKES ITS TOLL
JO
STATUS: EXHAUSTED
BONUS INFO: BEING A DAD IS AMAZING
HOPE
STATUS: ALSO EXHAUSTED AND CRAVING A SMOKE
BONUS INFO: HAPPY

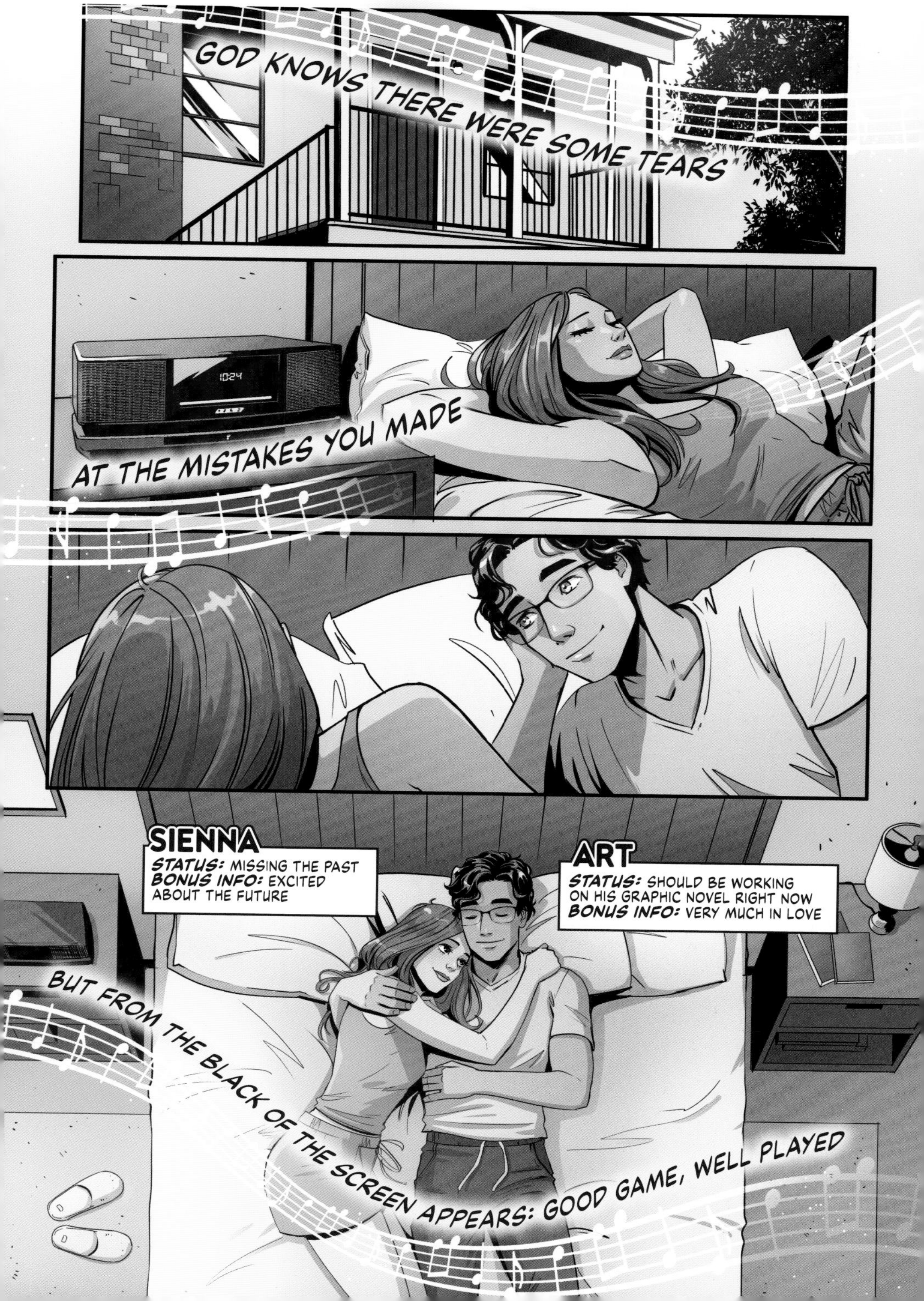
GOD KNOWS THERE WERE SOME TEARS
10:24
AT THE MISTAKES YOU MADE
SIENNA
STATUS: MISSING THE PAST
BONUS INFO: EXCITED ABOUT THE FUTURE
ART
STATUS: SHOULD BE WORKING ON HIS GRAPHIC NOVEL RIGHT NOW
BONUS INFO: VERY MUCH IN LOVE
BUT FROM THE BLACK OF THE SCREEN APPEARS: GOOD GAME, WELL PLAYED

"HOW TO"

OF MAKING A
4 PANEL COMIC

BY RACHAEL SMITH

WRITING

4 PANEL COMICS ARE KIND OF A SPECIALITY OF MINE, AND I'VE BEEN DOING THEM FOR A LONG TIME SO SOMETIMES IT'S HARD TO SEPARATE MYSELF ENOUGH TO EXPLAIN HOW I WRITE THEM, BUT I'LL TRY MY BEST...

4 PANELS IS NOT A LOT! USUALLY THE JOKE IS DIVIDED UP INTO 1) SET UP, 2) CATALYST, 3) BEAT, 4) PUNCHLINE. OR SOMETIMES IT'S THREE PANELS OF A SITUATION RAMPING UP AND THE FOURTH IS A PULL BACK AND REVEAL.

I TRY TO ALWAYS USE MY OWN EXPERIENCES AS INSPIRATION; LUCKY I HAD SO MANY RUBBISH JOBS AS A TEENAGER!

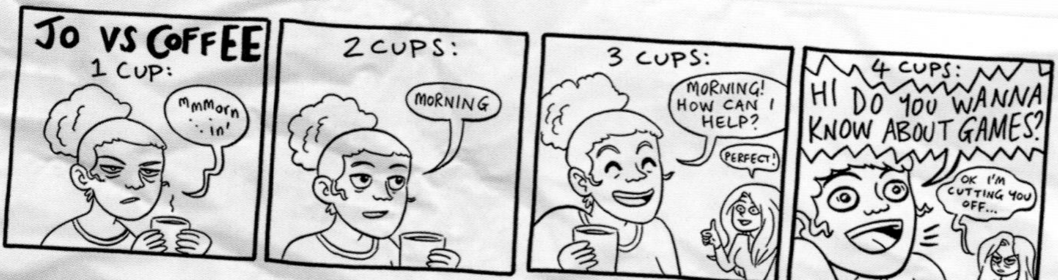
JO VS COFFEE
1 CUP:
mmmorn ... in'
2 CUPS:
MORNING
3 CUPS:
MORNING! HOW CAN I HELP?
PERFECT!
4 CUPS:
HI DO YOU WANNA KNOW ABOUT GAMES?
OK I'M CUTTING YOU OFF...

BECAUSE THE MAIN STORY IS ABOUT HOW CLOSE THE FRIENDS ARE, I WANTED SOME OF THE HUMOR TO COME EITHER FROM HOW WELL THEY KNOW EACH OTHER (JO AND THEIR COFFEE ADDICTION) OR THEM STICKING UP FOR EACH OTHER (HOPE PUNCHING THE MISOGYNIST GUY).

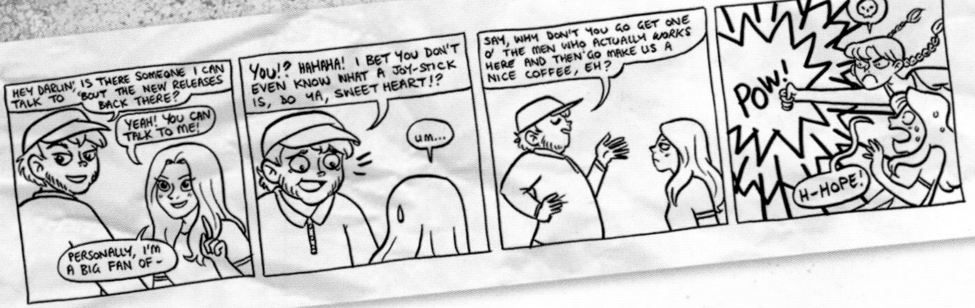
HEY DARLIN', IS THERE SOMEONE I CAN TALK TO 'BOUT THE NEW RELEASES BACK THERE?
YEAH! YOU CAN TALK TO ME!
PERSONALLY, I'M A BIG FAN OF-
YOU!? HAHAHA! I BET YOU DON'T EVEN KNOW WHAT A JOY-STICK IS, DO YA, SWEET HEART!?
UM...
SAY, WHY DON'T YOU GO GET ONE O' THE MEN WHO ACTUALLY WORKS HERE AND THEN GO MAKE US A NICE COFFEE, EH?
POW!
H-HOPE!

DRAWING

I LIKE TO DRAW ON BRISTOL BOARD PAPER BECAUSE IT'S LOVELY AND SMOOTH AND PREVENTS MY INK FROM SOAKING INTO THE PAPER AND SMUDGING.

I USE A BLUE COL-ERASE PENCIL TO MARK OUT MY PANEL BORDERS, AND THEN ROUGHLY DRAW EACH PANEL.

THEN I'LL GO OVER THE LINES WITH A KURETAKE FUDEGEKOCHI BRUSH PEN. A LOT OF MY PEERS USE A PENTEL POCKET BRUSH PEN, BUT I FIND THESE A BIT TOO CHUNKY FOR MY HEAVY-HANDED DRAWING! I WISH I COULD GET ALONG WITH THEM THOUGH AS THEY ARE REFILLABLE AND A LOT CHEAPER!

SID! STOP HITTING ME!
STOP HITTING ME!
YOU'RE THE ONE GETTING IN THE WAY OF MY FISTS!
OH! NOW YOU'RE IN FOR A WORLD OF PAIN!
THAT'S A GREAT VIDEO GAME YOU'RE PLAYING THERE, GUYS!
SOMETIMES I WORRY OUR NEIGHBOURS ARE GONNA CALL THE COPS!

I THEN SCAN THE DRAWING IN AND THE REST HAPPENS IN PHOTOSHOP. USUALLY THIS WOULD BE WHERE I ADD THE PANEL BORDERS TO KEEP THEM NICE AND STRAIGHT, BUT I WANTED THESE PARTICULAR COMICS TO LOOK ENTIRELY DRAWN BY HAND IN ART'S SKETCHBOOK, SO I DREW THEM WITH MY PEN SO THEY WOULD END UP A BIT WIGGLY.

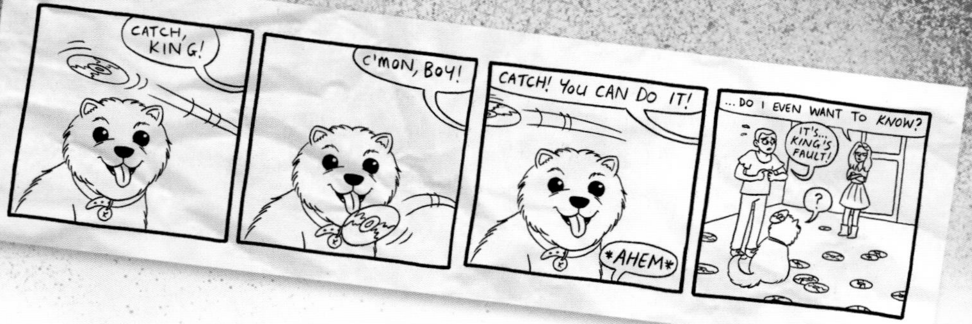
CATCH, KING!
C'MON, BOY!
CATCH! YOU CAN DO IT!
AHEM
... DO I EVEN WANT TO KNOW?
IT'S... KING'S FAULT!
?

IN PHOTOSHOP, I CAN GET RID OF THE BLUE LINES WITH THE TOUCH OF A BUTTON, AND THEN I CLEAN UP THE BLACK LINES SO THEY STAND OUT AGAINST THE WHITE. AND WE'RE DONE!

SIGNING OFF

IF YOU'RE HAVING TROUBLE GETTING STARTED I RECOMMEND DRAWING A LITTLE COMIC EVERY DAY ABOUT SOMETHING THAT HAPPENED TO YOU THAT DAY. IT COULD BE FUNNY, OR SAD, OR SCARY - ANYTHING! AFTER A WEEK YOU'LL HAVE SEVEN COMICS! AFTER TWO WEEKS - 14! THEY MIGHT NOT BE PERFECT, BUT NOTHING EVER IS, AND I'LL BET YOU ANYTHING THAT THE 14TH ONE WILL BE MILES BETTER THAN THE FIRST. THINK HOW GREAT YOUR 50TH ONE WILL BE! IT'S ALL PROGRESS.

GOOD LUCK!

LGBTQIA+ RESOURCES

THESE ARE JUST A FEW OF THE RESOURCES THAT MAY BENEFIT THE GROWTH AND DEVELOPMENT OF LGBTQIA+ INDIVIDUALS. FEEL FREE TO SHARE THESE RESOURCES AND FIND MORE THAT SPECIFICALLY RELATE TO WHAT YOU OR SOMEONE THAT YOU KNOW ARE GOING THROUGH.

Crisis Text Line
Crisis Text Line connects texters with trained volunteer Crisis Counselors to help resolve times of crisis. This service tries to match texters with Crisis Counselors who have shared lived experience.
Learn more: www.crisistextline.org

Trans Lifeline
Trans Lifeline is a nonprofit organization dedicated to the well being of transgender people. The hotline is staffed by transgender people for transgender people.
Learn more: www.translifeline.org

It Gets Better Project
The It Gets Better Project is a nonprofit organization with a mission to uplift, empower, and connect lesbian, gay, bisexual, transgender, and queer youth around the globe. Their website offers education, stories, and directory of local resources to help get the support your loved one needs.
Learn more: www.itgetsbetter.org

GLMA Health Professionals Advancing LGBT Equality

GLMA works to ensure equality in healthcare for lesbian, gay, bisexual, and transgender individuals and healthcare providers. They offer a directory for patients to connect with LGBT welcoming providers.
Learn more: www.glma.org

National Center for Transgender Equality

The National Center for Transgender Equality advocates to change policies and society to increase understanding and acceptance of transgender people.
Learn more: https://transequality.org/

Anti-Violence Project

AVP empowers lesbian, gay, bisexual, transgender, queer, and HIV-affected communities and allies to end all forms of violence through organizing and education, and supports survivors through counseling and advocacy.
Learn more: https://avp.org/

GSA Network

GSA clubs are student-run organizations that unite LGBTQ+ and allied youth to build community and organize around issues impacting them in their schools and communities.
Learn More: https://gsanetwork.org/

Brown Boi Project

The Brown Boi Project works to transform the way that communities of color talk about gender. They build the leadership, economic self sufficiency, and health of LGBTQ people of color--pipelining them into the social justice movement.
Learn more: https://www.brownboiproject.org/

REMEMBER, IF YOU'RE TRULY IN NEED, CHECK WITH YOUR LOCAL COMMUNITIES AND SHELTERS. YOUR HEALTH AND SAFETY IS THE MOST IMPORTANT THING AND KNOW THAT THERE ARE PEOPLE OUT THERE WHO ARE WILLING TO HELP.

CREATOR SPOTLIGHT

RACHAEL SMITH IS A COMICS CREATOR WHOSE WORKS INCLUDE WIRED UP WRONG, STAND IN YOUR POWER, THE RABBIT, AND ARTIFICIAL FLOWERS. SHE ALSO WORKED ON THE DOCTOR WHO: TENTH DOCTOR COMIC SERIES AND IS MAKING DAILY COMICS AT THE HASHTAG #QUARANTINECOMIX.

KATHERINE LOBO IS A COMIC ARTIST AND ILLUSTRATOR FROM COSTA RICA. SHE'S WORKED FOR A VARIETY OF INDIE CREATORS AND PUBLISHERS INCLUDING BOOM! STUDIOS AND COMIC EXPERIENCE. MORE RECENTLY, SHE WAS THE ARTIST FOR BULLET, CURRENTLY PUBLISHED IN TAPAS.

JUSTIN BIRCH IS A RINGO AWARD NOMINATED LETTERER BORN AND RAISED IN THE HILLS OF WEST VIRGINIA. LETTERING COMICS SINCE 2015, HE IS A MEMBER OF THE LETTERING STUDIO ANDWORLD DESIGN AND HAS WORKED WITH NUMEROUS INDIE PUBLISHERS. JUSTIN STILL LIVES IN WEST VIRGINIA, ONLY NOW IT'S WITH HIS LOVING WIFE, DAUGHTERS, AND THEIR DOG, KIRBY.

ACKNOWLEDGMENTS

First and foremost, I would like to thank my Mum for always encouraging and inspiring me to do what I love. I hope I'll be a Mum like you one day.

I'd like to thank Chris, my editor, for thinking of me for this project in the first place. It was an absolute joy to work on knowing that I had his support every step of the way. And I will of course be forever grateful to Katherine Lobo and Justin Birch for making my words come so wonderfully to life.

Huge thanks to my friends who piled into my kitchen to read the first draft of the script aloud to me whilst I sat and made notes on the dialogue. Those would be: Heather, Iain, Readle, Richard, Liv, Rachel, and Rob. I learned so much that night, about my characters, about my story, and about how dreadful we all are at American accents.

Speaking of Rob, I'd like to thank him specially for his sterling support while I was writing this book. Rob, I love you so much. It's really rather nice of you to love me back.

Finally, thank YOU. Yes, YOU! For reading this book. I hope it made you feel like hugging your friends, or at least asking them if they fancy a burger sometime.

Rachael Smith

First of all, I would like to thank my husband, Serg, who was always by my side, supporting me and giving me his artistic feedback, as well as my little Sofi, who always came to my desk to make my work days more fun, with her comments and her encouragement.

I'd also like to thank Chris, my editor, for trusting me to draw this graphic novel, and for all his patience and flexibility. Many thanks to Rachael Smith too, for writing this story with so much heart, and giving me the opportunity to illustrate it.

And of course, many thanks to the entire Mad Cave team for helping me through the process and for all their kindness and support.

And thanks to everyone who, i n one way or another, accompanied me on this journey, especially to El Zarpe, my buddies group, Dan Mora, César Acuña, Daniel Mora, and Serg Acuña, because I started with them on this artistic path, and they are still stuck on me like uncomfortable chewing gum.

Katherine Lobo